Orchard Valley,
Wilbraham - MA.
April 14, 2020

Shirin Dastur Patel

FALSE FLAG IN AUTUMN

Michael Bowen

FARRAGUT SQUARE PUBLICATIONS

First Edition: November 2019

10 9 8 7 6 5 4 3 2 1

False Flag in Autumn is a work of fiction. Louisiana does not have seven congressional districts, or a San Eglise Parish, or any elected official remotely like Chad Bilbo. Except for widely reported news events mentioned as background, nothing in this story actually happened. But fiction is truth liberated from the tyranny of fact.

False Flag: "A political or military act orchestrated in such a way that it appears to have been carried out by a party who is not in fact responsible."

Oxford Living Dictionaries, def. 2

RUMPSEY DUMPSEY

August to October, 2017

"Rumpsey, Dumpsey
Colonel Johnson killed Tecumsey!"

1840 Democratic Party campaign slogan celebrating vice-presidential candidate
Richard M. Johnson for firing the shot that killed the Native American leader
Techumseh

Chapter 1

In June, 2019, a nice young man in a blue suit asked me "when was the last time you smoked marijuana, ma'am?" I told him the truth – semester break during my sophomore year at Tulane – because you don't lie to the FBI. I have no objection to the truth, but I don't let it push me around. That's why I get assignments like the one that started everything almost two years before, in August, 2017.

The video playing on Seamus Danica's computer screen showed a matronly, bespectacled woman at a podium. The background made me think of a junior high multi-purpose room with a floor-to-ceiling partition that can be stretched across the floor to divide it into two separate areas. The woman's caramel-colored skin wasn't quite as dark as mine, but her bushy silver hair told me she was African-American rather than Creole/Cajun like yours truly. She spoke in a minimally inflected voice, like you might use to announce table assignments for a PTA's pot-luck supper.

"Good afternoon. My name is Letitia Dejean. I am the chancellor of North Central Louisiana Agricultural and Technical University.

"You may have heard that some players on A and T's Water Moccasins football team announced earlier today that they will not play in this Saturday's game against the Red River University Bobcats unless two administrators are fired, funding is provided for additional faculty positions to be filled by non-white professors, increased sensitivity and diversity training is required, and compulsory trigger warnings are adopted for all courses in all departments.

"These demands will be taken under advisement for appropriate study. Meanwhile, any members of the football team who fail to participate fully in this Saturday's game will have their athletic scholarships withdrawn and will be expected to vacate the athletic dormitory by the end of the month. Failure by any coaches to participate fully in practices and games will breach their contracts, which will in consequence be terminated forthwith.

"That concludes our response. Unfortunately, we will not have time for questions. Thank you for coming, and have a pleasant day."

"Fantastic," I murmured.

"Spectacular," Seamus agreed.

"Dynamite."

"An atomic bomb."

"When did it happen?"

"It hasn't happened yet," Seamus said. "You're going to make it happen."

Didn't gape, exactly, but I swallowed hard. Seamus ended the conversation with, "I'll see you in the Atwater Room after I pick up your briefing book from the excellent nerds."

'Excellent nerds' is Seamus's homage to Lee Atwater, the man behind the Willie Horton ad that sank Dukakis in the 1988 presidential election. He used an army of them.

My name is Josephine Robideaux Kendall – Josie to Seamus, Rafe (my husband), and the two-hundred or so close friends I have in the Washington power class, among media, congressional aides, and (technically) on the White House staff. I say 'technically' because my close friend at 1600 Pennsylvania Avenue actually hates my guts. He still calls me 'Josie,' though, and I still call him 'Hank.' It's that 1600 Pennsylvania Avenue thing.

If I ever write my memoirs, the title will *not* be *Nancy Drew Goes to Washington*. I'm not an earnest, high-minded, idealistic *naïf*. I'm a hard-nosed political apparatchik who can make things happen in D.C.

I love politics. I love every part of it. If politics caused cancer, I'd be dead, no question. Electoral politics, governance politics, lobbying politics, bureaucratic politics, how-a-bill-becomes-a-law politics, White House basement politics, media politics – *le tout ensemble*, as we sometimes say in Baton Rouge. If there's a rehab program, I'm not interested. I gave up smoking (mostly) at twenty-five, but I won't give up politics until a priest sprinkles holy water on the urn holding my ashes. If my grade school catechism is right, I may keep a hand in even then.

Growing up in a political family hard-wired me, and my first toe in the Washington reflecting pool had me hooked. I interned on the staffs of a couple of congressional committees during term breaks at Tulane, and I found even intern-level intrigue a lot more exciting than anything the NCAA had to offer. After graduating, I worked for Congressman Jerome Temple until he inconveniently decided not to run for re-election. Now I'm toiling away at the Majority Values Coalition, which tries to push values held by people with lots of money into the majority. Someday I will work in the West Wing of the White House. You can take that to the bank. I didn't make any short lists during President Trump's transition, but I should be in the mix for several more transitions. *Dum spiro spero*: "While I breathe, I hope."

In the meantime, I have to help Seamus keep the lights on at MVC. So I was sitting expectantly seven minutes later, on the window side of the Atwater Room's tapered oval conference table, when he came in and tossed me a freshly burned thumb drive ('briefing book' in old-school lingo). Before I could ask a question starting with 'why' – Seamus doesn't like questions that start with 'why' – a 60-inch screen dominating the opposite wall flickered to life. Seamus and I gazed upward at a male face showing the treadwear of fifty-plus years, a warm, down-to-earth smile, and eyes the stunning blue of a clear sky in early autumn.

We were teleconferencing with Calvin Kirby – an extremely wealthy man with an extremely wealthy wife, an extremely wealthy extended family, and very definite ideas about America: what it should be, what it could be, what he wanted it to be. He was not just rich but *real* rich, in a world where a lot of people in public life can be bought cheap, or scared easily, or both. He had the ability to do what he wanted and not think twice.

His whole torso appeared on the screen, but his face monopolized my attention. For a thousand dollars I couldn't tell you the color of his sport coat, and if I said he had on a pale blue shirt I'd mostly be guessing. He had graying brown hair that I would have sworn were real if I hadn't happened to know it was a superbly woven toupee that had cost roughly the gross national product of a small third-world country. The rug comforted me a little. That touch of vanity offered a hint of vulnerability in a guy who could send shivers through governors, senators, and assorted prime ministers in countries ending in -stan.

"Good to see you again, Ms. Kendall," he said, beaming like the salesman he had been since age sixteen.

"A pleasure as always, Mr. Kirby."

"Has Seamus explained what you are to do?"

"*What*, yes; *why*, no."

"Why is simple," Kirby said. "We need to make Letitia Dejean a credible opponent for Chad Bilbo in Louisiana's 7th congressional district."

"I see. And I'm guessing that's not just because Congressman Bilbo is a 24-four carat bastard with an ego the size of the Hope Diamond."

"We don't really go in much for aesthetic judgments." Kirby shared a wry, crinkly-eyed smile with us. "It's because he has acquired an unfortunate sensitivity to the environmental downsides of fracking. Some of my relations and I own options on frackable land that without the fracking is –"

"Worthless," I added for him.

"That would be one word for it."

"So it's a matter of principle," I said.

"I'm so glad you understand." Kirby chuckled like an indulgent uncle who enjoys high-spirited teasing from his sassy niece. "I won't kid you. At one level, it's about money – just like everything else. But it is not *just* about money."

"Right," Seamus said.

Kirby squinted and his eyes warmed up a degree or two under his bristly eyebrows. His whole face radiated earnestness and vision. The true-believer resonance in his next words would have alienated half the politicians in the country.

"There isn't one damn thing in the entire Middle East that's worth a single drop of American blood," he said. "Much less an occasional threat of nuclear war. Except Israel, and unlike our other so-called allies Israel can defend itself. With a little effort, a little risk, a few dollars from petty cash, and a little *imagination*, the United States can meet as much of the world's demand for oil as we want. We can set the price. We can tell everyone from Algeria to Iran, 'Go ahead and live in the twelfth century if you want. Just don't try it here. Because we don't need you anymore.'"

"Bilbo playing tree-hugger doesn't come as a complete surprise, though," I said. "Louisiana sells lots of oil and gas that it gets the old-fashioned way, and it doesn't want more competition, from fracking or otherwise."

"No doubt," Kirby said, nodding. "My hope is that if Bilbo gets a good primary scare, he might find his way to a less parochial position on the issue. Somehow, I see a possible change of heart lurking in his crass, shallow soul."

"Got it," I said.

"Good. I love a quick study."

I blitzed through the thumb drive during my flight to Baton Rouge that afternoon. All the usual stuff, of course, providing a data-trail on Bilbo's political life to date. The crown jewel, though, was a vintage reprise of the Wrong Man campaign commercial that had jump started his maiden run for Congress eight years before:

Tight shot on an open garage door. Super at the bottom of the screen: DRAMATIZATION OF ACTUAL EVENTS. Dolly in to show thug in hoodie and mask rifling tool box at the back of the garage. Sudden blast of white light on the thug, who whirls around, startled. Off-camera, Bilbo's voice: "Drop your weapon and put your hands in the air!" Thug levels a pistol toward the camera. Barrel flash from the thug's pistol and roar of gunshot. Three gunshots from off-camera. Thug falls. Cut to black-and-white photograph showing bullet hole in a wooden joist next to the garage door. Super at screen-bottom: ACTUAL POLICE FORENSIC PHOTO. Cut to Bilbo, lowering a handgun. Voiceover in the kind of baritone that Hollywood trailers use: "Three shots, under fire. Three hits. The thug missed. Chad Bilbo didn't." Cut to gurney rolling toward camera with thug's covered body on it. An African-American sheriff's deputy in khaki uniform with highly polished brown boots walks at the head of the gurney, shaking his head. DEPUTY: "Looks like you done messed with the wrong man, son." Cut to Chad Bilbo, looking solemn and confident. "My name is Chad Bilbo. I defended my home and my family, and I will defend you in Congress. I ask for your prayers and your vote."

Wow! Not a new idea. Goes back to at least 1840 in American elections, and probably before that. The 1840 effort didn't work, but Bilbo's variation on the theme had. Well executed, you might say.

All I had to do was make an apparently decent, smart, and well-educated but totally obscure woman into a political rock star capable of scaring Chad Bilbo. As my flight touched down in Baton Rouge, I did *not* think *how in the HELL am I going to bring this off?* Because I knew. The answer may have scared me, but during the primary and election seasons we'd just been through I'd gotten used to scared.

Chapter 2

"'Young Conservative *Federation*,' not '*Association*,'" G.G. Mason earnestly specified, in about the 65th second of our face-to-face that evening. "We feel that 'Association' has excessively collectivist connotations."

"'Federation,' I dutifully noted. "Got it."

I knew Gideon Gamaliel Mason inside *and* out the moment I laid eyes on him – and not just because the thumb drive had included a brief biographical sketch: senior at A&T; double major in political science and agricultural economics, pulling a three-eight GPA in both; and head of the YCF. I knew a lot more than that. *When your eighth-grade classmates were doing essays on the three branches of government, you did a five-pager on the committee system in Congress. You started door-to-door lit-drops when you were fifteen. Constituent services aide for a congressman is the very bottom of the Rayburn Building food chain, but you would crawl over broken glass to get a gig like that.*

I knew all that because I'd been that same kid.

The unbridled lust that he politely but unsuccessfully tried to banish from his eyes the first time he saw me came as no surprise. For healthy straight males, I'm what the devout nuns at Carondolet Academy sometimes called 'a near occasion of sin.' Glossy black hair; Creole complexion and cheekbones; breasts as generous as the ones that other Creole Josephine had used to turn Napoleon's head; dark eyes with some *éclat* to them, and a smile with perfect white teeth.

Clearly used to being the smartest guy in the room, Mason just as clearly sensed that he might not be ready for the likes of me. Hair the color of corn stubble in autumn, combed like a 1950's frat boy's without the Brylcream. Skin not quite rice-white but showing the geek-pallor that comes from spending a lot more time in Wi-Fi hotspots than on running tracks or hiking trails. Under six feet tall – call it five-ten-plus – and could have used some more beef on his thin arms. Preppy checkered shirt and khakis, and looking like he'd have felt more comfortable if he'd been wearing a tie.

"Thank you for taking some time to see me," I said, fingering the ecologically sensitive cardboard coffee cup that A&T's student lounge had given me. "As I mentioned in my call, when I looked at YCF's website – very professional, by the way; I love the quotes from Burke – I noticed the panel discussion you're planning on campus diversity controversies."

"Yeah, that's a big deal here. Everywhere, I guess."

The three panel participants listed on the site were a little light in buzz potential. I hoped that would give me the opening I needed.

"I'm wondering whether you might be interested in a fourth panelist who could attract some additional attention to your event." I paused to assess. He was interested all right.

"Please tell me you don't mean Congressman Chad Bilbo, that closet liberal who wants to become Governor Chad Bilbo."

I love it when pretty boys play hard to get.

"No, no – not a D.C.-insider type at all. And I don't mean a mouth-breather with white supremacy baggage, either."

"So what kind of profile are you talking about?"

"Louisiana-local. Lives in Baton Rouge now, but cut his political teeth in Plaquemines Parish. Colorful, you might call him. Media-bait. Gives a good sound bite. He's a guy who'd push an MTV commentator fully clothed into the swimming pool if the party got a little dull."

"No violence," Mason said hastily, with a suddenly alarmed expression. "I don't want any rough stuff." For a moment I thought he was checking out my breasts. Then I realized that he was looking for evidence of a hidden recorder.

"Only a figure of speech," I assured him. "I just mean . . . he's the kind of guy who's apt to keep things lively, traffic in the kind of repartee that could go viral. In a good way, of course."

Mason's eyes lit up, but he came back down to earth pretty quickly.

"Um, we, uh, I mean, one thing is, we don't actually have a lot of money."

"I wouldn't worry too much about that. Majority Values Coalition is very excited about your organization. Decide what you feel you can invest in an additional panelist. Whatever it is, we'll try to find a way to make it work."

That would have set off an alarm bell even in Forrest Gump's head, but if one rang for Mason it wasn't loud enough.

"Uh, yeah. Okay." He bowed his head, then looked back up. "Who's this panelist you have in mind?"

I took a deep breath. My conscience was bothering me and, believe me, we're not talking about an overly delicate conscience. Then I thought about the Wrong Man commercial and forged ahead.

"Darius Zachary Taylor Barry," I told him. Uncle D for me, but I didn't mention that. "You might be a little young to recognize the name, but every political reporter in Louisiana over forty knows him."

Mason whipped out an iPhone and started thumbing keys. Researching my Uncle Darius right there in front of me. No apology; no, 'please excuse me for a second;' just double-thumb research in between sips of coffee. I kept my expression carefully neutral. Mason didn't. I picked up excitement, astonishment, and deep concern flashing in turns across his face as he clicked and scrolled. The sequence ended with excitement.

"It says here that he's a convicted felon."

Picky, picky, picky.

"That's true," I acknowledged. "Here in Louisiana, a politician with a felony conviction doesn't belong to a very exclusive club."

Mason grinned. The governors he'd grown up under mostly hadn't gone to prison, but he knew what I was talking about.

"He does seem . . . quotable," Mason allowed.

"Definitely not constrained by the strictures of political correctness. He'll for sure raise your panel's 'wow' quotient."

"Okay." He re-holstered his phone. "I'll have to run this by my board, but I see a way forward here."

I slipped one of my cards across the table to him.

"Absolutely get the board thing. With your conference only four weeks away, of course, the sooner the better. Look forward to hearing from you."

My appointment with Chancellor Dejean wasn't until the next morning. After leaving Mason, though, I walked across campus toward the main administration building anyway, just to get a feel for the place.

The only sleepier campuses in America must have compulsory chapel. Fall semester classes weren't yet under way in late August, but even so. I saw signs for pep rallies and frat/sorority rushes, but no BLACK LIVES MATTER banners, no SAY NO TO RAPE CULTURE! posters, not even any red circle/slash-over-WHITE MALE PRIVILEGE broadsides. MATRIARCHY NOW! or THE PLAGUE OF WHITENESS? Forget it.

Didn't bother me a bit. Show me a hundred millennials paying for college with checks their daddies wrote, and I'll show you fifty who think life is just a reality TV show with a lame premise. If I have a shoulder-mounted camera and a place to stand, I can make the little darlings dance like Pinocchio on speed.

The administration building reminded me of YCF's proposed panel: serviceable and safe enough, but nothing that would make your eyes pop. Mauve and cream paint that could've used some freshening, molded fiberglass chairs of Crayola red and blue, beige carpet just this side of threadbare, and no one had varnished the blond woodwork recently. A&T's alumni apparently weren't dumping tax-deductible contributions into its capital budget. Good news for me.

I picked up a copy of the campus newspaper, the *A&T Pelican*. Eight pages. Pretty much what you'd expect. High hopes for the upcoming football season; Greek life as lively as ever. A fierce debate over whether there should be *any* designated smoking areas on campus was the closest thing to political controversy I could find.

We can fix that. I pulled out my phone to call Uncle D.

Chapter 3

Letitia Dejean in real life looked about ten times better than Letitia Dejean on a low-quality iPhone video, and she sounded ten times better than whoever had overdubbed her voice with words she hadn't actually spoken on the recording Seamus had shown me. She had the kind of hearty, engaging smile I don't normally associate with PhD's, but then I haven't met a lot of people with doctorates in Animal Husbandry.

"Well, Ms. Kendall, we *are* living in interesting times."

"Amen to that," I smiled. "Sometime around 11:00 on election night it seemed like every political rule I ever knew had been repealed and replaced by ones I'd never heard of."

"I guess we'll learn as we go along," she responded warmly. The smile she flashed now told me it was time to get down to business. "In your call, you mentioned an organization called the Educational Integrity Foundation."

"Right. EIF is a client of my employer, Majority Values Coalition. They've asked us to scout out some special universities where EIF's modest resources might get a little more traction than at some of the usual suspects. They're looking to produce major returns in terms of raising the tone and beefing up the substance of higher education."

"And since A and T is pretty much off most people's radar, we're on your list?"

"Blunt, but correct," I said. "Traditional, real world-oriented education; serious faculty focused on student instruction rather than star-turns at symposiums; a place where the inmates don't run the asylum; that kind of thing."

"Guilty as charged on all counts." She nodded once, but meaningfully. "Our professors don't have time to turn out papers on 'Hidden Patriarchy in Self-Isolated Communities.' Does EIF have any specifics in mind?"

"Well, they want to work out the details in close collaboration with each institution. The basic idea is providing seed money to enable student-interactive, labor-intensive research projects. EIF hopes that at least some of these projects would attract sustaining federal grants."

Dejean's eyes lit up. My stilted, carefully prepared spiel had pushed two hot buttons near dead center on any academic administrator's console: autonomy and federal grant-bait. She wasn't a babe in the woods like Mason, though. She asked the question he hadn't.

"And what would EIF want in exchange? Specific course offerings? Some more conservative muscle in our mission statement?"

"EIF doesn't want to coopt A and T, and even if it did, it knows it couldn't do that for three hundred or four hundred thousand dollars." I shook my head earnestly, the way I used to do with Sister Clare Scholastica when I was hoping to get off with two demerits. "With any university it works with, EIF just wants a better model for other universities to follow."

"A noble aspiration," she said in a carefully neutral voice.

"EIF thinks that in the arena of higher education, a focused administrator can make an impact that ripples all the way through society. I mean, look at S.I Hayakawa, for example."

"Ms. Kendall," she said with yet another smile, "you are way too young to remember Professor Hayakawa. I can barely recall him, and I'm betting I have thirty years on you."

"No, you're right. Someone at EIF told me about him. Quite a story, though."

She gave me a look a lot like the one I sometimes got from Sister Clare.

"What do you need from me?"

Chapter 4

By dint of heroic effort, disregard of speed limits, and remarkably good luck, I made it home to Georgetown by 6:30 that evening. Rafe had my cocktail ready – a simple, refreshing gin and tonic, in honor of it still being August.

"Bless you, my son," I said to Rafe, who's twenty-four years my senior, as I folded gratefully into my favorite English country armchair. Before taking a sip, I admired him standing there, with hair as white as mine is black and a gut as flat as a table top. He's a D.C. veteran with a southern pedigree that shows up in a number of ways – never offending anyone unintentionally, for example, and (as I'd found out some time before) shooting straight enough to hit a moving mammal at four hundred-fifty yards with a hunting rifle.

"The project must be going well," he said.

"Mason called me just before I caught my flight to tell me his board had signed on. Release goes out Monday. He'll get quick calls from a couple of old Louisiana scribblers I've tipped off. I've given him talking points that even an undergraduate couldn't screw up."

"How about the A and T end?"

"Dejean completely bought the EIF tease," I said. "She has her development people pulling together data for a submission."

"And then there's Uncle Darius."

"He's chomping at the bit," I said. "'Sonofagun/ We'll have big fun/On the bayou.'"

"Mm-hmm," Rafe said, with a smile showing skeptical concern that only I would have spotted. "Uncle Darius and 'fun' are practically synonyms."

"He is a calculated risk," I admitted.

"I'm not sure that 'calculated' and 'Uncle Darius' are customarily used in the same sentence."

"You have a point." Big sip. The cold liquid, the gin's heat – such a comfort. "Let's think of Uncle D as a bullet that has to be fired only when absolutely necessary, and aimed very carefully when discharged."

"Inspired metaphor," Rafe said.

"Thank you."

"No matter how carefully you aim, you wanna think about what's behind your target. After bullets hit what they're aimed at, they sometimes keep on going."

My eyebrows went up, the last of my G&T went down, and I bestowed on my beloved husband my best penetrating gaze.

"Have you heard something about Uncle Darius that I should know?"

"No, I've heard something about Congressman Chad Bilbo. From Theo McAbbott."

Theo McAbbott writes thrillers that Rafe beats up, puts back together, and then sells to a publisher. Before he wrote thrillers, he worked as a special agent for the FBI. Like basically everyone in Washington, starting with GS-3 clerk-typists, Theo has been known to serve as a conduit for getting information from one person to another with no one's fingerprints on it.

"Okay, now you have my undivided attention, dearest," I told him.

"Turns out Bilbo, who isn't exactly known for his concerns about agricultural and technical education, has tasked a staffer with a full-scale work-up on Dejean, and made inquiries about her with both the Justice Department and the Department of Education – all in the last month or so."

"What a startling coincidence," I said, acknowledging surprise at something that should never be surprising in my line of work. "According to Seamus, that's about when EIF started taking a close interest in her – suggesting that Bilbo is both well informed and at least verging on paranoid."

"Well, no one can stimulate paranoia like your Uncle Darius." Rafe shrugged.

"This is true." I sighed and rattled the ice in my empty glass.

Darius Zachary Taylor Barry jumped hip deep into Louisiana politics right after he finished his tour in Vietnam, figuring that the chances of being killed on the Plaquemines Parish hustings were only a little greater than in Nam. He kept the .45 Uncle Sam had issued him because he thought it might come in handy. It did, though mostly as a deterrent.

Uncle D has always been what you might call "old school." He started out as a precinct captain and a brawler (but in the context of Louisiana politics I repeat myself), busting his knuckles on the chops of rival Democrats trafficking in new-fangled ideas about updating voter registration rolls and similar mischief. His kind of Louisiana Democrats eventually became Republicans, and he made the transition without a qualm.

He is fond of saying that my mind is like the rapids on Louisiana's Tagiapahoa River: fast but not deep. Uncle D did his level best to pick up the male role-model slack after my Papa died when I was twelve. I had the usual teen spells of *I hate your rules!* and he vocally favored dealing with them in traditional southern fashion. There is one person on Earth he's afraid of, though, and that is his sister, who happens to be my Mama. She said as long as I wasn't a thief, a bully, or a snitch, the *fouet* would stay in the kitchen closet. She admitted I was a rascal and a scamp, but she told him that St. Augustine's mom, Monica, was a rascal and a scamp and she got to be a saint without ever feeling a whip.

I never held the retro-parenting stuff against Uncle D. He called in chits to get me my first D.C. gig. And looking back on it, I'm not the soul of patience and wisdom Mama is, and there were times when I would have been tempted to give me a lick or two if I'd been in her shoes. So I can't really blame him for that.

He served twenty-three months in prison because an Assistant United States Attorney dug up a statute that takes a dim view of promising political influence in exchange for an attaché case full of hundred-dollar bills. Incarceration did not rehabilitate him.

In short, I was deploying a man who's about as discreet as the Incredible Hulk, has the tact of a 2 a.m. tweet, and blusters like a drunk at the end of the bar. He could provoke profanity from anyone short of the Pope, even on a calm day.

I knew as well as Rafe did what was coming.

Chapter 5

In politics spontaneity is critical, so it should be well rehearsed. If I couldn't prep a natural like Uncle D in a week, though, I'd quit politics and look into retail shoe sales. That gave me plenty of time for other aspects of the project. In light of Rafe's little bombshell, I decided to drill even deeper down the Chad Bilbo shaft.

Only a political science major who still gets carded at bars would call Bilbo a "closet liberal." His criminal justice policy is 'lock 'em up and hang 'em high.' He's fond of noting that the recidivism rate for executed convicts is zero. He'd cheerfully put abortionists and people who blow up abortion clinics in adjoining cells on death row. He thinks global warming is a hoax and homosexuality is a choice. He'd have welfare recipients earn their food stamps sweeping streets. His answer to the 'problem of mass incarceration' is, 'Why is that a problem?'

Two things got Bilbo the 'closet liberal' tag from Mason: (1) Bilbo's eminently pragmatic, home-cooking views on fracking; and (2) his weakness for massive infrastructure spending. I'd call the second an obvious position for someone with his name on a hundred million-dollar company in the infrastructure business, but I wasn't drinking from the same, undiluted ideological wellsprings as Mason.

Neither, of course, was Calvin Kirby. He figured that after a stiff primary challenge had brought Bilbo home to Jesus, everyone could kiss and make up. Someone – I didn't yet know who – had spotted Letitia Dejean's political potential and touted her to Kirby. Next thing you know, Kirby had set up the Educational Integrity Foundation under the appropriate section of the Internal Revenue Code and the expert tutelage of Seamus Danica.

I called my old boss, former congressman Temple, who's now earning an honest living consulting about renewable energy projects. He always had a soft spot for me and he knew I would take 'off the record' seriously, so he was happy to give me twenty minutes on the phone.

"Brother Chad was not one of my favorite colleagues," he said. "I tried to make allowances, because he's a member of what I call 'the Lucky Sperm Club.'"

"You mean a rich daddy?" I asked.

"Yep. Inherited a hundred twenty million dollars and in seven years ran it up to a hundred twenty-two million. Would have been way better off sticking the whole pile in some little-old-lady index fund."

"I'm guessing that led to lots of Freudian stuff like deep-seated insecurities and compensation issues," I said.

"Bingo, Ms. Kendall. Where do I start? He was always trying to measure up to dad. He lied about how much money he had, bragged about what a great negotiator he was – even though he couldn't negotiate his way out of a bicycle shop if he started with all the spokes – and shed two wives looking for a shinier trophy spouse. Let's see . . . . He bragged about his many intimate recreational experiences. And then, of course, he paid someone an unconscionable amount of money to provide him with a head of hair that looks like nothing you'd ever find in nature."

"It was very kind of you to make allowances."

"Basically, he's just the guy on the country club patio on his second mint julep telling business associates how simple the world is – if you just don't pay attention to professors and bureaucrats. But he still had a vote in committee and on the floor so, yeah, I made allowances."

"Is the dad thing why he wanted to get into Congress?"

"That was always my guess," Temple said. "Sort of a 'they *have* to respect me now' kind of deal. He hired speechwriters who knew how to throw red meat to a crowd, then he basked in the hoots and the hollers and the cheers. Got to Congress and found out it's a lot of work, but not if you never do any."

If it were easy, Kirby wouldn't need me.

Chapter 6

Late September, 2017

Uncle D in place, check. The rest of the panel in place, check. Campus police officers standing around as if they might actually do something useful, check. Two of Uncle D's friends, Jay-Hondra Washington and Billy Hank Tucker, occupying the outside seats at the end of the first row, check. (Jay-Hondra looks like an NFL defensive end; Billy Hank looks like he steals lunch money from NFL defensive ends on their way to school.) Yours truly in a discreet spot stage right, shouldering a major league video camera, check. Lights nice and bright, check. Six-by-eight-foot American flag hung vertically behind the panelists, check.

After welcoming the crowd, Mason asked everyone to stand for the pledge of allegiance. I caught about forty audience members booing, and made sure I had clean shots of them to cross-cut during editing with shots I'd already taken of the flag. After everyone sat down, Mason introduced the panel: Professor Ursula Dallas (African-American, late forties, from A&T's Sociology Department, and looking like she was comfortable in front of a microphone); Professor Bart Julius (white, early fifties, from the Political Science Department, and looking like he'd run over his mother to get to a microphone); and Uncle D. There was supposed to be a fourth panelist, but Professor Shaleel Muhammed Khalil had withdrawn from the panel to protest Uncle D's addition to it.

I watched Mason as he glanced at an iPad in front of him. *Okay, kid, stick to the script, don't kill anyone, and we'll be fine.*

"We're going to begin with white male privilege," Mason said. "Ninety seconds. We'll start with Professor Dallas."

She spent ninety-three seconds sharing her views in an emphatic but reasonably modulated tone. She explained that white male privilege was an intellectually fruitful construct for exploring something or other. I tuned out after 'exploring,' so I didn't pick up any more of her comment.

Professor Julius then said that, 'as the token conservative on the campus,' he thought the first comment, 'while certainly not without merit,' had overlooked implicit racial and gender bias 'secreted in the terminology itself.' That generated gasps, boos, and angry shouts. Smoothly ignoring them, he concluded with a knowing smile and a neat little sound bite: "It's a matter of words, but words matter." A line worth stealing; I made a mental note of it.

Deep breath. Uncle D now had the floor. Uncle D's job was *not* to enlighten, to educate, to persuade, to convince, to inspire, or to participate in a constructive dialogue. Uncle D's job was to provoke. You can provoke people by saying outrageous things, but Uncle D doesn't do that. He says reasonably sane things in a way that unfailingly triggers the blind-fury reflex of whatever crowd he's addressing. It's a gift.

"I'll tell you what," he drawled, "back in nineteen-sixty-six, I wish I'd had a few ladies to share the privilege of being drafted to fight in Vietnam with. The bullets them Cong was firing didn't know what color I was, so I have a hard time seeing where privilege entered into it. When I got back, I went over to LSU and asked them to give me a bachelor's degree because I was a white male, and those fellas told me no, I'd have to get admitted first, without any affirmative action help, and then pass the same courses as everyone else."

Jay-Hondra and Billy Hank threw their heads back and roared, along with maybe twenty percent of the rest of the crowd. The remainder reacted at first with stunned silence. Uncle D's words weren't just heretical, they were *unthinkable* on a college campus. Then came the uproar. Jeers, curses and, after a false start or two, a chant. *What's the enemy? White supremacy!* I panned across the audience, picking up every angry face, every snarling mouth, and every shaking fist.

The campus cops remained studiously immobile until Billy Hank stood up, went to the nearest chanter, and asked him to please quiet down because his shouting was making it difficult for Billy Hank to hear Mason introduce the next topic. (He may not have put it quite that way.) *Then* the campus cops started moving and the chanting gradually died away, like a wave at a baseball game when the crowd just can't quite get into it anymore.

It went like that with each topic Mason introduced.

"The problem of mass incarceration," Mason intoned. Blah-blah-blah/Yada-yada-yada, and then Uncle D: "Well, as the only member of this panel who has actual experience with incarceration, here's my solution. Don't sell drugs. Don't hijack cars. Don't knock over gas stations and liquor stores. Problem solved! You're welcome! Next issue." Uproar.

On the subject of choice: Core-of-personal-autonomy/Need-for-balance, and then Uncle D: "Seems to me like it depends on what you're choosing. In a history class I flunked I learned that John C. Calhoun was pro-choice on slavery, and I am definitely not pro *that* choice." Uproar.

Mason managed somehow to get things more or less under control each time, but then he reached the final topic, the oppression of people of color. After fervent but carefully modulated protest/standard-issue academic boilerplate, Uncle D got the floor: "That is truly a concern. The very idea that we would build a wall to keep people of color in this country. Oh, wait a minute. We're building a wall to keep non-white people *out* of the country, aren't we? People who are risking their lives to get here. Guess those non-white folks voting with their feet aren't as 'woke' as y'all here are."

The reaction to that one went way, *way* beyond uproar. Within seconds it presented a picture-postcard of activists on their feet and filling the venue with feral, frothing outrage. Screams of "Fascist!" and "Racist!" and "Terrorism!" I kid you not: "Terrorism!"

All I needed now was a money shot before fade-to-black. I gave Uncle Darius his cue. Cupping his right ear theatrically, he pretended to hear one student shouting, "You should find out what 'mansplaining' is and stop doing it!" He repeated the imaginary comment into the microphone and then answered, "Oh, I know what 'mansplaining' is. It's the same thing as 'libsplaining,' except with logic and *co*-herence." On our digital film, we'd add that exchange in subscript, because by that point we had achieved the distilled essence of free speech: no one could understand a word anyone else was shouting.

Co-herence did it. Six students charged the stage. The campus police ran for cover. Jay-Hondra and Billy Hank did not run for cover. They jumped up, turned around, and from under their chairs pulled old-fashioned syphon bottles with squeeze triggers, like people once used to spritz carbonated water into scotch. On each side they squirted the first attacker in the face. We were one whipped cream pie in the puss short of perfect slapstick.

I got every blessed second of it on camera. Truly beautiful. I felt like Monet after putting the last brush-stroke on *Water Lillies*.

Chapter 7

Half a dozen attendees posted crappy, muddy-sounding videos that they'd taken with their mobile phones. We went up at two a.m. with a professional, high-quality, digital recording that I'd improved with some judicious mouse clicks. Not much of a contest. By the end of day-two we were in the middle six figures and we had cable news producers panting over the phone. *Earned media*: the two most beautiful words in the English language.

Even so, Seamus was in classic fuss-budget mode. We were watching the same feed on our computers, he in D.C. while I was at Mama's house on St. Philip Street in Baton Rouge. He allowed that what we had so far was "stupendous, colossal," which is Seamus-speak for not bad. But he was stewing about a second act.

"Where are the grievance junkies?" he demanded.

Seamus thinks that any culture war will involve deeply sincere, profoundly committed, idealistic partisans who would give their very souls for their vision of what's right. They're amateurs with an attention span equal to roughly three news cycles. He calls these people 'halo polishers.' It will also involve professional activists who are in it for the long haul. Activism is who they are and what they do. The causes change, but their attitude doesn't. He calls this group 'grievance junkies.' Grievance junkies give a protest legs.

"They'll come," I assured him. "Uncle D is on Rush Limbaugh's show today, and our video is still trending."

Bingo. Late that afternoon, just about the time overwhelming indignation from about ten percent of the student body was threatening to plateau, unmistakable signs of grievance-junkie incursion appeared. Dueling manifestoes. Meetings that excluded white students or relegated them to the role of silent spectators in the back of the room. And, of course, lists of non-negotiable demands.

The administration responded by inviting protest leaders in for discussions, participating in screaming psycho-dramas called 'conversations,' and promising to consider the demands. This wasn't enough, of course. Sit-ins, teach-ins, and demonstrations outside (and sometimes inside) the administration building ensued.

I spent over a week in Baton Rouge, touching base with various targets of opportunity. My most productive chat involved Delia Derryberry, Republican assemblyperson from a district that included parts of Ascension, Assumption, and Iberville Parishes and chair of the Louisiana Assembly's Committee on Higher Education. Ms. Derryberry allowed that she would get in touch with a handful of A&T regents to let them know that many of her colleagues on the committee took a very dim view of students and 'outside agitators' hijacking universities.

The message apparently came in loud and clear to Letitia Dejean. While continuing a placatory approach with the students, she refused to fire anyone, or ask for anyone's resignation, or order the Young Conservative Federation into sensitivity training, or commit to spending dime one on any of the demands.

Five days later came the answer to my ultimate prayer. The frustrated grievance-junkies got the football team involved. That brought things to a crisis, which is exactly where I wanted them.

I told Dejean on behalf of the Educational Integrity Foundation that, by a remarkable coincidence, EIF's views were the same as Assemblyperson Derryberry's. I added that, while A&T's submission really excited EIF blah-blah- blah, it would be hard for donors to see the point of throwing money at adolescents who apparently didn't grasp the basic idea of university education. I also shared some thoughts which, out of habit, I had written down in a script that read a lot like the voiceover Seamus had shown me in his office.

I expected a pretty tense conversation with Dejean. When I sat down to talk with her, though, I noticed a Wikipedia printout headed "S.I. Hayakawa." Hayakawa had been a semantics professor at the University of California – Berkeley. He became dean in the 'seventies after his predecessor was forced out for being too soft with campus protesters. Hayakawa was not soft with campus protesters. Long story short, he went from dean to folk hero and from folk hero to United States Senator. I thought *my work here is done.*

It was. Dejean's response to the protest came off like a dream. Money and support poured in from alumni. The football team caved. The protest lost steam. Dejean suddenly found herself an icon of adult common sense. Rumors about a run for public office spread. When she refused to confirm them, they spread faster. Majority Values Coalition had delivered big time for Calvin Kirby.

Mama gave me a hug. Uncle Darius gave me a big grin and a hug. When I got back to D.C., Rafe gave me a vodka martini.

"Guess you had big fun on the bayou," he said.

"Thanks. I'm trying to feel guilty about shamelessly using an earnest young man who was a political virgin."

"He's not a political virgin anymore," Rafe pointed out.

"Well that's something, I guess."

Rafe drew on a Monte Cristo and waited a beat to see if I'd ask for a puff. I didn't.

"You ginned up a protest out of thin air. You used political contacts to manipulate the university's administration. You made Letitia Dejean a plausible primary opponent for Chad Bilbo. What are her chances of actually beating him?"

"Not much. The seventh district demographics have changed a lot in the last few years, but probably not enough."

"So he pretty much has a lock on the Republican primary?"

"That's the beautiful part," I said. "Louisiana doesn't have party primaries in congressional races. The primary is a free for all, and the top two finishers go to a run-off if no candidate gets fifty percent."

"So if she keeps him under fifty percent in the first round," Rafe said, "who knows? As the baseball gurus say, anything can happen in a short series."

"Amen. Anyway, for our purposes she doesn't have to beat him. All she needs to do is scare him."

I had confected a news story that was true without being real. A lot of reporters had sat on their butts and let a political hustler like me spoon feed a narrative to them. And that's not my fault. Just like a spikes-high slide into second base: It ain't pretty – but that's the way the game is played.

Chapter 8

October, 2017

I had just noticed the American flag outside the Library of Congress fluttering at half-staff when Rafe phoned to tell me that I might get a call from Phoebe Riverdale. Half-staff because a few days before someone named Stephen Paddock had murdered fifty-eight people and wounded more than a hundred at the Route 91 Harvest Festival Concert in Las Vegas. But half-staff for killings at a school or a church or a political rally had gotten pretty standard by now. I'm almost surprised that it caught my attention.

I knew better than to ask why Phoebe might call. Except with publishers, Rafe isn't a detail guy. He just makes the connection, and then the people connected are on their own.

Rafe's literary-agent work is like the book in a Broadway musical: it takes up a lot of time, but it's not really the point. What is the point? Well, that's complicated.

Start with a group of whip-smart twenty-somethings with the ink still wet on their JDs from Harvard Law or MAs (Political Science) from Tufts or BSs (Economics) from Stanford or even BAs (Communications/Public Policy) from Tulane. (That last one would be me.) These newbies go to work for members of Congress or congressional committee staffs or executive agencies or news organizations, where they quickly learn that lots of brainiacs roughly as smart as they are come to work in D.C. every single year. Two or three, though, don't just have book smarts but gut smarts, or some other special aptitude that gives them a higher ceiling than their peers.

Rafe tries to spot them early on. He's pretty good at it. He has his share of swings and misses, but it's like baseball: hit 300 and you're in the Hall of Fame. He arranges to run into them, cultivates them, guides them, introduces them to people they should know – the usual Washington stuff.

Over time, some of Rafe's protégés rise. Not to cabinet secretary necessarily (although one actually has gone that far), but to, say, deputy solicitor in the Labor Department or senior producer on CNN or coordinating data analyst for the Office of Inspector General or communication staff in the West Wing – my friend Hank Sinclair, that sniveling little weasel, for example. Rafe stays in touch with them, remembers them at holiday time, creates little synergies where he puts two of them together because he sees they can do each other some good.

Then, when it works the way it's supposed to, someone in Raleigh-Durham or Silicon Valley or South Korea discovers that he needs to confer with one of Rafe's protégés or one of their bosses or someone else in that orbit. This person talks to an obscenely overpaid lobbyist, who talks to Rafe, who talks to the appropriate protégé, who talks to the lobbyist's client, whereupon the lobbyist pays Rafe a consulting fee, or buys five thousand copies of a book written by one of Rafe's clients, or does something else really nice for Rafe that involves money.

That's why Rafe told me to expect a call from Phoebe.

Rafe or no Rafe, Phoebe would have done just fine. With Rafe's nudges, though, she did just fine faster than she otherwise might have, landing herself a job in the Communications Office of George W. Bush's administration at the ripe age of twenty-three. She went from there to Fox News. Hit a little speed bump by side-stepping over to NPR when the fanny patting at Fox got old. She kept at it, though. Now and then she'd write a breezy little, wryly humorous think piece that Rafe would get onto the op-ed page of the *Post* or the *Times* or, failing that, into *Impolitic* or *Rotunda* on-line. He helped her get a collection of these published in paperback (*Anagram City: Matters of State and Matters of Taste*) so that she could send free copies to about four hundred people who wouldn't necessarily read them but who'd remember that they'd seen her name on the cover of a book.

Next step: one of the CNN daily news shows took her on as a reporter and occasional panelist. By now she was one big score away from having Fox, MSNBC, and CNN in a bidding war over her for weekend anchor and prime-time host-in-waiting (with Fox, presumably, throwing in a no-groping clause as a sweetener). The point is, Phoebe got her calls returned.

Chapter 9

"Josie, how are things going?" she asked when we connected.

"On the record, no comment. Off the record, things are going great."

She laughed.

"There's someone I'd like you to meet," she said.

"Where and when?"

"Don't you want to know who it is?"

"Any friend of yours, Phoebe. I'm wide open this afternoon."

"How about the Newseum at one?"

Huh? We each have a perfectly good office in Washington and instead of using one of them we're going to meet at a tourist trap crawling with eleven-year-old munchkins wearing Day-glow orange t-shirts so that their harried field-trip chaperones can keep track of them? Apparently, she and her source didn't want anyone connecting them to me. What's next, a dead-letter drop on Embassy Row?

"You got it, Phoebe. See you then."

In Washington you have friends and then you have "friends." Phoebe and I were "friends." First-name basis; wished each other well; I would have lent her a hundred dollars in a pinch without a second thought and vice-versa. But neither of us would have called the other about, say, a problem pregnancy or an addiction issue or insecurity about our husbands' fidelity. Not actual friends, in other words. Just "friends."

Until January 12, 2017, when their divorce decree became final, Phoebe had technically still been married to one weasel-in-the-West-Wing Hank Sinclair. During the Trump transition, before the divorce was officially done, Hank had called me for a meeting. He was on the transition team, though way at the end of the bench, so his call got my hopes up.

Turned out all he wanted was a roll in the hay. I still remember the let-down. There I was, sitting across a desk from him, close enough to appreciate the ultra-fine weave on his two hundred twenty-five dollar white cotton broadcloth dress shirt featuring cufflinks with the presidential seal; allowing myself to hope, when – *wham!* – he propositioned me.

Now, I don't get all sideways about such moves. They happen. Hank, though, came up a bit short in the finesse department. After two polite 'no's' and one almost-as-polite 'that's enough,' he got a little coarse for my taste.

"Look, Josie, I'm on the transition team. I'll have a job in the White House. It's not like you've never stepped out on that relic you call a husband. You're going to sleep with me and we both know it. Let's stop wasting time. Just be a good little power groupie and hitch up your skirt."

What hurt was that his crack about my cheating on Rafe once was true. I don't rationalize it. Don't excuse it. *Just a fling, didn't mean anything, right?* No, not right. Dead wrong. I screwed up, period, and I'm still ashamed of myself for it. It's not going to happen again, and it's sure *as hell* not going to happen with my hips under a self-important, Ivy-League loser.

"Hank, this is the real world, not the third season of *Veep*. I'm not going to cheat on Rafe, and even if I were single and interested, I would never sleep with a friend's husband."

"Saint Josephine," he'd said, smiling his Hollywood smile. "Right. Who do you think you're kidding?"

That tore it.

"'Whom,'" I'd said before splashing a tumbler full of water on his face and walking out.

So, as you can see, Hank Sinclair is on my scut list and I'm on his.

Chapter 10

At five minutes before one p.m. I strolled into the Newseum, a monument to the Washington news media's image of itself as Fearless Watchdog and Savior of Free Institutions. Just past the admission area, Phoebe introduced me to Vernon Czlewski (*Ches-LEV-ski* – in a political family you learn to pronounce people's names right). Mid-sixties, very sparse light brown hair, skin the color and texture of saddle leather, five-eight on a good day, with the reedy, care-worn body of a survivor. His most striking feature by far was his eyes: so dark brown they seemed almost black, piercing, and moving constantly to survey his surroundings.

"Nice to meet you, Ms. Kendall," he said as he flashed me a two-second smile.

"You too, Mr. Czlewski," I said.

"Call me Vernon, please. Using my Slavic moniker all the time might add ten minutes to our conversation."

"You got it, Vernon."

He snapped his first question as soon as we began pretending to look at exhibits.

"Do you know who Slow Willie Woodbine was?"

"No."

"He was the burglar that Chad Bilbo gunned down to start his political career," Vernon said.

"Oh, right." I nodded, embarrassed about not knowing Woodbine's name. I should have. "The incident in Bilbo's famous Wrong Man campaign ad. He dramatized it pretty well."

"'Dramatized' is one way to put it."

Vernon's tone sounded a touch gravelly, with a soft, southern accent that wrapped his provocative words in a comforting glow. Phoebe had her lips firmly sealed under her patrician nose.

"All ears," I said.

"Slow Willie owned two guns: a .357 magnum Colt Diamondback revolver, and a Remington pump-action twelve-gauge shotgun. He did *not* own a Walther CC semi-automatic pistol."

"Is that what he fired at Bilbo?"

"According to the police," Vernon said, looking at me appraisingly.

"Was the Walther one of Bilbo's guns, then?"

"Walther is a German make, and Chad Bilbo has always been Mr. Buy American. He wouldn't touch a kraut gun with a frog gig."

"Any idea where the gun came from?" I asked.

"Well, you might say it came from me." I took a stab at poker-faced but was pretty sure I didn't make it. Vernon continued. "I've owned pawn shops in Louisiana for going on forty years, including one in Baton Rouge. A fella looking at a nickel and a dime for aggravated battery pawned that weapon for money to pay his lawyer."

'A nickel and a dime' means five to ten years, so the battery must have been pretty aggravated – a loan-shark special with a baseball bat, maybe.

"I'm guessing he never got the gun out of hock," I said.

"Got off with eighteen months. I sold the Walther around the time that cat got his first taste of chipped beef on toast in the prison cafeteria. Sold it to a young lady for exactly one hundred eighty-five dollars, cash."

"I guess she was maxed out on her American Express."

"The damsel in question was on welfare, food stamps," he said after an honest chuckle. "Not ordinarily flush with legal tender. And that's not the only curious thing."

"Okay . . . ."

"Darned if that dadgummed gun didn't get stolen from the young lady not a week after she bought it. Snatch-and-grab while she was walking out of a KFC."

"Well I'll be switched." I figured I might as well play along with the down-home dialect game.

"She reported it to the police, but of course they couldn't do much."

Vernon's eyes asked whether I was keeping up.

"So she was a straw buyer," I said, to show that I was. "Buying for someone who couldn't legally buy a gun himself, or didn't want a record of him buying it. Then she covered herself by reporting it stolen."

Clasping his hands behind his back, he smiled at me.

"You think like a cop," he said.

"I'd slap your face, but I just did my nails." In Louisiana, threatening to slap a fella's face is damn close to flirting. "Any idea who the straw buyer was buying for?"

"If I had to take a wild guess, I'd go with Caleb André Regine Delacroix. Black fella. Real good looking. Dresses like a GQ cover. Goes by Card on the street. From his initials, you see."

"Yeah. I'll bet he earns his living selling home and automobile insurance."

"So close. Crack, heroin, and other opioids. Didn't mess with marijuana except as a loss-leader, to get those middle schoolers started. I believe the young lady was a steady customer, of the crack persuasion."

"Was Slow Willie part of Card's organization?"

"Not exactly. Slow Willie's bread and butter was breaking and entering. He could snap a standard residential door lock in seven seconds like it was a toy. He was big-time down on the hard stuff, and he thought transporting or dealing was a sucker's game. But he'd do some freelance work for Card now and then. Debt collection, site security, street intelligence."

"Sounds like you and Slow Willie knew each other real well," I said.

"We got along. Started out with us doing business together and sort of blossomed over time. Kind of cat I'd share a beer or a joint with. You know?"

"Sure." I also knew what kind of business a burglar and a pawn shop owner would have been doing together.

"Slow Willie had himself some hard-and-fast rules," Vernon said. "Rule one was, never take a firearm with you on a breaking-and-entering. Big penalty-enhancer – plus, it's a good way to get yourself killed."

So apparently either Slow Willie broke his own rule and brought a gun onto Bilbo's property, or Bilbo's gunfight narrative didn't match up with what actually happened – to say it politely. A tingle ran through me. Just what I needed: jump feet first into a tinfoil-hat conspiracy swamp that might be fake news from top to bottom. I felt Phoebe's eyes on me, so I glanced at her.

"I'll wait for you out on the smoking plaza," she said.

Phoebe doesn't smoke.

"Did they find Slow Willie's fingerprints on the Walther?" I asked.

"They found the Walther clutched in his right hand, but the latex gloves he was wearing sort of cut down on fingerprint potential. They did find powder residue on the glove from the back-flash when the gun fired."

"I guess that fits then," I said.

"Fits like a glove, you might say."

"You liked Slow Willie, didn't you?"

"That's a fact," Vernon said. "The whole thing has grated on me ever since the Holiness Full Gospel Church choir sang *Standin' in the Need of Prayer* over Slow Willie's grave. I actually made a couple of quiet little inquiries early on."

"What did you find out?"

"Not much. 'Fore I knew which end was up the *po*-lice were down on me like a front-end loader full of quarry stone. Something about stolen property in my shop."

"Imagine that."

"Probation," Vernon said, "but they told me I'd hear the big steel door slam for sure if it happened again. So, you know, it hasn't happened again."

"Any documentation for any of this?"

"The death certificate for the straw buyer is a public record. Seems she tragically overdosed on heroin about a week before Slow Willie messed with the wrong future congressman."

"I thought you said she was a crack addict."

"I did. Funny thing, right? It's just one damned funny thing after another in this little affair." Vernon paused for a couple of beats. "Interested?"

"Oh, I'm interested all right."

"Phoebe knows how to reach me," he said, then gave me a sad smile and began strolling away.

I found Phoebe on the smoking plaza, not smoking. She turned her cobalt blue eyes toward me, her expression wry and a bit sheepish.

"I keep telling myself that getting used to cigarette smoke might help me when I interview Ivanka Trump," she said.

"Ivanka? That's quite a get for you."

"I have a 'yes' in principle. And if she's still smoking, prissy body language might turn her off."

"Anything for a story," I said. "Let's head back inside."

"So what do you think of Vernon?" she asked as we began to move.

"Could be huge – *if* we can figure out what actually happened, and prove it."

"Those ifs still come up quite a bit in the news game. If you wanna get technical about it, we do *try* not to run with stuff that didn't actually happen."

"Right. Leave fake news to the professionals." I smiled a professional smile.

"I think Vernon has more hard evidence to back up his story than he's shown so far," Phoebe said.

"What's he waiting for?"

"Cover and commitment."

"Commitment I get," I said. "He doesn't want to risk that big steel door unless someone is really going to go after the story. But if he thinks I can give him cover, he's kidding himself."

"I'm the cover he's hoping for," Phoebe said. "He thinks that maybe if I get enough evidence, I can break the story without his name coming up. He believes the cops will think twice about nailing a whistle-blower on a story that a national news network is running with – especially if that story is part of a political campaign."

"Well *this* couldn't get much clearer, could it?" I asked. "You give Vernon cover, and I give you cover. If there are campaign commercials blaring a charge against a politician who's running for re-election, CNN can just report the accusation as part of the campaign story. Wouldn't even need to claim that it's true."

"That's about the size of it," Phoebe said crisply and unapologetically. "The thing is, Trump's media strategy has worked. The opinion guys can scream about him nonstop, but on the news side we've gotten downright gun-shy. No news director in Washington wants a 4 a.m. tweetstorm ginning up the fake news calls. There's no room for a mistake, much less a discredited story. Trump doesn't care how much we loathe him as long as we're scared – and we are."

So, Phoebe was using me, and not making any bones about it. Welcome to D.C. You know how you can tell you're being used in Washington? You're in Washington.

"I need to get my boss in the loop," I said. *And Kirby,* but that I didn't say. "I'll be in touch."

Phoebe looked at me with a touch of concern.

"Are you okay with this, Josie?"

"On the record, I'm fine. Off the record, I've just been handed three sticks of dynamite with a lit fuse."

Chapter 11

"What does Seamus think?" Rafe asked in between bites of salmon with Creole sauce.

"'Atomic bomb!' But he agrees we can't drop it until we have serious evidence."

"Look at Seamus getting religion all of a sudden!" Rafe exclaimed. "Evidence! How scrupulous! How about the client?"

"Conflicted. Bilbo thinks he can beat Letitia Dejean, so he isn't budging on the fracking issue. The client feels that he needs some serious motivation."

"Like a smear. Not just a run-of-the-mill 30-second spot, though. Has to be a smear that generates attention from major news organizations," Rafe said.

"Yeah. But Calvin Kirby is highly principled. He only wants to smear people with stuff that at least looks like it might be true."

"Nice to have standards. So, on with a quest for evidence now, right?"

"Bingo. I've talked with Uncle Darius about getting a peek at the sheriff's file on the original investigation."

"A legal peek?" Rep asked.

"As legal as anything involving Louisiana public officials ever is."

Rafe savored another forkful of the salmon. It takes a topping well and I'm good with Creole sauce, so it was definitely worth savoring. While we ate, I reflected. I'm a grade-A multi-tasker. A worry began to simmer. Rafe put down his fork and looked at me.

We were thinking the same thing.

June 14, 2017, Alexandria, Virginia, Eugene Simpson Stadium Park. Sixty rounds of rifle fire split the still morning air, squeezed off by a loony lefty who hated President Trump. Four Republican congressmen and two security officers wounded – and Louisiana's own

34

Steve Scalise damn near killed. Bad as it was, the atrocity might have turned out vastly worse if the security officers hadn't heroically charged the gunman, running toward the fire instead of away from it, and taken the bastard out.

A lot of people in Washington will say "I was there" if they were even in the same zip code when some head-grabbing incident went down. Well, I was *not* at Eugene Simpson Stadium Park during the shooting. I was only *heading* there. The closest I'd gotten was three blocks away, where a cop informed me that I wouldn't be getting any closer for a while.

I reached Rafe in his car. He'd heard about the shooting before I had and tried to call me, but couldn't get through because I'd been on the phone with a chatty contact at the NRA. So he'd jumped in his Ford Escape, put a Winchester 12 gauge and a box of goose load on the back seat, and raced toward the scene to defend his woman. That's the way they raise boys down South. When he answered my call, I told him he could take dragon slaying off that day's to-do list.

What if I'd gotten to my spontaneous baseball field meet-and-greet half an hour earlier? What if I'd taken my shower the night before instead of that morning, or hadn't lingered over my French roast and the *Washington Post* on-line? Did Eugene Simpson Stadium Park and Stephen Paddock/Route 91 – and all the half-staff-causing rampages in between them – just mean we were living in crazy times and that's it? I mean, cliché du jour, right? Or have we gotten two fingers away from 1968 crazy: American cities in flames, combat troops double-timing down urban streets, Martin Luther King, Jr. and Bobby Kennedy falling to assassins' bullets within months of each other?

What if I fell down Phoebe's rabbit hole and actually stumbled into a truth that would be very inconvenient for some powerful people? I mean, not to put too fine a point on it, what might happen *to me*?

"So," Rafe said, his fork still down and a yarn ready to unfold, "Slow Willie is tangentially linked to a high-flying pusher named Card. Some DEA agent in Louisiana presumably had Card on his agenda."

"Drug Enforcement Administration." I nodded. "Makes sense."

"Any agent worth his salt must have had a snitch somewhere in Card's vicinity."

"Maybe the snitch was Slow Willie," I said. "Suppose Card found out, and decided that Slow Willie had to get chalked."

"What the hell does 'chalked' mean?"

"Turned into a body on the ground that the police outline in chalk."

"Okay, yes, exactly," Rafe said. "Anyway, instead of killing Slow Willie himself, Card tells him to plant the Walther in Bilbo's garage, to frame Bilbo for something or other. Then Card tips Bilbo off."

"Slow Willie walks into an ambush, and Bilbo goes to Washington. But he's got blood on his hands. 'Rumpsey Dumpsey/Colonel Johnson killed Tecumsey!'"

"Card gets Bilbo to do his dirty work, but Bilbo is the big winner. So now Bilbo feels he owes Card a favor."

"It works," I said.

"Doesn't mean that a word of it is true, though," Rafe cautioned. "We're just making stuff up."

"Have to start somewhere." I shrugged. "The next step is to find out if there's an agent. I know Theo was FBI, but do you think he might have some DEA contacts?"

"Doubt it," Rafe said. "The FBI is in the Justice Department, and DEA reports to Treasury. Friendly rivals without the friendly. Worth a try, though. Let's give him a call after dinner."

We did. As usual, Theo McAbbott was charming, genial – and pessimistic.

"I'll make some calls," he said, "but the two outfits basically try to stay out of each other's way. If I strike out, what's Plan B?"

I let out a long, deep breath.

"Plan B is gonna have to be Hank Sinclair."

DEFAULT TO WINK

November, 2017

"Never write if you can speak; never speak if you can nod; never nod if you can wink."

Martin Lomasney, after whom Lomasney Way in Boston is named

Chapter 12

I was at work around 11:00 a.m. on Monday a week later when Fed Ex delivered Uncle D's package. I still hadn't heard from Theo. I eagerly pulled the rip-tab on the express envelope: Thirty-seven photocopied pages, taken from the report of the East Baton Rouge Parish Sheriff's Department on Slow Willie Woodbine passing away while he burglarized Chad Bilbo's garage.

The written statement the cops had taken from Chad Bilbo said he'd been working into the small hours, fussing with some trout flies in his basement, holding them with a fishing rod section above an aquarium tank while examining them from below the tank to check out what they'd look like to a trout through two feet of fresh water. He'd finally gotten six new flies fixed up just the way he wanted them and had decided to take them out to the man-cave part of his four-bay garage so he could lock them in his Plano. (Quick swim in Google: 'Plano' is a brand of high-end tackle boxes.) Bilbo said he never went outside after dark these days without his high-intensity tactical flashlight and Smith & Wesson .38 caliber Police Positive revolver, so he'd plucked those items from his gun cabinet and started his trek.

Just outside the house he'd noticed that the garage service door was ajar. He'd made a mental note to chew Mary Barbara out for that, because that was a real firm house rule: that door stayed closed and locked at all times, except when you were going in or coming out. Then, as he'd stepped through the service door, damned if he hadn't heard furtive little noises over in the far bay, where he kept his tool boxes and his Plano, as if someone had maybe noticed his flashlight beam and was trying to cut his profile down to zero or so. Bilbo said he guessed it wasn't the smartest thing he'd ever done, but it rankled him that someone was violating his property and it might take the Sheriff's Department half an hour to get out there and damned if he was going to wait all night in Louisiana's summer heat, so he'd crept further inside. Sure enough, little on-and-off glimmers of light over in that far bay, as if someone were using the glow from his cell phone to find his way without knocking over something that would produce a real racket.

Well, at that point adrenaline had kicked in. That's all he could say. He'd padded behind the three vehicles in the garage – Mary Barbara's Escalade, his Corvette, and his Yukon Denali XL. He'd gotten that tactical flashlight up above his left shoulder, and shone it into the fourth bay where he thought he had an intruder on his hands. He'd barked, 'Drop your weapon and put your hands in the air!' What he'd gotten in return was a bullet whistling past him in the dark. Naturally, he'd returned fire. Three shots. It all happened so fast. Couldn't say how the intruder was standing or what his position was, except the muzzle flash seemed to come from up high. Bottom line, the intruder had missed and Bilbo hadn't. Bilbo said he'd hustled over to check frantically for a pulse, but there was none.

Okay. Consistent with the infamous campaign commercial – no surprise there. But the commercial had flashed something about an "actual forensic photograph." Page, page, page and there it was. There they were, actually. Two photos, one horizontal format like the one in the campaign commercial, and one vertical. Sure looked like a bullet hole in the joist beside a garage door to me, with splintered cracks radiating out from it. A third photo provided a close-up of the vertical, this one showing a measuring tape beside the joist. The tape said the hole was a shade over five feet from the ground. An annotation written in neat block letters beside the bullet-hole read:

Angle ≤ 3° ↓

Dist. = 14`

Ten more photos. Four, from various angles, showed Slow Willie lying dead. Latex gloves on his hands, pistol clenched in his right fist, slumped with his upper body against the base of a wide metal work table that looked about four feet high. Two showed the garage's fourth bay after removal of Willie's body. On the part of the work table above and just to the right of the chalk outline of Willie's outside shoulder sat what figured to be Bilbo's tackle box, end-on to the camera. It opened from the top instead of the front, and three tiers of trays for flies and other tackle rose elegantly upward in gulf-wing fashion. The last photo recorded the full chalk body outline on the garage floor and against the lower front of the work table. I said a little prayer that I was sorry for my flippant crack to Rafe about chalk outlines. Slow

Willie had indeed gotten chalked, and it wasn't pretty.

Page, page, page. Mary Barbara Bilbo's statement. Short and sweet. She'd been sound asleep; awakened by gunfire; didn't want to call 9-1-1 until she knew what was going on, so she'd grabbed her own Smith & Wesson .40 caliber and hustled downstairs. Didn't know where to look at first; called "Chad? Chad!" until he yelled that he was in the garage. As soon as she got through the service door, he'd yelled to her that he was okay but that he'd just shot a burglar and told her to call the sheriff, not 9-1-1, because it wasn't an emergency anymore. Call the sheriff's office and tell them that he'd just had a target-shooting contest with a burglar and the burglar had come in second.

Next two pages, lab reports: gunpowder traces on the latex glove on Slow Willie's right hand; ballistic test matched the bullet recovered from the joist to the pistol in Slow Willie's right hand.

Next page: no recoverable fingerprints except the Bilbos', which naturally showed up all over the garage and the service door.

A few more pages in, I found a summary of Slow Willie's record. He was known to the police, as the saying goes; multiple arrests but only one conviction, and that was for a misdemeanor that looked pretty chicken-shit to me.

On the next page a report of the search of Slow Willie's body and clothes: lock-pick, slim-jim, Samsung mobile phone, no wallet but two hundred eighty dollars in tens, twenties, and a couple of fifties stuffed into the right pocket of his jeans.

Autopsy report: Slow Willie was five feet, eight inches tall, weighed one hundred fifty-eight pounds, African-American, and had died of three gunshot wounds – technically, of one that had clipped the edge of his heart before the two that had punctured his lungs could do the job. No traces of drugs in his system.

That was it. No chats with neighbors, no canvass to see if someone might have been out walking his dog in the vicinity or having a joint where his wife or parents wouldn't see him, no follow-up on whatever recent calls showed up on Slow Willie's phone. Self-defense, open and shut. A man's home is his castle, and Slow Willie had picked a bad time to cross the moat.

As far as I could tell, I had wasted forty-five minutes of my life. Then the phone on my desk rang. Checked caller ID. Prayer answered: Theo.

Chapter 13

I didn't even bother with hello. "Give me good news, Theo," I said when I answered.

"The best, Empress." (Calling me 'Empress' is an allusion to that other Creole Josephine. Theo thinks it's a real knee-slapper.) "Your beloved husband is over here telling me how much blood, sweat, and tears my latest thriller is gonna need before we can show it to the publisher without embarrassing ourselves. I'm hopin' you can come over for a latish lunch so he'll ease up on me a little."

That would be yes. The only reason for Theo's blarney was that he had something for me that was too hot to say into a phone with a one-in-ten-thousand chance of being eavesdropped on by a Hoover Building techie or an NSA worker bee. I stuffed the Slow Willie file into my briefcase and within seven minutes I had my Ford Fusion rolling out of the parking ramp for MVC's building and pointed toward Lake Bancroft, Virginia – a kind of suburban oasis within the Beltway with views and boats and birdlife that no one would expect in a place this close to the Pentagon and downtown D.C..

When I got to Theo's house I found Rafe and him in high spirits on a rear porch that was screened-in during the summer but now, in November, was enclosed by Themapane windows as well. Ignoring the lake view behind them, the two of them actually were poring over a marked-up typescript strewn on the table between their beer bottles and the remains of their sandwiches. Theo produced a mug of hot coffee and a BLT on whole wheat for me and I thanked him sincerely.

"You made record time, Empress," Theo said, glancing at his watch. "We have about twenty minutes to kill before the ideal moment for a little walk down to the dock."

"Perfect," I said as the dock-walk part of his comment zoomed over my head and I handed him the file. "While I eat, you read and tell me what I'm missing."

"To figure out what you're missing, I have to know what you've caught."

"Nothing much, I don't think."

With a game grin, Theo burrowed into the file while I nibbled at the BLT. My hopes leaped when he raised his eyebrows from time to time. I didn't really get excited, though, until he paused, looked thoughtfully into space, then murmured, 'excuse me for a sec' and strolled back into his house. When he returned he had a dog-eared, beaten-up book with *Criminal Metrics: Investigating Crime by the Numbers* embossed on its hard cover.

"I used to carry this stuff around in my head," he mumbled apologetically as he began to page through it. "But that was ten years and three books ago."

I ate my BLT patiently. I sipped slowly as I watched him flip pages and scrawl an occasional note. I was about done with patience when he finally spoke up.

"Funny that the service door was ajar," he said. "An experienced burglar would never leave a door partially open after breaking in. Might as well hang a little sign on it saying, 'Burglary in Progress.'"

"Okay," I nodded. Not exactly a smoking gun, but better than anything I'd thought of.

"Plus, the powder residue from the Walther backflash is a little too precise for my tastes."

"You mean the residue on the latex glove Slow Willie was wearing?"

"Mm-hmm," Theo said. "You have to wonder why they didn't find any on his wrist or forearm. Not saying it couldn't possibly have happened. Don't believe I'd bet on it, though. And don't get me started on the perp prints that aren't there."

"How could Slow Willie have left prints if he were wearing latex gloves?"

"He was wearing the gloves during the burglary," Theo said. "At least, let's say he was. But was he wearing them when he snapped the clip into the Walther? Because there were no prints found on the clip, either. How about when he loaded the bullets into the clip? No prints on the bullets – not even partials."

"I guess he could just have been real careful," I said.

"Could be," Theo agreed. "Or maybe someone a lot more careful than Slow Willie loaded the weapon in the first place. Plus, the tackle box was open. Bilbo wouldn't have left it that way, and Slow Willie sure wouldn't risk a burglary to steal some trout-fishing flies. Put it all together and Rafe's theory that Slow Willie was there to plant the gun in Bilbo's garage starts to look plausible."

"I saw notations next to the shot of the bullet hole in one of the photos," I said. "Kind of wondering about that."

"Me too," Theo said. "That's why I ran in and got the book."

He riffed through the file, pulled that picture out, and turned it so I could see it. He put the end of his Mark Cross pen on the annotation I'd noticed on my own run-through:

Angle ≤ 3°↓

Distance = 14′

"Slow Willie was five foot eight, and that bullet hole is just a tad under five feet off the ground," Theo said.

"So he was firing from shoulder level," I suggested.

"A gun held at shoulder level for a five-eight shooter would be about five feet off the ground, maybe even a little less, if anything," Theo explained. "Unless the shooter is a complete no-neck, which Slow Willie wasn't."

"If someone five feet eight inches tall and standing straight up fired a dead level shot straight from his shoulder," I said, "wouldn't that be consistent with hitting a joist fourteen feet away five feet off the ground?"

"Yeah," Theo said, "but the weapon here wasn't fired dead level. The shooter fired it at a slight downward angle. Three degrees, or maybe a little less, but something."

"Hmm," I said.

"According to *Criminal Metrics*, a three-degree downward angle would lower the impact point by half an inch for every horizontal foot the bullet traveled. So for a shot that covered fourteen feet, that's seven inches lower – meaning the hole should have been a little less than four and a half feet off the ground."

"Any chance he squeezed off a round while he was holding the gun over his head or some crazy movie thing like that?" I asked.

"Well here's my problem with that." Theo stood up and backed toward the window-wall behind him, spreading his arms wide at his shoulders. "Pumping three thirty-eights into a little guy like Slow Willie while he was standing straight up would have slammed him big time *backwards*." Theo stepped briskly backwards and hit the glass hard. "The tackle box was behind him, just to his right. His arm should have knocked that tackle box six ways from Sunday and spread trout flies all over hell's half acre."

"Which didn't happen," I said.

"Right you are, Empress. I think Slow Willie was *crouching* – which is what I'd sure be doing if I saw someone in a bad mood comin' my direction with a pocket cannon."

"If you're right about that," I said, "then Slow Willie couldn't have fired the shot from the Walther that hit the joist in Bilbo's garage."

"Can I get an AMEN?" Theo asked with Gospel-tent enthusiasm.

I felt a sudden chill in my gut as I wrapped my mind around the reality that our crazy theory about Slow Willie's death could actually be . . . the truth.

Three things turn average voters off: taxes, snakes, and conspiracy theories. The Las Vegas shooter had stopped firing and killed himself an hour before the cops broke in. *That's just weird, dude!* The hard drive from one of the computers in the room was missing. *Can you spell CIA?* ISIS said it was behind the attack and everyone official instantly denied it. *Because that's what they want you to think, man.*

I *hate* those Twilight Zone scenarios. Only geeks living in their moms' basements like them. Everyone else plays them for laughs or just checks out as soon as you start making noises about them. And here I was on the verge of peddling the idea that a veteran member of Congress had conspired with a bad-ass drug dealer to use first-degree murder as a campaign strategy.

"Empress," Theo said, "how would you like to take a stroll down by the dock?"

Chapter 14

I slipped my down-filled vest over the wool sweater I was wearing. Theo grew up in Michigan, so his flannel shirt was all he needed, but November in northern Virginia feels nippy to a Louisiana girl like me.

Nice, leisurely sixty-foot walk down a slight grade to a weathered, wooden pier stretching a good twenty feet into the lake. As I admired the trees on the far shore beginning to show some autumn color, I noticed a man on the water's edge maybe fifty yards to my right. He swished a fly-fishing pole over his head to send line curving high, then arcing elegantly over the water, and then dropping gently toward the surface – trying to tempt a bass to leap from the water and snatch the tied fly at the end of the line.

Lake Bancroft is known for its bass fishing, but I didn't see the angler having any luck. Maybe he'd been out there quite a while, or maybe he thought our arrival would spook any fish in the neighborhood. Whatever, after glancing over his shoulder at us, he reeled his line back in and started disassembling his rod and reel. Once the reel was detached and stashed in a tackle box and the pole pulled apart and slipped lovingly into a fiberglass case, the fisherman headed back into the woods behind him. I kept looking in that direction, drinking in the breathtaking beauty – almost like being on vacation – until I saw the man come out of the woods, much closer to Theo's dock, walking toward us. Just over six feet, looked like. The fishing vest he wore couldn't hide his nice, trim build, and from the peppy way he was walking over uneven ground, he was in decent shape.

As he closed the distance between us, he started to look vaguely familiar, except that he had on a pair of nerdy-looking black horn-rim glasses and I couldn't think of anyone I knew who wore those. When he took off his floppy, canvas hat and wiped his forehead with a glen-plaid sleeve, still ten healthy strides from the end of Theo's dock, I recognized him: Hank Sinclair. Maybe the glasses were his idea of making himself inconspicuous so that he could avoid autograph requests from adoring groupies. I popped up and waved my right arm with pom-pom girl enthusiasm while I pasted a sunny smile on my face.

"Is that you, Hank?" I called in a sorority rush-week voice. "What in the world are you doing here? Thought you'd be in Texas helping get that wall built."

"Always good to see you, Josie," he called back with a hint of Brahmin nasality while caressing the right arm of the glasses with his index finger. "I prefer fly fishing, even for bass, to golf at Mar-a-Lago."

By the time he reached the dock he'd taken the glasses off and stashed them in his shirt pocket. We gave each other *pro forma* hugs. I smelled sweat but not fish on his face and neck. Then we sat down on Theo's deck chairs near the end of the dock.

"Let's skip the foreplay," Theo told Hank. "It's put up or shut up for me, and you're the closest thing I have to a deliverable."

"Fair enough," Hank said. "The DEA agent working Caleb André et cetera, better known as Card, during the three years or so leading up to Slow Willie Woodbine's untimely death, was named Dominic Kappa. Went by 'Dom' in New York and 'Nick' in Louisiana."

Whoa. Just like that.

"He still with the DEA?" Theo asked.

"He is not." Hank ran the fingers of his right hand through light brown hair which I could tell had gotten a hundred twenty-dollar style job within the last week, even though sweat now matted it in an appealingly carefree way. "For several years he has been in charge of security for Global Martial Arts Promotions, Inc., headquartered in Vicksburg, Mississippi."

"Well, now, *that* is an interesting career move," Theo said.

"Put in his twenty, cashed in, and moved on without taking a slug," Hank shrugged. "Can't say I blame him."

"Have you by any chance been in touch with him?" I asked.

"I most certainly have not," Hank answered, flashing a thousand-dollar smile.

Almost coyly, Hank slipped off the fishing vest. Laying it front-down on the dock, he started unzipping a rubberized pouch that stretched over most of the back. The pouch struck me as a good place to stash fish, if he'd caught any.

Taking his time about it, he extracted from the pouch two manila file folders, both wrinkled and shopworn. Thick rubber bands around each of them. Not a flash drive, not a floppy, not a server. Two file-folders stuffed with paper, as in *The Eighties just called; they want their props back.*

Boldface type on the first folder's tab read: **CALEB ANDRÉ REGINE DELACROIX ("CARD").** The second folder's tab read: **DOMINIC KAPPA ("DOM" "NICK").**

In my imagination I could see the scene playing out without even closing my eyes. Hank carefully manipulating those folders, just as he had flexed his fly rod and cast his line out over the still lake in a lazy S that gradually uncurled into a looping arc – and Josie leaping straight up out of the water like a sleek, lithe bass, jaws wide open, to grab that succulent-looking fly and the wicked hook it was wrapped around. *Knowing* the hook was there but hardwired with a deep hunger for political action that kept me from caring.

He had me, the sonofabitch.

Without loosening the rubber bands, he lifted the Card folder with his left hand and the Nick folder with his right so Theo and I could see big, red initials stamped on the front of each of them:

CI

Congressional Influence.

Grinning, Hank watched me salivate over the things, yearning for them like a junkie for a fix. Just the existence of the files with that stamp was useful information, but I figured the stuff inside might be even more valuable. Hank had displayed them to see how badly I wanted them. Now he knew.

"I can't let you look inside these," he said.

"Not yet," I responded. Not a question.

He winked.

Chapter 15

"We are in very deep fertilizer," I told Seamus less than an hour later.

"Oh, I wouldn't go that far," he said philosophically. "True, we don't have enough evidence yet to go live with 'Please call Congressman Bilbo and ask him not to commit any more murders.' But if you can get anything more than the time of day from this ex-DEA guy we might be headed out of the fake news woods."

We were not communicating.

"Seamus, we are in shit up to our earlobes. We're being sucked into something way bigger than smearing a congressman. Someone in the West Wing wants to use us in a scheme that has 'special prosecutor' written all over it."

"They're mostly amateurs over there these days," Seamus shrugged.

"That's what worries me most. I'd rather aid and abet a pro any day."

"Okay." Seamus shrugged again, but this time he at least squared up and made eye contact. "What do you think this fiendish plot is?"

"Don't have the least idea, except that it somehow involves Bilbo. A White House staffer doesn't take a long lunch hour to go fishing. Hank Sinclair was on the clock. And he didn't pull sensitive files out of Treasury Department archives by saying 'pretty please.' He has some major pull behind him. Finally, he didn't hand me a key name on a silver platter just for the exercise."

"He wants a *quid pro quo*," Seamus said. "Welcome to Washington."

"Maybe what he wants in exchange is for us to use the information and create a mile-wide trail while we're doing it."

"Fair enough," Seamus said, as if he were being a good sport. "What I'm hearing is that the White House doesn't have the guts to take down Bilbo in broad daylight so they tasked Hank to manipulate us into doing it. Let's say you're right. Fine. We'll take him down and be proud of it. We'll issue a press release. We'll make it a photo-op when we paint Bilbo's silhouette on the cockpit door of our F-16."

This was getting frustrating.

"If this were only about Bilbo," I said, "they wouldn't need us. A few strategic leaks to Phoebe would raze Bilboville to the ground and sow its fields with salt. This is much more serious stuff. Hank, and whoever is running him, wants the fingers pointing at us, not them, when the *merde* hits the fan."

"Yeah, I got that the first four times you said it. But when do you expect to have a clue about what the 'serious stuff' actually is?"

"When Hank tells me what he wants in exchange for letting me sit in some Old Executive Office Building nook so he can page through those two files with me and try to feel me up while he's at it."

"Fine," Seamus said. "That's when we'll know something. Right now, we know nothing."

"But if we wait until then it might be too late." My head spun as I projected a dozen possible scenarios and tried to find a low-risk path to follow.

Seamus slumped.

"So," he said, "what are you saying? Should we should bail on the Bilbo thing?"

"In the long run, for sure."

"What is this 'long run' you speak of?" he asked, giving me a mischievous grin. "I'm not familiar with that concept. Let's talk about the short run."

"In the short run, we might have a little time to try to get a handle on what the hell is going on before we get compromised. So –"

"Great! 'Damn the torpedoes, full speed ahead!'"

"I'll fly to Vicksburg tomorrow morning," I said, nodding.

Chapter 16

"Understand one thing up front," Nick Kappa said the next morning from behind his desk. "To me, all politicians are whores."

"Why, shame on you, Mr. Kappa," I said. "Imagine a Louisiana boy disrespecting prostitutes that way."

He liked the joke. His chestnut eyes sparkled on his flat-nosed, rock-chinned face – a face that could have graced a Wanted poster or a prize-fight flyer. He flexed massive shoulders encased in a chalk-striped gray wool jacket. His bald head nodded. He reached a beefy hand across a cluttered mahogany desk.

"*Bella donna*," he said, "you and I are going to get along just fine. Sit."

I'd had the devil's own time finding Global Martial Arts Promotions, Inc. on my drive from Vicksburg's airport. GMAP had a six-room suite in the southeast corner of the third floor of an eight-story building with **BEDFORD OFFICE TOWER** over its entrance and various Bedford mining, construction, and forestry companies as its other tenants. Way out in the boonies, the building had a street address on something called Bedford Place, but when the rental car's cut-rate GPS told me I'd reached Bedford Place, all I could see between me and a glass and concrete building a hundred yards away was puddle-specked red and brown clay, road-graders and bulldozers painted black and yellow, and a giant tire standing upright. By "giant," I mean a grown man could have stood on another grown man's shoulders on the inside of the tire without either of them feeling cramped.

I'd finally stumbled onto a two-lane asphalt ribbon leading to a guard booth and a parking lot cunningly concealed behind the building. I stayed shaky about the address until I actually found GMAP's name in white plastic letters stuck on black felt on the directory in the building's reception area. The receptionist had me sign in, but when I told her I was there to see Kappa she just pointed to a telephone on the desk with a list of extensions beside it.

Kappa's handshake was a nice, polite clasp. He didn't try to crush my bones just to show me who was boss, even though his DEA experience had probably taught him to take charge from the start of a conversation. There were no plants on his desk or the window sills, no aquarium behind his swivel chair, and no *objets d'art* in sight unless a heavy crystal ashtray next to his phone counted. The closest thing to decorations on the walls were framed posters touting "cage matches" and "fights to the death."

"Slow Willie was a rarity among snitches," Kappa said after we'd gotten the preliminary fencing out of the way and he had a cigar going. "Drugs were a moral thing with him: sell white kids anything they're dumb enough to buy, but don't sell hard stuff to blacks and don't sell *anything* to black teenagers. I dropped some cash on him – jacksons, not benjamins – and ran interference for him when he needed it, but he wouldn't have given me squat just for that."

"I understand he did some work for Card, though," I said.

"Man's gotta make a living. Place like Baton Rouge, hustling hot laptops can only take you so far. But he wouldn't *deal* for Card. Wouldn't buy for him and wouldn't mule for him."

"Because of that moral thing," I said.

"Exactly. Story is, one time his mama caught his little brother with a lump of crack. Sent the kid outside for a switch and he says he's not havin' it, he's too big for lickings now. Well, mom calls Slow Willie, who comes over and straps little bro's fanny 'til hell wouldn't have it. Tells him whether he's fifteen or twenty-five, there's plenty more where that came from if he even thinks about crack again."

Kappa waved away an accumulating cloud of rich, blue smoke. With his face visible again, I could pick up a nostalgic glow in his eyes. Residual fondness for Slow Willie, or just longing for 'back when I was a cop?' Couldn't tell.

"You figure being a snitch had anything to do with Slow Willie getting shot?" I asked.

"I wore out two pairs of shoes trying to prove Slow Willie's death was a hit that Card had somehow orchestrated," Kappa said, narrowing his eyes. "Know what I came up with?"

"Not enough, apparently."

"Nada. No word on the street about how the same thing could happen to you if you cross Card; no one who'd admit to even seeing Card or any of his flunkies in the same area code as that girl who bought the Walther and then bought the farm; no rival dealers who'd give me tip one; no disgruntled former associates. I mean *nothing*. Only time in my career I ever got totally whitewashed."

I searched for some encouragement in *nothing*. Didn't find any.

"A friend of mine with a background in law enforcement," I said, straining a bit for careful phrasing, "found some anomalies in the crime-scene data."

"'Anomalies'," Kappa snorted. "Investigate the scene of a firefight and you'll have anomalies crawling out your ass. A real gunfight doesn't look like on TV. One guy might stand like a statue instead of ducking for cover. Another might spray lead all over the neighborhood, shooting behind him while he's running away."

"'Look like on TV,'" I mused out loud. "In Bilbo's statement to the sheriff, he came across to me just like someone on TV."

"I'd go along with that, even without seeing the statement in, like, five years," Kappa laughed. "As I remember, he left out the part about wetting his pants."

"How do you know he did that?"

"I don't '*know*' – I wasn't there. But a civilian facing live fire for the first time in his life? I'll give you eight to one."

"Not taking *that* bet," I said.

"First time I read Bilbo's statement I said to myself, 'This guy is the dumbest SOB in the State of Louisiana.' Risking a bullet for a full toolbox or whatever else he had in that garage. What a moron!"

"And yet, Bilbo apparently did take that risk."

"That's a fact," Kappa said. "That comes right after gravity in the way the world works. Every blessed day of the year, smart people do stuff so incredibly stupid a crack whore wouldn't even consider it. If they didn't, guys like me would starve to death."

Time to fire my last bullet (so to speak).

"Did you give up on Card after three years just because you kept drilling dry holes, or did someone else cross that off your list for you – maybe because he was getting calls from a member of the House Appropriations Committee?"

I was afraid that question might piss him off, but it didn't. He chuckled, shook his head, and in a broad grin showed me teeth so perfect you knew they'd come from an orthodontist. Then he got up from behind the desk.

"Let me show you Bedford's shed," he said. "Excuse me. Its 'Heavy Equipment Containment Facility.'"

Exiting the suite and rattling down terrazzo stairs instead of taking the elevator, he ushered me outside into the bright and chilly November air. Three determined strides brought us to the edge of the work yard.

"Do you mind going through a little muck?" he asked.

"Won't be the first time," I told him. A lot of the stuff I do in Washington involves going through muck.

We strode gamely into the yard. Dodging puddles and squishing a bit in churned up mud, we made our way past the giant tire. Maybe twenty yards beyond it, we slipped through sliding doors into a massive building made of treated pine that still smelled richly of resin, with a steel roof and a concrete floor. As sheds go, it would have made a pretty good airplane hangar. At least forty feet high, with enough length and width for a track meet.

It needed almost every inch to shelter the truck inside. 'Truck,' singular. I'd never seen a vehicle anything like that big in my life. An Abrams tank sitting next to it would have looked like a scale model. Mustard yellow with black trim. The top of the truck's cab sat two stories off the floor. I had to crane my neck to see it. A literal two-flight staircase built into the body of the truck led from just above the ground to the doors on either side of the cab.

"Something, ain't it?" Kappa asked.

"That would be yes."

"Mining dump truck. Ore and slag hauler. Anything-else hauler too, for that matter. That tire outside is the spare for this baby. Costs a cool four hundred fifty thousand dollars. The tire, not the truck."

I thought he was putting me on.

"You mean that thing is an actual *tire*? I just assumed it was a fiberglass mock-up, painted to look like a tire and stuck there in the yard as some kind of branding."

He grinned and started walking toward the back of the truck. I followed him. Only when we'd almost reached the end did I spot an eight-man crew doing tote-that-barge/lift-that-bale stuff. Under the watchful scowl of an African-American foreman, a brown-skinned man with what I pegged as Mediterranean features sat in a forklift whose thick, steel arms lifted a dozen fifty-pound burlap bags to the cargo bay's lip. The other six, evenly divided between African-Americans and Near Easterners (or maybe Hispanics, I guessed), stood in the bay and hoisted the bags into it. They'd been doing that the whole time I was standing at the front, but the sides of the cargo bay were so high that I couldn't see them in there. I couldn't even hear them clumping around.

Kappa and the foreman made eye contact. The foreman's scowl darkened.

"Don't get tight-assed on me, Eli," Kappa said in a joshing tone. "Just impressing a visitor. Fertilizer isn't a trade secret."

Shaking his head dubiously as Kappa led me all the way to the back of the truck, Eli turned his scowl toward the bay.

"Keep your eyes to yourself, Haji," he growled. "Your job is up there in that bay, not down here."

Nodding toward Eli, Kappa spun around and walked back toward the sliding doors with me in his wake.

"I just wanted you to see that," he said. "I could have described it and recited the dimensions, but the best words I could come up with wouldn't have given you a real idea of the thing."

"You got that right," I admitted. "Which one is Haji, by the way?"

"Eli calls them all 'Haji.' Keeps things simple."

"Uh *huh*," I said.

"I'll tell you one thing. If Trump ever gets his wall built, Bedford takes a hit. The illegals are the only ones who really put their backs into it."

I let that one pass without comment.

Fishing a large Swiss Army Knife out of his trouser pocket, he flicked out a file with dull edges.

"Soon as we get back on concrete," he said, "I'll see if I can get the worst of that mud off your shoes. Chilly as it's been the last couple of days, I didn't think the mud would be quite this sloppy."

"Not necessary," I said. "I can handle it."

"I insist," he said. "Southern hospitality. Won't take five minutes."

"That is very kind of you." I would much rather have skipped the gentlemanly gesture, but I didn't have a good excuse and I didn't want to march through all that mud without getting an answer to the question I'd asked: Congressional Influence or not?

As we passed the tire, the unmistakable smell of sunbaked rubber wafted over me. In something like wonder, I looked up close at the thing. Tread wide enough and deep enough that I could have fit my hand in the spaces defining its surface. The whole thing so much bigger than my wildest idea of a tire that, even with the evidence staring me in the face, I had trouble wrapping my mind around it. Kappa abruptly stopped.

"Here's the thing," he said. "That tire is just standing out here in the yard for all the world to see. Twelve-foot diameter. But bright people look at it from a distance and have no idea what they're seeing."

"I think I hear you saying that the answer to that last question I asked back in your office is obvious."

He didn't wink, he smiled – but the smile meant the same thing.

Chapter 17

Even after Kappa's mud-scraping, my navy pumps didn't look like shoes I'd wear to anything classier than a demolition derby. This was supposed to be just a day trip, so I'd only brought four pairs of shoes, and one of them was now out of commission for the duration. I decided to drive barefoot back to the airport, like I was sixteen again, and then dig out clean shoes in a ladies' room at the terminal.

That plan lasted until I checked my phone for messages.

Hank Sinclair's voicemail had come in about the time Kappa had fired up his cigar. Heart rate ramping up a bit, I returned the call. Got voicemail – which I wouldn't have if the call-back number he'd left were for a West Wing land line. I would have reached a live secretary. I left a message that I was returning Hank's call, that I'd be available until my flight took off in about four hours, and that I was looking forward to speaking with him.

Seamus had left a message about the time Kappa and I had started our mud-march. I got him on the first ring.

"I think the second shoe is about to drop," I told him. "I'm playing phone tag with Hank Sinclair."

"I was actually calling you about something else," Seamus said. "You're still in Vicksburg, right?"

"Yes, heading for the airport."

"Something has come up." Seamus paused – seldom a good sign. "Looks like Dejean is starting to get some traction. She's being interviewed for thirty minutes on Polly Mathis's show tomorrow morning."

I whistled. PMS With Polly Mathis was simulcast on NPR and WBRL with a statewide feed every morning at 7:00 and every evening at 8:00. Fluent in four languages, boasting degrees in both political science and engineering, Mathis brought a ton of 'tude to her top-rated show. Don't know whether she qualified as a genius, but she definitely qualified as a pain in the butt. She loved playing '*gotcha*' with her guests.

"Has Dejean gotten enough traction to have a communications adviser?" I asked.

"Closest thing to that is your buddy from A and T," Seamus said. "You know – Joe College, the kid."

Mason. I came within an eyelash of dropping an f-bomb at that news. Someone who thought Bilbo was a closet liberal would have had to overcome some daunting philosophical qualms to back Dejean. But a chance to eat at the grown-ups' table can have that effect.

"So what I was hoping," Seamus said, "was that you could make your way to Baton Rouge and, you know –"

"Yeah, I know." I sighed. "But he's not going to be happy about advice from an interloper."

"He'd be even less happy about pissing off a major campaign contributor. I've already arranged for him to get the word."

"Okay."

"Dejean and college boy will be at the Hampton Inn in downtown Baton Rouge. I'll text you contact information for them. I can book you into the place too, unless you'd rather stay with your mom."

"Yeah, I'll stay with Mama," I said distractedly. "And I'll let you know when I hear back from Hank."

"Safe travels," Seamus said, his voice brimming with hearty cheer.

Vicksburg to Baton Rouge is two and a half hours if you drive sensibly and legally. I made it in one hundred twenty-eight minutes flat, and I would have shaved off another five minutes if I hadn't slowed down to read the phone number Seamus texted me and then call Mason.

"When you get the prep-call from Polly Mathis' producer," I told him, "she'll ask you whether there's any topic that Doctor Dejean would rather Mathis didn't bring up in the interview. The candidate might want to consider saying she'd prefer not to discuss questions being raised about Bilbo killing that burglar just before his first campaign."

"That's helpful," he said, not sounding like he felt particularly helped.

Then I gave him a couple of other really basic tips, like tracking down prices for staple grocery items. Anyone with any business working as a communications adviser in a congressional campaign would have known them without being told, but Mason hadn't. We settled on eight p.m. for my meeting with Dejean.

For the rest of the trip I propped my laptop open on the passenger seat and serially dialed up talk shows on satellite radio. Listening to them is the only time I ever feel like a liberal, closet or otherwise. No way I could duck the chore, though, any more than an MBA working in finance could skip the *Wall Street Journal.*

Usual stuff, at first: double-standards applied by the lamestream media. Middle-school kid suspended for bringing a Bible to class. Rape committed by an illegal alien who would have been deported first if a sanctuary city hadn't sheltered him. Murder rates at record highs in cities run by Democratic mayors. Jane Austen bumped from the required reading list at a New England college because the characters in her novels weren't diverse enough.

Then I picked up a Nashville-based regional guy named Slippery Elm, who was teasing a topic I hadn't heard anyone feature for a while: the court fight over the Trump administration's moving-target directives limiting immigration from several predominantly Muslim countries. Months before, the Supreme Court had temporarily vacated lower court injunctions blocking Trump's initial directives, but then he'd issued a new one and at least two lower courts had blocked *it*. (The Supreme Court would ultimately reverse *those* orders as well, but that lay in the future.)

"How long have our federal courts been chewing on this bone," he twanged, "trying to figure out if we have to let everyone from a terrorist area in here who wants to come? Eleven months? Tell y'all what, I'll bet I could decide that case in eleven *minutes*. Maybe they should concentrate on deciding whether people with male body parts can get dressed and undressed in front of teenage girls – but then they can't even get *that* one right. Well I'll say this. The judges who let those people into our country got clocked nine-to-nothing on the temporary rulings. Nine-*zero*. I mean, you have to work at it to lose nine-*zero*. So thank the good Lord those injunctions were set aside. But now it looks like we're right back where we started. More important, the people those judges let into our great country *are still here*. If some of those people let in by those hard-left judges without being checked out properly decide to blow up a shopping mall – well, then, brothers and sisters, those judges will have black robes on their backs and American blood on their hands. And if *that* happens, pardon my French, but you mark my words: there will be hell to pay. Yessir. Hell to pay."

His first caller on the topic was "Esther Sue from Moberly." Classic. "My husband is pretty conservative, and he thinks those judges should be hanged. I'm more of a moderate, so I say they should just be hanged from low trees." Slippery guffawed at that one but I couldn't muster a smile. Smearing a congressman is one thing; lynching judges just doesn't tickle my funny bone.

Chapter 18

Baton Rouge. The city where I grew up, where my Papa died, first beer, first love, first taste of politics, first heartbreak, all that stuff. I get back here two or three times a year, but for some reason this spur-of-the-moment return was plucking a nostalgia cord that usually doesn't resonate with me. Not sure why. Maybe Esther Sue from Moberly.

After catch-up chat with Mama and Uncle D, I got to work on a status report for Seamus. Hank Sinclair's call led the first paragraph, which reminded me that he'd never called me back after I'd returned his call. Then I flashed on something I'd missed in my morning talk with Seamus. I punched speed dial. Hard.

"Josie!" Seamus said with Rotary Club level geniality. "Arrived safely?"

"I'm going to ask you a question. I want a yes-or-no answer, and I want the truth. Did our buddy Hank call you today after I called him back?"

"I did get a call from Hank today," Seamus said. "So, yes."

"And I'm betting he told you what he wants in exchange for a peek at the two files he teased me with, right?"

"Yes, that did come up. It's been a little hectic around here, and I hadn't gotten around to sharing that with you yet."

"Uh-huh," I said. "What does he want?"

"Right," Seamus said. "Basically, he wants all the footage you took during that panel discussion where your uncle did his star turn."

What the fuck?

"Well," I said tentatively, "I can't imagine what he wants with it, but offhand I don't see any harm in giving it to him, after we've reviewed it ourselves."

"To that point, Josie," Seamus said. "It's, ah —"

I could not *believe* this.

"You've already given it to him!" I barked. "Are you kidding? With no guarantee we'll get the files from him?"

"Uh, yeah," Seamus admitted. "Go ahead and yell at me, if you like. But dammit, Josie, I *am* your boss. I mean, technically."

"You are totally in the wrong here and you know it, Seamus Danica."

"I hear you. It's just hard to say no to the White House."

"You *have* talked with MVC's lawyer about this, haven't you?"

"Well, no, not yet."

"Is it on your agenda?"

"It is now."

"Okay." I sighed. "Look, Seamus, in light of this little bombshell, I'm going to have to stay down here at least through tomorrow and try to flesh some things out. We're playing with fire and we should get some idea of how hot the flames have gotten."

"Fair enough," he said. "And thanks for not telling me to not fuck up again."

"I would have," I said, "but I'm at Mama's house and I'm too old to get my mouth washed out with soap."

Chapter 19

Dinner took up roughly half the time between the end of my Seamus chat and 7:40, when I left for the Hampton to meet Dejean and Mason. I devoted the other half to retrieving the raw footage of Uncle D's A&T adventure and giving it an initial run-through. Damned if I could see what Hank Sinclair or anyone else could do with this stuff, beyond what Seamus and I had already done with it.

Uncle D offered to drive me downtown. The idea didn't thrill me, but he'd already put on a tie so I went along with it.

Mason greeted me in the lobby with wary warmth. He still sported light brown dress slacks, and his dark brown belt still matched his shoes. Above the waist, though, he'd dropped the 1958 preppy look in favor of a black t-shirt featuring white icons on the front:

♂ ↑, ☼

"'Man up, snowflake,'" he said, pointing to the icons one by one, when he saw me looking at it.

"Yeah, I see what you did there."

I carefully assessed the people and surroundings as I walked into Letitia Dejean's suite. That's right, suite. For an overnight stay. In addition to Mason, Dejean had two other people in her entourage, a black woman with 'graduate student' written all over her and a white man who needed only leather elbow patches on his tweed jacket to look like a professor from central casting. The combination of suite and posse meant that Dejean was raising lots of money for a rookie longshot – and that she had no idea how quickly that delicious cash flow could dry up.

I gave her the highlights of *Interviewing for Dummies*: never start an answer with 'first of all,' avoid words like 'all' or 'never' or 'every,' that kind of thing. Mentioned that Mathis's first question figured to focus on challenges to Bilbo's account of the garage gunfight – the one thing Mason had told Mathis's producer Dejean would prefer *not* to discuss – and told her how to hit it out of the park. Ended by telling her that anytime Mathis said, 'So what you're saying is,' push back with, 'Here's what I'm saying.' and then use her words instead of Mathis's.

Dejean was a quick study. Seventy-five minutes flew by.

"I think you're set," I said as I stood up. "Good luck tomorrow morning. Just remember: never give an interviewer an even break."

As I was heading for the door after smiles and handshakes, Mason jumped up, with clear designs on escorting me to the lobby.

"No problem," he said when I started to demur. "No problem at all."

Okay, you want to talk.

On the way down, Mason told me how much he'd learned from tonight's session and how lucky he felt to have a chance to work with me. When we got to the lobby, he seemed on the verge of something besides sucking up to me, so I started paying attention. Right then, though, I spotted Uncle D standing on 4th street outside the hotel, leaning into the driver's side of a harvest gold Camry and having what looked like a frank and candid exchange of views with the driver.

"Mr. Mason," I said, "I would deeply appreciate it if you would hold that thought for just one second. I need to run outside and see to something – but I'll be right back, I promise."

I hustled out the door in time to hear Uncle Darius in full cry.

"Listen, Abdullah, I am not interested in a debate. The next time I catch you following my niece, or even looking like you're thinking about following my niece, I am gonna put my fist so far up your bony ass that you'll never have to worry about prostate cancer. Now get your towel-hat, camel-jockey ass outta here."

After checking in both directions for cops and not seeing any, I decided to go around the back of the Camry. Good call: that vehicle was lurching forward and down the street at a fair clip by the time I made it all the way across the sidewalk.

"Josephine!" Uncle D yelled. "Do you know that –"

"We will discuss this later, Uncle D," I said. "Right now I need you to come in and say hello to the young man who arranged for you to be on that A and T panel where you had so much fun."

He choked off his rant and followed me back inside without a whimper. Beamed when he saw Mason's t-shirt. They shook hands and did everything short of chest bumping each other.

"Is our car right outside, Uncle D?" I asked.

"No, I had to stow it in a garage around the corner."

"Why don't you go get it and bring it around then, if you would be so kind? Mr. Mason and I have one more thing we need to discuss."

"At your service, Josephine." Uncle D headed for the door while I offered a silent prayer that he'd make it all the way to the car without getting arrested.

"I apologize for that interruption," I told Mason. "Was there something else you wanted to tell me?"

He hemmed and hawed for just a second. Then he managed to spit it out.

"Something I wanted to ask you, really."

"Ask away."

"Do you know a Hank Sinclair?"

Chapter 20

I figured I'd better drive us home. Uncle D wasn't knee-walking drunk, but he didn't strike me as stone-cold sober, either. He wasn't any too happy about sliding from behind the wheel, but I told him that even though I think a snitch is one of the lowest forms of human life, if he gave me any static, I was going to tell Mama on him. That sealed the deal.

"Uncle Darius," I said as soon as I'd turned the car onto Fourth Street, "you are the very best uncle a girl could have, and I thank the good Lord for you every single morning. But this isn't 1970. You can't just go around treating everyone with dark skin as a Muslim, and treating everyone you think is a Muslim as a terrorist."

"I've been in politics long enough to tell Hispanic from Arab, young lady." He was a mite cross. "I can tell a Haitian from a Dominican, for that matter – and I can get both of them to the polls with a sample ballot."

"Fair enough." I tried to sound abashed. "But being Arab doesn't necessarily make him a terrorist."

"I take your point, Josephine," he said, "although I will note for the record that the United States isn't being attacked these days by Polish Lutherans or French Presbyterians or Indian HooDoos."

"Hindus."

"Whatever. Point is –"

"Point is," I said, "that young man might have just been out looking for a hooker. Or a hookah. Or both."

"He was following you," Uncle D said. "I first noticed him this afternoon, about forty seconds after you pulled into the driveway."

"What?" I did *not* see that one coming.

"Same vehicle, same license number. He drove past the house before you'd gotten your stuff all the way inside. Then he must have gone around the block, because less than a minute later he drove past again, and on that second run he slowed down like his fuzzbuster had just lit up."

That made me stop and think. Uncle D can go way over the top without even trying, but he doesn't just make stuff up. Not important stuff, anyway.

"That drive-by is why I wiggled my way into your expedition this evening," Uncle D continued. "Thought it was at least 50-50 that I'd spot that rice burner again on our way downtown, and sure enough I did."

"I see," I said. *My God.*

"Now, I know the years you've spent in Washington have made you a little delicate about certain things," he said, "so instead of clocking him a couple and blowing his tires out, I let him off with just a talking-to. Think of that as an early Christmas present from me to you."

"I thank you for that, Uncle D."

I frowned as I looked straight ahead. A gentle rain had started, making the pavement glisten.

"Rain-slick pavement is like a pretty girl," Uncle D said complacently. "The more beautiful it looks, the more dangerous it is."

I heard his words, but my mind was elsewhere. *Why hadn't I spotted the tail? And who in the world would go to the trouble of putting a tail on me anyway? Chad Bilbo would have sent a good old boy who'd blend in, not someone who'd stand out like a Manhattan debutante at a hoe-down. Hank Sinclair would have used a professional operative, not a rank amateur sure to get spotted on his first pass.*

Hank Sinclair. Just pulling the name from my mental Rolodex started dominoes toppling. Hank had leveraged raw footage from the A&T event out of Seamus. Then he'd apparently contacted Mason. What could he have wanted Mason to tell him about that footage? Only thing I could think of was identifying people on it.

"Uncle D," I said, "first, I owe you an apology. I should have known you wouldn't pull a stunt like that street scene without a good reason. I am truly sorry, and if you want to chew me out, you go right ahead."

"I'd only be pretending to scold you, Josephine," he said. "I couldn't bring myself to do it properly. But you said 'first'. What's second?"

"Second is that as soon as we get home, you and I have some work to do."

Chapter 21

I woke up the next morning in a crappy mood. Uncle D and I had gone through my raw footage of the A&T melee – sorry, *conference* – in obsessive detail. He'd picked out one face and sworn up and down it was the cat he'd called Abdullah. So now I was *real* worried, but I still didn't know what I was worried about.

I'd called Mason before going to bed to find out what Hank wanted from him. Got voicemail, left a message, and by the time I started breakfast he still hadn't called back.

Dialed up Polly Mathis's interview of Letitia Dejean on the radio while I was eating cream cheese on a toasted bagel and Mama and Uncle D were digging into bacon, eggs, and toast. The show went like a dream, which improved my disposition a bit. Dejean was a quick study all right.

"That sounds like it might've been your work, Josie," Uncle D said as he deftly wiped egg yolk dripping from the left corner of his lips.

I smiled with the kind of becoming modesty you learn growing up as a girl in the south. I still had a half-smile on my face as I helped Mama wash the breakfast dishes. Only a half-smile, though. Mason still hadn't called me back.

"So," Mama said, handing me a spotless white plate to dry. "You've got yourself a real interesting situation here."

"That's a fact, Mama."

She walked over to the only drawer in the kitchen that she'd kept locked when I was growing up. Opening it, she took out a black case with a Bakelite cover, about the size of something you might have on your dresser to hold paste jewelry and inexpensive earrings. She opened it on the counter next to me. Inside I saw what she called her "home security system:" a palm-sized, twenty-five caliber Colt automatic pistol with ivory handles. I knew it was loaded, with a cartridge in the chamber and the safety on.

"What's your next step?" she asked.

Funny, but I hadn't had the first idea about what to do next until Mama asked that question. Then, the second she asked it, the answer popped into my head, as clear as Gordon's Gin in the middle of July.

"I'm going to try to find myself a pawn shop," I said. "But I think I'll leave the gun here."

Chapter 22

It took me until after ten a.m. to track down Bond Street Consignments, Inc./Licensed Pawnbroker. I found it on Florida Boulevard instead of Bond Street, I'd call 'Consignments' just a regular lie, and I put the odds on 'Licensed' at no better than 50-50.

It seemed like the right time to be looking for Slow Willie's old friend, but Vernon Czlewski hadn't publicly associated himself with any of Baton Rouge's numerous pawn shops, at least as far as I could tell from Google and Mama's old Yellow Pages. I'd gotten his phone number from Phoebe, but no answer when I called it. I wasn't going to just sit around Mama's house stewing, though, so I drove down to look around Government Street and Florida Boulevard, which Baton Rouge would have called its "pawnbroker district" if cities bragged about hock shops.

Got shrugs and headshakes at the first three shops I tried, along with the feeling that pawnbrokers don't think much of people who ask questions about pawnbrokers. The fourth gent I talked to said he thought either Bond Street Consignments on Florida or Pledge and Payday Loans on Airline Highway might be Vernon's sole surviving Baton Rouge enterprise. I had no interest in hauling all the way out to Airline Highway if I could help it, so I had my fingers crossed real hard when I pulled up down the block from the Florida Boulevard address.

I saw two East Baton Rouge Parish Sheriff's cars slanted to the curb outside. I had a feeling, somehow, that I'd found the right place.

No point in acting bashful, so I just sauntered up and strolled in like I owned the place. Walking to the door took me past an alley where a rangy black due who looked down on his luck was urinating. You see stuff like that any day of the week on Capitol Hill if you know where to look, so I wasn't close to fainting when I entered the shop. I just felt like I knew the neighborhood a little better.

Vernon stood behind a waist-high glass display case in the back. The two other men and one woman in civvies in the shop didn't strike me as customers. One of the men, standing right next to Vernon, had an enormous black binder open on top of the display case. Each page of the binder bristled with heavy pasteboard tags stapled two across and five down. He would mash his left index finger onto a tag as if he were trying to squash a bug, then look down into the display case for eight to ten seconds, then move his finger to another tag and repeat the process. The other man and the woman had clipboards holding legal-size sheets of paper. They moved through the store, checking everything from banjos to tie pins against their lists.

None of them looked happy to see me. The display case where Vernon was standing held three glass shelves of handguns. The binder was most likely a gun register now undergoing intensive police scrutiny. I mentally tagged the long pages on the clipboards as hot property lists. I'd walked in on a roust.

As I approached, binder-guy looked up. I read 'No hookers north of Convention Street' in his watery brown eyes, so I knew right where I stood.

"Do you have business here, Miss?" he asked.

"'Ma'am', actually," I said, smiling and showing him the plain gold band Rafe had slipped on my finger right here in Baton Rouge, several years before. I wasn't going to take the hooker-look lying down. "I was hoping to speak with the proprietor."

I sensed the cop-ette coming up behind me. Trying not to show it, I tensed.

"May I see some ID, *ma'am*?"

"Of course," I said, and immediately reached down to unlatch my tan leather Kate Spade purse.

I let it fall open so Lady Kojak could see that I didn't have a gun stashed there. With deliberate movements I pulled my smooth brown leather wallet out, unsnapped it, and flipped over the inside flap to show my D.C. driver's license in one plastic window and my Rayburn Building Congressional Pass in the one below it. The pass was four years out of date, but it still came in handy at times – like now, for example. Cop-ette shared an expression with Deputy Hardass that dialed him back a couple of clicks.

"Uh, ma'am," he said, skipping the verbal italics, "Mr. Czlewski will likely be tied up for quite a while here."

"I see." I flashed a bright, sunny smile at binder-guy and turned toward Vernon to address him myself. "Not a good time?"

"I am a sinner seeking grace," he said, looking right at me with a philosophical smile. Then he spread his arms out to each side and let his chest bow forward as he began to sing in a thin tenor. I didn't recognize the spiritual from anything I'd stumbled over in my occasional glances at Catholic hymnals. The second and fourth lines of the verse he sang, though, were the same: "'Standin' n the need of prayer!'"

They rang a faint bell, and at first I couldn't understand why. I figured that Vernon was trying to tell me something but . . . . *Trying to tell me something. DUH!* Just like that, it came to me. At our first meeting, Vernon had mentioned the choir of the Holiness Full Gospel Church singing "Standin' in the Need of Prayer" at Slow Willie's grave. *Loud and clear, Vernon.* I knew the next place I was going.

"All right, then," I chirped. "I'll just stop by some other time when y'all aren't quite so busy."

Chapter 23

Walking to my car, puzzling about why the officers in Vernon's shop were wound so tight, I started when a voice barked at me.

"Hey! You dere! What happenin' in dat shylock shack?"

My head swiveled to my left, toward the voice. I saw the guy I'd spotted in the alley, but now he was on the sidewalk, and up close he didn't look so down on his luck. A black guy, six foot two at least, hard-eyed and hard-muscled, stone-cold expression, and not a speck of stubble on his face. His eyes darted left, right, and back, constantly, not in a panicky way but like a quarterback checking off his receivers one by one while avoiding a rush.

He still had the ratty patchwork quilt draped over his shoulders, and baggy olive-drab pants from a military surplus store served as his trousers. Under the quilt, though, he wore a dress shirt that might have come from any D.C. lobbyist's closet. His shoes sealed the deal: supple, chocolate leather slip-ons, either Hugo Boss or a damn good knock-off.

I generally take aggressive panhandling in stride, but this guy just plain scared me. *Why didn't I take Mama's gun?* As my trembling fingers twitched toward my purse, I felt a rising wave of nausea. Three or four pedestrians using the sidewalk gave the guy a wide berth as they kept right on walking and studiously didn't notice me.

"I axed you a question," he barked.

"Roust," I finally managed. "Three cops, doing a hot-sheet check and eyeballing the gun register."

"Dey have a warrant?" he asked, now in a calmer voice.

"I don't know, but the proprietor didn't look like he was bellyaching."

He snickered. "You mean Mr. C."

"Right. Vernon Czlewski."

He nodded at that. His eyes flickered with interest, presumably at my knowing Vernon's name. Then he averted his gaze as if he were thinking something over and didn't want my charm and good looks to distract him. The next thing I heard was a minute *'ping.'* He reacted by quickly yanking a sleek, oversize iPhone from the left pocket of his army pants and glancing at what figured to be a text message.

"Sheeyit!" he hissed. He swiveled to confront me with a look of sharp and urgent alarm. "Get back! Right now!"

The next thing I knew, he'd thrown himself on his belly onto the street behind my car and was hauling ass under the chassis of my rental faster than a cockroach when the lights come on. Elbows and knees digging into the asphalt. Hurt just to look at him. In what couldn't have been more than seven seconds he was all the way underneath. I heard his voice now as if he were talking in a tunnel.

"No runnin', no crouchin', don't be lookin' scared," he told me. "Just step back toward the storefront 'dere behind you. Like you just come out to get a smoke. Got 'dat?"

"Sure, sure, I got it."

Now I was the one with eyes darting left and right and back. I expected squealing tires coming around the corner and volleys of gunfire any second.

"See anything?" he asked, in the same tunnel voice.

"No."

"You be my eyes out 'dere, okay? You don't be goin' nowhere, dig?"

"Right," I mumbled distractedly as I looked over toward Vernon's shop eighty feet away and the cop cars in front of it. I calculated how long it would take me to cover that distance and leave this cat to whatever fate the text had warned him about.

" 'Kay, den. Anyone come up to you, on foot, in a car, on a horse, any ole way at all, an' acks you if you seen someone look like me, you say, 'Yeah, he ran into that pawnshop down the street.' Got that?"

"Got it," I said. "Pawnshop down the street."

I figured I could cover the distance in less than ten seconds. Didn't see any way he could slither out from under the car and plug me in that time. But I didn't hightail it. Inertia compounded by paralytic fear, I guess.

I started counting, the way I did when I was eight years old. *One locomotive, two locomotive . . . .* Seventy-two seconds passed. Nothing happened. No squealing tires, no black sedans careening around corners, no sinister bad asses in hoodies walking toward me with a menacing gaze, no rattling gunfire. I just stood there.

A nondescript, almost generic SUV turned the corner two blocks away onto Florida Boulevard. Not much traffic that time of day, or I might not have noticed it at all.

"Car coming," I said, trying to speak without moving my lips.

"What kind?"

"Big SUV type thing. Durango or something. Faded red."

"Comin' fast or what?"

"Normal speed, I guess. Speed limit, maybe a little over. Like he doesn't wanna get a ticket."

"Okay," came the calm, controlled voice from under my car. "Be cool, now. Jus' stay where you be, okay? Don't be lookin' at that Durango. Keep yo' eyes on that pawnshop, like you waitin' for the pigs to go for donuts so you can stroll in wid' no frisk. You cool wi' dat?"

"Sure." Didn't sound very cool to me, but it was the best I could do.

I sensed the Durango slowing down to a glacial pace as it got closer. Just past the front bumper of my car it stopped. A palsied shake rattled my right knee. I heard rather than saw the front passenger window coming down. A black guy who looked maybe nineteen poked his head out.

"Git yo ass over here, bitch!"

I walked to the edge of the curb, but didn't step into the street. If the passenger door even started to open, I'd head at flank speed for the pawnshop

"Whatch y'll want?" I asked. "I'm not hookin'."

"Thass jus' fine, bitch, 'cause we ain't payin'. You haul that shiny ass o' yours all the way over here."

I gestured toward the sheriff's cars.

"Can't. Law up there told me to stay here. He tell me I don't dare take one step off this sidewalk 'til he comes back. So if we've got business, we gonna do it with me right here."

He looked toward the sheriff's cars, seeming to notice them for the first time. Then he turned his blank face back to me.

"Lookin' for a tall brothuh, uptown faggot type. You see a cocksucker like 'dat? 'Cause if you did, you best be tellin' me, hear?"

"Yeah." I nodded. "I saw a tall black fella. Wouldn't call him a fancy dresser, except he had himself a real nice pair of dress shoes. About two minutes ago, he walked into that pawnshop down the street, where them law is parked. Just walked right into it." Goodbye D.C. diction, hello Lu-sana. Didn't even think about it. Just happened.

I pointed this time toward the entrance to Vernon's pawnshop. He looked in that direction. Looked back at me. Gave me a cold stare. Spat on the pavement.

"Sheeyit," he said.

The window went up and the Durango moved away, just creeping at first then slowly accelerating toward normal speed. The SUV stopped at the corner beyond the sheriff's cars, then turned left. I stepped back from the curb.

"Just drove off," I muttered, barely loud enough for the guy under my car to hear. "Hung a left on North Fifteenth."

"You be sure 'bout 'dat?"

"I'm sure."

"Guess 'dose pigs done scare him off. If he been thinkin' 'bout circling back, he be turnin' right up 'dere."

He took his time crawling out from under the car. I could tell he was trying to spare his knees and elbows. Once his head cleared the tailpipe, he reached back under the car to retrieve the ratty blanket, then pushed himself up deliberately, shaking his head and cussing under his breath. Bloody skin showed through tears in the shirt's left elbow, and the right knee on the pants had torn. Then he turned around, bent over, and retrieved something from the street. Couldn't see what it was.

He took three or four steps in my direction, tossing a tiny black box up and down in the palm of his right hand.

"What this be doin' stuck underneath that Jap piece of shit you be drivin'?"

He held it up for me to see. About two inches long, less wide and thick.

"No idea," I said. "Didn't know it was there. The car is a rental."

"Who you rent it from? Da CIA?"

"What do you mean? What is it?"

"Issa trackin' dealie," he said. "It be sendin' out microwave shit or somethin', and somewhere 'dere be some asshole lookin' at where you goin'. He know you be here an' he know where you been 'fore you get here."

"I wouldn't think the CIA would care that much about me." I sketched a clueless-female shrug.

"This ain't no CIA shit. If real spooks be trackin' you they be usin' somethin' 'bout a tenth this size, an' they stick it up someplace where no one be scrapin' it off wid his black ass, you dig?"

"Uh, sure."

He looked searchingly over my shoulder to check out the scene at Vernon's pawnshop.

"This be cheap-ass tracker shit you buy on 'da web, maybe," he went on. "Look to me like some muthafucka wid' a low budget wanna know where you have yo' pretty little ass parked."

"I guess that's right." I gulped.

"So who might 'dat be?"

"Dunno," I said. I knew exactly who it was. "I've had this car a full day now – parked downtown, parked in my Mama's driveway overnight. Coulda been anyone, but I don't know who'd want to."

"You 'n I know that be bitch-jive, but you wanna stick wid' it you go right ahead, for now, anyway. You coulda hauled ass on me an' didn't, so I not be pushin' it, dig?"

"Sure."

"An' Card don't be no fool, so wid' pigs just down the street, I won't be bitch-slappin' you anyway, for maybe gen'ral encouragement."

"Okay. Thank you for that."

"Want me to get rid a dis fo' you?" he asked.

"I would very much appreciate that."

"Okay den." He tossed the thing in his hand again. "You think of 'da fucker 'dat planted 'dis, you let Mr. C know. You do 'dat for me?"

"Sure." I nodded earnestly.

He sauntered off, toward Bond Street Consignments, shrugging the blanket into a more convincing shapeless drape over his shoulders. It took him five or six paces to get back the shambling shuffle of a junkie street person. About a yard short of where the first sheriff's car slanted toward the curb he stopped, looking up at the sky like something scary was happening to his body. Wobbled toward the curb. Bent over, putting his hands on his knees, looking like he was gulping air into tortured lungs.

Then, without warning, his right hand darted out and just barely reached the inside of the sheriff car's front bumper. If I'd blinked I would've missed it. That done, without a backward glance, he continued on past the pawnshop, hands now empty.

By the time I'd gotten behind the wheel of my rental, I'd figured out three things. First,

I'd just met Caleb André Regine Delacroix. Second, I never wanted to see him again. And third, he and Vernon Czlewski knew each other.

I told Siri or Alexa or whoever to find me a route to the Holiness Full Gospel Church.

Chapter 24

The words "HOLINESS FULL GOSPEL" arched in nine-inch gold and white letters over the word "CHURCH" on the display window of a plain storefront on TJ Jemison Boulevard. Beneath the arching words two tan crosses flanked an image of a Bible. The storefront itself was wedged in between Honest Abner's Rent-to-Own Home Furniture and Dave & Ralph's Bail Bonds and Notary Public. Smaller lettering below "CHURCH" promised Sunday Service 10:00 a.m. and Table Fellowship/Bible Study on Wednesday and Saturday evenings.

Inside were maybe a hundred fifty square feet of worn, brown floorboards in front of a bedsheet curtain. A round table sat on one side of the door, and a square table on the other, each flanked by two folding chairs. Two big Bibles with black covers and red fore-edge pages rested on pine bookstands on each table. A wicker basket lined with green felt sat next to each Bible. Two one-dollar bills and a fistful of change decorated the bottom of the nearer basket.

When no one came out to greet me after twenty seconds or so, I strolled over to the round table. Dropped a single into the basket, sat down, and opened the Bible. Isaiah. Great. Knew next to nothing about him, except that he gets read a lot during Lent. Just barely remembered not to cross myself, and slipped my St. Monica brooch underneath the top of my dress. Started reading. Something about a "suffering servant." I can relate, Izzy.

I'd made it through four verses or so when an older man with a fringe of gray hair around his shiny brown scalp ambled through the curtain and turned toward me. He was African-American with a healthy dose of Creole by my take, wearing navy blue slacks and a white shirt. No tie. His well-polished black shoes were high end. I guessed Johnston and

Murphy's, so apparently those baskets got filled with some regularity.

"Good morning, child," he said as I rose to greet him. "I am Reverend Carmichael."

"Good morning, Reverend. My name is Josie Robideaux Kendall. I'm an acquaintance of Vernon Czlewski."

"I see." The minister tried to hide a flash of recognition, but I learned how to play poker from Uncle D and the reverend didn't stand a chance.

"I just came from his shop," I said. "He had some visitors with badges. They were searching the place."

"That is a misfortune for the gentleman. Is that what has brought you here?"

"Well," I said, "if you happen to know who his lawyer is, I think it might be a good idea to call him. I don't think the police will be giving him the opportunity, unless they arrest him and take him to jail."

"I see." Carmichael fussed gold-rimmed spectacles onto his face, and his eyes now glinted at me behind them. "Did he ask you to come see me?"

"Not directly."

"'Not directly'?" Carmichael said, shaking his head. "Allow me to ask you again: Why have you come here?"

The dime finally dropped.

"I am a sinner seeking grace," I said.

"I see." The two words this time came not from Carmichael but from a woman who stepped through the curtain and strode toward us. African-American, without any strain of Creole or Cajun that I could see. Above her black, ankle-length skirt she wore a black shirt with a Roman collar.

"Good morning," I said.

"I am Reverend Sojourner," she replied. "You did well to come here. Reverend Carmichael, perhaps you could show our visitor around our church, while I make a phone call."

"Certainly," Carmichael said. "Would you come with me, please?"

I followed him through the sheet curtain into a largely open space. Folded card tables rested on their sides against the walls, with folded metal chairs nesting four deep in the spaces between tables. Plain crosses, two in dark wood and two in blond, adorned the walls. In one corner sat piles of canned food and dry cereal, much of it still in paper grocery bags.

"This is our table-fellowship space," Carmichael explained. "You would be most welcome to join us on Wednesday or Saturday evening, if you wish."

"Thank you very much, but I don't think I'll still be in town then."

"Let me show you our worship space."

He led me through an inconspicuous door to a set of maple stairs. He mounted them deliberately, pausing at the top to take two deep breaths. I followed him into a large room with maple-trimmed white walls. This one had only one cross, at the front, freestanding and about seven feet tall. A maple pulpit stood maybe six feet in front of the cross, facing eight rows of eight folding chairs each. On a whiteboard mounted on the wall behind, above, and to the right of the cross I saw titles and numbers of hymns, hand-printed with calligraphic elegance.

Against the wall to the pulpit's left, two modest risers provided space for a choir of perhaps twelve members. A rack on the wall behind the risers held hymnals with individual names on white slips of paper Scotch-taped to the front covers. The slip on the cover of one of the hymnals read, "Brother Czlewski."

Hurrying would have seemed out of place here. With urgency roiling my gut but without haste in my steps I crossed to the choir area and picked up Vernon's hymnal. *Standin' in the Need of Prayer* appeared as Hymn Number 283.

Held to the page by a speck of tape was a tiny plastic chip with specks of copper at the bottom. Maybe a half inch by a quarter inch and only microns thick. More than anything else, it reminded me of a photo card for a digital camera, but not as big.

I glanced over at Carmichael's carefully non-committal expression. I delicately detached the card from the hymnal page. I held it up between the tips of my right thumb and index finger, giving Carmichael a chance to object to my taking it. Not a murmur, not a muscle twitch. Then he winked.

Chapter 25

Back behind the wheel of my rental car, my breathing turned shallow and fast and I started sweating all over. The tracking device under my car had to be Kappa's work; apparently, he was into more than martial arts promotion. He must've deliberately taken me to see Paul Bunyan's dump truck so someone there could get a good look at me. And all that shoe-scraping nonsense gave someone a chance to plant the tracking device under my car. I remembered the workers in the truck whom the foreman called "Haji," which is a lot more likely label for a Muslim than for anyone from Latin America. Syrian refugees? And then there was Abdullah, as Uncle D had called him, who had been able to follow me without my spotting him – an easy trick if he were just tracking me on a computer.

I saw an East Baton Rouge Parish Sheriff's squad car hustling up from behind me, and I held my breath until it had zoomed past, flashing red and blue lights to nail some schlub who'd jumped a red light. Then an old white Crown Victoria whisked past my parking space, and I wondered if it was an unmarked car. I told my psyche to knock it off, that the Executive Branch of the United States government and the Louisiana constabulary weren't planning their days around me. My psyche didn't seem impressed.

My phone rang. Mason. Shit. Swiped and answered 'Josie Kendall!'

"It's Mason, returning your call," he said, his voice all clipped and arm's-length.

"Thanks for getting back to me. I'm real interested in what Hank Sinclair asked you about when you and he finally hooked up."

"Uh, *yeah*." Deep breath at Mason's end. "He kind of said, you know, that it was pretty confidential, you know?"

I don't enjoy slapping newbies around, but I told myself it was really for his own good.

"Okay, look, Mason. You and I are for Letitia Dejean. Hank Sinclair is for Hank Sinclair. Plus, everything behind Hank's dazzling blue eyes is 'pretty confidential' in his mind, including his recipe for French onion soup. Now if you'll work with me here and I can figure out what's going on, maybe I can get you some information that will impress the candidate."

"*Okay,*" he said after a *long* pause. "He sent me the raw footage you shot of the conference at A and T."

"And?" I prompted.

"And he asked me to get him names for as many of the protesters who showed up on it as I could. I got him a bunch of names, but there were at least eight I couldn't identify. He pushed me hard on one, but I couldn't come up with a name for him to save my life. I'm sure he wasn't a student."

"Dark complexion, oily-looking black hair, dark brown eyes, piss-ant little excuse for a moustache?" I asked, describing 'Abdullah.'

"That's the one. Same way Mr. Sinclair described him."

"Thank you *very* much," I managed. "Give my best to the candidate, and y'all have a real good day now."

I didn't need any GPS help to find Matrixarchy, Inc. on Whitehaven Street, even though I hadn't been there in ten years. Owned by two sisters who called themselves 'the Nerd Chicks,' it specializes in computer games and 'computer maintenance services.' Services like cleaning out hard drives that have been corrupted by incautious clicks on naughty sites. The Nerd Chicks are neither nosy nor talkative about any depravities they stumble over in the process.

This business model produced revenue spikes when the Louisiana Legislature met. The ladies charged an arm and a leg, but no legislator whose computer they laundered ever had to field any inquiries from the vice squad. Shy lawmakers would use Uncle D as an intermediary, and he had me act as a cutout a few times until Mama got wind of it and scorched him with an ass-chewing that would have impressed a chief petty officer.

Bells above the door announced my entrance. Once my eyes adjusted to the dim interior, I saw half the Nerd Chicks – Veronica – talking to a high school kid navigating between grunge and goth. He was saying something about "a game based on that Wonder Woman graphic novel where she has a hard landing in her invisible airplane and when her head clears she has a discipline kink but she gets frustrated because she can't find a man brave enough to spank her."

"You're totally making that up," Veronica said, "and I have an actual customer, so no more fantasy-fun until you're ready to buy something."

Taking that as a cue, I stepped forward.

"Good morning," I said, glancing at my watch. "Barely. You probably don't remember me –"

"Josephine Robideaux," she said. "Though you're probably married by now. You always struck me as the type who'd do that sooner or later."

"Guilty. Kendall."

"Well, we don't judge, but shame on you anyway," she said, mischief sparkling in her battleship gray eyes. "I read somewhere that crazy uncle of yours was up to his old tricks – but maybe that was just fake news."

"He totally is," I said.

"Good for him. What can I do for you?"

I held up the chip I'd scavenged from Vernon's hymnal.

"I need some help with this," I said.

"What is it?"

"That's the first thing I need help with."

She took the thing from me and examined it critically.

"You do understand that we don't deal in antiques, right?" she murmured.

"I hope that means you can at least tell me what it is."

"The thing looks like a data card from the mobile phone that Orville Wright used to call mom with the good news from Kitty Hawk." Her words tumbled out like lemmings racing off a cliff edge. "Ten years old if it's a day. Where in the world did you get it? No, wait, don't answer that." She turned her head so that she could shout over her right shoulder. "Mary Cary, I'm sending someone back to you."

Returning the card to me, she jerked her thumb toward the back of the store. I negotiated my way through a swinging gate in the counter and threaded in between gray metal, ceiling-high racks arrayed with electronics and games you could play on them. I reached a white-painted wood door marked in red

PRIVATE!
NO ADMITTANCE!
THIS MEANS YOU!

I knocked politely, got a sweet-sounding "Come in!", and pushed through the door. Mary Cary, her hair half blue and half a bright coppery color, sat at a splintery wooden table splattered with paint splotches and cluttered with drives, servers, cannibalized computers, and what looked like one actual working desktop PC. She smiled at me, but just as I opened my mouth and took my first full stride toward her, the bells at St. Augustine's started to peal, chiming the noon hour. Mary Cary held up an index finger to tell me to wait, then made the sign of the cross, bowed her head, and began softly praying the Angelus. I didn't know the words anymore and it wouldn't have felt right faking it, so I just stood there. After about two minutes she opened her eyes, crossed herself, and looked up at me with a a smile that gave a momentarily rejuvenated, forever-twenty-one look to a face that had left twenty-one behind at least two decades ago.

"What do you have there, dear?" she asked.

"Veronica said it was a data card from a phone," I said, handing it to her.

"Where did you get it? Wait, don't answer that." Handling it with painstaking care, she laid it in her left palm and turned it over with her right thumb and index finger. "I don't suppose you know the pass-code, do you? It would be numeric, probably five digits."

That one stumped me at first, but then inspiration struck. "Hang on," I said, taking out my own phone. I checked the telephone keypad screen and told her, "Try 4-7-2-2-3," the numbers corresponding to G-R-A-C-E. "Only an educated guess."

"Well," she said, not sounding overly hopeful, "miracles do happen."

Hoisting herself from her worn leather chair, she stepped with a spry hop to a four-drawer, custard-colored filing cabinet parked against the farther wall. She rummaged in the top drawer for half a minute or so, pushed it shut with a *moué* of disappointment, and opened the second drawer. Her rummaging this time produced what looked to me like the guts of an old-timey mobile phone: palm-sized, curved in a modest forward arc, and without a screen or a case.

She waited until she'd gotten back to her work table to worry the data card into it. Then she pushed some buttons so fast that I didn't have a prayer of telling which ones they were. Two seconds later I heard recorded sounds that echoed thinly as if they were coming from the far end of a wind-tunnel:

> *Indistinct noises.*
> *First voice:* "Drop your weapon and put hour hands in the air!"

Second voice: "No gun, boss! Hands up! No gun!"
Three gunshots, a split-second apart but distinct, interspersed with a brief, gurgling scream.
Pause.
First voice: *Looks like you done fucked with the wrong cracker, boy.*

"Are you paying for this out of your own pocket, dear," Mary Cary asked, "or will you be billing a client?"

"Billing a client for sure," I mumbled, still trying to wrap my mind around what I'd just heard.

"In that case, the charge is two hundred fifty dollars. Plus thirty-five dollars for a copy of the recording, if you want one."

"Sure, and yes on the copy," I said. "Just out of curiosity, how much would it have cost if I were paying for it myself?"

"Same price," Mary Cary said serenely. "But I would have gone to confession this Saturday."

I found a FedEx store and shipped the original phone card to M. Anthony York, my lawyer in D.C., with a scrawled note on the back of one of my business cards telling him to keep the item safe until further instructions. I shipped the copy of the recording to myself at MVC, with PERSONAL AND CONFIDENTIAL written on the label.

Three shots, not four. All through my flight back to Reagan National that night, that gut-chilling reality echoed pitilessly in my head. I would have thought by now that I could spin just about anything, but I couldn't spin that. Chad Bilbo hadn't shot Slow Willie Woodbine in self-defense after dodging a bullet Slow Willie fired. He'd ambushed an unarmed man, and murdered him in cold blood.

The phone card would prove nothing in court without Vernon. He'd have to testify that he'd found that stuff on his voicemail sometime after Slow Willie bought the farm. The jury would have to believe him, and it would have to buy the theory that Slow Willie had accidentally speed-dialed Vernon's number while fumbling to use his own phone as a mini flashlight. Without that, the stuff on the data-card could have been put there twenty-four hours before I found it by a good actor and a sound-effects tech.

But we weren't in court. We were in Josie's head, where no doubts lurked. Bilbo had already hidden in the garage before Slow Willie broke in. As soon as Slow Willie had cornered himself by the work table, Bilbo had jumped out with his Smith and Wesson ready. A *pro forma* challenge, just in case anyone might overhear; then three shots. Three, not four.

What about the Walther CC bullet buried in the garage joist? Bilbo himself could have fired that any time after Card got the gun to him. Wearing a latex glove while he did it would account for the gunpowder residue, assuming that he could have worked the glove onto Slow Willie's right hand after killing him.

Reclining my seat, I closed my eyes. Boy did this suck. Go to the cops? They'd need Vernon, who needed cover, because when he'd raised some questions without any he'd ended up on probation for a felony and threatened with hard time. The road to cover for Vernon ran through Phoebe, who had asked for cover from me in the form of campaign commercials that she could run stories about without vouching for their truth. But how could MVC gin up issue ads unless Vernon was willing to authenticate the recording? Bilbo would claim it was fake news, and damned if I could blame a blessed soul for swallowing that.

If there was any alternative way forward, it figured to be in the Kappa/Card files that Hank Sinclair had teased me with on Theo's dock – assuming that Bilbo was the congressman behind the Congressional Influence initials on the file folders. So I had to get them, and how could I do that after Seamus had given Sinclair our only bargaining chip for free?

Chapter 26

"Thoughts, ASAP. Seamus." That email, with a Word document icon, popped up at 10:28 the next morning. A little over an hour earlier FedEx had delivered the package with a copy of Vernon's phone card, except not to me. After my lawyer, Tony York, called to confirm that he had gotten the original card that I'd sent to him, I had checked the tracking number for the MVC copy online, wondering why it hadn't hit my desk yet. FedEx had delivered the envelope at nine-fifteen, but Seamus had signed for it and taken it, apparently viewing PERSONAL AND CONFIDENTIAL over my name on the envelope as just a casual suggestion. When I'd strolled down to Seamus's office I'd found a closed door and felt a *'Don't even THINK about knocking'* vibe.

Now, after stewing for an hour-plus, I clicked on Seamus's email icon, bringing up a crudely sketched storyboard headed 'Bilbo versus The Truth.' Simple concept: Contrast the story from Bilbo's Wrong Man campaign commercial with the phone card version. Cut back and forth. Then, at the end: "Call Congressman Chad Bilbo and tell him we need an independent investigation into what REALLY happened in his garage that night."

It looked pretty damn good for less than 75 minutes' work. After making it "that fatal night" and marking up a couple of other things just to show I was paying attention, I took a deep, purposeful breath and this time marched down to Seamus's office instead of strolling. His door stood open, but I knocked anyway. Beaming as he looked up, he beckoned to me to come in.

"What do you think?" he asked.

"Atomic bomb," I said. "Thermonuclear device. But –"

"I think it needs a little something," Seamus said. "Make it sing."

"Seamus, we can't go on the air with these charges unless we can be sure Vernon Czlewski will back them up."

"You know what I mean," Seamus said. "Slather it with Josie-juice. Give it that special Josie touch."

"We can slather it with anything you like, but right now all we have is the equivalent of proof that the moon landing was staged on location in New Mexico. If fact checkers go after this, our client is going to get creamed, and so are we."

Seamus settled back in his ergonomic mesh-and-tubular steel swivel chair. A savvy, hustler's smile spread ominously across his face. Seamus was 59, but at times like this, exuding confidence and pumping creative juice like water spewing from an open fire hydrant, he didn't look a day over 58. Old-school paunch, smoker's cough, highway map on his upper nose courtesy of Jameson's, lame combover with hair that Grecian Formula had given up on – and at this moment he looked as serene and content as a leprechaun on St. Patrick's Day.

I sank gingerly into the nearer of the two guest chairs in front of his desk. He casually waved aside whatever I was going to say next. He paused for a breath and then continued speaking in a calm, unhurried voice.

"Take my modest little effort and sex it up as only you can," he said. "Do that stuff you do that makes a fifteen-second issue ad just grab people by the balls and squeeze until they scream for mercy."

Chapter 27

"Go," I said to Rafe as I pushed the Timer Start button on my watch.

Picking up a latex glove from the box I'd bought at CVS on my way home from work, Rafe stepped behind Theo, who was sitting behind me at our dining room table. Without a hint of hurrying, he held the glove with the thumb and first two fingers of each hand as he reached down and began working it deliberately over Theo's hand. He snapped the wrist into place. I pushed STOP.

"Nineteen seconds," I said.

'That works," Rafe said. "Bilbo could have worn a latex glove when he fired a shot from the Walther into the joist in the garage. He could have done that hours before the burglary – even the day before. The backflash would have put powder residue on the glove. Then, after he shot Slow Willie, Bilbo would have had plenty of time before Mary Barbara got to the garage to pull that contaminated glove onto Slow Willie's hand, where the police found it."

"And a matching glove onto the other," Theo said, as he turned the latex glove inside out and pulled it from his hand. "It does work, except for fingerprints."

"Huh?" I asked.

Theo reached into the black and yellow Kelty backpack he'd brought to our home and pulled out an oblong tin box. From the box he took what looked like a miniature reading light, a munchkin paint brush, and a circular plastic container that, when opened, turned out to be half full of gray powder. He sprinkled powder on the inside-out tip of the glove's index finger, then delicately dusted with the brush. Even before he focused the light on the fingertip, I could make out sketchy whorls suggesting a fingerprint.

"No sure thing," he explained, "but latex can accept a very nice print, especially if you have a trained CSI tech using a professional fingerprint kit instead of me fumbling with the kind of Junior G-Man toy they advertise in comic books."

"Mm-*hmm*," Rafe murmured.

"So, Bilbo couldn't be sure his own prints wouldn't be picked up if he messed with the glove we think he slipped onto Slow Willie's hand," Theo continued.

"Of course!" I damn near squealed that. "That's why Bilbo put that Mr. Compassion stuff in his police statement about rushing over to Slow Willie and frantically checking for a pulse. That could explain his prints all over the gloves."

"All over the *outside* of the gloves," Theo said. "But Bilbo's fingertips would have been pressed against the *inside* of the fingers for the gun-hand glove, if he'd had that glove on when the fired the Walther. He could have left a print *inside*."

I said a word that I wouldn't have used in front of Mama.

"What are the chances of that?" I asked.

"Who knows?" Theo said. "But more than zero. Now, maybe he never even thought about it, but if he had, would Bilbo have been willing to take that risk, however small it is?"

"To get to the White House," Rafe said thoughtfully, "sure. But to become a back-bencher in the House of Representatives?"

"How about measuring up to dad?" I interjected.

We all looked at each other. The answer stared us in the face: Maybe.

Much as I wanted to, I couldn't just blow Theo's objection off. Bilbo was a bully; and bullies are cowards. Hard to see him taking even a tiny risk with the death house at stake. So I couldn't get to a hundred percent on *Bilbo did it.* To be honest, I was having trouble with ninety. Even a soft ninety.

Tough, I thought, remembering the chilling sounds and gut-churning words from that phone card. *Suck it up, girl.* When I handed Seamus my re-draft of "Bilbo Versus the Truth" at 4:30 the next day, it dripped with Josie-juice. Of course, I included a memo repeating my warning about how we didn't dare go public with this until we could corroborate it. Seamus grinned.

"Point taken," he said. "If I had an ass as nice as yours, I'd cover it too."

I did *not* post a wail about that crack on *#MeToo*. I *was* covering my ass, and I couldn't blame Seamus for calling me on it. Instead of pouting, I just put a little bite into my trademark Creole smile, nodded, and went back to my office to wait and see what happened.

For quite a while, nothing did.

A LUXURY PURCHASED
WITH IGNORANCE

December, 2017 to August, 2018

"Optimism is a luxury purchased with ignorance. I've never been able to afford it."

Richard Michaelson

Chapter 27

December, 2017 to March, 2018

Realclearpolitics online aggregates news and opinion across the ideological spectrum for political junkies – me, for example. Every morning, and again every afternoon, I run down its list of twelve to fifteen articles. Each time I did that after handing Seamus my Josie-juiced contribution, I braced myself for a tease about "Bilbo Versus the Truth." Seamus actually hitting the bricks with that thing would mean collateral damage, with part of the collateral named Josie. *Nada.* Day after day, week after week, for more than three months, not a peep, not a whisper. Not even a wink. After a while I almost stopped worrying about it.

Reality provided me with other things to worry about. Mama and Uncle D came up for Christmas through New Year's. Mama living under my roof meant that I went to Mass four times – about half my annual quota. Some team that wasn't Tulane or LSU won the NCAA College Football Championship. Another team that wasn't the New Orleans Saints or the Washington Redskins won the Super Bowl.

Three times over the first two weeks of March I came across pieces echoing the fever-swamp radio commentary I'd heard back in November on my way from Vicksburg to Baton Rouge: What if people who shouldn't be here but who got into the country while the courts were playing ping-pong with Trump's refugee hold launched a major terrorist attack? Three times in ten working days by three different writers working on three separate publications is no accident. It means insiders are calling reporters and commentators with deep-background leaks about real or pretended hyper-sensitive intelligence assessments.

Mid-morning on the Ides of March in the Year of Our Lord 2018, my phone pinged with a text from Rafe: "Icebreaker @ 6 w/Richard Michaelson re: poss bk?" I texted back a thumbs-up. If there's one thing I know how to do, it's break ice. If I were any better at it, the Coast Guard would draft me.

Rafe would have pissed me off if he'd suggested that I Google Richard Michaelson, so it's a good thing he didn't. I'd never met the D.C. legend, but I knew him by reputation. True, he was known these days mostly to a dwindling core of dyed-in-the-wool Washington-history mavens – but that club includes me. Had to be in his mid-eighties now, and he'd retired from the State Department before I was born. He'd taken early retirement so that he could angle politely and sometimes not so politely for Secretary of State, National Security Adviser, or CIA Director.

Part of his angling had involved deploying his intimate feel for how D.C. works, and a web of contacts rivaling even Rafe's, to clean up embarrassing little messes on Capitol Hill and in or near the White House. Some of those messes had involved deaths that hadn't resulted from natural causes. Michaelson was smart, just as a whole lot of people in Washington are smart. He had one gift, though, that's less common here: he could look the truth in the face, without blinking, without evasion, no matter how gut-wrenching it was. He might spin you from here to Sunday, but he'd never spin himself. People still sometimes quoted his aphorism that one sin national security never excuses is believing your own propaganda.

In the early 'nineties, according to Rafe, Michaelson could probably have copped a cabinet post if he'd turned a bombshell document over to a political hack with a senior position in the White House. Instead, he'd snookered the hack into burning the thing without realizing it. Then he'd told him what he'd done.

I assumed the book Rafe hinted at would present ideas seasoned by Michaelson's real-world, on-the-ground experience, along with some unclassified anecdotes. After a 30,000-foot overview of the book pitch, though, our cocktail chat moved smoothly on to other things. About forty-five minutes in, we were sitting comfortably in the living room, real wood fire going courtesy of Rafe and a warm, fuzzy glow on the day courtesy of half a brandy old fashioned each. We had been chatting about the fall midterm elections, and speculating over how many Republican congressmen were in trouble.

"Hard to know which way it cuts on the midterms," Michaelson said then, "but the White House staff has the devil's own time hanging onto people."

My ears pricked up. *Huh?* Michaelson made his out-of-nowhere comment placidly, without a hint of a tease. His facial features, sagging a bit now instead of displaying the sculpted look that I remembered from pictures of him during his pre-retirement years presented a portrait of benign candor.

"Highest turnover rate I've ever seen," Rafe agreed.

Setting his drink down, Michaelson pulled from his inside coat pocket two sheets of paper folded lengthwise. With the kind of default frown you sometimes see in older people, he laid the first one face down on the arm of his chair, and made a show of studying the second. He had to trombone his arms to examine it, so without getting nosy I could see that it listed names, titles, and dates. Given the context, I guessed it was a West Wing exit roster. A taste for such precision struck me as a bit anal in casual conversation, but Michaelson had a reputation for that.

"They've lost an average of three people a month going back to September," Michaelson murmured, as if he were doing sums in his head. "Not clerk-typists. GS-Twelve and higher and Schedule-C appointees. Major players, walking away from the biggest table where they'll ever have a seat."

Stating the obvious seemed to be my assigned role, so I did it.

"Sounds like a toxic work environment."

"Two sides to that coin, of course," Michaelson said. "Another term for 'toxic work environment' is 'land of opportunity.'"

Is he sending out a feeler? Rafe gave me a sidelong glance, took a measured sip of his old fashioned, then shifted his eyes again to meet Michaelson's.

"You are subtlety its very self, Richard," Rafe said, his southern accent a bit more pronounced than usual. "But someone overhearing this conversation could be forgiven for jumping incautiously to the conclusion that a possible gig in the land of opportunity might lurk in Josie's near future."

"I'm just a superannuated Cold Warrior," Michaelson said dismissively, shrugging as he sketched a sly smile. "My name doesn't show up on the email list-serve for anyone who matters these days, so where would I get inside information like that? If you held a gun to my head, though, I suppose I'd say that I wouldn't be shocked if such a thing happened. Of course, I don't shock easily."

Gob-smacked. *Holy shit.* I'd been working, hoping, and praying for a shot like this since I enrolled at Tulane. My mind started racing. My mouth raced even faster.

"Would *you* take a senior-staff position right now if they offered you one?" I just blurted that out.

"Certainly, if it were a position my country needed me to fill." Michaelson's shrug suggested that this answer was self-evident. "If my country needed me, I wouldn't feel I could say no."

"Very big 'ifs'," Rafe commented. "Washington right now is full of people who say they'll serve their country when it has a president it deserves."

No mistaking the brief flicker of contempt that lit Michaelson's almost black eyes for an instant. When he spoke, his low-key tone had some bite to it.

"Our country doesn't need anyone special when it has a president it deserves. In that situation, most any well-meaning bachelor of arts will do."

"Hold that thought," Rafe said. "There's a title in there somewhere."

Michaelson finished his drink and stood up, smiling enigmatically.

"I'll get you a detailed proposal on my idea by the end of next week," he said. "Settling on a title will leave only the detail of writing the book itself."

"Don't be dour about it," Rafe joshed. "Writing is a job for optimists."

Michaelson smiled at Rafe and then at me, not cryptically this time but with what seemed like genuine warmth.

"Optimism is a luxury purchased with ignorance. I've never been able to afford it. Thank you for your hospitality and an enjoyable evening."

Chapter 28

With iron discipline I contained myself for a full ninety seconds after our front door closed behind Michaelson. Then I burst.

"Do you think he really knows something?"

"Richard Michaelson seldom chatters," Rafe said, "and when he does the chatter isn't idle."

"But Michaelson has 'deep state' woven into every fiber of his being. Why would a Trump underling use him to feel me out?"

"Maybe an underling was using him to *warn* you about an overture that a rival underling has in mind for you," Rafe said. "After all, the default setting for the current White House staff on any given day is open civil war. The various factions spend more time shamelessly undercutting each other than fighting Democrats."

"If it was a heads-up," I said, "it worked. I'm paying attention, even if I can't help wondering, Why me?"

"The more interesting question isn't 'Why you?' but 'Why now'? You were a solid candidate for, say, a communications staff position during the transition, and all you got was an indecent proposal. Why are you suddenly a blip on radar screens you weren't showing up on before?"

"Operation Bilbo?" I asked. "Except that we're nowhere close to a clean kill on that one. I've moved pieces all over the board, but no checkmate yet."

"Well, Michaelson didn't come here for a brandy old fashioned," Rafe said. "He must have – *hello*. Look at that."

I followed his eyes to the right arm of the chair where Michaelson had sat. The page that he'd set aside so he could study his West Wing exit roster still lay there, face down. Senior moment? *Not a chance in hell.*

Rafe grabbed the page and flipped it over. I looked around his bicep at it. One word leaped out at me, stamped in red in the upper corners on both sides: DINAR.

DINAR is a security designation at least three levels above TOP SECRET. It supposedly limits the legal viewers of a document to the president and no more than forty other people whose jobs give them a need to see it. The very existence of the DINAR classification is confidential. Super confidential. Hyper confidential on steroids. But pretty much everyone who works in Northwest D.C. knows about it.

In other words, Richard Michaelson had just completed a leak approximating the Johnstown Flood. Rafe and I were probably committing a felony just by looking at this piece of paper. Because of Michaelson's finesse, though, we'd have a shot at plausible deniability.

After the DINAR tease, the rest of the page seemed anti-climactic. Four columns of numbers and dates, with the dates going back to August, 2017 and running through January, 2018. The numbers were mostly 20KLbs or 10KLbs. Centered at the bottom were the letters ANF.

"Well," Rafe said after studying the thing, "if 'Lbs' is pounds and 'K' is thousand, then something highly confidential happened to about eight hundred thousand pounds of ANF – whatever 'ANF' is."

"Uranium?" I guessed, fearing the worst. "Fissionable material? Something you could make nuclear bombs with?"

"Hard to believe that four hundred tons of anything like that has been moving around without anyone except whoever leaked this to Michaelson knowing about it."

"That's why he really came here," I said. "Not mainly to alert me to a possible West Wing job feeler, but to get this into our hands."

"To get it into *your* hands," Rafe corrected me.

"Which gets us back to why me and why now? Questions we don't have answers for."

"If Michaelson is right," Rafe said, "we'll have answers for them soon."

Chapter 29

April, 2018

Perfectly prepared shrimp creole made with fresh Gulf Coast shrimp, served on Wedgwood china with Moet-Hennessey champagne in Waterford stemware, on a Gulfstream IV jet cruising six miles above the ground from Washington, D.C. to San Antonio, Texas. In San Antonio we'd board a spacious helicopter painted British racing green with black and white checkered racing flags fore and aft for trim, which would ferry us to the Alamo Dome. We were on our way to watch the final round of the NCAA men's basketball tournament from a luxury suite.

By "we," I mean Rafe, Seamus, Calvin Kirby, his oldest son, Alan, Kirby's entourage (executive secretary and a taciturn ex-SEAL), one cook, two waiters, and me. Ten of us altogether aft of the cockpit, and we were nowhere close to crowded. I've flown commercial on puddle-jumpers smaller than this plane.

I had no idea why I rated this treatment. If Kirby were softening me up for a project even edgier than the Bilbo exercise, it was working. As the punch line from an old political joke puts it, everyone has a price and they were getting close to mine. By now I was game for anything short of high treason.

"Congratulations," Kirby said in his resonant baritone as he flashed me a warm, winning smile.

"For what?"

"Full flip-flop on fracking from Congressman Bilbo. He has seen the light, and is now on the side of truth, virtue, and sound public policy."

"Did *not* see that one coming," I admitted.

"Seamus here leaked a taste of your masterpiece to the only member of Bilbo's staff who doesn't have his head up his ass," Kirby explained. "Some internal polling and a come-to-Jesus meeting with the congressman finished the job."

"Well hallelujah," I sort of yelled. "I had no idea I was this good. Uhh, that is, that *we* were this good."

"Take the credit and enjoy it," Seamus said. "You ginned up a kerfuffle at the expense of campus snowflakes, you pulled a nice woman from obscurity and made her a lead story, and you dug up evidence that had eluded experienced detectives – maybe because they weren't looking for it, but even so."

"Thank you. I'm glad Congressman Bilbo won't be standing in the way of fracking development any longer."

"The stakes are way higher than a few hundred million in oil revenue," Alan Kirby said, shrugging as if a nine-figure payoff were chump change. "One of our major political parties sees its mission as taking money from people who have earned it and giving it to people who haven't. The other thinks its mission is to deny money to people who need it so it can be kept by people who don't. Their real purpose in each case is to buy votes from the people who end up with the money. Both of them are intellectually and morally bankrupt."

I cocked a right eyebrow at that. He sure hadn't pulled that riff off of an Excel spreadsheet.

"Look at the guy who won the last election," Seamus said.

"The last election wasn't won, it was lost," the senior Kirby said. "Like most American elections. If you're one party's candidate when the other party's nominee falls on his face – or hers – then you take office by default."

"But on the rare occasions when someone actually manages to *win* a presidential election instead of just backing into victory when the other candidate face-plants," Alan said, "he doesn't just take office, he takes power."

"Reagan showed that when the moment meets the man, outright winning can be managed if you push the right buttons," I commented.

"Which is generally a matter of having the right people pushing them," Calvin Kirby said with a smiling, sidelong glance at his son. "You've got a keeper on your hands here, Seamus. Don't fuck things up."

Whoa. I glanced at a Lucite-fronted bookcase built at roughly chest level into the bulkhead behind the Kirbys. Machiavelli. Hobbes. Hayek. Russel Kirk. Thomas More.

Jordan Peterson. Patrick Dineen. At least one of the Kirbys didn't limit his reading to *Forbes* and the *Wall Street Journal.*

"Have you had any more encounters with that drug dealer, Card, who shows up in your reports?" Alan asked then.

"Nope. And I'm not looking forward to the next one. Pure thug."

"Hard to avoid thugs in politics, though," Calvin said. "Every day Washington looks more and more like Las Vegas East. At least among the politicians that the media touts as presidential timber, how many do you think are more than three degrees of separation from a mobster?"

"Loaded question," Seamus said. "On a wild guess, not many."

"Symbiosis," Alan said. "The war on drugs alone is the most massive transfer of wealth from Americans to third-world countries in our history. Couldn't happen without the complicity of the current political class."

"That's what keeps Card in high-end designer shoes all right," I said.

Calvin and Alan both smiled. Their smiles were equally enigmatic, Alan's crinkling under real hair less gray and more eye-catching than the hand-woven variety worn by his dad. I knew Alan was thirty-one or thirty-two. He wasn't breathtakingly handsome, but he had the build and looks suggestive of a Hollywood man's man from the 'forties or 'fifties, before Tinseltown heartthrobs got all sensitive and vulnerable. I knew that in between his bachelor's at USC's Marshall School of Business and his MBA from Stanford he'd earned his chops ferrying supplies in Kirby helicopters to oil drilling platforms off the Louisiana and Mississippi coasts, and pitching in on the North Slope in Alaska.

What I hadn't known until this flight was that he wanted to be President of the United States. Now I had no doubt that he saw himself at the podium on a January 20th in, say, 2028 or 2032, with his right hand raised and his left hand on a Bible, eyeball to eyeball with the Chief Justice. And that maybe he saw his dad there even sooner.

Can't possibly happen? The last time I said that about presidential politics was November 7, 2016, and it will be a long damn time before I say it again. Sitting across from the two Kirbys, I felt that special, charismatic, shimmering excitement generated by proximity to real power. Not the power of a congressman or a senator or even a cabinet member. The thing its very self, as Rafe might put it.

"Pushing buttons is all down the road a bit," Calvin Kirby said. "For now, let's just enjoy good food, good friends, and the luxury of optimism."

'Luxury of optimism.' I imagined Richard Michaelson chuckling politely in the background.

I called Phoebe with the bad news on our first full day back in D.C. I kept it barebones: MVC's best judgment now was that Letitia Dejean was a flash in the pan whose funding was about to dry up. That would mean no TV/radio money for attack ads accusing Bilbo of murder. *So no campaign ad cover for your scoop.*

"So you flipped him, huh?" Phoebe asked.

"I can't comment on speculation."

"Just so you know," Phoebe said, "I'm not dropping the story. If I can get corroboration from any credible source, I'm going to break it wide open, and that skillfully engineered flip-flop will turn into an epic fail."

"Good luck with that, Phoebe. I sure wish I could be more help."

"Thanks for nothing, Josie."

She broke the connection. I felt lousy, as if I'd flirted with a good friend's ex after a bad breakup. I thought for a second about sharing the rogue DINAR document with her as sort of a consolation prize. So far, though, I couldn't make any sense out of the thing myself, so how could I expect her to get anywhere with it?

Chapter 30

May, 2018

Every once in a while I wonder whether all the political morons in the country are Republicans. During the first week in May, though, the Louisiana Democratic Party generated Exhibit 6,256 for the case that stupidity is bipartisan. With Letitia Dejean gaining traction against Bilbo, showing his potential vulnerability, the Dems decided to get a "real" Democrat into the race – one of those people who has shown selfless devotion to the party for years. Who has sat through countless county meetings and done thankless, behind-the-scenes grunt work at state conventions. Who has burned up cell-phone minutes and gas getting out the vote. And who has lots of experience losing to the likes of Chad Bilbo.

Now the anti-Bilbo vote would be split. With Kirby dollars drying up for Dejean after Bilbo's fracking flip-flop, of course, she was probably doomed anyway. Still . . . . I mixed myself a G-and-T.

On the last day of May, I finally got the White-House-staff job tickle Michaelson had vaguely alluded to. Introducing herself in a robust Alabama accent as Vanessa Sara Lee, the tickler told me to call her Nessa.

"Only if you'll call me Josie."

"Deal. So, we're creating a new position here: something like communications assistant for foreign policy/domestic policy liaison."

That was bullshit, but I didn't mind. What she really meant was that she didn't want me to know what job was opening up, because then I could have figured out who was about to leave.

"Sounds like a promising idea," I said.

"Way too early for short strokes, but if it happens, does it sound like the kind of thing that might interest you?"

"Absolutely. If my country can use me, I wouldn't feel I could say no." I made a mental note to send Michaelson a royalty.

"Great. Why don't you shoot your CV over, just in case?"

No sense playing hard to get. I launched it into cyber-space less than a minute after she'd finished giving me her email address.

Chapter 31

June, 2018

On Flag Day, Seamus asked me to come down to his office. He asked very politely, so I wondered if I was about to get fired.

False alarm. It was worse.

Seamus introduced me to Baxter Haskel, whom he described as a "constituent services aide" in Congressman Bilbo's office back home. This meant that whatever Haskel had come to talk about was something Bilbo didn't want to disclose to his Washington office – where some staffers had gotten a preview of Bilbo Versus the Truth. Most likely, then, it also meant that Haskel didn't know about that threat – um, prototype ad. So this situation basically sucked.

Bax Haskel had a United States Marine Corps signet ring on the third finger of his right hand, a WWJD – "What Would Jesus Do?" – band on his right wrist, and a prosthesis where his left hand should have been. Didn't take Sherlock Holmes to put that one together: Marine ROTC at a fundamentalist Christian college, career-ending wound in Iraq or Afghanistan, and pit-bull loyalty to the congressman who'd given him a veterans-preference billet in his local office.

"Bax says a reporter in town is sniffing around a cock-and-bull idea about something fishy with that tragic incident in Congressman Bilbo's garage before he was first elected," Seamus explained.

"Phoebe Riverdale?" I asked.

"How did you know?" Haskel looked astonished at my insider acuity.

"Wild guess. Phoebe grabs at straws a lot, and she's looking for a big score to take her to the next level. But she's too smart to get behind a smear she can't substantiate. So as long as there's nothing to the rumor, I'd say the congressman doesn't need to worry."

"She has hinted that there's some kind of documentation behind the rumor," Haskel said. "Hard evidence or something."

"Do you know of anything that might fit that bill?" Seamus asked me.

"*Nada*," I answered, shaking my head. "Unless it's that thing I sent back from Baton Rouge – but calling that 'documentation' would be a huge stretch, even for the fake news media."

"Could you give me a look at that, whatever it is?" Haskel asked.

"Love to," Seamus said. "Absolutely love to. But it's in the hands of a client. I took exclusive control of it from the time it reached this office, and I can guarantee you no one made a copy of it at this end."

"That's unfortunate," Haskel said. "Very unfortunate."

"Not necessarily," Seamus said. "The client in question greatly values the important contribution Congressman Bilbo is making to America's energy independence. There'd be no risk of Phoebe Riverdale getting a whiff of it even if it were something to worry about."

Bax Haskel didn't like it and I couldn't blame him. But there wasn't a blessed thing he could do about it.

July, 2018
By Bastille Day I was getting antsy because Nessa hadn't touched base. I'd gotten to where I jumped every time my phone buzzed. That's what I did around 2:30 p.m. and – another anti-climax.

What showed up on Caller ID was 'DOMINIC K.' Kappa. I answered in my default voice: bright and cheerful.

"It's Kappa," he said. "This may sound off the wall, but I just heard a rumor about something that might or might not have happened when you visited down here a few months ago."

"Oh?" I said in a voice of naive innocence. "What might that be?"

"It's a little confused, but my favorite version has it that one of Bedford's valued human resources took it into his idiot head to follow you down to Baton Rouge after your visit here. Anything to that?"

"Well, I sure didn't notice anyone. My Uncle Darius thought he spotted a tail, but Uncle D has been known to overreact." All true. Not the whole truth, but you can't have everything.

"None of my business, of course," Kappa said, "but if a Bedford employee did go off on a frolic of his own, you might want to make a formal report to Homeland Security. FBI, even. In fact, I strongly recommend it. You know, just in case."

"Good thought."

Early August, 2018

Nothing happens in D.C. in August except this August, when something did. Seamus told me about it as he wandered into my office without knocking. He was looking at the kind of pink telephone message slip that I would have thought people stopped using sometime in the nineties.

"Do you know a guy named Quentin Balegan?"

"Senior staff at the White House," I said. "Reputation for sharp elbows. I've never talked to him, but I know the name. I think he accents the first syllable, by the way: BAL-e-gan."

"He couldn't reach you and then he couldn't reach me, and he's apparently never heard of voicemail, so he left a message with the receptionist." He handed the thing to me. "If this is that next step up the ladder you've been dreaming about, let's hope the dream doesn't turn into a nightmare."

I shook my head, poor-mouthing my own chances so that it wouldn't hurt if nothing ever came of that tickle back in June. If this were a real follow-up, it would have come from the first person who'd contacted me.

"It ain't Nessa Sara Lee, so . . . ."

"Call him back anyway," Seamus said, already in mid-exit. "You miss a hundred percent of the shots you don't take."

I returned Balegan's call, of course. Reached him on the first try. After half a minute of introductions and pleasantries, he got to the purpose-of-my-call part.

"What can you tell me about Cavour, Louisiana?"

"Small burg in Slidell Parish in the northeast part of the state," I said. "Destination for Italian immigrants decades ago, and their descendants still have a strong presence there. Solidly Republican."

"Red wine, red votes, and red necks. So that would figure."

"What would figure?" *Seriously?*

"Hank Sinclair has been tasked to do an advance there in mid-September," Balegan said.

"I have a world of respect for Hank, of course, but I don't know that he's ever actually done an advance before. Plus, there's the fish out of water thing. I'm wondering if I could pass your name on to him so that he could prep for the job by having a little chat with you."

Go to hell was one of two plausible answers to that. I gave him the other.

"Sure. Anything I can do to help."

He thanked me and hung up.

Late August, 2018

"So," Rafe said as we careened toward Labor Day Weekend with no further word about any West Wing job, "what are the odds that they're just jerking you around?"

"Seventy percent, and that's a hard seventy. I think something totally different is going on."

"There's more in play than head-hunting, that's for sure." Rafe sipped a bourbon-and-sweet. "You got a world-class leak from Richard Michaelson, followed by a world-class-cubed leak from Quentin Balegan."

"Who almost certainly is the one who used Michaelson as a cutout to get the DINAR document to me to start with."

"Inference: Hank Sinclair is involved in something Balegan thinks is a very bad idea." Rafe raised his eyebrows to ask if I agreed, and I nodded to show I did. "Instead of queering it himself, which he could manage with an exit memo if he were willing to risk his job over this, he thinks he can maneuver you into doing that for him – presumably because of the surgery you successfully performed on Congressman Bilbo's testicles."

My turn for a slug of diluted Jim Beam.

"Thing is," I said, "it's hard for me to imagine some power player in the White House basement in charge of ramrodding a high-risk project stroking his chin and saying to himself, 'Finesse, instincts, and guts. *I've got it!* Hank Sinclair!'"

"Power players don't always operate that way," Rafe said. "One day King Henry the Second mutters, as if he's talking to himself, 'Will no one rid me of this turbulent priest?' Next thing you know, Thomas á Beckett has his brains splattered all over Canterbury Cathedral."

"I get that," I said. "No project formally approved. No National Security Decision-Action Memorandum. Word just gets around that the president would be happy if such-and-such problem got solved. Someone sees this as a big chance to move up the depth chart, doesn't have the operational experience to appreciate the gigantic risk he's taking by working as a cat's paw – that could be Hank Sinclair looking in a mirror."

"Whereas you, by contrast, know exactly what the risks of letting yourself be used as a cat's paw are," Rafe continued. "Maybe you should just get out of the picture. Give Phoebe the DINAR document along with some informed speculation and otherwise keep your head down. 'Thanks, but no thanks. You folks made the Hank Sinclair mess, you clean it up.'"

Bullseye. Bailing out was the best option. No sooner had I reached that clarity, though, than I flashed on those two security guards at Eugene Simpson Stadium Park charging toward the gunman instead of running away from him. And of Rafe, driving toward the sound of the guns. And, for that matter, of a high-class kleptocrat who planned to kill me going to asshole heaven courtesy of a .30-06 fired by my beloved husband.

Rafe had made his comment to cover me in case I decided to bail out and wash my hands of the whole ordeal. If I did, he'd unconditionally support me. But he'd also be disappointed. The thought of disappointing him was the deciding factor.

"Not gonna do it," I said. I told him about Kappa's call, which I hadn't mentioned before, because in the larger scheme of things it had seemed pretty trivial.

"Josie, he wanted you to create a paper trail that might someday sic the FBI on designated scapegoats."

"Right. And I guess that's what really settles it for me. I'm not the bravest girl in the world, I'm not the most selfless patriot who ever sang *The Star-Spangled Banner*, and I don't have the most sensitive gag reflex in Washington. But everyone has a choke-point, and somewhere between DINAR and Dom Kappa, these jerks have triggered mine."

Brave words that came from my gut, not my head. They made me feel good. They didn't make me feel smart.

"In the immortal words of Spiderman," Rafe mused, "'With great power comes great responsibility.'"

"Strictly speaking." I said, "I don't have any power. Just information."

"In Washington, information is power."

"Touché." I bowed my head briefly in graceful submission. "Except we can't do a blessed thing without some facts we still don't have, and I don't know how to get them."

"I have an idea about that," Rafe said. "Let's discuss it after dessert."

"Can I ask for a hint?"

"Of course you can," Rafe said. "There's no harm in asking."

THERE'S NO HARM IN ASKING

September, 2018

"[Women] have occasionally sought damages for mental distress and humiliation on account of being addressed by a proposal of illicit intercourse. . . . [Recovery] was generally denied, the view being, apparently, that there is no harm in asking."

Judge Calvert Magruder, "Mental and Emotional Disturbance in the Law of Torts," 49 Harvard Law Review 1033, 1055 (1936)

Chapter 32

I called Vernon Czlewski the morning after Labor Day. Got voicemail, left a message. He called back an hour later.

"Just wanted to let you know that I may be heading back to Baton Rouge later this month," I said. "Something has come up."

"Dee-light-ful. I can give you a good price on stainless steel flatware or a wedding dress only used twice."

"I might take you up on some knives and forks," I said. "Another thing I thought I might do down there is chat with Card."

"We don't travel in the same circles."

"Oh, I'd be flat out astonished if *you* knew how to reach him," I said, which was technically a barefaced lie. "But I'm thinking your lawyer might know how to get in touch with his lawyer."

"Possible, I suppose," Vernon said. "I can guess why you want to talk to Card. But why would Card want to talk to you? You know, just in case his lawyer asks my lawyer."

"I have some information he asked me to pass on to him."

"That's a little light in the detail department, but I guess it's the best you can do. Let's go with it and see what happens."

I sat back in my chair, stretched my arms over my head with my fingers joined, closed my eyes, and took a good, deep breath. That one was easy. The second act is always harder. I called Kappa, expecting to get voicemail. He picked up on the second ring.

"Did you make that report?" he asked.

"Sure did." Barefaced lie number two for the morning. "Homeland Security, but no follow-up at all. I have the feeling it might have dropped through a crack."

"Maybe," Kappa commented. "But it'll show up in a hard drive somewhere."

"Here's the thing. I'm heading down to Baton Rouge before the end of the month. I could hop down to New Orleans while I was at it. I'm wondering if a face-to-face with the FBI field office might generate a little more interest. Or do you think that would just be a waste of time?"

Pause. Pregnant silence. I imagined Kappa thinking about me mentioning him to the FBI as the source of a rumor I was reporting, and then wondering whether I really was as dumb as he apparently thought I was. He finally spoke up.

"Couldn't hurt," he said. "Good luck with it."

"I'm guessing I should keep your name out of it if I possibly can."

"Up to you, but they might think you're trying to borrow credibility if you invoke an ex-fed."

"Probably right," I said.

The next day I called Mason. Got voicemail. Left the same message: I'd be in Baton Rouge before the end of September, and would he find it helpful to talk to me? I knew the answer – he wouldn't. Didn't expect a call back and didn't get one. The point was just to put my upcoming visit into one more dataset.

That afternoon, I figured it was time for Push and Shove to be formally introduced. I told myself not to rush things. I had no idea which strand on which information web – Vernon's, Card's, Mason's, or Kappa's – would tickle Hank Sinclair when it vibrated, or how long it would take. I had a sudden urge right out of nowhere to waltz down to Seamus's office and bum a Marlboro. I resisted it. I turned the desk calendar in front of me to the next day and wrote: "2:00 p.m.: Call Hank Sinclair."

Turned out that I didn't have to wait that long. My phone rang the next morning at 11:58. I answered with the lilt I use to suggest that talking to this particular caller will be the highlight of my day.

"Ms. Kendall?" Voice probably female, but I couldn't be sure. Very low-key, flat affect. Definitely no lilt.

"Yes, this is Josie Kendall."

"Please hold for Mr. Sinclair."

Whoa. This was official. This call would be noted in a computerized data base with the time the call was placed and the time it ended. It could be found by any White House task force trying to sniff out leakers. It would be subject to disclosure to any American citizen – a reporter, for example – willing to make a Freedom of Information Act Request, as well as to any congressional committee willing to subpoena White House call logs. Hank knew all that, and yet he was still making the call the old-fashioned, record-generating way instead of on his own mobile phone. *Hmm.*

"Hey, Josie," Hank said in a genial, Skull and Bones Club voice. "How's everything going?"

"Downright peachy, tiger. How about with you?"

"Just grooving on the vibe, baby. Living my dream."

"What can I do for you, Hank?"

"How would you like a ride on Air Force One?"

HELL-O.

"That would be . . . a lot," I said.

"Don't want to over-promise," he said. "But I'm heading out to your old stomping grounds next week to do an advance on an event in the first half of October. First stop, Baton Rouge. If the presidential visit I'm advancing for comes off, I might be able to get you on board. Could be some people along on the same ride who'd like to talk to you."

Steady, girl.

"What a remarkable coincidence," I said. "I'm heading out to BR around that time myself."

"No kidding. What's on your plate?"

"Oh, this and that." I kept my voice slow and casual, but my pulse rate spiked. "Kick the tires. Maybe find some reading material."

"Reading material," Hank said. Said, not asked.

"Sure. Never can tell what you might stumble over in a city full of interesting people. By the way, Seamus did get you that footage of the A and T conference that you asked about, didn't he?"

"Sure did."

Dead air while Hank waited for me to say something. *Okay, now, Josie. Whip that rod forward with a nice, soft touch, sending the line in a gentle parabola over the water so you give him a good view of the juicy-looking fly at the end.* I finally spoke up.

"I'll be staying at the Hotel Indigo."

"Traveling solo or *en famille?*"

"Rafe has to stay in Washington to work out exit strategies for a couple of junior trumpkins. *Quelle dommage*, but there it is."

"You wouldn't be teasing me now, would you, Josie?"

"Do you know what happens down in Louisiana to girls who tease?" I asked him teasingly.

"Well, well, well," he said. I could almost see his smile. "Why don't you keep some time open on the day of your arrival? Let's see what happens."

"Looking forward to it, Hank."

Gotcha, you sonofabitch.

Chapter 33

I saw the shackle first. A brown leather cuff started at Hank's left wrist and extended a good four inches up his arm. A silver chain went from a ring on the cuff to the handle of the attaché case he was carrying. Pretty nice attaché case, too – oxblood leather with highly polished brass fittings.

An expletive came right to the edge of my lips. I'm not prissy, but everybody doesn't like something and I don't like handcuffs and chains. As I opened the door to Suite 418 all the way, though, I managed to pull my eyes from the shackle and look Hank in the face.

"Well good evening, Hank, and welcome to Baton Rouge." I showed him into the suite's main room. "How was your flight?"

"No complaints." With his right hand he produced a handkerchief and wiped a charming little sheen of first-date sweat from his forehead.

"Let's see, you're one of those scotch-and-soda boys, aren't you?"

Without waiting for an answer, I started mixing mini-bar Johnny Walker Red with tonic water. I could do that in my sleep, so I didn't have any trouble glancing over my right shoulder to keep an eye on Hank. He set the attaché case upright on a coffee table in front of a dark-toned sofa. Then he fished a small key from his right pants pocket and fussed with it clumsily until he'd gotten it into the lock on his wrist-cuff. A clockwise quarter turn, a barely audible *click*, and he worked the cuff off. He left it hanging on the attaché case's handle.

Really? Not kink, just self-importance? It's not like he was walking around with the nuclear launch codes. His case presumably held files on an ex-cop and a run-of-the-mill street criminal, but here he was acting like a twelve year old boy's idea of a CIA agent.

Strolling over to him, I gave him his drink. He didn't even try to civilize the ogle he laid on me. Gaped appreciatively at my breasts, then raised his eyes to meet mine.

"Looks like you brought some interesting reading material," I said.

"We aim to please."

I sank onto the couch just as he was craftily raising his left hand to cop a feel. I patted the cushion beside me. He sat, but with an expression hinting that he didn't appreciate the coy-mistress routine. Deftly, and with a measure of finesse, he undid the top button on my alabaster-white silk blouse. Only used a thumb and index finger and got it on the first try.

"Steady, tiger," I said, offering him a lingering squeeze as I wrapped his hand in mine. "I'm not asking for dinner and a movie first. But I am dying for a brief glance at reading material exciting enough to require bondage gear."

"Tit for tat?"

"I'd prefer *quid pro quo*."

"That makes it seem kind of mercenary."

"We're both whores, darlin'," I said. "I'm not a tease, but I'm not an idiot, either. Cards on the table."

Hank set down his drink and used his thumbs to work triple-digit combination dials on either side of the attaché case's handle. *Click, snap*, open. Laying the case flat on the table, he pulled the lid up and took his laptop from inside. That revealed the two bulging manila file folders that he'd shown me on the dock at Theo's place, complete with the oversized, red-stamped CI initials.

"Well bless my soul, Hank Sinclair," I said, "you are a man of your word."

He beamed. His eyes lit up over teeth white and even enough for a Crest commercial. Standing, he hastily unfastened his belt and undid his pants. His trousers and tighty-whities had fallen to all the way to his ankles when three angry, pounding raps boomed at the door.

Chapter 34

"Open this door, Josie!" Rafe's voice. "Open up, goddammit!"

Sinclair's face turned whiter than the Daughters of the Confederacy. His eyes widened. His nostrils flared. His lips quivered. He opened his mouth, but no sounds came out.

The main thing he knew about Rafe was the rumor that my beloved husband had gone old school on a shadowy one-percenter named Jerzy Schroeder who'd slipped between the sheets with me. The police had neither turned up a scrap of physical evidence linking Rafe to the execution – uh, excuse me, *murder* – nor shaken the cast-iron alibi provided for Rafe by Theo McAbbott. They'd chalked the killing up to a conveniently deceased crony capitalist/racketeer and rival of Schroeder's (who, to be fair, most certainly would have killed Schroeder if he'd had the balls). The D.C. insider attitude had settled on, *maybe, maybe not, but no-harm/no-foul.* After all, what's one less shadowy one-percenter?

Now, to be clear: (1) I had cheated on Rafe with Schroeder; (2) Rafe had found out about it; (3) Rafe had killed Schroeder; but (4) Rafe had done that not to vindicate his husbandly honor but to keep Schroeder from killing me (which he'd been right on the verge of doing). The handful of people who knew that last part didn't include Hank Sinclair.

"Is that you, Rafe honey?" I called, coloring my voice with a quiver of panic. "Simmer down, now. I'll be right there."

"What's he doing here?" Hank stage-whispered as he fumbled at his pants. Nothing feigned about the panic in *his* voice.

"No idea," I whispered with *faux* urgency.

"Open this door, woman!" Rafe barked to the accompaniment of two more thumps. "Right now! I mean it!"

"I'm comin', lover. Just chill." I turned back toward Hank, and lowered my voice back to whisper. "Get outta sight. I'll talk Rafe down, then waltz him into the bedroom and you can get discreetly on your way."

I had expected Hank to hobble to the nearest closet, like any sensible tryst-meister would. That, however, would have required more presence of mind than he had at the moment. He knee-flopped onto the couch, his unbuttoned pants sliding back down over his underwear, which had never made it back over his buttocks. Then he frantically clambered over the sofa's back – fanny as bare as the day he was born.

I hustled over to the door and opened it.

"Rafe, darlin'," I squealed delightedly as I pointed toward the couch. "What a wonderful surprise to see you here. I thought I was in for a long, lonely evening."

"Don't hand me that, Josie!" Rafe barged into the room, slamming the door behind him. "Where is he?"

"Where is who, honey?" I asked, dripping with innocence.

"The weasel who belongs to that dispatch case, for starters. And don't tell me it's yours."

"Why it most certainly is mine," I said, girlishly stamping my foot as I quietly pulled off the rubber bands around the two manila file folders. "I bought it after I got my year-end bonus in January."

"That execrable piece of *nouveau riche* cliché crap is *yours*?" He picked it up and shook it violently, creating a shoulder-high mini-blizzard of CONFIDENTIAL/ HIGHLY SENSITIVE/INVESTIGATIVE PRIVLEGE paper. "You expect me to believe that?"

"Rafe, this isn't like you." I pointed at my left cheek to cue the next bit of business we'd rehearsed. "You're hurting my feelings."

"I'll hurt more than that, you whore!"

Rafe tried to slap me. He really tried. Did his dead level best to smack my cheek convincingly, but Lord love him his heart just wasn't in it. Best he could manage was a glorified love-pat. I extended my arms and clapped my palms together as hard as I could. That produced a good, loud SLAP!

"Rafe, you hit me!" I wailed. "How could you do that after everything I've done for you?"

As I gave my best impression of pathetic, choking sobs, I pointed to the bedroom. Rafe looked puzzled for a second but got back on-message pretty quick.

"What was that?" Rafe barked. "That noise in the bedroom? Is he in there?"

"Rafe, honey," I panted between sobs, "there's no one in that bedroom!"

"There won't be for long, I promise you that," Rafe snarled.

He bolted for the bedroom. I scurried around behind the sofa and kicked Hank, mooning in frozen fear, in his bare fanny. Just couldn't resist.

"Get a move on," I whispered fiercely. "You've got about five seconds."

I would have bet everything I own that that boy couldn't move anything like as fast as he did. Out from behind the couch lickety-split, holding his pants closed with his left hand, and grabbing the computer with his right. He paused to look with an eloquent combination of uncertainty and panic at the paper scattered all over the carpet.

"Never mind that," I told him. "I'll work out a way to get it back to you as soon as I have Rafe snoring in post-coital bliss."

With that I jerked my head toward the bedroom as if I'd heard Rafe about to emerge. That was all Hank needed. He aimed his nose at the door and ran like the Yankees at Chancellorsville.

"Where are you, you sonofabitch?" Rafe yelled from the bedroom, just for general motivational purposes.

Hank actually sped up, which I wouldn't have thought possible. He fumbled at the doorknob, what with having both hands full, but he got the door open and disappeared into the hall.

Rafe came out of the bedroom, grinning like a farm boy walking through the rye under a harvest moon. I put a finger to my lips, because I figured Sinclair might be lingering outside our door regularizing his trouser situation. I allowed sixty seconds for that, then turned toward Rafe with a beam as wide as his. The high five we exchanged stung a lot more than his half-hearted stage slap but, believe me, it was a good sting.

"How long do you figure we have?" Rafe asked.

"Well," I said, "let's say five minutes to get back to his room."

"First thing he'll do is pick up the phone, right?"

"Don't think so. First thing he'll do is some panic-thinking."

"You're right," Rafe said. "He'll sit on his bed with his elbows on his knees, running his fingers through his hair. He'll try to calm himself." Rafe paced back and forth, mimicking a male in self-calming mode. "Fix a drink from the mini-bar. Take a healthy swallow. That should get a little spunk back for him."

"He may need more than one drink for that," I said. "But whatever. Then he'll start to go through his options."

"Which will all be bad," Rafe said. "Secret Service protection starts way above his pay-grade, so he can't show up back here with a couple of those boys."

"They'd probably be sampling the local hookers about now anyway," I said. "The nearest FBI field office is in New Orleans, so no help from them for at least three hours."

"No help from them until tomorrow at the earliest," Rafe said. "You won't find more *per capita* contempt for the White House anywhere in the federal bureaucracy than at the FBI these days."

"Plus," I said, "an FBI report would guarantee Hank getting fired and probably indicted. So for cops he's down to local police and hotel security."

"And he'd only call them as a last resort," Rafe said.

"Agreed. That leaves calling me or sitting there and hoping for the best."

"Which means he'll call you."

"So," I said, counting minutes on my fingers. "Wardrobe rehabilitation, travel time, all that cogitation, a couple of variables in there . . . ."

"I'd say the over-under is twenty-seven minutes from when he walked out the door," Rafe said.

"I'll take the over," I said, nodding.

Chapter 35

If Rafe and I had been playing strip poker, I'd have been stark naked. Hank's call came at room-exit plus twenty-three minutes.

"Hello?" I said in a worried whisper.

"Josie, you need to bring those files to me right now." Hank's voice, one level short of panicky. "I'm in room –"

"Are you out of your mind? I can't leave this room. I'll be standing up for breakfast as it is. Rafe is in in the shower or I couldn't even have taken this call."

"Josie, those documents are United States Government property, and misappropriating them is a felony."

"Government property that you brought here and then left behind when you got caught with your pants down," I said. "So let's have no chat about misappropriation. Whenever you want those files, you just march up here and knock on the door. I'll hand them to you with pink ribbons tied around them."

"I can't come up while he's still there! You said –"

"I know what I said, darlin', and I'm sticking with it. Rafe will come out any minute feeling real hangdog about smacking me the way he has. I know what to do with male guilt. Just give me an hour. Strike that. Seventy-five minutes to be safe. I know my man. By then he'll be sleeping like a baby on knockout drops."

I paused, mainly because hearing people sweat is one of my guilty pleasures. I resisted the temptation to twist the knife. No snark about his creepy shackle. I just listened to the sweat. Imagined him trying to find the guts to come back at me with something tough. Five seconds. Ten. Finally, he spoke up.

"All right. One hour and fifteen minutes."

He rang off. I gave a thumbs-up to Rafe, who was sitting about a foot away.

We'd already gathered the documents and stacked them in two neat piles on the coffee table. Rafe took Kappa's file and I took Card's. In less than an hour we could get through them and use our Scannable app to take pictures of any important pages. Then I'd stuff them back in the attaché case, hand the case off to Sinclair when he appeared at the door, and try real hard not to kick his ass again while he slunk off.

Well, that was the plan.

"Come on in, Hank," I said seventy-eight minutes later. "We need to talk."

Not the original plan. Two tidbits that Rafe and I stumbled over, followed by ten minutes of brisk discussion, had made us drop Plan A like a bad date.

I came across tidbit number one almost without realizing it. I was blitzing through the Caleb André *et cetera* file, waiting for key words to jump out at me from the gray, telegraphic government prose.

Snitches have to be compensated with money, drugs, or favors. Every penny, gram, and dropped charge has to be accounted for to the satisfaction of green-eyeshade types in the Inspector General's office, all of whom apparently underwent excessively rigorous toilet training. DEA agents do *not* leave snitches out of their confidential reports.

Three snitches appeared in the Kappa reports in Card's file, but only one of them amounted to anything: Code name NATHAN; Code number 09-7312A457.

On the page stamped with document control number CARD 00353, I felt a tingle without knowing why. Focused. Re-read the last two pages. Bingo. Snitch code-number 09-7312A457 had gotten two hundred dollars for bust-worthy information three days *after* Slow Willie bought the farm. Which meant that Slow Willie *wasn't* the snitch telling Kappa about Card's opioid supermarket. No reason for Card to have set up a high-risk plan to chalk Slow Willie.

After I'd explained my searing insight, Rafe spoke up with tidbit number two.

"Brother Kappa has a more interesting employment history than we thought. Seven months before his retirement, the DEA pulled him out of active field work and stuck him on desk duty in Toledo, Ohio."

"Punitive transfer," I said. "What they'd do to someone they wished they could fire but couldn't."

"Couldn't *yet*," Rafe corrected me. "The *de facto* demotion came after the beginning of an internal investigation of Kappa for conduct unbecoming a narc."

"A little too much snitch money sticking to his fingers?"

"Nope," Rafe said. "Suspicions that he was improperly getting money from a non-government source."

"Bedford Industries?"

"Pretty good for a wild guess," Rafe said. "And it gets better. Or maybe worse. Brace yourself."

"Braced."

"The DEA had a snitch tattling on Kappa. They were using odds and ends that the snitch gave them to build the case they were cobbling together. The last tip from that snitch came five days before Slow Willie was killed."

"So Slow Willie was a DEA snitch all right – but he was snitching on Kappa," I said. "And apparently they couldn't finish the case once he was gone."

"Which is too bad, because here's one more factoid. Most of the martial arts fighters that Global Martial Arts Promotions, Inc. has under contract are either convicted felons or Blackwater alumni – in other words, mercenaries."

I suddenly felt like a security guard finding a taped-over lock on a door at the Watergate Hotel.

"Conclusion," Rafe continued, reading my mind. "Kappa is working with Hank on something sinister. We don't know who's running them – maybe someone higher up on the White House staff, maybe someone rich and ruthless in the alt-right, maybe someone else. We don't know what the project is. But we do know that it's something a lot bigger than a four-term congressman getting away with murder – and whatever it is, Kappa/Bilbo/Bedford is critical to it."

"Holy shit, Rafe!" I panted as the implications gut-punched me. "This is a world-class cluster-fuck! We have to do something about it."

"All *we* can do is the usual Washington stuff." Rafe's eyes narrowed. "Tell Phoebe. Have Theo mention it to one or two of his buddies at the FBI. Drop a word in the ears of a couple of my protégés. Hope that someone bites and follows up."

"Do we use Hank?" I asked.

"He's scum under a rock." Rafe said this thoughtfully, as if he were adding up the pros and cons of a fantasy baseball deal. "He's serving a nefarious purpose that he's probably not savvy enough to recognize. He'd throw you under the bus in a heartbeat if he thought it would move him one rung up the West Wing ladder."

"So we use him."

"We do."

Chapter 36

That's why I invited Hank in and said, "We need to talk," when he knocked on our door.

His face turned purple.

"Give me those fucking files, goddammit! You gave me your word!"

"I'm going to give you the files," I said. "But we have to talk, so haul your fucking ass in here. And watch your language. You're talking to a lady."

I turned and walked toward the couch. He didn't really have any choice but to follow me. Before he could take more than half a step in, though, he remembered how scared he was.

"Where's your husband?" he demanded.

"You don't have to worry about Rafe."

I reached the couch. I let Hank get a good look at the two precious files stacked next to his attaché case on the coffee table. I pointed at the chair opposite the couch. Rafe and I had moved the other chair into the kitchenette, and we'd centered the remaining chair in the area that the two of them had occupied. We wanted Hank to feel like a suspect in a squeal room.

Hank scowled. Gritted his teeth. Licked his lips. Took about four steps into the room and stopped.

"What would you do if I just grabbed the things and walked out?" he asked.

"I'd start making phone calls."

Shoulders sagging and facial expression constipated, he shuffled over to the chair I'd indicated and slumped into it. I sat rather primly on the couch. Enter Rafe from the kitchenette. Hank jumped like a startled jackrabbit.

"I have to apologize for losing my temper," Rafe said suavely as he circled behind Hank to stand towering over him to his right. "Josie has explained that you and she were just having a professional discussion about a political matter, with nothing untoward going on. I'm afraid I jumped to conclusions. Sorry."

Rafe extended his hand. As slowly and tentatively as if he were defusing a bomb, Hank clasped it. A combination of wariness, bafflement, and plain old terror distorted his face. Handshake completed, Rafe smiled and walked over to sit beside me. Cue Josie.

"Hank," I said, "you are in way over your head on something. You need an exit strategy before 'plea bargain' hits the top of your option list."

"What are you talking about?" He managed a weak smile.

I told him about the tidbits from the file, and said we knew Kappa was in on something with him. He tried for a poker face, but his expression had more Tells than Rossini's opera. He opened his clasped hands.

"Follow the money," I said. "The money trail here leads to Bedford Industries. The question raised by Bedford-equals-money is, money for what? I have a couple of clues on that for you."

I described the sudden outbreak of talk radio and inside-the-beltway commentary on Syrian refugees allowed into the country by lower courts. His Prussian blue eyes widened with sudden panic. *Sonofagun!* I thought. *You were in on that! You were one of the people getting the word out to the wingnuts!* Then I went over the kid who'd followed me. The one I was supposed to spot and report, generating a Homeland Security paper trail.

"Which probably doesn't come as a complete surprise to you, Hank," I concluded, "because you jumped through some hoops to confirm that he was at the A and T conference last fall."

I looked at him steadily. He looked at me steadily, but he had to work harder at it than I did. Time for the last schmear of vanilla frosting on the devil's food layer cake we were fixing here.

"And then," I said, "out of a clear blue sky, someone gets the bright idea of having the president visit northeast Louisiana in the first half of October."

"Interesting," Hank said, not batting an eye. "So what?"

"I don't know what, Hank," I said. "That's just the thing. I'm not sure you know what either. I'm guessing that all Kappa has told you is the bare minimum you have to know to take care of your specific assignments. But you know more than I know."

"And you'd like me to tell you." He said that with a definite smirk.

"I'd love for you to tell me, but I don't expect you to do that."

"Then what do you expect me to do?"

"Basically, what you did earlier tonight: run for the hills, covering your ass on the way."

"Are you serious?" he demanded. "You think I'll go to the president with conjectural drivel that sounds like it's out of a made-for-TV movie?"

"Hank," I said wearily, "we both know that you couldn't get the secretary for the deputy chief of staff on the phone, much less the president."

Hank had somehow misinterpreted my metaphor. Why would we want him to tell the president anything? We wanted him to do the same thing I'd done with my phone calls, except on the D.C./deep state spider's web: tickle as many strands as possible, in the hope that one or two of them would shake someone who could pick up a phone and yell, "Abort!" I decided to leave the plain-English explanation to Rafe.

"We have something a little closer to your speed in mind," Rafe said in his friendly, coaxing, soft-sell voice. "Paper the file. Punch up the report on your advance work here with a paragraph about rumors of something afoot in northeast Louisiana. Send blind copies to the Secret Service and Homeland Security. Then do a separate, much more comprehensive report."

"A *piece de resistance*," I said.

"A masterpiece," Rafe continued. "Thirty pages with an executive summary and a brace of exhibits – the kind they taught you how to do at the Kennedy School. Put in what Josie has told you and what you know that she hasn't told you. Identify possible risk scenarios, including the one that you actually think may be in play here. Throw in some probability assessments to make it sound like you have serious sources from the intelligence community: say, hard thirty percent; soft sixty percent; that kind of thing."

"Do that one on your home computer," I interjected.

"Absolutely right," Rafe said. "Nothing traceable to your office."

"Send a PDF of the thing to your immediate superior for approval," I said.

"But without waiting for him to approve it," Rafe said, "which he won't – he probably won't even read past the executive summary – circulate hard copies discreetly to two people on the White House staff that you trust and to two people in agencies whose employees carry guns on the job."

"There probably aren't two people on the staff that he trusts," I pointed out.

"Good point," Rafe said. "Make that two people that you distrust less than you distrust all the rest."

Hank glanced from Rafe to me and back, as if he were following a rally in a tennis match.

"I see," he finally said, after a pause of two or three beats.

"You getting all this, Hank?" I asked.

"Sure." His voice sounded numb and shaken at the same time. "So . . . that's it?"

"That's it," I said. "Take your files and be on your way. Don't forget the shackle."

Hank stood up gingerly. He shambled over to the coffee table and loaded the files back into the attaché case. Got a death grip on the handle, lifted the case, and started for the door. I let him get about halfway there before I asked my last question.

"By the way, what's the exact date for the president's possible visit to Cavour, Louisiana – the one you're doing this advance for?"

He stopped and, without turning all the way around, glanced over his shoulder. "Information that valuable has a price," he said.

"Name it."

"Give me everything I left here."

Seriously?

"It's all there, Hank," I said, gesturing toward his attaché case. "We didn't hold back a thing. Scout's honor."

He smirked as he shook his head. Really. He'd just gotten his ass kicked from here to Sunday and he smirked.

"Have a nice life, Josie."

Exit Hank. As soon as the door closed behind him, I pulled out my mobile phone, counted slowly to ten, then punched in a number.

"Phoebe Riverdale," a no-nonsense voice answered. "What's up, Josie?"

"You got yourself one hell of a story, girl, that's what's up. And the murder in Chad Bilbo's garage is just background."

Chapter 37

Rafe and I checked out the next morning. Because I am Evangeline Barry Robideaux's daughter, I compulsively looked through the hotel suite to make sure we left with everything we'd brought. Checked every closet, every shelf, every drawer, every cabinet, whether we'd used them or not, checked under the bed, under the couch, just as Mama did. Nothing, nothing, nothing and . . . *Huh?*

A thumb drive, shiny blue plastic with a hint of silver, lay forlornly on the carpet behind the couch. Souvenir that Hank had dropped when he was cowering there on the verge of being caught *in flagrante?* Had to be. That must have been what he'd come with and discovered he didn't have.

Thirty seconds later Rafe and I were on my laptop, checking out the part of the contents that wasn't triple-encrypted behind the cyber equivalent of a chastity belt. *Hmm.* Collection of videos, stills, and text-PDFs: the singer Madonna ranting on Inauguration Day about bombing the White House; the comedian Kathy Griffin holding a mock-up of Trump's severed head; assassination scene from a modern dress New York production of *Julius Caesar* in which Caesar looked a lot like Trump; descriptions in encyclopedic detail of the Eugene Simpson Stadium Park shooting and the Las Vegas mass murder; exhortations from ISIS/ISIL about lone-wolf attacks; more diatribes against Trump from Hollywood types.

"Wow," Rafe said mildly. "I wouldn't want that stuff found on *my* computer."

". . . found on your computer . . . ." I murmured.

"But can you seriously imagine Hank Sinclair somehow planting compromising data on someone's computer while he's running around down here doing an advance and aspiring to adultery?"

"No, I can't. That sounds like more than that boy has in his bag. But I sure can imagine him having a copy of something somebody else is going to plant – or already has planted."

"*Whoa!*" Rafe said. "Josephine Robideaux Kendall, you are absolutely right." He paused thoughtfully for a moment, then asked the obvious next question. "Where do we go from here?"

"You go back to D.C.," I said. "I stay here in Baton Rouge for a bit."

"Doing what?"

My turn to pause, because I couldn't believe what I was about to say. Then, quietly, as if it were an offhand comment of no particular importance, I got it out.

"Well for one thing, I'm going to go to confession."

Chapter 38

Sister Clare Scholastica and I shook hands at 11:00 sharp the next morning. I donate five hundred dollars to Carondalet Academy every year, which I figured didn't hurt, but she probably would have met with me anyway.

Her hair had gone completely gray in the eleven years since she'd last given me two demerits. She'd also acquired a few wrinkles. She still presented the mixture of wary understanding and don't-bullshit-me firmness that I remembered. Same twinkling gray eyes behind the same rimless glasses, same half-smile that didn't give much away, same dry voice, same tone that was correct without always rising to polite.

After the usual opening – *Welcome back to Carondalet which will always be your home, thank you for your continuing support* – we were seated across her desk from each other and she got to, "What can I do for you?"

"I need to talk to whoever is handling operational stuff for Syrian refugees at the Archdiocese," I said.

"Can you tell me why?"

"I'm afraid that some of the refugees may be in danger."

"Ah," she said.

She didn't cross-examine me, probably because she knew I was incapable of lying to her. She picked up the receiver of her old-fashioned dial phone and pushed one of the five buttons along the bottom.

"The name I can do," she said. "Getting you a conversation with him might be a challenge, but we'll see." She held up a finger as she began to speak into the phone. "Ms. Irwin, please get me Sister Benedicta at the Arch, and buzz me as soon as the phone is ringing. Thank you."

We smiled at each other for ten seconds. She seemed to notice my St. Monica brooch. What showed in her eyes might have been either approval or amusement. I think I'll go with approval. Her phone buzzed and she picked up. After four more seconds, she spoke.

"Benedicta, this is CS at Carondalet . . . . Great, thank you, sister. How about you? . . . . Wonderful. Listen, do you have anyone over there who's handling food, shelter, and clothing for Syrian refugees in this area? . . . No, not oversight so much. More rubber-meets-the-road stuff, day-to-day logistics. . . . Thank you, Sister. Blessings and peace."

She hung up. She hadn't made a note. She hadn't even picked up a pen.

"Father Xavier Kempton," she said. Then she rattled off a phone number and an email address. I'd seen that coming, so I was ready, copying them down on a mini legal pad with a cheap, serviceable Bic.

"Thank you, sister. Do you happen to know Father Kempton?"

"Nope. I'll give him a call, though, just for luck. He's a Jesuit, so watch out. You have that lapsed-Catholic whiff about you. He might feel moved to a little evangelization."

"I wouldn't say 'lapsed.' I'd call myself more of a relaxed Catholic."

"Just don't tell him you want him to hear your confession. I'll guarantee you he's heard that one before."

Well, so much for that bright idea.

I called Kempton's number and got voicemail, so I left a message that included a reference to Sister CS. A monsignor once told me that a non-trivial percentage of the people who contact priests out of the clear blue sky are crazy. I hoped that the call Sister CS had promised would win me at least a provisional non-lunatic presumption. Kempton called me back before noon, so apparently it did.

"Good morning, Ms. Kendall. Returning your call. You have a concern about Syrian refugees?"

"Yes, Father. Not just a concern. I have hard facts making me fear a serious crime implicating the refugee community is being planned."

"I see." He paused. "Have you shared these concerns with law enforcement?"

"Selectively," I said, figuring that what Rafe was already doing back in D.C. qualified. "But the FBI, the Department of Homeland Security, the Central Intelligence Agency, and the Secret Service get an average of thirty-seven tips about terrorist activities per day. We can't count on my report reaching the top of anyone's in-box in time."

"Okay," he said.

Next, he'd ask what these hard facts were. I didn't want to recite them over the phone, but I was afraid that saying so would get me a Loony Tunes tag. So I preempted the question.

"Father, I'd really like to meet with you soon to discuss this."

"I got a heads-up about possibly hearing from you," he said at last. "You apparently have Washington connections that actually could generate concrete information about the refugee situation. I'm also told that you're not exactly obsessed with the truth but you don't lie just for the fun of it."

"Well," I said cheerfully, "it's nice to be loved."

"I'll take you at your word. Do you know where Saint Francis Borgia Church is?"

"I can find it, and probably get there in less than an hour."

Twenty-five minutes later I was sitting in a folding metal chair with fifty-pound bags of rice stacked high behind me and Father Kempton's well-tanned face, light brown hair, and clear blue eyes in front of me. Not much taller than I am, he presented himself with a coiled, oddly detached intensity, almost in the Zen zone. We were in the basement of a nineteenth-century church built mostly of custard-colored brick. Peeling linoleum on the concrete floor, gaudy murals brightening otherwise drab concrete walls.

"We eat what our guests eat," Kempton explained, offering me bottled water and a plate of chicken and cooked rice, emphasis on the rice. I figured I might earn some cred by accepting, so I did. I remembered to bow my head and say grace first. That got a smile from the padre.

In between forkfuls I told him what I knew, working my way from Hank Sinclair, to 'Haji' and 'Abdullah,' through Bedford Industries, with a little inside-baseball stuff about planted media topics thrown in for good measure. He listened with polite skepticism.

"Anything else?" he asked.

"That's what I know," I said. "Here's what I think."

I paused, giving him a chance to tell me not to bother. Instead, elbows on his knees, he slightly spread the hands clasped in front of the open expression on his face. With a deep breath I plunged in.

"I think that at least one White House staffer is working with an outside group to orchestrate a false flag attack – some kind of terrorist act that can be blamed on refugees who would have been kept out by Trump's exclusion orders, but who came into the country because judges initially blocked the orders."

"When and where?" the priest asked.

"The best I can do on that is somewhere in northeast Louisiana in the first half of October."

Kempton dropped his forearms down to his knees – slightly less defensive body language. I looked into his eyes to make sure they hadn't glazed over. They hadn't.

"Assuming every word out of your mouth is Gospel truth," he said, "where do I come in? What do you want from me?"

"For starters, confirmation that some of the refugees actually have found work at Bedford."

"Certainly possible," he said. "We try to arrange employment for them, and so do their own communities. Not very efficient. Trained engineers working as fry cooks, that kind of thing. I don't know about Bedford specifically, but sure, that could happen."

"The second thing I need is a channel to someone these refugees will listen to. Someone who can tell them they're being used, they're right on the verge of being thrown under a Caterpillar mining dump truck, and if they get instructions to drive that truck *anywhere* in the first half of October they'd better go on strike."

"Not sure how I can help you with that," he said, shaking his head. "Our guests are mostly Christians. The Christian refugees think the Muslim refugees want to kill them, and the Muslim refugees think the Christian refugees are spies. The Muslims are more likely to trust Trump himself than a Syrian Christian."

Streaking for the end-zone with time running out, and then suddenly dropped on the three-yard line by a blind-side tackle. *No. Not taking no for an answer, dammit.*

"There has to be some way," I insisted. "Some Muslim equivalent of you for the Muslim refugees, some Christian refugee who can talk with a Muslim refugee, *something*. We can't just sit back and let this happen."

Kempton smiled. A real smile, warm and genuine. A hint of condescension to it, but admiration as well.

"My office is in the rectory attached to the west side of the church," he said. "No guarantees, but I'll do what I can. I have morning Mass at seven-thirty on Tuesdays. Can you get to my office at eight-fifteen sharp?"

"I could even get to seven-thirty Mass if I had to."

"You're a very intriguing woman," he said. "I'd like to hear your confession someday."

"How much time do you have?"

Chapter 39

"Right on time," Kempton said when he spotted me waiting on the rectory porch at 8:06.

He flashed a card at a sensor next to the door, waited for a click, then opened the door for me. He and a receptionist named Dolores at a desk behind a long, high counter exchanged good mornings. After grabbing a handful of mail from her, he led me briskly to an office about ten feet down a narrow hallway from the reception area. He rather pointedly left the door open, making Dolores our *de facto* chaperone. Tossing the mail on an ancient but thoroughly clean and dusted wooden desk, he picked up what looked like a long black shawl draped over the back of the guest chair. He handed it to me.

"Do you know how to wear one of these?" he asked.

I opened it out. It was a hijab.

"Can't be too complicated," I said.

I laid it across my shoulders and lifted the middle part to cover my head, all the way to my forehead and a little over. So far so good. Folding the ends to overlap across my chest and cover my throat was trickier than it sounds, but I managed it.

By the time I had the hijab on, Kempton had pulled his Roman collar off, stashed it in the shirt's breast pocket, and unbuttoned the top button. Now he took a royal blue sweater from a pegboard hanger behind the desk and slipped into it. He picked up an iPad and tucked it under his left arm.

"Okay," he said, concern showing in his caramel colored eyes. "Let's go."

I followed him out of the rectory and across a rain-damp parking lot toward a two-story detached building, yellow brick like the church, that reminded me of a dormitory. Repurposed convent? Probably. Instead of flashing a card at the front door of that building, he pushed a doorbell button. A buzz sounded and we went in.

The guy at the desk eight feet inside the door definitely was *not* a receptionist. He was a guard. Retired cop veneer mixed with an ex-Navy vibe, and an expression that said you'd make his day if you took a swing at him. He didn't have a gun, but he looked like he didn't need one.

"Good morning, Father."

"Morning, Pete," Kempton said. "Rajiha here yet?"

"Not yet," Pete said.

"All right. We'll wait for him in the refectory."

Across an open space behind the desk, through double doors, into a dining room large enough that calling it a 'refectory' didn't sound pretentious. Most of the tables were eight-foot long Formica-topped numbers with folding legs of gray, tubular steel. Metal folding chairs dotted the spaces along them. Kempton led me to a far corner where one table of dark wood sat in between pew-like benches made of wood that was almost as dark but not quite.

"Don't say anything about Islam," Kempton said as he flipped the iPad open. "No matter how benign it seems to you. Rajiha has a short fuse. If he hears anything that strikes him as blasphemous, he's liable to storm out."

"Got it."

Kempton made a quick sign of the cross and began studying the screen – reading that day's eight-page Morning Prayer online instead of from a breviary, I assumed. He'd scrolled for about thirty seconds when something near his left hip pinged. He pulled out his phone and examined it.

"They're here," he said, closing the iPad and rising. "Sit tight. I'll bring them back. Don't offer to shake hands. If they offer, go ahead, but don't initiate."

"Understood." *Eyes on the prize, Josie. You're not here to witness against religious misogyny. You're here to . . . to . . . to what, exactly? Put the Apocalypse off for one more month, I guess.*

I had less than two minutes to stew. Before I knew it, Kempton was striding back into the room, accompanied by two dark-skinned men. The older of the two was both taller and thinner than Kempton – and the 'thinner' part is saying something. He wore a black, pin-striped three-piece suit, and I could have put lipstick on by the reflection from his glossily polished shoes. A suspicious scowl dominated his face. The other man's head came to Kempton's shoulder. Late teens, early twenties, tops. Looked nervous, scared even, but was trying hard to hide it. He wore blue jeans, a New Orleans Saints jersey, and brown leather sandals.

I stood up as they approached the table. *Bow?* Oh, why not? With hooded eyes I inclined my head and shoulders slightly. Seemed to go over well. The kid responded with just a bashful nod, but the older man came to a full stop and returned the bow, making sure that his head didn't go quite as low as mine had. Kempton introduced the older man as Walid Rajiha and the kid as Fahd al-Moallem. He said that Rajiha was his counterpart for the Muslim refugees who'd found their way to Baton Rouge, and al-Moallem was a refugee himself and served as one of Rajiha's liaisons with the other Muslim refugees.

We all sat down. Rajiha favored me with an accusing glare.

"You are with the American government?" he asked.

"No, I have nothing to do with the government," I said. *And vice-versa.* "I work with a . . . private organization."

"What does this 'private organization' do?" he asked in a staccato voice.

"We try to impact policy and legislation, and make our clients' voices heard in political campaigns."

"Ah!" he said delightedly as understanding brightened his eyes. "You are bagmen!"

Uncomfortably close.

Kempton intervened.

"Ms. Kendall has some information that she thinks you might find important," he said.

"Right." I nodded. "I believe that some powerful people are trying to fake a terrorist attack that can be blamed on Syrian refugees – possibly one or more refugees working at a company in Vicksburg, Mississippi called Bedford Industries."

Rajiha's grin vanished into thin air. Al-Moallem's eyes widened and he opened his mouth. A glare from Rajiha and the kid's mouth closed as fast as Rajiha's smile had disappeared.

"'Powerful people,'" Rajiha said. "Powerful people like Trump?"

"I don't think President Trump knows the first thing about it. People whose names you wouldn't recognize, but who have enough muscle to make it happen."

"You said 'Bedford Industries'?" he demanded.

"Yes."

Rajiha turned toward the kid and shared what sounded like some no-nonsense Arabic with him. No idea what he said, except that I picked up the word 'Bedford' pronounced phonetically. The tone, though, was what I'd use to accuse someone of stealing camels. Al-Moallem responded in Arabic, in a voice that struck me as defensive and tentative. After a couple of sentences, Rajiha cut him off with a quick wave of his left hand. He turned back to me.

"We know nothing about this," he said. "No Muslim refugees who have come to reception centers in Louisiana since the Trump administration began are working at any place called Bedford Industries."

I kept my expression carefully neutral. *Bullshit is my business, Chester. I know it when I smell it. But what could I do? I'll tell you what you* can't *do, girl. You can't say, 'Nice try, Josie' and wait for BOOM. Why not throw a Hail Mary?*

I looked directly at al-Moallem. Arabic and smatterings of English might be the only languages he knew, but the odds were against it.

I started speaking to him in French. Not schoolroom French. The French you learn if you grow up in a house where French toast for breakfast is *pain perdu pour le p'tit déjeuner* and napkins are *serviettes* and the thing you don't get beaten with if your Mama doesn't like corporal punishment is a *fouet* and the entire conversation when you had Sunday dinner with your paternal *gran' père* and *gran' mere* was in Creole French. I read understanding in Fahd's eyes and in the surprised way his mouth opened.

"Any refugee at that company is in danger of being set up to take the blame for a fake terrorist attack," I said (in French). "The refugees shouldn't run. That will just make them look guilty. But they need to talk to someone they trust about anything they've seen or heard or been told to do that seems suspicious – following an American woman from Vicksburg to Baton Rouge, for example, or loading something besides fertilizer into a mammoth mining truck. And from now on, if anyone tells them to do anything like that, I'd recommend saying, 'Not my job, boss. *Je ne m'en fiche pas.*'"

Al-Moallem's face suddenly took on a serious and determined look. Rajiha, meanwhile, had gone into full glare mode at my first French words.

"What is she saying?" he loudly asked in the middle of my monologue.

"She's talking about her admiration for Syrian culture and history," Kempton said with a face straighter than a West Pointer at attention. "She's saying that one of her relatives was named after Saint Ignatius of Antioch. And she hopes that Fahd will find his time in the United States instructive and fulfilling."

Rajiha scowled. He followed the scowl with a gruff, "We go now." Fortunately, that came three seconds after I'd finished my spiel.

"I'll show you out," Kempton told the two men as he stood up.

I stayed where I was until Kempton returned, which didn't take long. Rajiha apparently wasn't in a mood for long goodbyes. I'd barely gotten the hijab off and folded when I saw the young priest strolling back in my direction.

"I'm not sure Rajiha was being completely honest with you," he said.

"He was lying through his teeth. He thought I was a cop, trying to trick them into spilling something that would tie Syrian refugees here to whatever is going on in Vicksburg."

"What did you actually tell Fahd, by the way?"

"Basically the same thing I told you, except I left out the pawnshop owner who fences stolen goods and the pusher who knows him and a retired FBI agent who sometimes colors outside the lines."

He grinned.

"There *is* such a thing as too much information," he said.

Chapter 40

I'd done everything I could. With a clear conscience I could improvise some road-warrior work at Mama's for the rest of the day, hanging around Baton Rouge in case Vernon suddenly got chatty or something else local broke. Then I'd watch *Game of Thrones* that night with Mama and catch a flight back to D.C. the next morning. (After six years full-time in Washington, *Game of Thrones* is a little tame and sentimental for my tastes, but Mama likes it.)

That plan was looking real good until Kempton called shortly after 11:00 a.m.

"I just heard from Rajiha," he said. "He asked me for your number. Do you want me to give it to him?"

"Yes, please. Thank you."

Rajiha called me twelve minutes later. As soon as I'd spoken my name he said, "We must meet."

"Where and when?"

"As soon as possible," he said. "If a male family member can accompany you, we could meet at my office."

Whoa. Didn't like that idea at all. I remembered his scowl and his attitude from earlier that morning. For all I knew, in his eyes I was still a cop or a spy or both. Going to see him someplace with an acute shortage of disinterested witnesses struck me as the kind of incredibly dumb thing heroines in action stories do just to move the plot along. Plus, 'male relative' meant Uncle D, and I could just see him rehashing the War Against the Barbary Pirates. I assumed that any place serving alcoholic beverages was out, and in Baton Rouge that didn't leave a lot of public-space alternatives. So I defaulted to the obvious.

"How do you feel about seeing me at my Mama's house?"

"Would your father be present?"

"My father died when I was twelve, but my uncle could be here." I said that with a golf ball-sized lump in my throat, hoping against hope that here at home Uncle D would behave himself for fear of Mama braining him if he didn't.

Pause. I could almost hear Rajiha frowning. He finally spoke.

"Yes, that will do. One p.m.?"

Quick look around. Could we get all the bourbon, scotch, and gin out of the living room in ninety-four minutes? Close, but yes. I gave him the address.

"See you then."

Worked out just fine. Mama provided a sweat-beaded glass pitcher of peach tea, then made herself scarce. Uncle D put on a clean shirt and, in the spirit of southern hospitality, left his .45 in his bedroom. Rajiha brought the cat Uncle D had dubbed Abdullah along, and introduced him as Tariq. The four of us sat down around Mama's living room coffee table at 1:00 p.m. sharp. One sip of peach tea to be polite, then Rajiha came straight to the point.

"This morning," he began, "you spoke to Fahd in French about 'loading something besides fertilizer' on a large mining truck. What were you alluding to?"

"The day I saw the truck, workers were loading fifty-pound bags of fertilizer into its cargo bay. If they start loading dynamite or TNT or something like that onto it, I'd be worried."

"But fertilizer doesn't alarm you?"

"Should it? My husband and I have ten pounds of fertilizer stored in our garage right now, and we don't exactly treat it as hazardous material."

"Ten pounds is no concern," he said. "Two-hundred tons of ammonium nitrate fertilizer in a confined space, if ignited, could cause an enormous explosion."

"That's what wiped out the Murrah Federal Building in Oklahoma City back when you still had to use a car seat, if I remember correctly," Uncle D rumbled.

"Correct," Rajiah said.

Shit. I took a real deep breath. Not comfortable about putting the stuff from the DINAR document on the table, but I couldn't see any way around it.

"I've seen a confidential document summarizing deliveries of something called 'ANF' to Bedford Industries," I said. "Not two hundred tons; twice that much. Let's say 'ANF' is Ammonium Nitrate Fertilizer. And as long as we're making stuff up, let's say the deliveries have been signed for by the Syrian refugees you told me weren't working there. If that stuff makes a loud noise about a week from now in the same zip code as the President of the United States, then –"

"That would be a major provocation," Rajiha said.

"That's one way to put it," I said. "Another would be 'Reichstag Fire.'"

His brow wrinkled. Eyes that looked like miniature polished onyx stones laser-focused on me as the reference clicked. I can generally tell when someone believes me, and I can almost always feel the vibe when they're sure I'm lying. It looked to me like Rajiha hadn't made up his mind yet.

"Can you show me this confidential document?"

"No."

"Why not?"

Because that would be espionage. Giving a reporter a peek is one thing. Disclosing a highly classified document to an agent of a hostile power – which Rajiha just might be – is another matter entirely.

"Because it's locked in a safe in Washington, D.C."

"No copies?"

"No."

Frown from Rajiha. Not quite a scowl this time. Maybe we were making progress.

"Why are you telling me this?" he asked then.

"Because I don't want the American midterm elections in November to be deformed by a false-flag terrorist attack orchestrated by White House cowboys and then blamed on people who had nothing to do with it."

"You said this morning that you're not with the government."

"I'm not."

"But you must have contacts in Washington," Rajiha said. "That's how you make money – and how you get looks at sensitive documents."

"Yep."

"Surely you could get this information to somebody who can stop this plot without scapegoating the refugees."

"I'm putting this in the ear of anyone in Washington who'll listen to me," I said. "But I can't guarantee 'stop.' I can't even guarantee second thoughts."

His head nodded but his eyes said 'bullshit.' The longer I talked, the more he doubted me. In his view, I could be a key part of the very plot I was describing – someone sent down here to cleverly manipulate the refugee community into doing something that would make it look guilty when the attack came off.

Make it look guilty when the attack came off. I had an idea. I was going nowhere fast, so I figured I had nothing to lose.

"I can't show you the document, but there's one thing I can show you," I said.

From my briefcase across the room I pulled my laptop and the thumb drive Hank Sinclair had left behind when he'd high-tailed it out of my hotel room. Flipping the laptop open on the coffee table so that Rajiha could see it, I popped the thumb drive in and pulled up the myriad anti-Trump images Rafe and I had reviewed. Rajiha visibly recoiled from the texts and pictures. His face showed that he had no trouble imagining the trouble they could cause.

"I could have made up the fertilizer documentation," I said. "I didn't, but I could have. But you're seeing this stuff with your own eyes. If anything close to this happens to be on the computers of some of those Syrian refugees at Bedford Industries, then either the plot I'm worried about is real, or we have a mighty interesting coincidence on our hands, don't you think?"

Now Rajiha smiled. Not a bad smile, really. A bit chilly for my tastes, but a definite improvement over the thundercloud frown I'd gotten used to from him. Turning his head toward Abdullah – excuse me, Tariq – he favored the lad with some rapid-fire Arabic. At least judging from the tone of his response Tariq pushed back a bit, but Rajiha was having none of that. Twenty seconds later Tariq, with obvious reluctance, produced his own iPad from the backpack at his feet. Rajiha opened it on the coffee table and gestured for Tariq to boot it up, which he did. Rajiha took it from there.

The first couple of minutes produced nothing noteworthy. Rajiha's trek through Tariq's Safari search history turned up mostly CNN, Al-jazeera, and ESPN soccer stuff, plus the inevitable videos of cats playing piano, and only a little cheesecake verging toward soft-core porn in the blush-worthy department. Then, fingers flying over the keyboard, Rajiha brought up the main screen, clicked on Apple Photos so fast I would have missed it if I'd blinked, and then blitzed through file after file, his eyes seeming to glow in the excitement of the hunt. On the seventh one he hit pay dirt.

Sitting back and sending Tariq a reproving glance, he gestured toward the screen with the back of his right hand. Madonna, Kathy Griffin and a fake severed head, followed in order by everything on Hank Sinclair's thumb drive. Tariq stammered confused and indignant denials, all the more touching because they were undoubtedly true.

Rajiha turned his attention back to me.

"No Syrian born of woman could possibly be stupid enough to have downloaded this garbage intentionally," he said. "So it must have been infiltrated into the computer, probably through an attachment to some of the girlie stuff."

"And probably not just to Tariq's computer," I said. "Probably on the computers of some of the other refugees who aren't working at Bedford – except that they are."

Rajiha grinned. Honest to goodness, no kidding grin.

"I would tell you I'm sorry for lying to you about that," he said, "but I don't apologize for strategic lies."

"I don't blame you. I would have done the same thing if I thought I were talking to a cop."

"Do you know who planted this?"

"No," I said. "But what matters is that it was planted. The question now is what to do about it before the president gets to northeast Louisiana next month."

"Do you have any suggestions?"

The answer stuck in the back of my throat when I started to respond. Destroying evidence is a felony, so *suggesting* that someone destroy it must be a felony too. So far, I'd gotten through this mess without doing anything obviously indictable. I wanted it to keep it that way. Uncle D to the rescue.

"That's a puzzler," he drawled. "A real head-scratcher. The computers and the fertilizer both. Hillary Clinton's lawyers are all real smart, though, at least for Yankees. You might want to call them and see if they have any ideas."

It took less than two seconds for the pieces to fall into place in Rajiha's head. He grinned at us. Then he winked.

Chapter 41

"I've talked to Theo and a couple of others," Rafe told me that night when I called him right after dinner. "No scribblers yet. Thought you might want to give Phoebe the first shot."

"Mulling that over, but I can't see anyone running with the story as long as all we have is a date range and a piece of paper."

"Probably right," Rafe said. "How are things at your end?"

"I've warned the designated scapegoats. Don't know what else I can do."

A buzz signaled another call coming in. I ignored it. Rafe didn't.

"You'd better take that," he said. "Might be Vernon, and you said you halfway expected to hear from him."

"You're right. I'll call you back."

I swiped my screen to take the in-coming call.

"I need your help." Mason's voice, sounding pretty shook.

"Where are you?"

"In custody. Slidell Parish Jail in Cavour. This is my one phone call."

"*Jail?*"

"They arrested me in a brothel."

"Getting arrested in a brothel is a parking ticket in Louisiana. Unless there's blood on the floor or something."

"Long story. Anyway, they say they're going to hold me until a hearing tomorrow unless I can post bail. Three hundred dollars. You're the only one I could think of who might be able to figure out some way to get the money legally from the campaign fund somehow."

You're so young. Two things kept me from blowing him off.

First, this didn't compute. Louisiana cops in some parishes might do brothel busts if their skim from the pimps is coming up short or if it's close to election day and the sheriff needs to goose the Bible-thumpers. But three hundred dollars bail for a Louisiana resident without any drugs on him caught indoors with a party girl was ridiculous. Something very strange had to be going on here.

Second, on a clear night if you have a fast car and a driver with no fear, Cavour, Louisiana is about thirty-five minutes from Vicksburg, Mississippi. Probably three times that if you're driving a giant mining truck in the opposite direction, but definitely doable.

"All right, GG," I said, "just hang on and sit tight. I'll think of something."

I got a touchingly emphatic *"Thank you!"* from Mason. I barely caught the last word, because I was already scrambling.

"Where are you off to in such a hurry?" Mama asked as I grabbed my purse.

"Slidell Parish Jail up in Cavour, with a stop at an ATM."

"Wop Heaven!" Uncle D yelled. "Right with you as soon as I get strapped."

"*Honte a toi,* Darius Zachary Taylor Robideaux!" Mama said sharply. "You know better than to talk like that in this home."

"Sorry, sis, but that's what they call it. Highest concentration of Italian- Americans in Louisiana outside of New Orleans."

"I don't care what they call it, mister. You're in the home where my sainted husband and I brought Josie up – not lolling around some political clubhouse in Plaquemines Parish."

"It just slipped out, sis." Uncle D actually looked contrite. "But whatever, we have to get up there. You coming? You can DVD *Game of Thrones.*"

"DVR," Mama said distractedly. "Darius, for all I know they may still have a warrant out on you in Slidell Parish. You stay home and watch the house. And DVR my show. I'll go with Josie."

Mama hustled into the kitchen. When she hustled back out, she had her Kindle cradled in the crook of her left arm and her purse in her right hand. The purse bulged with something she'd added in the last thirty seconds, and I didn't have to ask what it was.

Chapter 42

I wasn't really looking for company. The more I thought about it, though, the more it seemed like it wouldn't be such a terrible idea to have Mama along for the ride. She knows as many Louisiana politicians as Uncle D and, unlike Uncle D, she hasn't punched any of them.

Daylight saving time was still in force, so we had mellow sun for a good share of our two-hour-plus drive. Mama toggled her gaze between James Lee Burke's Louisiana on Kindle and God's outside her window. Rural Louisiana can be breathtakingly, heartbreakingly beautiful, but I kept my eyes on the road. I was pushing Mama's Fusion as close to eighty as I could, and past it when I dared.

The Slidell Parish constabulary got all our attention from the moment we rolled into Courthouse Square in Cavour. It isn't the most impressive building in town, but its alternately blackened, bleached, and gray stones have a certain custodial charm. Not much going on at nine p.m., so once we stowed Mama's gun in the glove compartment and waltzed in, it didn't take long to state our business and get to work. I posted Mason's bail and a deputy brought him out front while Mama indignantly asked the desk sergeant what this blessed state was coming to.

By nine thirty, we were sitting with a very pale GG Mason back in Mama's sensible sedan, creeping away from the square while we looked for his car. (He had walked to the whorehouse, and was a little shaky on where he'd left his jalopy.) I was bursting with questions for the lad, but Mama beat me to the punch.

"All right," she said, "now that you've seen the inside of a jail cell you are a true son of the Pelican State. You can put that on your resumé. But what in the name of Philistine foreskins is going on?"

"Okay," he sighed. "I was over in San Esprit, doing stuff for the candidate. About ten o'clock this morning I got a tip that Mr. Sinclair had come to Cavour all the way from Washington and was talking with the sheriff and the chair of the parish board of supervisors and all kinds of other people."

"Hank Sinclair," I muttered. *As in, the guy who's doing advance work for a presidential visit.*

"Yeah, him. Trump is back supporting Bilbo, so I thought maybe I should run over here and see if I could find out what was going on."

"Initiative," Mama said approvingly.

"Well, I didn't do anything special. Didn't stalk him or anything. Just sort of asked around."

"Uh-*huh*," I said. "Including asking around in a whorehouse?"

"Not exactly. I mean, no. Around four o'clock or so he went to his car and I figured he was about to head out of town. You know. Mission accomplished, whatever. But before he could get in this other guy approaches him. Kind of a bullet-head type. If it hadn't been for the sharp suit he was wearing I would have pegged him as a cop. At one point he looked over his shoulder directly at me, and it kind of gave me the creeps."

I described Kappa.

"Yeah, that could have been him," Mason said.

"What happened next?"

"The two of them go over to a different car, parked maybe a block away on Gambetta Street. Great big black thing. They get into the front seat, but they don't go anywhere. I couldn't read their lips, but from their body language they were having a real animated discussion."

"How long did that go on?" I asked.

"They were still going strong at four thirty, when another guy comes up behind me and taps me on the shoulder. I jumped like a cat. Hadn't heard him approach, and had no idea he was there. He was even bigger than the guy talking to Mr. Sinclair, but he was kind of dressed like a slob and didn't have the cool the other guy did, y'know?"

"Sure."

"Anyway, he asks am I the one looking for data on what Hank Sinclair was up to in Cavour? That's the word he used. 'Data.' I said I'm interested, sure. He says for ten bucks he can put me onto someone who'll give me the whole story. I managed to scrape up a five and five ones."

"You should have asked if he took credit cards."

"Yeah." Mason managed a good-sport kind of smile and seemed to relax a little. "Anyway, he gives me an address on Shirley Avenue, a residential flat over a diner. Tells me to ask for Anna Maria. I go there. An older woman wearing a ton of make-up asks me in. She fixes me a drink, and starts telling me a lot of things about Mr. Sinclair's visit that I already know."

"And then cops join the party," I guessed.

"I'd been there about five minutes when they came hammering at the door. Next thing I know, I'm in jail, charged with 'frequenting a house of assignation.' I feel pretty stupid for falling into that trap, 'cause it seems so obvious now."

"Don't beat yourself up too much," Mama said. "If it hadn't been that, they would have arrested you for loitering. You'd been fingered for a roust."

"Anyway, I tell them this is an illegal arrest, I haven't done anything. The top cop says tell all that to the judge when I see him in the morning, but meanwhile I'm being held on three hundred dollars bond. Altogether they fool around with me for well over an hour before they'll even let me make my one phone call."

Hoo boy.

We'd completed our first circuit and just turned back onto Saint Louis Street, approaching Courthouse Square from the opposite direction. Glancing up, Mama pointed through the windshield at a banner stretched fifteen feet in the air diagonally from the northeast corner of the square to the southwest corner. Clearly legible in the bright street lights illuminating the town's main intersection were red and green letters on a white background:

CAVOUR COLUMBUS DAY PARADE
FESTIVAL AND FIREWORKS
OCTOBER 8, 2018

Of course. This figured to be the event for the possible Trump drop-by that Hank had come to Cavour to advance for.

When I heard Mason saying, "That's it," I twisted around to see him pointing out the window at a small Chevy parked three storefronts down from Garibaldi Avenue. His car, apparently.

He started to get out.

"Not so fast," Mama said. "There's a black Lexus SUV sitting with its engine running about twenty feet from the other side of your car. It's right under a street lamp, so probably whoever belongs to it wants us to see it. Does that look like the crate Sinclair and bullet-head climbed into?"

"Uh, yeah."

Mason suddenly sounded a bit subdued. Didn't blame him. Mama discreetly opened the glove compartment to extract her gun. Didn't blame her either.

I thought if I edged our Fusion forward, maybe I could get it in between Mason's Chevy and the Lexus, close enough that Mason could hop into the Chevy and *vroom* off before the Lexus could do anything about it. Before I could go anywhere with that plan, though, the front door on the passenger side of the Lexus opened and a big dude got out. White, expressionless. Not Kappa. Wearing denim cut-offs, sandals, and a pink-sunset Margaritaville t-shirt. Dressing like a slob? I could see calling it that.

He walked steadily toward Mason's Chevy. Stopped about three feet short of the left rear fender, in the street, and just stood there, like an illustration of 'conspicuous' on an English as a Second Language flashcard.

"Well," I said, "we have ourselves a real interesting situation here."

"Amen," Mama agreed. "Can't really see calling the police, all things considered."

"Whatever it is," Mason said, "I guess I have to face it."

He gulped. Give him credit, though: he started again to open the door.

"Just sit tight," Mama told him. "I don't like the odds in a scrap."

"Here's an idea," I said, without much conviction. "What if I do a little NASCAR number and blitz our Fusion past the Lexus so fast all they see is a blur?"

"They'll follow us," Mama said. "He already has the engine running."

"Right. But if I hang a left at the end of the block and then another left at the next street I come to, we'll have about five seconds when they can't see us. You and GG can get out and slip into the darkness. Then I'll burn rubber. They'll almost have to follow me. While they're chasing my tail lights, you two can get someplace safe."

"But maybe they leave Sir No-Neck here, or drop him off to look around on foot, while Bullet-head in the Lexus follows you," Mama said.

She had a point.

Not sure how our risk assessment would have worked out, but what happened next mooted the question. Kappa suddenly leaned halfway out the Lexus driver's side window. He banged the heel of his hand on the door loud enough to wake up a senator during a filibuster, and yelled at the dude by Mason's Chevy.

"Tug! Move! Move move move!"

By the second 'Move!' the dude – Tug, apparently – was hustling big time, and by the third one he'd reached the Lexus. Good thing for him, because Kappa by that time had the Lexus swung around in a tire-screeching U-Turn with the passenger side door open. The guy jumped into the moving car and slammed the door. We saw glaring, blood-red tail-lights for three seconds, followed by nothing special as the Lexus careened to the left around the corner and disappeared.

By then my adrenaline-drenched brain had generated nine thoughts. Talking faster than most folks are used to down south, I shared three of them with Mama and Mason.

"Kappa engineered a roust to keep GG here overnight. Why? So GG couldn't tell anyone about seeing Hank Sinclair and Kappa together until tomorrow morning."

"How do we know that last part?" Mama asked

"We don't. I'm making shit up."

"Josephine Robideaux Kendal," Mama said sharply, "you were raised better than that."

"Sorry, Mama. I'm stressed out. Point is, that last part is an educated guess."

"Okay, then. But you be watching that mouth of yours."

"We need to get you and GG into rooms at the Slidell Planter's Hotel," I explained. "That way, GG can make his court appearance tomorrow morning, and you can get my bail money back."

"How much time do you think I'll get?" Mason asked forlornly.

"The prosecutor will dismiss the case before you say 'not guilty'," I told him. "If he doesn't, the judge will do it for him and chew him out in the bargain."

"Oh."

"What will you be doing all this time?" Mama asked, looking at me with an obvious measure of concern.

"Steering with one hand and talking to a reporter with the other."

"You want to take Colonel Colt here along with you?"

"No, you hang onto that in case you need it." I waited three seconds for them to get out and neither of them did. Combining nerves with impatience I asked, "Any more questions?"

"One," Mason said. "What does 'in the name of Philistine foreskins' mean?"

"First Book of Samuel," Mama said crisply, swiveling around in the seat to fix steely eyes on him. "David had to produce foreskins from a hundred Philistines before Saul would let him marry Michal. He came up with two hundred, just to be safe. You getting the picture here?"

"Uh, sure."

"This wasn't bread falling from the sky or the Red Sea conveniently drying up. This actually happened. Maybe not two hundred Philistines, allowing for Mediterranean exaggeration, maybe only ten or twenty. But a pretty good mob got their throats slit and pieces of their male parts cut off so that David could get himself a girl. You with me?"

"Sure." Mason looked a little pale.

"Thirty percent of the registered voters in this parish could tell you that story by heart. They read their Bibles cover to cover every blessed year. And son, if you plan on going very far in Louisiana politics, you'd better get a slug of that Bible into your head too."

Chapter 43

I for sure planned to call Phoebe, like I'd told Mama, but I punched in Rajiha's number first. No answer. I spewed my message into voicemail. If the NSA was listening, well *write a memo, boys, and put it someplace safe.*

"This is Josie Kendall, calling about ten o'clock on September twenty-seventh. A dangerous guy named Dominic Kappa, who is hip-deep in whatever is going on at Bedford Industries, just left Cavour, Louisiana in a great big hurry. If Bedford is where he's headed, by now he's probably less than a half hour away. Has another bad-looking dude with him. He had pressing business in Cavour when he took off, so I'm guessing he got a call about something super-urgent happening at Bedford. If your boys are up to something there, I'd exfiltrate them right now."

Quite a mouthful, but I got it out. Took a deep breath. Punched in Phoebe's number. No answer. *You call yourself a reporter?* I didn't expect her to be at her desk at 11:00 p.m. her time, but dammit shouldn't she still be up, checking websites and ready for tips?

No time to think about that. At the voicemail prompt I just self-debriefed at about a hundred fifty words a minute.

"Phoebe, this is Josie. I have about six things here, so I'm just going to spit them out – all on deep background.

"First, someone in the White House is dreaming about having Trump do one of his spur-of-the-moment jaunts on Columbus Day, October 8th. Destination is Cavour, Louisiana in Slidell Parish. No idea whether it will come off, but someone in the West Wing is pushing for it.

"Second, Hank Sinclair, is up to his –"

"Josie, take a deep breath. I just picked up." Phoebe's voice.

"'Bout time, girl."

"I've heard rumblings about an impulsive presidential trip in early October, so that checks out. How do you know it's Columbus Day in Cabour?"

"Cavour. V as in vasectomy. Hank was there today doing some kind of half-assed, low-profile advance for it. And what the hell else besides Columbus Day could rate a presidential visit to a town with four stoplights?"

"Okay. You actually saw Hank in Cavour?"

"Not exactly. I talked to someone else who saw him there."

"I see," Phoebe said. "And can I talk to the person who actually saw him?"

Pause. Hesitation. Doubt – not a setting often used on the Josie dial.

"I'll have to check with him on that," I said.

"How fast can you check with him?"

"Depends. Right now I'm driving hell-for-leather *away* from Cavour hoping I can somehow preempt a much bigger story."

"And how do you plan to do that?"

"For starters, by giving you this lead. After that, I don't have the faintest idea. I'm making this up as I go along."

"Okay." I could tell Phoebe started to snap at me and stopped herself. I could actually hear her taking calming breaths like she'd probably learned in some how-not-to-be-an-asshole self-improvement course. When she spoke again, her voice was firm but calm. "Josie, what do you expect me to do with this?"

"Wait," I pleaded. "I haven't told you yet that one of the guys Hank met out here is the dirty ex-cop tied to the Slow Willie Woodbine killing. Or about an illegal arrest he arranged. Or about how this all might be part of a head-grabbing October surprise."

"Fine. Let's say you tell me about all that. What am I supposed to do while I'm waiting for my Pulitzer Prize?"

"Check your White House contacts, one of whom I hope will wonder what in the *hell* is going on out here and push an *abort* button because now the media is onto it."

"Well," Phoebe sighed. "I appreciate your candor. You just officially became the confidential-source equivalent of 'slam-bam-thank-you-ma'am.'"

The pitch of my tires' whine went up an octave. I'd just rolled onto the Vicksburg Bridge across the Mississippi River, headed for the Magnolia State.

"Phoebe, goddammit, hold on. I'm just –"

"You're just using me to squelch a story by having me look into it. If it works, I hope you at least have the decency to call and ask, 'Was it good for you too?'"

I started to break in, but Phoebe was on a roll.

"Hank being in Cavour may be actual news," she continued. "Not Nieman Award stuff, but something I could put together with a fact here and a fact there and get on the air with. The Dom Kappa/Slow Willie angle will take a lot more digging before it goes anywhere. The rest of what you're peddling sounds like what Trump means when he accuses us of trafficking in fake news."

"No, Phoebe, I wouldn't –"

"Maybe you would and maybe you wouldn't, but at the moment that doesn't matter. What matters is that there is only one piece of hard news in everything you've said, and I'll need an eye-witness who'll go on the record before I can do a blessed thing about it. If you can get him to give me a call, you know my number."

I sputtered for three seconds before I realized that I was sputtering into a dead line. I glared at my phone in disgust as I hit dry land in the State of Mississippi.

Well, Josie, THAT'S what you get for letting the truth push you around.

Chapter 44

Every instinct I had screamed that I should turn around and hightail it back to Cavour. If Rajiha couldn't be bothered to check his messages or do what I'd recommended if he did check them, what was I supposed to do about it? Hell, maybe if Kappa ended up littering the Bedford property with three or four corpses *that* would generate enough attention from the Phoebe Riverdales of the world to just possibly stop a Columbus Day tragedy.

Then I saw red and blue lights flashing maybe a quarter mile ahead on the shoulder of the road. Lights from at least two patrol cars, meaning that the first cop on the scene had found it prudent to call for reinforcements. This late on a weeknight, the highway I was on wouldn't typically see much traffic. Kappa had peeled out of Cavour like a drag racer, so I figured he'd gone pedal to the metal once he hit the highway. Put those together and there was, what, a ten percent chance that the car the cops had stopped was Kappa's.

Maybe even fifteen.

But what if Rahija *had* gotten my message and had phoned a tip to the Mississippi Highway Patrol about someone auditioning for a *Fast and Furious* remake on this highway? Then we were talking, what, maybe eighty percent?

As I approached, I slowed down and pulled as far to the left as I could, so the cops would know I was giving them plenty of room. I cruised past and gaped. Couldn't make out faces in the dark, but the car they'd pulled over sure looked like a black Lexus SUV. I imagined the first cop there, thinking he'd be handing out a routine speeding ticket for twenty miles over, then seeing the two hard cases in the Lexus; asking if they were armed; getting the truth, because if they lied about that they were toast; finding out that between the two of them they had a regular arsenal of high-end small arms; and deciding to call for back-up.

So, problem solved, right? Wrong. The traffic stop bought some time for Rajiha's crew, but I couldn't see it ending up with Kappa and his playmate in a holding cell. Kappa was too smart to try bribing the cops, and the hardware figured to be legal. In another ten minutes they'd be scorching pavement toward Bedford again. I asked myself what I could do with the extra ten minutes I'd lucked into. The only thing I could think of was to scope Bedford out and see if I got any bright ideas.

I remembered from my last adventure how to find the access road. A little trickier in the dark, but I managed it. At the end of the road I could see a light on in the hut at the guard station. That gave me an idea: drive on up, click into clueless female mode, say I'd gotten myself hopelessly lost, and ask for directions back to Louisiana. While the guard was mansplaining, I'd see if I could pick up some subtle clue, some tic of body language or tonal nuance, that would tell me whether he was nervous about something – intruders on the property, for example.

I pulled up to the lighted hut and, sure enough, there was my subtle clue: it was empty; no one home. That meant the guard was probably out looking for something, which meant there was probably something to look for. Not good.

Second subtle clue: the barrier arm was up. The most logical explanation for that was the guard reporting something suspicious on the grounds to Kappa, and Kappa telling him to check it out while Kappa hurried back, and leave the gate up so that Kappa could blow through without having to worry about it. Call me Sherlock.

Right then, with my head on a swivel, I stumbled over my third subtle clue: someone tied up on the ground about sixty feet beyond the guard hut. As I gazed through the windshield with my brights on, I could just make out a writhing, oblong lump, stretching well over five feet along the ground. That made it either a Jurassic era caterpillar or a human being who'd just had a real bad experience.

I pulled the Fusion forward to about ten feet from the guy, stopped, and jumped out to help him. I found myself hustling big time all of a sudden, because I thought I'd just figured out Rajiha's plans for Bedford and its mining truck. Namely, *Boom!* He was going to close all the vents and windows in the heavy equipment storage facility, do something to make the fertilizer in the mining truck hot, beat it, and hope he was far enough away when the facility and everything in the neighborhood, maybe including the main building and the guy writhing on the ground, exploded.

If I had it right, in other words, his boys were actually going to commit a terrorist attack uncomfortably close to the one the false-flag guys were trying to frame them for. Not as spectacular, but with plenty of visual interest for TV news cameras and ugly enough to serve the purpose.

Shit! I thought Rahija was smart!

As I got closer, I could make out a black guy on his belly, hog-tied, hands and feet tied behind him with the same rope. Looking about 30 and sporting a cheap, off-the-rack security uniform, the stocky guard looked madder than a wet hen. Whoever trussed him had used a sock stuck deep in his mouth to gag him, but it wasn't tied to his head so I got it out pretty fast.

"Knife in my belt!" he gasped. "Left side!"

Cost me a few seconds and a broken nail, but I found it.

"What happened?" I asked as I started sawing at the hemp around his wrists.

"Perimeter alarm went off," he said. "Couldn't get a visual, so I ran down here to check things out. While I was running I radioed the boss for authorization to call the cops. He said, 'Negative! Absolutely no cops!' just before I get smashed on the back of my head and the lights went out. You the police?"

"If I were any farther from police, I'd be doing time." The severed rope slackened and fell away from his wrists.

"Well I thank you."

Rolling to his fanny, he took the knife from me and went to work on the rope still binding his ankles.

"Any idea where the folks who knocked you out got off to?"

"Could be wrong," he panted, "but the desk console in the guard hut back there might tell us somethin' 'bout that. I'll run back and check it. I'll radio the boss again on the way."

Blue-bright halogen lights blared from the far end of the access road.

"Don't think you'll need the radio," I said. "Company is coming."

"Nailed that one, missy," he muttered. "That's the boss for sure."

He jumped up and ran back toward the hut, waving his arms. I hurried to the Fusion and drove it forward and to the right, out of sight, well off the access road, and into the parking lot behind Bedford's main building. I swung the car around so that I could exit back along the access road as soon as Kappa's SUV was no longer blocking it. Then I cut the lights. Where I was parked he shouldn't notice me and I figured there'd be a least a brief conference at the guard hut, so I gave myself time to call Rajiha again. I spoke into his voicemail as calmly as if every nerve in my body weren't screaming *Go! Go! Go!*

"An explosion in an almost deserted building at Bedford won't be as bad as one at a crowded parade, but they'll still spin it into a terrorist attack. If that's your Plan A and it's not too late, you'd better come up with Plan B. You are now officially on your own, because I'm getting the hell out of here as soon as I have a clear road to drive on."

Chapter 45

At least that was the plan.

Seconds later, the SUV shot forward and screeched to a stop inches beyond where the access road intersected the edge of the Bedford parking lot. There wasn't enough room between the Lexus and the building for me to squeeze through, so I'd have to circle around the front of it by driving into the construction yard itself. That meant waiting for Kappa and friend to get a comfortable distance away from their vehicle before I moved. Stomach roiling like a shrimp boil, I sat tight.

Kappa and Tug, both brandishing the kind of pistols people carry when they're not being shy about it, jumped out of the front seats. The guard leaped out of the rear seat on the passenger side.

"Cover the front!" Kappa yelled at the guard.

Then Kappa and Tug raced toward what I could now clearly see was a service door on the west side of the heavy equipment containment facility. As soon as they opened the door, I touched my St. Monica brooch, said a quick prayer, and gunned the Fusion toward the muddy construction yard beyond the parking lot. At the sound of my engine revving, the guard, now about forty feet away, spun his head in my direction, gaping at me over his right shoulder. Fortunately, I was the least of his problems, so I only had his attention for half a second.

As soon as I had all four tires off pavement my front tires started to spin a bit. That didn't bother me. I know how to work a stick-shift lever and a steering wheel in mud. I shifted to second, spun the wheel left, gunned the engine, got an encouraging dab of traction, stalled, cussed, reached for the key to re-start and –

Then I felt a vibration rolling in waves along the ground and up through the floorboard until it made the soles of my feet tingle. *This is it.* The first stage of a gigantic explosion, I thought. I turned the ignition key on pure reflex, with my eyes squeezed shut. The engine didn't catch on the first try, but so what? Engine running or engine stalled, I figured I had only seconds left on Earth.

Oh, God, Rafe, please be proud of me. I did my best, I really did.

But no explosion came. Instead, the sound of muffled gunshots and rattling, metallic *CLANGS!* from inside the building snapped my eyes open. *What the fuck?* The vibrations continued, now seeming to shake the ground seismically, even as my own body shivered with fear and pent-up adrenaline in my stalled car.

A sudden loud rumble gave way to a massive, air-shredding *Crack!* and the main door of the storage facility splintered outward into flying shards and kindling. The mining dump truck, all two stories of the damned thing, crashed through the main door and into the open. I saw it rolling slowly but inexorably forward, like an elephant doing a cake walk. Going about ten miles an hour at first, it started gaining speed, the laboring engine roaring and whining over the crack of debris being crushed. And there I sat in a motionless car, stuck in a muddy construction yard only a dozen blessed feet from the first usable asphalt beyond the Lexus. Even once I got the car started again, though, it might as well have been a dozen yards.

The guard already had his sidearm pulled. He raised his arm to aim the gun at the cab of the mining truck. I leaned as far out of the Fusion's window as I could.

"Duck!" I screamed. "That thing is gonna blow big-time!"

The guard hesitated. He looked back at me. Then his head turned back toward the truck.

"Get behind something!" I howled. "DO IT NOW!"

He made one more quick turn toward me, then back to the truck. He squeezed off three fast shots, firing haphazardly at a moving target at least twenty feet away. The first one pinged off the top of the cab and the next two went higher.

"Get DOWN, you idiot, RIGHT FUCKING NOW!"

The guard didn't take his eyes off the truck, but he flinched as he rapid-fired four more blasts, all banging off the front lip of the payload bed. That volley apparently emptied his clip, because the next thing I heard was *click.*

So far so good, but I still didn't see how this could end well for the driver. Kappa and Tug couldn't be too far behind the truck. I didn't imagine either of them sustaining a six-minute-mile pace for any considerable distance, but they could surely manage it for a hundred-yard spurt. That's all they'd need to sling lead from in front of the truck – and I had a feeling they'd be better at it than the guard.

I suddenly realized that I had a weapon myself. Not a handgun, but a smartphone whose camera could stream video. I climbed out of the Fusion and pointed my phone at the advancing truck, video running.

Without an eyeblink to spare, the mining truck gave me something to film. The front of its payload bed started rising, not all the way up, but high enough for loose fertilizer to start pouring from the back of the bed onto the ground in a dramatic dump. *Lots* of loose fertilizer.

Running out of the storage building, Kappa and Tug reached the remnants of the shattered door just in time to smack knee-deep into what had to be five tons of fertilizer blocking the entrance in a mound at least two feet high, and running the entire width of the opening. They were literally in deep shit, going nowhere fast. The top of the payload bed lowered a bit, closer to level but still with a definite downward slant. Fertilizer continued to spill out, but was now tumbling at a more measured rate that was making a royal mess behind the truck as it drove but was no longer piling up in two-foot mounds.

Kappa and Tug blazed away at the truck, but from behind it. Bullets *thokked* into fertilizer still in the payload bed, *dinged* against the top of the bed itself, and caromed noisily off the outside frame of the truck – all with roughly the effect that a marble hurled by a slingshot might have on a tank. Kappa then started firing at the truck's rear tires, but the tipped payload bed made that a tough shot. If any of the bullets actually hit rubber, they didn't penetrate.

By now the behemoth was lumbering at about twenty miles an hour and still steadily dropping fertilizer as it went. Barely skirting my Fusion, it reached the long access road, pulled onto it without caring about whether it was moving on asphalt or mud, and plowed on. Sideswiped the Lexus with a grinding scrape, pushing it over onto one side like an NFL lineman sacking a college quarterback.

I desperately wanted to get out of there, but as long as the mining truck was taking up the entire width of the access road, I didn't see any point in getting back into the Fusion for take two on my escape attempt. Nothing to do but keep filming and hope for the best.

The fertilizer kept coming, steadily and aromatically spilling from the payload bed. By the time Kappa, Tug, and the guard had failed in a furious effort to right the Lexus, the mining truck was smashing the guard hut and lumbering toward the highway.

I finally had an open road to drive on, but now I also had company. Kappa had noticed me and the Fusion. His face twisted with rage, he stormed over to me in his shit-caked Florsheims.

"I need that car, bitch!"

Twenty minutes before, I probably would have wet my pants. Something had changed, though. I'd thought I was about to die and I hadn't. Now I had something even more dangerous than a weapon. I had an idea.

"You got it," I said resignedly, flipping the fob to him. I used the next ten seconds or so to forward my footage to Rafe.

Kappa swung behind the Fusion's wheel, started the engine, and then made the car hop and promptly stall by stomping on the gas.

"Stick! Shit! A stick!" After that he said some more unseemly words.

He jumped back out of the car and circled around the front to the passenger side, jabbing an index finger in my direction as he moved.

"Drive that car after those towel-hats or you are dead!" he screamed. "Go!"

I hustled to get behind the wheel. *We'll see how Josie performs under pressure, won't we?*

Chapter 46

I managed to restart the car on the first try. Then I did the downshift-wheel-left-gun-it-reverse-downshift-wheel-right-gun-it-again thing, got some decent traction without too much trouble, and finally bumped onto the access road. Turned out that driving on fertilizer wasn't any picnic, but it was easier than driving on mud. Struck me as a moot point anyway, though, because by now the mining dump truck had disappeared.

"Which way on the highway?" I asked Kappa.

I kept any hint of sass out of my tone. There are two times when a human male is most dangerous: when he's all set to go and you say no; and when you say yes but he isn't up to the occasion. I figured that in the dark recesses of Kappa's psyche, what he'd just been through came pretty close to the second.

"Right," he said.

I turned right. I had just about enough time to get the Fusion up to fifty when we saw the truck. Off the road, off the shoulder, through the guard rail, and nose first down an incline and into a drainage ditch.

"Stop!" he yelled.

Obedient as a lamb, I brought the Fusion to a gradual stop on the shoulder, ending up about ten feet from where the truck had taken its header. Kappa flew out of the passenger door and ran toward the truck. As he moved he fished a clip from his coat pocket, fit it into the bottom of the grip on the gleaming chrome automatic in his right hand, and spanked it home.

When Kappa reached the truck, though, he seemed to get wary, maybe thinking the thing could be booby-trapped and worrying about how to avoid tripping over an improvised explosive device. What with his sudden caution, it took him a good five minutes to satisfy himself that the driver and anyone who was with him had long since taken off.

He turned around to look back at me, an oddly quizzical expression on his face. He appeared to realize suddenly that the two tons of steel I was sitting in was a lot more muscle than the ounce of lead he could fire through the windshield at me if I decided to downshift and squash him between the Fusion's grill and the side of the truck. I suppose that wouldn't have been such a terrible idea – but I had another one that I liked better.

As Kappa trudged back to the car, I got out because I thought the conversation we were about to have might not lend itself to close quarters. He stopped at the passenger-side fender, staring at me across the hood.

"Did you know about this?" he asked.

"How dumb do you think I am? If the crew working at Bedford had told me about the mess they planned to make, why would I drive into the middle of it?"

"Then why did you come here?"

"Because I couldn't figure out what you and a White House aide expected to happen tomorrow morning that was important enough to keep a college boy locked up overnight so he wouldn't blab about seeing the two of you together in Cavour," I said. "When you broke off our stalemate in Cavour in such a hurry, I decided the answer would have something to do with wherever you were headed."

"Did you come to any conclusions?"

Oh, I came to some conclusions all right. I concluded that your Plan A went to hell this afternoon when you finally bullied Hank Sinclair into admitting that he'd lost the thumbdrive with the compromising evidence on it. Which triggered Plan B: tomorrow morning was supposed to see a hot tip leading to a raid on Bedford that would scoop up paperwork, fertilizer in highly suspicious quantities, hard drives with kill-Trump stuff on them, and refugees who could be blamed for the plot this all suggested. Then, not quite a week later, in early October, word would get out that the feds had thwarted a planned terrorist attack on the Columbus Day parade in Cavour. You'd spin that into an October surprise based on a planned false flag attack that was stopped before the flag got to half-staff. Not as good as an actual attack, of course, but not bad for a Plan B.

I didn't say any of that, of course. I lied through my teeth.

"Nope. Whatever is going on is way over my head. All I got for my trouble was forty-five seconds of cell-phone footage that is now sitting up there in the cloud, waiting to be downloaded by people I trust."

Interesting reaction from Kappa. He didn't turn pale or go bug-eyed or get mad. If anything, he calmed down a little. Gave me a slight nod, along with one word: "Okay."

"So here's the deal," I said. "You've got yourself a world-class fiasco on your hands. I see you spending the next week or so doing full-time damage control."

"What's your point?"

"You clean up your mess whatever way you think best. Not just the fertilizer mess but the big-picture mess as well. I'm not going to go around blabbing about it. My footage won't be posted to YouTube or sent to any reporters. If any cops question me, though, I'm telling them the God's-honest truth – so if I were you, I'd keep Josephine Kendall out of it."

"There had to be a catch," he sighed.

"Oh, that's not a catch, that's just friendly advice. Here's the catch."

I paused. He looked at me dead on, eyes as hard and cold as Card's.

"Okay," he said. "Spit it out."

"If a single one of those refugees gets arrested, all bets are off. If a single one of their apartments or computers or sock drawers gets searched, all bets are off. If there is a single peep – print, digital, or electronic, from Breitbart to the *New York Times*, from the alt-right to the *Huffington Post* – about heroically thwarting a planned terrorist attack by Syrian refugees, then all bets are off. If that happens, I'm going to pull out every stop on the organ. Smart people pay me lots of money to pull those stops because I am very good at it. You don't want to be in church when it happens."

"That sounds like a threat."

"It's more than that," I said. "It's a good, old-fashioned, back-country bayou threat."

He looked at me like I was a skinned steer hanging on a meathook and he was trying to calculate how much hamburger he could grind out of me. Nothing for me to do but double-down.

"I can guess what you're thinking," I said. "'Kill her and blame it on a firefight with the people in the truck. Ditch the gun, fix the guard, brazen it out.' Bad idea. You're an ex-cop. You know you can't ad lib a homicide cover-up on the fly. Too many ways to fuck it up. You've got guns on record from the traffic stop, and if you can't account for all of them, you'll flunk the smell test right there. Too many people know too much stuff for you to pass off my corpse as collateral damage – and besides, I have friends who'll put the FBI on this. No way you're gonna snow those boys. So just take the deal on the table and live to fake another day."

Kappa dropped the hard look and tried a different one. Call it intrigued and calculating. I read hate in it for sure, but not just hate. I also saw . . . what? Some kind of respect.

I'm not sure which one bothered me more.

Chapter 47

I returned Kappa to Bedford, then hauled my own weary bones back to Cavour. On the way I called Rafe so he could debrief me. I probably came across as one cool customer, but that owed more to shellshock than nerve. I was close to wiped out, running on fumes. Once I got to the Slidell Planter's Hotel where Mama and Mason were holed up for the next morning's hearing, I gave Mama the whole story as well. That was pretty much all the talking I had in me at the moment. I figured there was no point in having Mason call Phoebe anymore, so I didn't bother telling him to do it.

I slept hard and woke up sore all over from the adrenaline-fueled tension that had wracked every muscle I owned the night before. Sore, but surprisingly refreshed. I was still alive, and eight hours before, Vegas would have given pretty good odds the other way.

We got to court early for Mason's appearance. Before the Honorable Anthony Puricelli took the bench, Mama went back to his chambers to say hi, which was just good manners since she'd met him once at a campaign rally seventeen years ago – and in Louisiana politics that made them BFFs. She may have said more than hi. When Judge Puricelli's clerk called the case, the assistant district attorney barely got "May it please the Court" out before Puricelli jumped in.

"Skip it. Sophie needs a break."

The court reporter, who had been hard at work for twenty-three seconds, obediently took her fingers off the keys of her machine. The judge leaned forward.

"In the next minute," he said to the prosecutor, "one of two things is going to happen. Either you are going to dismiss this steaming pantload of crap you call a case, or I am going to have the sheriff bring Anna Maria in here, even if she's still in her nightgown, so that she can sit on that witness chair and explain, on the record and under oath, exactly what went down yesterday."

"Your Honor," the prosecutor said.

"Back to work, Sophie," the judge said.

"Your Honor, the People move to dismiss the charges against GG Madison."

"Mason," the judge corrected him.

"Right. Mason."

"Case dismissed." The gavel banged. "Court is in recess."

High fives and fist pumps outside the courthouse. Everyone loves winning, and I'm no exception.

My exhilarated rush lasted until Mama and I got to her Fusion. I saw a sun-glinted reflection in the front passenger seat window. I almost stopped cold. It was my own reflection, but for a split second I thought I saw Kappa's face instead of mine. I actually glanced over my shoulder to see if he were lurking in the vicinity, but there was no sign of him. As I climbed into the car, I thought about why my psyche was messing with me. I didn't have to think long.

Yeah, I'd done some hard things that needed doing. I'd pitched in to keep bad stuff from happening. I'd call it a decent week's work, even if it wasn't in the same league as Rahija dreaming up a super-gutsy plan or young refugees coming under fire while they executed it.

But I'd also made a deal with a thug. I'd hold up my end of that deal if Kappa held up his, because in my universe, deal-keeping isn't just what you do, it's a big part of who you are. That meant sitting on inflammatory information that three federal agencies, Phoebe Riverdale, and a solid chunk of the American people would really like to know, in exchange for keeping innocent people from becoming scapegoats for the Beta version of a nasty October surprise. I'd done it because in my cold, clinical calculation, that was the best deal I could get.

Calvin Kirby had talked about politicians being only three degrees of separation from a mobster. I was now one degree. Kappa had negotiated with me as an equal. He was right. We were peers. We'd both had cards to play, and we'd played them.

I had an answer to that, and I tried it on for size: *You don't do politics with choir girls.* True enough. But that didn't mean I liked what I saw when I looked at my own reflection.

WHAT HAPPENED WHILE
NOTHING WAS HAPPENING

October, 2018 to June, 2019

"'I've been in Washington about thirty years,' Mark Salter, a former chief of staff and top campaign aide to John McCain says. 'And here's the surprising reality: On any given day, not much happens. It's just the way it is.'"

Mark Leibovich, *Citizens of the Green Room: Profiles in Courage and Self-Delusion* (Blue Ridge Press New York 2014)

Chapter 48

A welcome lull followed all the Cavour excitement, and nobody welcomed it more than I did. For four months the story was what *didn't* happen.

Nothing went *Boom!* in October; and I couldn't turn up a solitary whispered syllable of a thwarted terrorist attack by Syrian refugees. The closest thing to an October surprise was a 'caravan' of asylum-seekers traveling from Honduras with designs on finessing their way into the U.S. by seeking refugee status. It sure didn't have the impact that a Columbus Day 'terrorist attack' supposedly by Syrian refugees would have.

Letitia Dejean didn't beat Chad Bilbo, who eked out 50.9% of the vote to escape a runoff. Hank Sinclair didn't get fired, even though he'd made a total hash of out of the biggest assignment of his career. Neither Nessa Sara Lee nor anyone else followed up on the West Wing-job tease, and my own follow-up with Nessa got a polite brush-off. I decided that I'd be riding pink unicorns to work before I got a job on the White House staff.

In early February, 2019, after thinking about it long and hard, I decided to make something happen. On a cold but sunny Tuesday morning I walked into a coffee shop called Grounds for Impeachment two blocks from Phoebe's office. Over lattes with precious foam art on top, I gave her the copy I'd kept of Vernon's three-shots-not-four phone card. Just for luck I turned over the local cops' incident report that Uncle D had scrounged up. On deep background, I explained how I'd gotten the card and how it fit in with Theo's analysis of the report.

Why did I do this? I really don't have a good answer, because I had at least one good reason not to. Calvin Kirby was happy about Bilbo's fracking flip-flop and would have been pissed off big time if he'd found out I was rocking that little boat. Maybe it was just disgust at the idea of Chad Bilbo sitting in a gilded second-tier Rayburn Building office, looking in the mirror every morning and telling himself that he'd measured up to dad when he'd had to kill a guy to get there. Or maybe I was letting the truth push me around.

"Will Vernon back this up?" Phoebe asked.

"Once you're willing to go public with the story."

"I can't take this on the air without authentication, and he's the only one who can authenticate it."

"I see the problem for sure," I said, managing to avoid a shrug. "But you've been poking at this thing hard enough to worry Bilbo. Maybe if you keep at it, you'll turn up enough to make Vernon's authentication the last piece."

"Maybe."

"But what do I know? I'm just a deep background source."

"By the way," she said innocently, "did you know that someone is shopping the missing hard drive from the Las Vegas mass murder around?"

"No idea. What are the chances that it's real?"

"On a wild guess, zero. The sales pitch screams phony."

"What's the pitch?" I asked, my juices flowing in spite of myself.

"That it includes an operational plan from an ISIS cell for the Vegas mass murder. An ISIS cell in Mexico."

Shit. Mexico, whose border we'd supposedly have walled off by now if Trump could just get his way.

"I thought the formal conclusion was that Paddock, the killer, acted alone."

"Yep," Phoebe said. "Acted alone, for an unknown reason. But of course the government reached the official conclusion without the missing hard drive."

"Or did it?" I intoned, and then started humming the *Twilight Zone* theme.

"Exactly."

"Who's trying to peddle it?"

"Whoever it is, they're doing it through at least two layers of cutouts." Phoebe finished her latte and stood up, carefully stashing the envelope with the phone card in it in her purse. "Just thought you'd like to know."

Chapter 49

April, 2019

Our mail on the first Monday in April notified Rafe and me that the IRS was auditing our 2016 and 2017 income tax returns. It rudely instructed us to produce every piece of paper we had relating to every penny earned or spent in those years. It would mean lawyers' bills and hours poring over files and chatting with bureaucrats on power trips.

After we'd exchanged the customary expletives, we started thinking.

"It's baffling," Rafe said. "My home office was an audit red flag in the old days, but I thought that was ancient history."

"Yeah, I know," I said. "The way I'd heard it, budget cuts have left the IRS without enough auditors to go after anyone except Russian ex-pats who report sixty thousand a year in income while living in penthouses and spending ten thousand a month on bling."

"We don't even make all that much by D.C. standards." Rafe shook his head, looking handsome under his distinguished white mane. "And we actually report what we make."

At that point, this thought-provoking development provoked the same thought in both of us, simultaneously: *We have pissed somebody off.*

May, 2019

In early May, a nice piece of business fell in Rafe's lap. Someone from a company that makes medical stents – things that keep clogged arteries open – called Rafe to say that he'd really, *really* like to talk with a "senior, savvy, knowledgeable staffer" at the Office of U.S. Trade Representative. He said that Teddy Maltz on the White House staff had given him Rafe's name.

Can do, said Rafe. A week later, five thousand-dollars landed in Rafe's business bank account. Not bad for twenty minutes work. Thanks to Teddy Maltz. On the White House staff.

Later in May, on the other hand, by order of the President of the United States, the government formally withdrew Richard Michaelson's security clearance. I learned about it the day after it happened – not by reading it in the *Washington Post*, because the withdrawal didn't make much of a splash, but in a phone call from Hank Sinclair's administrative assistant, a rather tedious young man whose name I didn't bother to remember. He told me that this information was *highly* confidential, but Mr. Sinclair thought I'd like to know.

"Really?" Phoebe ribbed me when I called her with the *highly* confidential information. "Not even Hank himself? A glorified secretary?"

I was surprised at how much the news pissed me off. I usually adopt a take-a-punch/throw-a-punch attitude toward the bullshit that goes down in Washington. Idealism is for eighth-grade civics. But Michaelson had served his country as Deputy Chief of Mission in places where the Cold War got very hot now and then. At least once that I knew of he had calmly ordered destruction of code books and top-secret documents while Kalashnikov bullets ricocheted off the security glass that was the only thing between a screaming mob and our embassy in a Near Eastern country. And here he was being gratuitously insulted by someone who wasn't fit to carry his briefcase.

"It seems so petty," I said to Phoebe.

"It seems so *random*," Phoebe replied. "Michaelson hasn't been running around hawking Trump/Russia-collusion theories on cable news or smearing the president on op-ed pages. It's now a felony to show him classified information, but if he's leaked top-secret documents to anyone recently, I sure haven't heard about it."

Oops. Phoebe waited for me to bite. I didn't. I sought refuge instead in a comforting bromide.

"Well, if they're trying to intimidate Michaelson, I doubt that this will do it."

"If all they wanted was to chill Michaelson, they wouldn't have made a point of sharing the news with you," Phoebe said. "You're the one who's supposed to get the message here."

Chapter 50

June, 2019

On the first Wednesday in June Nessa called me from the West Wing. Actually, her secretary called me and asked me to hold for Ms. Lee. Which I did. I have a long memory, but I don't sulk.

"Nessa! Great to hear your voice! Been a long time."

"Sorry, Josie. I'm really, truly sorry. I should have kept you updated more than I have, but you know how things can get."

"What can I do for you, Nessa?"

"Okay. I *know* this is incredibly short notice, and I'm sorry about that too, but could you possibly make it to an initial interview this Friday?"

As in *two days* from now. 'Short notice' qualified as a world-class understatement. Working in the White House, though, means not having to mean it when you say you're sorry, at least until the House Judiciary Committee votes on the third article of impeachment.

"Can do. What time and where?"

"One-thirty, in Conference Room E3602 in the Old Executive Office Building."

"Okay, great. See you then."

I worked late whipping up a five-minute PowerPoint of Josie's greatest hits, with a heavy dose of Letitia Dejean and nary a whiff of Bilbo Versus the Truth. I also got canned answers ready in case the interview included obvious lobs like, "What are the three most important rules of political communication?" (Answer: know your audience, know your audience, and know your audience.) I showed up ten minutes early with a bright smile, a navy suit jacket, ivory skirt – not *too* tight, not *too* short – and a silk blouse with just the top button open.

As conference rooms go, E3602 is a glorified closet with bilious green walls that could have been improved aesthetically by scribbling random excerpts from Warren Harding's speeches on them. Fortunately, Nessa and I only had to share it with two other people. Quentin Balegan, the guy who'd called me about helping Hank Sinclair with the Cavour advance, was bald, bearded, and forty-something. He had a blasé smile and the kind of two-thousand-dollar suit you own if you hang out at K-Street lobby shops during your periodic sabbaticals from public service. The other communications hand was Jake Hurden, blond, mid-twenties, with a New York look and an ingratiating, don't-hate-me-because-I-went-to-Princeton demeanor.

Interesting to put a face and body with Nessa's name. I'd never seen her before and my web browsing hadn't turned up any pictures. Mid-thirties and a little plump, with carrot-red hair that she wore with bangs in front and piecrust curls in back. I thought of her as basically what Scarlet O'Hara would have looked like if *Gone with the Wind* had been a documentary. She had two smiles: tolerantly bemused, and puzzled. In the next half hour I'd see both.

Why am I here? Couldn't help asking myself that question. I don't mean I wondered why I had bothered to come, when there was a ninety-nine percent chance that Nessa was just jerking me around. I knew the answer to that: a one percent chance of a job in the White House, even in a toxic work environment and with a president who's up to his ears in hot water, easily justified showing up.

What I *was* wondering was why Nessa and whoever she took orders from were going to all this trouble to keep me dangling. For Rafe and me, 2019 had seen carrots (the referral to Rafe and my shot at a White House job coming back to life) and sticks (the audit and the special notice about withdrawing Michaelson's security clearance). You use carrots and sticks to motivate people. Fine. What were they trying to get me to do? Keep my mouth shut about last October's failed surprise? That was old news (or more likely non-news). If not that, then what? In short, *why am I here?*

I hadn't come up with an answer when Nessa turned to Hurden with a question that got my attention.

"Where's Hank? Wasn't he on the list for this meeting?"

Balegan answered in the time it took Hurden to open his mouth.

"Hank is running around trying to sell a presidential campaign appearance that he wants to get scheduled for next year."

"Over a year from now?" Nessa asked, using the puzzled smile.

"Mm-hmm. He's told me three times this week that he's going, quote, 'balls to the wall' on the thing."

"Huh," Nessa said with an expressive eye-roll. Two *weeks* qualifies as long-range planning for most campaign appearances.

"Want me to call Hank?" Hurden asked.

"No." She sighed and smiled. "Let's soldier on without him."

Soldier on we did, for a snappy twenty-five minutes. Smiles, assurance that former Congressman Temple spoke highly of me, compliments on my outstanding *curriculum vitae* (that's what Hurden called my CV, going full Latin on everyone), my PowerPoint, and then some back-and-forth. It ended with Nessa asking, "If you could tell a rookie in White House communications three things, what would they be?"

"One," I said, "all mics are hot. Two, Congress isn't the enemy, Congress is the opposition. The enemy is the media. Three, the truth is fine, but don't let it push you around."

That's called knowing your audience. Nessa beamed, Balegan fist-pumped and mouthed "YES!", and Hurden did a double take. Then Balegan noticed Hurden fingering his iPad keyboard and ungently jumped on him.

"Do *not* write that down, junior. Anywhere. Don't even print it on a whiteboard when you're trying to impress the next batch of interns. People take pictures of those things. Just keep it in your head."

Somewhat sheepishly Nessa said something about hoping to call me "within a few weeks" about a follow-up. A. Few. Weeks. Seriously? *Sigh*. All three stood up to shake hands. Balegan had his mobile phone out and was already speaking into it before we reached the door.

"Hey, Hank," Balegan said into the phone, without lowering his voice, "thanks for skipping the interview just now. Your absence really moved things along. Second time around for this idea, I know, but if you'd like local insight on that long-range campaign stop, give me a call because I just talked to some."

Nessa's expression told me she realized this was a bit raw even by Trump West Wing standards.

"Boys will be boys," she sighed.

I managed a return smile for her but I had to work at it. Balegan had just gone out of his way to make sure I knew that Hank Sinclair was pitching a 2020 election campaign appearance by the president for next summer in the rough vicinity of Louisiana. That could have been happenstance, of course. Sure it could. And I could have been a Benedictine abbess.

Two weeks later the nice young man in a blue suit and I had the chat that I mentioned earlier about my adolescent flirtation with marijuana. The semester-break indulgence I shamelessly confessed to him hadn't been my first but, thanks to Mama, it was my last.

When I'd come home the next day, Mama could see I'd gotten baked in the last twenty-four hours. She'd marched me up to her bedroom for a little heart-to-heart. She informed me that I had a compulsive personality. If I thought I was one of those people who could limit pot to an occasional weekend spree, I was kidding myself. Keep it up and soon I'd be toking too regularly to compete for the kind of Washington job I wanted, so I needed to make a choice right then and there, and make sure it was a choice I could live with for the next forty years. Classic Mama-chat. It worked.

I didn't go into that part with the nice young man. He didn't ask. Instead he asked if I'd ever done any harder drugs and I said no. The truth again.

I let myself hope that the post-interview background check might be genuine good news, but I knew it was probably just another link in the neutralize-Josie chain. I still hadn't figured out why they were worried about me. Even worse, I wasn't sure how worried they were.

But I was just about to find out.

Chapter 51

Snip-CLICK. Not loud at all, but the sound woke me up even so. *Snip-CLICK.* Sitting up groggily, I automatically glanced at the digital clock on our bedside radio: 2:13. *Snip-CLICK.* The silvery blue moonlight soaking through our bedroom window cast just enough glow for me to make out my beloved husband, resplendent in his birthday suit, loading his Winchester twelve-gauge.

Afraid that I might freak out and maybe even yell, he raised his left index finger to his lips to shush me.

"I heard noises downstairs," he whispered.

Seemed to me like a *hell* of a good reason to yell, but in deference to Rafe I kept my voice low.

"It's probably just your imagination, or maybe a real vivid dream –"

The preliminary warning beeps from our house alarm interrupted me. Something had happened to trip the alarm, and unless someone turned the thing off within thirty seconds our home security system was going to wake up Georgetown. Eyes now wide open, I jumped out of bed, thoroughly awake and pumped from here to Sunday. Adrenaline I didn't know I had coursed through my body. I grabbed a robe from my closet. I may have been scared, but I didn't want to be scared *and* naked.

"Stay here!" Rafe stage-whispered assertively as he headed for the door.

That's bullshit. Deference has its limits. I followed Rafe but hung back a bit, so that I wouldn't get in his way if he actually ended up confronting a burglar – though only the dumbest burglar in creation would still be hanging around once those pre-alarm beeps had started.

I stayed in Rafe's wake as he headed cautiously downstairs. He can be as single-minded as a whore on payday, but Rafe isn't reckless. He took a good three seconds on each stair as he went down in the dark, pausing, looking into the interior blackness, and listening before he continued.

About four stairs from the bottom the warning beeps stopped and the full house alarm kicked in, ululating with ear-piercing shrillness. Rafe kept going just as he had been. It was a good ten seconds later when he called out "Light," looking over his shoulder at me and pitching his voice *beneath* the alarm's racket, so I could just make out what he said. I figured he wanted me to turn on the living room lights from the upstairs hallway, so I went back up a few stairs, found the switch, and did it. I flipped the hallway light on too while I was at it, then headed back downstairs. I was bracing myself for the deafening roar of a shotgun blast, but didn't really expect one. I figured our intruder had to be long gone by now. I was right.

Within a couple of minutes, between the two of us we'd turned on every other downstairs light and gotten a look at every nook and cranny on our first floor that could hold a burglar. None turned up. But we found the back door leading from the laundry room off our kitchen was ajar.

By then our land line was ringing. I answered it in the kitchen while Rafe punched in the code to turn the alarm off.

"This is Capital Home Security." Male voice, authoritative, no-nonsense. "Are you the homeowner?"

"Yes."

"What is your security password?"

"Monica."

"We have a signal of an alarm triggered at location two of your home."

"Yeah," I sighed. "We had unwanted company."

"Is the unauthorized entrant still present in the residence?"

"No sign of him."

"Is it possible that the wind or an animal pushed the location-two door open?"

Interesting question. I check it before going to bed every night to make sure it's locked, but one night in a thousand you can forget something routine like that. A quick inspection gave me the answer.

"Nope," I said, noting a small pane of glass smashed right next to the bolt and just above the inside door knob.

"Do you want us to dispatch local police?"

"Do we want the police to come, Rafe?" I asked, even as I formulated my own answer. D.C. Metropolitan Police policy is that a burglary no longer in progress, without anyone seeing a burglar still on the scene, gets priority just above donut shop drive-throughs. We couldn't expect to see a uniform for at least forty-five minutes, more likely twice that. Once there the cop would look things over, ask us if anything was missing (which we probably wouldn't know for sure by then), and prepare a report to make our insurance agent happy. Why go through all that in the middle of the night rather than sometime tomorrow, after we'd gotten a few more hours of sleep? I was in my last few seconds of mulling this over when I caught sight of Rafe, holding the extension phone from our front hallway and vigorously shaking his head: *NO!*

"No, you know what?" I obediently told the agent from Capital Home Security. "Just skip it for now. Report the alarm but say that the homeowners have asked to have an officer come by during the day to take a report. No need to send anyone right now. We're fine."

"Will do," the agent said. "Be safe, and let us know if you need anything. Good night, ma'am."

Click.

With the adrenaline ramping down, my head suddenly remembered that I'd been scared stiff, so *now* I started shaking. Rafe pulled me into a warm hug, the shotgun's barrel caressing my right shoulder blade in an oddly comforting way. After basking in the hug for a bit, I stepped back and looked up at his chocolate brown eyes. They were lit with a fierce intensity that I'd seen before. It wasn't lust.

"You look like a fella who's been thinking something over."

"Let me get a robe on while I'm running through it with you."

"First-rate idea."

We headed back upstairs at a pretty good clip. I had to hustle to keep up with him. The recap he began sharing with me on the way required my undivided attention.

"I heard noise downstairs *before* the alarm went off," he said. "So the burglar got into the house without tripping the alarm. He probably tripped it on his way out."

"But if he knew how to get into the house without setting the alarm off, why wouldn't he just go out the same way?"

"My guess is that he *wanted* us to know he'd been here. He wanted us to call the cops and generate a report. I don't know why, but we'll probably get a big clue if we can figure out what he took."

Chapter 52

Ninety minutes of inventorying told us he'd taken absolutely nothing. Computers safe and sound. TVs, radios, and electronics right where they were supposed to be. Sterling silver service that Rafe had inherited from his mom secure in its maple chest. Rafe's cashmere overcoat nestled in our basement cedar closet.

Rafe's home office was locked with no signs of forced entry. Household paper files neat as a pin. Rafe's leather camera case with the Nikon and three expensive lenses snugly stashed in the back of the hall closet. No hint that anyone had opened my writing desk in our living room – and if anyone had he'd overlooked the miniature manila envelope with the keys to our safe- deposit box, and that safe-deposit box was where I'd put the thumb drive that Hank Sinclair had dropped in his haste to exit my hotel room.

No one had bothered the firearms that the District of Columbia grudgingly allows us to have in our own home because the Supreme Court said it had to. We kept them in the bedroom, so that figured. But we checked, just to be sure.

Then I had one last idea. Without much conviction that I'd find anything amiss, after investing so much time in finding nothing, I walked over to the glass-doored kitchen cabinet where we keep our everyday plates and bowls and a smattering of other stuff.

"You think he wanted our antique salt shaker or something?" Rafe asked.

"Spare fobs for our cars," I said. "I keep them in here."

The two fobs lay right there, in the back-right corner of the cabinet's lowest shelf. I saw something else lying there too, though, and it didn't look familiar: a white-capped green plastic bottle maybe four inches long, lying on its side. I pulled it out and showed it to Rafe.

A white adhesive label on one side had "Wisconsin Avenue Pharmacy" printed at the top, followed in typing by

> Amlodopine 5 mg
> 1x/dy
> Dr. Lestrade 5 Refills Left

"What's Amlodopine?" I asked.

"Blood pressure medication."

"I didn't know you had high blood pressure."

"I didn't until just now."

Taking the bottle from me, Rafe pushed the cap down and then twisted it off. He shook a couple of tablets into his hand. I'm no pharmacist, but any pill that big had to be more than five milligrams. They were oval, and had a rough, pebbly surface.

"The burglar didn't come to take something," Rafe said. "He came to leave something. On a wild guess, maybe a high-powered prescription opioid painkiller with a phony label on the bottle."

"That we don't have a prescription for," I said.

"Right. Which could have been a real embarrassment if the police responding to the alarm report had stumbled over it because they had been tipped off about where to look for it."

"Maybe a lot more than an embarrassment. Someone who really wanted to might spin it into evidence that I lied to the FBI last month. Martha Stewart did almost a year for that."

"You're onto something there," Rafe said.

"Of course, we won't know for sure that it's opioids until we have it analyzed."

Rafe was moving toward the bathroom before I got the last two words out.

"We're not having anything analyzed," he said.

Next thing I knew Rafe had flushed the contents of the bottle down the toilet in our downstairs half bath. Just for good luck he soaked the label off the bottle and gave it to me to burn, then smashed the bottle itself into smithereens with a ball- peen hammer and buried the shards under used coffee grounds and dinner waste in our kitchen trash can. Call it the Hillary Clinton rule: If you're going to destroy evidence, do a proper job of it.

This wasn't just carrots and sticks any more. We were no longer dealing only with bureaucrats and politicians playing Washington games.

"You know what, lover?" I said to Rafe. "We are at war."

Chapter 53

No sense trying to get back to sleep, so we talked the problem through over coffee, bacon, and eggs at our kitchen table.

"It looks like someone powerful doesn't want me to talk about something," I said. "That has to be what this is all about."

"Yeah, Nixon's ethics without Nixon's competence."

"The problem is, I don't know what it is. I don't have the first clue why Hank Sinclair or Dominic Kappa, or whoever else it might be, is going to all this trouble to shut me up. And I don't know how to find out."

Rafe blinked, then got a sudden *bingo* expression that looked especially charming under bed-tousled hair.

"It doesn't really make any difference what they think you know, does it?" he asked, eyebrows raised and a slight shrug in his shoulders.

It took me a half second to see his point and agree with it.

"No, it doesn't," I said. "Not the slightest difference. We're under fire. We have to start shooting back. We can worry about why when the shooting is over."

Knives and forks clicked on china for a bit. Then Rafe raised his head and looked me straight in the eye. The words he spoke were measured and carefully calculated.

"I think the name of your first bullet is Vernon Czlewski."

It was a novel prelude to sharing love with your life mate, but as we ran water over our dishes and stacked them in the sink side by side, we let our bodies fall into the kind of spontaneously intimate touching that starts in the kitchen but begs for the living room couch, which is where we took it. The fear I'd felt, the comfort I'd taken in him ahead of me as we crept down the steps, the intrigue we'd shared as we searched the house, and the feeling that we were somehow in danger *together;* it all combined to give every touch, every kiss, and every stroke a thrilling sense of urgency. The erotic back-and-forth gave me a rush far beyond my physical pleasure – and that's saying something, because the sensual pleasure itself was over the top. Exhausted, we held hands as we headed back up to the bedroom to finally go back to sleep.

Our doorbell rang at seven thirty. It woke me from a naked-in-public dream that I didn't need any shrink's help to figure out. Showing up this early on a routine burglary follow-up was definitely not run-of-the-mill police response. Sometime in the afternoon would have been more like it. One more clue that we were officially under attack. I hurried downstairs, re-wrapping my robe in the process, checked our picture window, and reported to Rafe.

"Two uniforms from the Metropolitan Police plus a suit."

"A suit?" Rafe, trailing me by a few feet, shrugged into his robe as our doorbell chimed again. "One car or two?"

"Two. Second one is unmarked."

"Hmm." He knotted the robe's belt. "I'll get the door. Pick up as much about the unmarked car as you can from the window, but don't take any pictures."

Next thing I knew Rafe had opened our front door just wide enough to wedge himself in between it and our screen door. He belted out a cheery "Good morning!" while he did it.

"Good morning, sir." Female voice. "We're here about the burglary report from a few hours ago. May we come in?"

"You don't mind showing me some ID first, do you?" Rafe asked jovially. "I don't mean you two officers. I mean the gent here in civvies."

"He's sort of with us." Same female voice as before.

"Then he won't object to breaking out a badge." Pause. "Of course, if he *does* have a problem with that, then you two officers are welcome to come in and your acquaintance can wait here on the porch."

I picked up only garbled fragments of the response, which came in a male voice. One of the fragments was "warrant."

"Then by all means get one, Agent Nameless," Rafe said cheerfully. "Just hop back into your white Ford Crown Victoria with license number three-six-zero-two-one-two –"

"Three-six-one-zero-two-two," I said. "And not a D.C. government plate."

"I stand corrected," Rafe said. "Just jump on the radio and see if you can get a judge out of bed. For my money you're a DEA agent riding the coattails of hard-working police officers so that you can leverage their work into an improvised search of my home based on a phony tip from a rogue alumnus of your agency."

The uniforms and the suit stepped off of our porch for a caucus. My read of the earnest head-shakes and world-weary shrugs was that the cops weren't any too happy about having the narc along in the first place. The basic message was apparently, "Sorry, chum, our hands are tied." Bottom line, the uniforms came in while the suit went back to his car.

There's something magic about the guy I married. He'd just acted like someone who had Baggies packed tight with heroin stuffed under the floorboards. When the cops stepped inside, though, and he asked me to get them some coffee, they were the ones who seemed apologetic. By the time I got back to the living room with four mugs of French roast on a tray, they were halfway through filling in the blanks on their carbonless yellow report form. Rafe had apparently already told them that we'd found nothing missing. The woman cop finished the form and looked up.

"Do you mind if we take a look around, just to make sure?"

"Go right ahead," Rafe said.

They went right ahead. Seemed a little perfunctory about it if you ask me. In the kitchen, the male cop looked pointedly at the cabinet.

"Would it be okay if I took a look in there?"

"Help yourself," I said.

He opened the cabinet. Looked carefully inside. Pawed behind the bowls and plates a bit. Fingered the spare fobs. Stepped back. Rolled his eyes as he looked at his partner, disgustedly muttering, "Narcs."

"You're absolutely sure you heard noises downstairs before the alarm went off?" the female cop asked Rafe.

"Yes. One hundred percent level of confidence."

"Because the only way I know that anyone could break in without tripping the alarm would be to cut wires in two separate places simultaneously – which would be a pretty good trick."

"Capital Home Security is a fully digital operation," Rafe said. "You could disable the system temporarily with a focused hack on the software."

"He has a point," her partner said.

"Maybe," his colleague conceded. "But that would mean this wasn't some junkie doing a snatch-and-grab for a fix. This would have to have been a highly professional operation."

Rafe smiled at them over the rim of his coffee mug.

"Put that in your report, would you, please?" he asked.

CHOOSING ENEMIES

July, 2019 to June, 2020

"You choose your enemies; you don't choose your allies."

Raymond Aron

Chapter 54

July, 2019

I'm not brave. I'm spunky, but that's not the same thing. If someone makes me fight, I'll go at it tooth and nail, but I'll do everything I can not to fight if there's any way I can get out of it. When I waltzed into Vernon Czlewski's shop toward the end of the first week in July, it was spunk, not guts. I felt like I just didn't have any choice. They were coming after me no matter what, and damned if I was going to just bend over and enjoy it.

I picked out a respectable pile of stuff that I thought Father Kempton might find helpful for his refugees. Clothes, mostly. Almost a hundred dollars' worth altogether. Pretty steep price for five minutes of Vernon's undivided attention, but I was what brokers call a motivated buyer.

"Nice work," he said with a biting smile, as he sorted through the collection. "You didn't pick out anything hot."

"'Hot' is kind of a sore spot with me right now."

I told him about the burglary. That took care of the smile real fast. The sober expression replacing it matched the bitter words that came next.

"Like the fish said when it hit the landing net, 'I wish I'd never opened my mouth.'"

"Copy that, tiger." I shook my head in genuine sympathy. "Fat's in the fire now, though. You and I are looking at the same choice: play defense back on our heels, or go no-prisoners on offense."

"What's your idea of offense?"

"Talking to you, for starters."

Stepping back from the counter, he folded his arms across his chest.

"Talk."

"When you first went to Phoebe Riverdale with your Bilbo bombshell, you didn't give her enough to put the story on the air unless she could finesse me into making it a campaign issue."

"Which didn't quite happen."

"True," I conceded. "Meanwhile, though, she has come up with something more: a recording."

"Wonder how that happened?"

"No comment. Regardless, I'm betting it's enough to run the story – *if* she can authenticate it." I waited for three long beats while Vernon stood there in stolid, stone-faced silence. "Once the story is on the air, sending cops after you on any pretext is going to look like they're trying to squelch the whistle-blower on Phoebe's story because their bosses want to cover something up. If my experience is any guide, that means that you're at less risk on attack than you are just keeping your head down. I went on offense by talking to you. You can go on offense by talking to Phoebe."

"No sure thing, even if I do talk to her, though," he sighed after thinking it over.

"We're not operating in a sure-thing universe here." I gave him my Visa card. "Going on offense risks failure. Staying on defense guarantees it. Your call."

Next stop, Matrixarchy, the Nerd Chicks' shop where I'd found out what was on Vernon's phone card. I gave Hank's thumb drive to Mary Cary and stood by patiently (for me) while she plugged it into a computer and scanned to the encrypted part. After a good seven minutes of computer stuff, she whistled.

"This could be interesting," she murmured, her multi-colored hair hiding her face. "I've never worked on anything stolen from Mossad before."

"Um, actually –"

"Just an expression." She waved a dismissive hand at me and looked up. "This is going to take some work. And some time."

"How much time?"

"Two thousand dollars' worth, on a rough estimate." Mary Cary smiled beatifically. "With no guarantees – and I'll have to charge you even if I fail."

Had to think that one over. A couple of thousand was serious money. But after a burglary and an attempted framing I wasn't in a penny-pinching mood.

"How about a thousand guaranteed, plus another two thousand if you actually find what's on the encrypted part?" I asked.

I was hoping her eyes would light up, but they didn't. Just a hint of disappointment, seasoned with a nuanced glint.

"Give me a moment, dear. I'll have to pray about that."

She crossed herself, closed her eyes, and bowed her head. With nothing else to do, I said a little prayer of my own to St. Monica. Mama had always called her the patron saint of scamps and rascals. I wasn't sure whether that would put her on my side or Mary Cary's, but I said the prayer anyway.

Mary Cary's prayer took longer than mine, but she finally looked back up.

"You have to promise not to breathe a word about this to my sister," she said. "It will have to be our little secret."

"Cross my heart and hope to die."

"Five thousand if I turn up the material, with fifteen hundred guaranteed."

"The Holy Spirit is a hard bargainer."

"Don't be blasphemous, dear."

Well, she had me there. I nodded and smiled. We had a deal.

Chapter 55

"Another day in Baton Rouge?" Seamus asked when I called in the next morning with the news that my office at MVC would be dark for at least another twenty-four hours. "What's in Baton Rouge? Besides home cooking?"

"Opportunity," I said. "On this trip I'm charging my time here to 'Business Development.'"

"That's one of my personal favorites. 'Business Development' is great as long as you actually develop some business. Do you see that happening, say, sometime before the end of the current quarter?"

"I'm doing my dead level best, boss. That's all I can say."

"That's all I ask. That and chipping in to pay the rent. Remember, you don't have that White House job *yet*."

"As my beloved husband would say, Seamus, you are subtlety its very self. I'll call you with the first live one that turns up."

I ended the call with a thumb tap and sensed rather than saw Mama shaking her head three feet away.

"Sounds like you're getting some jazz from your brass," she said.

"Seamus is a teddy bear at heart. He has to kick my fanny every now and then when he catches me goldbricking just so he can say he did it. But he's the last thing I'm worried about right now."

"Yeah, I've sort of been picking up that Josie's-in-a-jam vibe from you ever since you got here yesterday morning."

We headed out onto the front porch so that I could give her a quick recap over spiced tea. It always helped to talk things over with Mama. I'd gotten my political genes from her.

Papa wouldn't even have voted if Mama hadn't made him, but politics had run in the blood of her ancestors going all the way back to Reconstruction.

Skepticism played unmistakably across her face as I wrapped up my story with the burglary. She gave me a long, thoughtful look over the rim of her china teacup. Filtered through the abundant green leaves of the elm tree dominating her front yard, a fierce midsummer sun picked up glints of silver in the steel-gray hair she wore gathered into a bun, and emphasized sparks of wary cussedness in her dark brown eyes.

"Hank Sinclair is afraid I'm up to something even more troublesome than interfering with the October surprise planned for 2018, but I don't know what intel I have or what project I could stop if I did know it."

"A conundrum demanding thoughtful consideration," Mama said.

"Which I am trying to give it."

"I can see that. Are you all in on that point, or are you holding some chips in reserve?"

"All in," I said. "I have to be." Then I looked sharply at her as I processed the Mama-vibe from her query. "Anything in particular provoke that question?"

"Someone named Czlewski called our land-line while you were in the shower and left a message for you. Said he'd be pleased if you'd join him for Bible study and table fellowship this evening at the Holiness Full Gospel Church."

"I see."

"Yes, Josephine Robideaux Kendall, I'll just bet you do see."

A cold shiver ran through me, defying the July heat. I'm plenty comfortable with political battles where the weapons are spin and strategic leaks and disciplined messaging. Back in Cavour less than a year ago, though, and then in my own home late last month, I'd found myself stumbling into a political battle where the weapons were actual *weapons*. Hated it. But 'all in' means you do it whether you like it or not.

"Mama," I said in what must have sounded like a quiet, faraway voice, "may I please borrow your gun this evening?"

Chapter 56

I enjoyed the table fellowship more than the Bible study. In Reverend Sojurner's view, I'm going to Hell for sure when I die. Just being a Catholic would pretty much guarantee it, even without the rascal and scamp stuff. Seemed to me she was over-reading the Book of Revelation, but I wouldn't have blown my cover by calling her on it even if I'd had chapter and verse at my fingertips.

Eating brightened things up. They'd set up all the card tables and pushed them together with chairs at each end and on either side. The rev began by explaining that Jesus had shared meals with prostitutes, tax collectors, and sinners, so I felt right at home. Grace seemed to go on a bit. Then came bread and soup and potato salad and pulled pork and bayou fish stew. The bread alone was worth the wait. Home baked, with a crisp crust and a nutty flavor – tasted better than anything I'd ever eaten outside home.

I sat next to Vernon. Card sat across from the two of us.

No more homeless-junkie look for Card. He wore a dove-gray, three-piece suit that he sure hadn't bought it off the rack at Men's Wearhouse. His shirt was richly textured, snow-white cotton broadcloth with French cuffs. A looped silver chain led from the right-side watch pocket on his vest down to a belt of highly polished black leather. I'd call the necktie exquisite. Pure silk of a rich, emerald green. His cufflinks matched the necktie perfectly. I'd never seen a straight male dressed that well in my life.

Wasn't sure of the protocol, so I improvised. After swallowing a dab of potato salad, I turned toward Vernon.

"Funniest thing," I said. "a tracking device turned up on the rental car I used last year when I was down this way. Well hidden. I could easily have missed it."

"That must be irritating," he said, with a quicksilver sidelong glance at Card. "Where do you figure you picked it up?"

"Well I've been thinking and thinking about that," I said. "Had to be at a place called Bedford Industries in Vicksburg."

My turn for a rapid look in Card's direction. His eyebrows didn't go up and he didn't suddenly lean forward or anything like that. But something in his expression subtly darkened. Bedford Industries wasn't a brand-new name to him, and what he'd just heard hadn't made him happy.

"Drivin' rented wheels," Card interjected, "you gotta be from outta town."

"For sure," I said. "I work in Washington for a company that helps people get their ideas out."

"That must be fascinating," Vernon said. "Working in our nation's capital, with all those powerful people. Any inside information you can share with us deplorables stuck in a backwater like Baton Rouge?"

"Rumors." I shrugged. "They're a penny a pound. Example: Some people think something might blow up – as in literally go *BOOM!* – during next year's election campaign, which would then get blamed on people the trumpkins don't like."

"Don't 'spose dat have somethin' to do wid da thingie you pick up in V-Burg, do you?" Card asked.

"Wouldn't bet against it," I said. "One thing's for sure, though. If something like that does happen, they'll be looking hard for people to take the rap."

Card nodded and stood up.

"Got to watch dat po'k," he said, "'less you wanna die young."

He went to each end of the row of card tables to thank the reverends in turn. From a pegboard cloak hanger on the farther wall he retrieved a snappy, black fedora. He stopped at a felt-lined wicker basket with a neatly printed FREE WILL OFFERING sign propped against it and dropped two hundred-dollar bills into it. Then, in a swirl of the sheet-curtain, he disappeared.

I started plotting my own graceful exit. Then a couple at the far end of the row got up, and Vernon announced that he was calling it a night as well. So, ditto Josie. Hearty handshakes, smiling thanks, a jackson in the basket, and we were on our way.

I could tell that Vernon still had some things he wanted to talk about, so I strolled in the direction of his dark blue Buick instead of my rented Malibu. Across the street I saw a Kelly green El Dorado with gold-flecked, wedding-gown-white trim. It looked like someone might be behind the wheel, but I couldn't tell for sure. Vernon paused at the driver side door of his Buick.

"I talked to Phoebe yesterday," he said. "She was very responsive."

"I'll bet she was."

"She left a message asking me to call someone at CNN I never heard of," he said. "Are we gettin' somewhere?"

"Definitely. The guy she wants you to call is a fact-checker, so she's already started the process of clearing the story. Look for a big splash before too much longer."

"Unless she hits a snag in that clearance process."

"If it's Phoebe versus a snag, bet against the snag."

That seemed to cheer him up a bit. His expression went from despondent hound dog to stoic beagle. He opened the car door and started to climb in.

"I hope I didn't come off as a cheapie on the free will offering," I said. "I couldn't match Card without my American Express. That was impressive."

Now behind the wheel, Vernon looked over his shoulder. He gave me a condescending smile.

"He was trying to impress some of the other diners," he said. "People who know Card's number. They see, hear, or feel anything they think Card might like to know, they text him. Calls it his 'street CIA.' He has snoops in church groups, neighborhood associations, and activist organizations. He does not do anything – and I mean *a-nee-thing* – without a stone-cold reason."

I thought about Card's scramble after getting a text the first time we'd met. I nodded as Vernon swung the door shut.

"The news I fed Card got more of a reaction than I expected," I said. "Any idea why it was such a big deal to him?"

After a long pause, Vernon gave me a meaningful look and spoke.

"Let's leave that question on hold until Wolf Blitzer introduces Phoebe Riverdale with the Bilbo story."

Chapter 57

I turned quickly and headed toward my rental. Not wary, not nervously reaching for Mama's gun. BR was my town, and it had never hurt me. I basked complacently in the mellow glow from the meal and talk I'd just shared.

So, naturally, I jumped at the sound of a voice from the twilit alley to my left.

"Good evening, Ms. Kendall."

I pivoted to face the alley, stepped backward toward my car and the street. The voice sounded white. I quietly opened my purse and started feeling around for that little .25 automatic. Found it, but wondered if I were kidding myself. Was it more of a security blanket for me than a weapon? I knew how to shoot the thing, but that didn't mean I could play Annie Oakley in real-life combat. You never really know if you can point a gun and fire it at someone until you actually have to do it.

"Who's there?" I tried to sound tough and poised. I didn't.

"You don't know us." *Us? Shit.* "We work for someone who'd like to have dinner with you. He told us to bring you to him."

"I just ate."

"That's okay, he's on a diet himself."

Two bulky figures stepped out of deep shadows into gloaming. I recognized the bigger one as Tug, the goon I'd seen in Cavour. So this was Kappa's party.

They took two measured paces toward me – close enough for me to see that they were both big dudes. Tug wore what looked like black biker leathers. His accomplice had a lightweight black windbreaker on over an ensemble that made me think he hadn't gotten the memo about disco being dead.

"Please tell Mr. Kappa that I very much appreciate his attention," I said. "I am otherwise engaged for the next hour or so, but if he would be kind enough to call me, I would be happy to arrange a meeting at his convenience."

"His convenience is pretty much now," Tug said.

Something about his eyes shook me. They weren't quite stone cold like Card's and Kappa's but they were cold enough, and I also thought I spotted a true-believer glint in them. Tug was hired muscle, but he was hired muscle who cared.

"As it happens," I said, "'now' is not convenient for me."

The two of them took one more pace toward me. My right index finger tightened on the automatic's trigger as I clicked off the safety with my thumb. Figured I was about to find out if I had what it takes.

"Let's just go see him right now. You come on along like a good girl, and no one gets spanked."

I managed "No" as I started to pull the gun out of the purse. I was either going to shoot this prick or fold like a cheap tent in a high wind. I had no idea which.

I wouldn't find out – not tonight, at least. A sharp voice split the darkness.

"Lady say no, cracker." Card. "No mean no. You be headin' out wid a quickness."

"Who the hell are you?" Tug asked, turning toward the voice.

"I be da wrong playuh fo' a coupla crackers like you ta' mess wid, dat's who. When somethin' bad go down here, da pigs don't be roustin' asshole tourists like you. Dey be comin' after Card. So you best be headin' out, an' right fuckin' now. Card'll chalk you two soon as fuck yo mamas."

They hesitated. Looked at each other. Tug jerked his head toward the far end of the street. They started moving away, their pace quickening as they went.

"Much obliged," I said, my whole body shaking with each pulse-beat.

No response. Not even a scrape of shoe-leather. I didn't hang around. I got in my car and drove away, past the El Dorado that still sat across the street. If Card had a stone-cold reason saving me, I didn't know what it was. But I gratefully accepted the result.

The next morning, I wanted nothing more than to get back to D.C. But I checked with Mary Cary first about her progress on the expensive little project I'd dropped in her lap.

"Let me put it this way, dear," she said. "This is going to take longer than I expected – and you've already got yourself a bargain."

"When should I check back with you?"

Pause.

"Next month," she finally said. "Perhaps after the Feast of the Assumption."

I flew back to Reagan National that afternoon. Empty-handed? No. Pushing a major story off the back burner and picking up a double-ton of useful information isn't empty-handed in my book. Without the key to Hank Sinclair's little secret, though, it kind of seemed that way.

Chapter 58

August, 2019

Phoebe broke her Bilbo story at the end of the first week in August. "A secret recording of a congressman's gunfight with a burglar raises a grave question: Were there four shots, as Congressman Chad Bilbo has always claimed, or only three – all of them fired by the congressman?" Almost four minutes of actual reportage – that's just short of eternity in TV news – on every CNN program through every news cycle from Tuesday's breakfast show to the late-night stuff watched only by insomniacs and political science majors.

The other cable news networks picked it up, along with NBC and CBS. (ABC apparently had other things on its mind.) The *Times* and the *Post* noted the story and started looking for fresh angles. Every two or three weekdays, Phoebe would dole out "new developments" that were new to everyone but her.

Letitia Dejean hadn't yet announced her intention to fight a rematch with Bilbo, but she got her matronly face on TV anyway with a pitch-perfect, facts-first-judgment-later statement. As the story neared the end of its second week, she released a copy of a letter to Louisiana's governor asking him to arrange for an "independent review of the circumstances surrounding William Woodbine's death." The governor said he'd think about it.

The story probably wouldn't have stayed alive after the college football season started except for Bilbo's tactically clueless response to it. He issued a statement pointing out that "law enforcement professionals" had already investigated "the incident." He denounced Phoebe's report as "fake news on steroids," and said CNN was begging for another libel suit to go along with the one it got from the Covington Catholic fiasco. In an interview on Fox News where he apparently expected three minutes of hanging curves and got two-seam fastballs instead, Bilbo shoehorned his favorite talking point into half his answers: "If there were only three shots, how come there were four bullet holes? Where'd that fourth bullet hole come from?"

The networks trotted out forensic experts to say the obvious: no one knew whether the bullet that made the hole in the joist was fired during the gunfight or at some other time. Then the crime mavens re-hashed the other 'anomalies' that Theo had spotted in the police report. The Monday after the Alabama Crimson Tide creamed its first gridiron opponent, the story still had legs.

On August 16th – which I'd verified with Mama was the day after the Feast of the Assumption – I left a message for Mary Cary at Matrixarchy. Short, vague, and not too pushy: "Hi, it's Josie. Just wondering how you're coming on fixing my thumb drive. Thanks."

I heard back around the time Letitia Dejean sent her letter to the governor. Seeing Mary Cary's number on caller ID had me practically gasping with anticipation.

"I hope this doesn't turn out to be a disappointment for you, dear."

"Couldn't you get through the encryption?" I asked.

"Oh, I got through that all right. Took forever and a day, but I managed it. But looking at what was encrypted, I didn't see anything that screamed '*bombshell!*' at me. Of course, what do I know?"

I may know zilch about computer coding, but I know a *lot* about the laws of political physics, such as the Presumption Against Disproportionate Security. The protection given a political person, place, or thing is *always* directly proportional to his, her, or its importance. If you see twenty-five Secret Service agents detailed to security prep for a speech, it's for someone higher on the food chain than the Secretary of Commerce. A front-line Marine regiment guarding a base in the Rockies means something more sensitive than shooting training films about how not to get the clap when you're on leave is going on at that base. Anything protected with encryption that a *savant* like Mary Cary needed weeks to chop through – well, it has something head-grabbing about it.

No sense sharing that insight with Mary Cary, though, so I didn't. I kept my follow-up response blasé and casual.

"Why don't you go ahead and send it to me and I'll see if I can make anything out? Along with your bill, of course."

"Actually," Mary Cary said, "I was wondering if you'd find it convenient to pick it up in person. That will simplify paying in advance."

At first I bristled at the idea. *Another Baton Rouge boondoggle?* I'd already played the 'business development' card for all it was worth. Then I realized that I might indeed be popping down to BR again in the very near future. The Bilbo story was in certifiable full swing on CNN, which made a visit to Vernon Czlewski overdue.

"Maybe I can make that work," I said. "Let's plan on sometime right after Labor Day. When I stop by to pick up the material, I'll have your check with me."

"No check, dear," Mary Cary said sweetly. "Cash."

Chapter 59

September, 2019

I was still waiting for Vernon to call me back on the Saturday of Labor Day weekend as Rafe and I tailgated outside Capital One Field, where the University of Maryland Terrapins would be taking on their first home opponent of the season. Nothing says fall like bloody marys and grilled burgers at 11:00 in the morning. Before arrival of the clients and contacts we'd be entertaining, Rafe and I didn't talk about the upcoming football game because, really, who cares? We talked about what some unimaginative wags had dubbed 'Bilbogate.'

"This thing may be evolving from a Grade A embarrassment into a slow-motion execution," Rafe said. "Do you think Bilbo can turn it around?"

"Have to go with yes on that one," I said. "Almost a year until he has to face the voters again. If all else fails, he can just brazen it out and hope for rain on primary day."

"How about joining Dejean's call for an independent investigation? Would you advise him to do that?"

"Only if he could be certain it wouldn't be independent."

Three days later, that's what Bilbo did. And Vernon finally called me back.

"I did my part, tiger," I told Vernon. "Turned you into a properly credentialed CNN whistleblower, and got you the cover that goes along with it. Time for you to hold up your end."

"Can't get up there anytime soon," he sighed. "And I'm sure as hell not getting into this over the phone. Can you come back down here?"

Trying to buy yourself two weeks? No sale. I'm onto you, and it's only noon in D.C.

"I can be there by later today," I said. "Where and what time?"

It took him a moment to realize I'd called his bluff, but he managed it.

"Spanish Moon on Highland," he said. "Why don't you hop on in there 'bout ten thirty? That late on a Tuesday night, I won't have any trouble finding you."

"Done."

I'd been going back and forth between D.C. and BR so often lately that it had begun to feel more like a commute than a trip: book flight, ' 'bye, honey' to Rafe, Uber, go through security, board, read Kindle for two hours, deplane, rental car, get to work.

The cigarette smoke at Spanish Moon went with the Dixieland jazz and brought back pleasant memories. I nursed a seven and seven and got into smooth versions of 'China Boy' and 'Tin Roof Blues' until Vernon appeared. He'd dialed his wardrobe up a notch, sporting a blue blazer and a textured blue silk tie. As we shook hands and he sat down at my table, he seemed genuinely glad to see me.

"I guess we've been through something together," he said.

"And we're not through it yet," I said, looking right into his eyes.

A waiter brought him a rum and Coke and called him 'Mr. Czlewski,' even though no one had taken his order.

"You came a long way for my theory about why Card got so focused when you mentioned Bedford Industries," Vernon said after a measured sip of his drink.

"This is true. I have my reasons."

"If any of this gets traced back to me, I'm a dead man."

"I won't exactly be a prime candidate for whole life insurance myself. I may be dumb, but I'm not crazy."

"Bedford Industries' basic business is leasing heavy equipment," Vernon said. He spoke reluctantly, with his eyes focused on the quintet now playing 'Columbus Stockade Blues.'

"Yeah, I've seen some of that equipment."

"Unless someone is watching extra close, of course, 'rented' heavy equipment doesn't actually have to go anywhere. If you have a Caterpillar mining truck in inventory, say, collecting six thousand dollars a month in rental fees for it for six months doesn't necessarily mean the truck ever actually left your premises."

"So if someone from the IRS stops by in the fifth month and sees a machine that's supposed to be out on rental," I said, "you just say, 'Oh, yeah, they returned that early. Cash flow problems or something.'"

"That's about the size of it," he said.

"I'm no entrepreneur, but with enough paper companies headquartered in the Cayman Islands, I can see how you could launder several million dollars a year in drug money with a setup like that."

"Add a zero," he said, shooting me his first smile since sitting down. "The string-pullers take out what they need in so-called 'consulting fees' or 'dividends,' they stash the rest offshore, and –"

"And Card never has to explain how he buys custom made suits and pimped up Cadillacs without any visible source of income."

"Right," he said. "Nor does Mr. Kappa."

Whoa! "They're *both* silent partners in Bedford Industries?"

"If they were any more silent, they'd be mimes."

"And the Global Martial Arts stuff is just a cover for rent-a-goons."

"On the nose."

"So when I told Card that I thought someone at Bedford had planted a tracker on my car, he could have gotten the idea that Kappa was using this narco-cash laundering front for some extracurricular project that could bring people a lot scarier than the IRS down on top of it."

"I would not be completely surprised if he drew that inference."

"Any idea what Kappa's unauthorized project is?"

"No comment," Vernon said, finishing his drink. "I'm completely committed to equality between the sexes. Why don't you get the bill?"

I called Rafe from Mama's house a little before midnight with a report.

"Do you buy it?" he asked.

"Yep. Don't you?"

"I'm a little shaky. Capital equipment that uses half-million-dollar tires would mean a great big start-up loan before anyone could launder any cash – and somehow I can't see First National Bank of Vicksburg signing on."

"You can borrow money from people in Vegas," I said, "especially if you know people in Brooklyn – and Kappa probably does."

"Fair point." He paused, in a way that somehow made me hear a troubled frown that I couldn't see. "When will you pick up your decoded bombshell?"

"Eight thirty tomorrow morning."

"I can't say I'm happy about you strolling around BR's mean streets with that kind of cash."

"Uncle D will be with me. He spent all night cleaning his forty-five."

"What can I say?'" Rafe sighed eloquently. "Pleasant dreams."

Chapter 60

"Mary Cary has led a sheltered life," Rafe murmured, fingering the three pages she had liberated from triple encryption. "I've never seen a PDB, but it's probably the only thing in town more explosive than this."

'PDB' is 'Presidential Daily Brief.' A Defense Intelligence Agency officer hand-delivers one each morning to the President, the Secretary of State, and the Secretary of Defense. Not on paper – on an iPad. And not to an aide – to the big three themselves. After each one has read it, he (or, sometimes, she) folds the tablet cover and returns the iPad to the delivering officer. No copies. No notes.

Sitting side by side at our dining room table, Rafe and I spread the pages out and started studying the first one. We found ourselves looking at a scanned copy of words hand-printed by someone clearly not trying for a penmanship prize:

> *GOODBYE MR. CHICKENSHIT*
> *Coopt R? (Doable?)*
> *Wait for IG report?*
> *Reliable replacement available/confirmable?*
> *Wait for r/c appt.?*
> *Message discipline crucial!*

That would indeed be gobbledygook to someone like Mary Cary, living a sane, balanced life outside the Beltway Bubble and worrying about property taxes and utility bills. To Rafe and me, though it was a chillingly clear first draft of a blueprint for orchestrating FBI

Director James Comey's ouster.

Comey had coined the term 'Chickenshit Club' to describe prosecutors without the guts to take tough cases to trial, so he was "Mr. Chickenshit." Deputy Attorney General Rod Rosenstein wrote a report scorching Comey for mishandling the Hillary Clinton email fiasco during the 2016 campaign. That made him the "R" that someone in the Trump administration was thinking about coopting but apparently couldn't, because Rosenstein then appointed Robert Mueller as a special prosecutor to investigate campaign collusion with Russia. Trump had fired Comey *without* waiting for the Inspector General's findings – "IG Report" on this page. Trump also hadn't waited for the session of Congress to end so that he could replace Comey with a recess appointment – "r/c appt." – that wouldn't require Senate confirmation right away.

"I love 'message discipline crucial,'" I said to Rafe. "This administration treats 'message discipline' as a loathsome disease. Careful planning doesn't do any good if the guy on top pops off in public with the first thing that comes into his head."

We turned our attention to the next page of block printing:

COURTING DISASTER
9-10/18
Prep wingnuts ≤ spring '18
Soft target
Preempt?
BTW parlay? Trek status/funding?

With twenty-twenty hindsight, I recognized this as an initial sketch of a false-flag terrorist attack operation that could be blamed on liberal judges who were soft on Islamic refugees – the one that I'd helped thwart. 9-10/18 suggested that it was planned for September or October of last year and, bingo, the planned Cavour attack had been scheduled for October 8, 2018. "Prep wingnuts" referred to leaking imaginary security assessments to talk radio hosts. "Soft target" presumably meant unguarded civilians, which again matched up with the failed plan.

"How do you read 'preempt'?" I asked Rafe.

"If I had to guess, I'd say that whoever drew this up hadn't decided yet whether to let the attack happen or to conspicuously prevent it at the eleventh hour. I'm not sure what 'BTW' and 'Trek' refer to, though."

"Me either."

I pulled the third page front and center:

IF YOU SHOOT AT THE KING
Time TBD. Spring? Summer? Fall?
Prep wingnuts DDAY - 60
VIMNAPA
WVa?/Wis?/Mich?/Ill?
PETN?/Semtex?

"'Shoot at the king'?" I read out loud. "Holy shit, Rafe. Were they talking about faking a presidential assassination attempt?"

As my husband grimly nodded, I thought for a moment about how wonderful it would have been right that minute not to have quit smoking.

"Nice of them to narrow it down to half the country for us," Rafe said. "West Virginia, Wisconsin, Michigan, Illinois. One red state, two purple, one blue. Any idea what 'VIMNAPA' is?"

"Nope. I'll Google it and see what I come up with. And I hope I get something, because right now we have a lot of sizzle but no steak. Triple-encryption will guarantee the attention of reporters and cops, but it's our word against Hank Sinclair's about where this came from."

"The first thing anyone we show this to is going to ask," Rafe said, nodding, "is why anyone planning bombshells like this would write it down in the first place. The President of the United States can't record a shred of info from the PDB. Why would a cabal of plotters carefully preserve first drafts of treason?"

"A good answer to that question isn't leaping out at me."

"Maybe you should ask one of your West Wing chums. Nessa, say. Or even Balegan."

'Or even Balegan.' Interview. 'Don't write that down. Anywhere. Not even on whiteboard. Pictures of those things.'

"What if whoever wrote this stuff didn't preserve a thing?" I asked. "What if Hank Sinclair did?"

"Why are you photobombing him into the picture?"

"I'm trying to imagine a scenario that fits the facts. Say we have two or three or four guys sitting in an office somewhere in the White House basement, in meetings maybe months apart. Maybe the same guys, maybe different, but Hank is always one of them. Out loud maybe they're talking about sports or girls or something, because they assume the interior decoration includes listening devices and their conversation is being recorded. While they're chatting, though, one of them is sketching the rudiments of one of these plans on whiteboard."

Rafe's face brightened. His eyes lit up. He snapped his fingers.

"Any notes have to go in a shredder, and probably the shredder waste goes into a burn bag," he said. "And of course, someone would erase the crude printing on the whiteboard. But before he does –"

"Right," I said. "Before he does, Hank somehow surreptitiously takes a picture of it." My turn to snap my fingers. "With camera-glasses! He was wearing those dorky horn-rims when he met Theo and me on the dock. They could have been camera-glasses. Except why would he have worn them to the dock meeting?"

"Maybe to get a picture of you next to Theo," Rafe said with more than a hint of anger in his voice. "You know, just in case it might come in handy someday."

"Which is the same reason he would have photographed the white board scrawl," I said. "In order to create his own, personal cover-Hank's-ass file."

"That's why his monumental fuck-up didn't get him fired," Rafe said. "Hank knows where a lot of bodies are buried, and he can prove it. And the pix also work as a Get Out of Jail Free card, if it comes to that. If any prosecutor gets too nosy about him, he can pull that file out and say, 'Let's make a deal.' Or he could have, before you relieved him of it."

"He probably has backup copies," I said. "As sniveling little shits go, that boy is *organized*."

Chapter 61

After thinking it over for a couple of weeks, I decided to tease Phoebe with our mini-trove of handwritten documents. I made sure not to overhype it. Just a tentative toe in the water. She reacted with a polite variation on, "Is that all you've got?" I answered with a coy, "Time will tell," because "Yes" didn't strike me as a promising response. I wasn't ready to hand her anything else, at least until some more shoes dropped.

About ten days after that, the Governor of Louisiana announced that he was appointing an independent prosecutor, a former judge named H. Marcus Lamarr, to look into the Slow Willy Woodbine case. That got a yawn from most reporters, but Mama told me Lamarr was a stand-up guy who wouldn't necessarily just roll over.

You could call that a shoe dropping if by "shoe" you meant "bedroom slipper." It didn't move the needle much. As weeks went by, nothing else moved it either.

The more time passed, the antsier I got about just sitting on our cryptic bombshell. I hate waiting for someone else to do something so that I can react. Rafe doesn't like it any more than I do. He has a habit of quoting the historian Livy: "Rome conquered the world in self-defense." We finally decided to get a little more proactive.

Over beer and pizza at our home in early November, we gave Theo a copy of the encrypted Hank thumb drive documents and the story behind them. We'd had some qualms. If the things turned out to be toxic, we didn't want Theo to get infected. We finally decided that it wouldn't hurt for someone reliable to have a spare set. You know, just in case.

"We mean it about the just-in-case part," Rafe said. "We're not asking you to do anything adventurous with them."

"What could I possibly do with them?"

"No idea," I said.

"How about another beer?" he asked, grinning.

The next day Letitia Dejean announced that she would challenge Bilbo again in 2020. GG Mason, now officially a bachelor of arts, would coordinate her campaign. He said something about 'crowd funding.' *Good luck with that one.*

I was still looking for some more buttons to push in December, when I got a call from Nessa Sara Lee. Her name on Caller ID produced the usual yips. My head knew I had no shot at a West Wing job, but my heart hadn't read the memo. I had to work at it to keep a tremor of hope out of my voice when I answered.

"Josie?" she said. "I'm just calling to let you know that I'll be leaving my position here at the end of the calendar year. Honored to have had the chance to serve and all that, but it's a good time to move on. It just is."

Right. Because __after__ you get subpoenaed would be a really bad time.

"I hear you, Nessa. Do you have something new lined up, or are you looking around? Or maybe thinking about just taking a little break?"

"Let's not get too far out over our skis."

So you've already picked out the office drapes at your new gig.

"Well best of luck, Nessa. I'm sure it's all going to work out for you."

"Thanks. . . . Uh, Josie?"

"Yes?"

"You're a big girl and you can take care of yourself, but if you don't mind one little word of advice, it wouldn't be a terrible idea for you to paper the file."

I processed that instantly and responded with no awkward pause.

"Copy that, sister. Live long and prosper."

Papering the file with exactly one sheet of premium bond on my personal letterhead took me an hour. After a paragraph of Miss Manners stuff, I got to the bottom line: I thought it best to withdraw my name from consideration for a position on the White House staff. Thanks for thinking of me, very flattered, best of luck moving forward.

I thought about copying Balegan but I didn't. Good move. In the darkest hours of the New Year's holiday hangover, Balegan quietly announced that he was leaving his job at the White House. Not at the end of the month. Right now. That day. No one noticed. Which was the idea.

That was about it until March – when it hit the fan.

Chapter 62

The 2020 primaries were in full swing, keeping me up to my ears in phone calls and bullet points, when I got a St. Patrick's Day text from Rafe: "Dinner 2morrow PM w/RM @ his condo?" I texted back a thumbs-up, without bothering to add "Book?" What else would it be about?

The dinner wasn't about Richard Michaelson's book.

I could tell even during cocktails that something was up. The table was set for four, not three, and Michaelson had a playful glint in his eye as we stood at the picture window of his elegantly modest one-bedroom unit in Washington Harbor. We were still at it when the doorbell chimed.

"Ah, our final guest," Michaelson said.

I raised a couple of quizzical eyebrows at Rafe as Michaelson strolled to the entryway. Rafe shrugged. We turned toward the door just in time to see Theo McAbbott walk in and shake Michaelson's hand. *HEL-lo.* When we'd mentioned Michaelson's name to Theo back in November, he'd hinted that it wasn't the first time he'd heard it, but I didn't think they moved in the same circles. Was our old buddy showing some initiative?

We'd know soon enough. Michaelson fixed a bourbon and sweet for Theo, went to the kitchen briefly to see how his rent-a-chef was doing with the meal, and rejoined us.

"Mr. McAbbott thought I might be able to help him with some technical advice on an idea he has for a thriller," Michaelson said blandly. "He wanted his agent to be in on our conversation."

"Working title?" Rafe asked Theo.

"*Courting Disaster,*" Theo said.

Direct quote from the thumb drive documents. Yep, Theo *had* taken the initiative on something. Now I had an idea of why we were here.

"*Courting Disaster*," Rafe said thoughtfully. "High body count that a heroic and omni-competent FBI veteran keeps from going any higher. Am I close?"

"Body count is negotiable, but you nailed it on the hero."

"Intriguing," Michaelson murmured, his face as innocent as a first-grader's. "Let's continue our discussion over salad."

We adjourned to the dinner table, where we found elegant arugula and frisee salads with pomegranate vinaigrette waiting for us. Michaelson did nothing to hurry things along. He actually seemed to enjoy the suspense radiating from Rafe and me as we passed around a basket of crusty bread. We had three healthy bites of salad each before he got back to the technical advice that Theo supposedly needed.

"I know far less about Russian and Chinese firearms than Google does, so I'm not sure my expertise will be much help," Michaelson said, "but I'll be happy to try."

"I can handle gun stuff just fine," Theo said. "What I need help on is satellite photographs. I need to know if the good guys in my story could figure out just from Star Trek images that Assad's government in Syria is tricking out three Russian tanks to look like American armor. If they could, that would save me about twelve hundred words."

"I saw my share of satellite photography during my State Department days, but that was more than thirty years ago." Michaelson glanced over his shoulder as a tall, thin African-American man in a crisp, double-breasted white chef's coat and gray pants brought a steaming white bone china bowl into the dining area from the kitchen. "Why don't you finish your salads and get started on the lobster bisque while I dig out one of the files I keep around for old times' sake?"

Excusing himself, Michaelson left the table and slipped into what I guessed was a combined bedroom and study. Diving immediately into the soup would have been bad manners even by today's Washington standards, so we held off on ladling the luscious-looking pink liquid into our bowls until Michaelson had returned with a brown accordion file. Fortunately, it didn't take him long.

He sat down with the file in his lap and nodded appreciatively when Theo filled the soup bowl at his place. After we'd each attacked the bisque, Michaelson pulled a print from the file and passed it around, then went back to work on his bisque while the three of us examined the thing.

I could tell I was looking at a big crowd of people mixed with trucks and cars, all crammed onto a road in a long line. Both sexes, all ages, civilian clothes.

"Part of the 'caravan' of Honduran refugees making its way through Mexico in October of 2018," Michaelson said.

"I'm surprised this isn't classified," Rafe said.

"That is a puzzle, isn't it?" Michaelson responded. "But I don't see CONFIDENTIAL or TOP SECRET anywhere on there. Do you?"

"Can't say that *I* do, anyway," Theo said. "And if this is state of the art, it might just do for my tank identification wrinkle. Might."

"For state of the art you really can't beat human intelligence," Michaelson said. "Let me show you an example of that."

Back he went into the file. The four more eight-by-tens he brought out now hadn't been taken by any satellite, and they weren't on standard copier paper. They were glossies, like you'd get from CVS if you had your vacation snaps printed there. Crisp, clear, outdoor shots, perfectly exposed and without a speck of grain. Aside from a bit of distortion suggesting use of a telephoto lens, they might have been taken in a studio.

The first photo featured the face and torso of a frowning, brown-skinned man with black hair and a bristly black moustache.

"That chap in the first photo is Bartolo Fuentes," Michaelson said. "He was one of the organizers of the Honduran 'caravan.' This was taken in early September of 2018 in Honduras. Once the 'caravan' started, Fuentes made it as far as Guatemala, where he was arrested and sent back to his home country."

We examined the rest of the four-picture set around tastes of lobster bisque. On the second, third, and fourth photos, Fuentes was just a fuzzy foreground figure. The photographer had focused on three men standing in an edgy group in front of a milling crowd about ten feet behind Fuentes. The one on the right was suntanned but clearly Anglo. The other two were darker skinned and just as clearly not Anglo. In the second photo, the Anglo held a well-stuffed duffel bag large enough that a Naval officer might actually go to sea with it. In the third, he had set the bag down on its end, in front of the two non-Anglos. In the fourth, the guy on the far left had picked up the bag.

"Payoff or a drug delivery?" Theo asked.

"On a wild guess," Michaelson said, "a turnover of two hundred eighty-seven-thousand dollars and change."

"That must be one hell of a camera," Rafe said.

"I have some sources beyond the photographs," Michaelson said with a shrug. "I wouldn't call it a payoff. More like funds to cover incidental expenses that might come up during a long trek through Honduras, Guatemala, and Mexico."

"Spook cash financed the caravan?" Theo demanded, astonished.

"No. I'm assured that no taxpayer funds were involved, as that could have become a bit awkward if it came out later on. The duffel bag holds private money."

I scarcely heard that last exchange. I couldn't take my eyes off the last picture, where I'd just spotted something. I didn't say '*Holy shit!*' out loud – that would have clashed with the occasion – but I gasped audibly.

"That's Tariq, isn't it?" Rafe asked, pointing to the guy next to the one who ended up with the bag.

"Either him or his twin brother," I said. "And not only that. The one standing immediately to his right is the goon that Kappa calls 'Tug.'"

"Worth a gasp all right," Theo said.

"That's not why I gasped." I pointed at the fourth picture's background. "See that guy dead center in the crowd milling behind Tug, Tariq, and friend?"

"The Yank who's giving the trio a real hard stare?" Rafe asked.

"Yes, him. One thing I've gotten from a youth misspent in politics is I don't forget faces. He's the bodyguard who accompanied the Kirbys on our flight down to San Antonio in early 2018."

At an inconspicuous signal from Michaelson, our conversation stopped cold, suspended in mid-thought. The chef reappeared to take our empty soup bowls and provide us each with a platter featuring what looked like Chilean sea bass.

"So what are you saying?" Theo asked when the kitchen door had again closed behind the chef. "That the Kirbys collaborated with Kappa to get walking-around money to Fuentes?"

"To get caravan money to someone, laundered through Bedford Industries," I said, suddenly wondering if Bedford had borrowed Kirby cash years ago for its initial stake. "Assuming the right people knew about it, and could be counted on to be appropriately grateful, serving as a channel for that kind of payment would be a prudent move for an operation that doesn't want a lot of pesky auditors pawing through its books. I think the Kirbys sent their guy to make sure Tug got to his photo-op without any of the cash going into his own pocket."

"Wherever the money came from," Michaelson said, "the pictures don't document a single dollar going to Fuentes. Just to someone in his general vicinity – conveniently within view of a photographer who must have been told about the handoff ahead of time."

"Leaving the rest of us to assume that the recipient was a Fuentes henchman," Rafe said, glancing toward me.

I could imagine the scenario as clearly as if it were a movie streaming right in front of me. *Boom!* (or near miss) in Cavour, Louisiana on October 8, 2018. Twenty-four hours later, Tariq showing up along with the other Syrian refugees at Bedford on perp walks, arrested for complicity in the actual or attempted terrorist attack. Then these photos splashed across news websites and front pages with a red circle around Tariq's face, showing him standing within sneezing distance of a caravan organizer and a bagful of money.

"This stuff could have flipped the script overnight," I said. "Reversed the media narrative. The Republicans might have held the House, and would certainly have gained at least one more seat in the Senate."

"Well," Rafe said with studied nonchalance, "at least now we know what 'BTW' on Hank's 'Courting Disaster' sheet means."

"'Build That Wall,'" I said. "Leverage a false-flag terrorist attack across the Mexican border to get wall-money appropriated, either in a special session before the election or a lame duck session after it. 'Trek' meant the 'caravan,' and a duffel bag full of cash answered the 'funding' question."

Michaelson smiled.

"Let's eat this superb seafood before it gets cold."

Chapter 63

April, 2020

We paid my lawyer, Tony York, a tidy sum to put together a formal report to the United States Attorney for the Northern District of Virginia. That's where Hank lived, and you have to start somewhere. We submitted it without (of course) naming Michaelson. Ten days later, an assistant attorney who sounded *maybe* three years older than I am interviewed me for twenty minutes over the phone. She didn't come across as especially excited. She said the office would follow up as appropriate.

Theo showed Tony's work confidentially to a couple of his buddies still serving with the FBI. The good news was that their eyes lit up; the bad news was that a lot of bureaucratic maneuvering lay between an excited FBI agent and someone actually opening an investigation.

When it was time to rattle Phoebe's cage with the new intel – which I also did without names – I was relieved that she didn't just blow me off. I suggested a quick lunch at Breadline, a local favorite near the White House, because it was always swarming with so many journalists, lobbyists, and politicos that I figured we wouldn't stand out.

"Hmm," she said over the cavernous din of the teeming café. "Double cutout. *Interesting*."

"The last person I heard say *'interesting'* in that tone was a sorority sister at Tulane after her first and last puff on a cigar."

Phoebe actually smiled at that one.

"This is a hook for sure," she said. "Hard facts, scary information. But this isn't going on the air until we've followed it up from three different angles and triple-checked everything that remotely resembles a fact."

"Understood."

"And that's going to take some time."

"I don't know how much time we have, but with the election coming up in November, it has to be less than seven months." Maybe I sounded a little melodramatic, but I felt like it was way too late for Beltway cool.

"I hear you," Phoebe said. "But that's the way it is these days."

"I'll leave it to you and just hope for the best, then. If it's any consolation, by the way, the Justice Department seems to be as gun-shy as the media."

"Same strategy, same result," Phoebe said. "The difference is the Hoover Building leaks more than toddlers during a diaper shortage."

I looked for a subtext in her comment. I found one.

"Speaking of leaks," I said, "I've never heard of any politically-sensitive activity in Louisiana being leak-proof. Any word about how Judge Lamarr is doing on his cold-case work involving Bilbo and Slow Willie?"

Phoebe's two-second hesitation told me the answer was 'yes'. After mulling things over for a few seconds, she decided to spit it out.

"Word is that Lamarr is turning over every rock he can find because he thinks Bilbo is as guilty as Judas Iscariot. He's having lots of heartburn, though, over the absence of Bilbo's fingerprints on the inside tips of the glove found at the scene with powder residue from the backflash. He doesn't like it, but he's not having much luck finding a way around it."

"Well," I said as I stood up, "if I stumble over an answer to that head-scratcher on my way back to the office, I'll give Judge Lamarr a call."

"You do that," Phoebe said.

So it looked like if anyone was going to make any headway anytime soon on figuring out 'Shoot at the King' from Hank's encrypted files, I'd have to be the one. Back at my desk I closed a seven-tab poll-analysis spreadsheet on my computer, shoved a stack of media reports aside, and ignored a rash of emails. I Googled 'VIMNAPA' with every permutation of 'Wisconsin', 'Illinois', 'Michigan' and 'West Virginia' that I could think of. Nothing helpful.

I had damn near sold my soul to some buddies from the good old days now working in the Trump Campaign to get a macro list of post-convention campaign stops under consideration. Plenty in Wisconsin and Michigan, more than a handful in West Virginia, and even a couple in Illinois. Googled 'VIMNAPA' with the city, town, or county associated with every one of the bloody things. Still zip.

I'd pushed every button I knew how to push and tried every manipulative, underhanded trick in the Josie playbook without much to show for it. I'd tried media, lawyers, and insiders and I couldn't get anyone to move faster than toothpaste.

I needed to think harder and more creatively. *Why only POST-convention possible campaign stops? Why should I assume that the 2020 surprise would be a false flag attack in autumn just because that was what they'd tried in 2018?* I should have asked myself questions like that. But I didn't, until it was almost too late.

Chapter 64

I spent most of the next two weeks spinning my wheels, hoping that something would grab my attention and somehow sharpen my focus. When something finally did, I seized on it, even though a normal person without Potomac OCD probably wouldn't have paid much attention to it. Mama sent me a link to an iPhone recording of what was supposed to be a private speech Bilbo had given to a roomful of his oil-and-gas buddies. Were they still royally pissed off about his fracking flip-flop? On the recording they'd sat on their hands, which meant they were probably also sitting on their wallets, so that looked like yes.

But that wasn't what set my political antennae quivering. The recording included a typical Bilbo throwaway line, the kind he'd never use in a speech he expected the general public to see, but that he sometimes dropped in more private settings to buff up his just-one-of-the-boys cred. After a standard rant against the idea that fossil-fuel use contributed to global warming, he'd said, 'That plumb misses the point. It's like a doctor prescribing arthritis medicine for a necrophiliac sex addict who said he'd just been feeling a little stiff.'

At least on the recording, no one guffawed. No one even giggled, and I don't think it was because none of them knew what a necrophiliac was. Guaranteed laugh-line before the Slow Willie story broke. Now all it drew were chair-scrapes and dubious murmurs.

This boy might be in real trouble.

THEN COUNT TO TEN

June, 2020

"Shoot to kill. Then count to ten."

Instruction from Homer Cummings, FDR's Attorney General, to FBI Agents dealing with Depression-era gangsters.

Chapter 65

In early June, Seamus dropped by my office to ask if I was free the next day.

"Wide open except for lunch."

"Good. I'd like to include you in a meeting with Campbell Flagman."

I blinked, surprised not to recognize a D.C. name important enough for Seamus to know.

"Who's he?" I asked.

"She," Seamus said.

"Ouch."

"Campbell Flagman is a consultant who's been hired full-time through the primary by Chad Bilbo."

"Ouch."

"You just said that," Seamus pointed out.

"I believe strongly in recycling."

When Flagman and I shook hands, I felt like I was meeting a high school junior who'd slipped the leash on a field trip. I would have carded her for anything north of a Shirley Temple. Her hair was shoulder length and shapeless, colored a half-hearted blond that didn't match her eyebrows. Her blouse/sweater/skirt *ensemble* had probably looked great on a mannequin in Forever 21's career-wear department, but on her it just looked like she was going through the corporate motions and fooling no one. Her nicely tanned face and an appealingly candid expression were marred by constantly shifting hazel eyes.

Which meant that this was a formidable lady. I'd checked her out. She might look sixteen but she was twenty-five and owned her own business. She did stuff with data mining that blew people's minds – not just politicians, whose minds are often easily blown, but also hard-headed business types who reportedly dropped eight thousand dollars a pop for her reports. She wasn't doing this on looks or charm or pizzazz, and she sure as hell wasn't doing it on *gravitas*. That left what she actually produced, so it must be good.

We sat around the head of a polished teak table in MVC's Sherman Adams room, with Seamus in between Flagman and me.

"I've done some analytics for Congressman Bilbo," she said, swiveling a computer around so that Seamus and I could look at it. You could have called the computer a 'laptop' if the lap in question were Shaquille O'Neal's. The screen showed lots of skinny red, blue, and green columns on a grid.

"Love the graphics," I said.

"I'll just hit the highlights," Flagman said. "Algorithms that we've beta tested and result-validated show that we can expect several key white constituent groups to break strongly pro-Bilbo: weekly church-goers, voters owning American-made cars, voters with hunting and fishing licenses, voters with only high school educations, NRA members, voters who make at least two tobacco purchases per week, small business owners, and blue-collar workers who don't belong to unions."

"So that leaves Dejean with school teachers, pacifists, and vegetarians," I said.

"How does this gibe with internal polling?" Seamus asked innocently, his face so cherubic you wouldn't dream he was channeling his inner asshole.

"We've found that economically feasible polling can't get granular enough to permit apples-to-apples comparisons," Flagman said. Translation: *Polling is SO twentieth century, dude.*

I shook my head just a fraction. I'd just turned twenty-eight, and apparently I was an old fogey. I *like* polling, talking to people who've voted in the last five elections, listening to campaign workers who put shoe-leather on the street. But 'analytics' was the hottest buzzword inside the Beltway after the 2012 election and, after all, it worked for Hillary Clinton.

Oh, wait a minute, it *didn't* work for her, did it? It flopped for her. Helped her lose an unlosable election. Phillippe Reines gave her the best prep job for a political debate since 1858, when Abraham Lincoln prepared himself to debate Stephen Douglas, and she *still* lost. As long as pols keep shoveling money into analytics, though, the Campbell Flagmans of the world will keep taking it. And good for them. They'll certainly spend it more wisely than the idiots who pay them.

Flagman continued speaking in a low, unhurried voice.

"As you can see from the metrics, a targeted get-out-the-vote effort will ensure Congressman Bilbo at least forty-three percent of the vote in a primary with three serious candidates. Even if one of the other two candidates beats that number, a third candidate guarantees a runoff by finishing in the high single digits."

"You following the math?" Seamus asked me with a sly wink.

"Yeah." *Forty-three for Bilbo leaves fifty-seven, so if the schlub who comes in third gets eight percent, that only leaves forty-nine for Dejean. No candidate over fifty means a runoff.* "But the establishment Democrats are backing Dejean instead of putting up their own candidate, and the only others in the race are single-issue oddballs who don't figure to pull one percent of the vote combined."

"One of those 'single-issue oddballs' is about to get a tranche of money and some professional help with ad buys," Flagman said. "We're computing him at eleven percent in a three-way."

"'Eleven percent in a three-way,'" Seamus said. "Sounds like me at a Fiesta Bowl after-party when I was in college."

"In a post-primary head-to-head," Flagman said, "Bilbo looks pretty good. Dejean's cash flow is checking in at nothing special."

"Fascinating," Seamus said. "Love the tease. But what does the congressman think MVC can contribute?"

"Not my department." Flagman shrugged. "I was only tasked to show why he has an eighty percent-plus chance of winning, and to ask you to meet with him."

"I think she means you," Seamus told me.

I had a nauseating feeling that he was right. He was.

"Yes," Flagman said. "Ms. Kendall."

"If I ask what he wants to meet with me about, you'll just say that's not your department, right?" I asked.

Again with the shrug.

"I was only tasked –"

"Got it," I snapped. "I can come to his office anytime today."

"The congressman would prefer to meet Wednesday of next week," Flagman said. "At his residence in the district. He'll be flying in for a District Work Session to coincide with the President's visit to the Siege of Vicksburg battle sites in Mississippi."

Bilbo doesn't HAVE a residence in the district. I almost said that out loud. Then I remembered the hunting lodge that he used as his official residence even though he didn't sleep there more than forty nights a year.

Tried to think of a polite way to ask whether the two of us would be properly chaperoned. Failed. Seamus to the rescue.

"Will Ms. Bilbo be there?" he asked.

"Yes," Flagman said.

Flagman had done her job so I saw her out. When I returned to Seamus in the conference room, he was shaking his right hand up and down, as if he'd just touched something a mite hot.

"Whew!" he said. "I'll bet she and Bilbo really get along."

"Do you think Bilbo would go to all that trouble just for a grope-fest?" I asked.

"No. He has something substantive in mind."

"Hard to imagine what."

Seamus beamed. His eyes twinkled. His fat, jolly cheeks bobbed. It was the scariest thing I'd seen since *Nightmare on Elm Street.*

"How close a look did you take at Ms. Flagman's analytics data?" he asked.

"Not very."

"Half of it was statewide," Seamus said. "Six to one he's thinking about a run for governor next time out of the chute. Looks like you're going back to Louisiana."

Chapter 66

Many is the limo I've ridden in less plush than Mary Barbara Bilbo's Cadillac Escalade. Not just leather on the customized captain's chairs in the middle row but the supplest deep maroon leather that wrapped my body like a swaddling cocoon. A/C banished the heat without any uncomfortable chill. Windshield and windows so delicately tinted that I didn't need sunglasses. Dvorak sandwiched between Mozart and Brahms on an HD radio station, wafting flawlessly over the car's speaker system.

Bax Haskel handled the driving – your taxpayer dollars at work. I could tell he remembered me, and I sure remembered him. Bilbo's Marine-veteran constituent services aide seemed to have a broad and elastic job description. One month he's prodding me for Phoebe's source and the next he's chauffeuring the latest Mrs. Bilbo – and me – around the district.

Mary Barbara charmed my socks off. Early thirties, chestnut hair with lots of bounce, soulful brown eyes, fetching dash of the Delta in her accent, perfect three-quarter profile of the model she had been before she'd caught Chad Bilbo's eye, and to all appearances absolutely fascinated by me. (That's about ninety percent of charming most people.) She asked me about myself and seemed dazzled by every detail.

"Carondalet!" she said delightedly. "The Ursulines! *Alors tu as un peu du francais, n'est-ce pas?*"

"*Tout a fait, mais peut-être pas á la Parisian.*"

We conversed in French for twenty minutes. My insides quivered when she brought up Hank Sinclair. I responded tactfully, but she had no trouble reading the subtext.

"*Moi, aussi, je le regarde comme un bas de soie plein de merde,*" she said.

We reached Bilbo's hunting lodge a little after 6 p.m., the Escalade's tires crunching pleasantly over a crushed-stone drive that wound close to a mile from the turn off the parish road we'd used for the last leg of our trip. Pines and magnolias lined the drive. Two mid-size sedans might have driven side by side on this road, but two SUVs would be trading paint.

Seeing the 'lodge' itself reminded me that Versailles had started out as a hunting lodge. Two stories plus basement. Tudor-style sprawl, arranged in an L with a rounded junction where a generous porch fronted an elegant entranceway.

"Don't pull into the garage, Bax," Mary Barbara said as we approached. "Just let us off at the porch steps and then park about two car lengths beyond that."

"Yes ma'am."

The garage that Baxter Haskel didn't use lay behind us, at the end of the L's short leg. Looked like a converted stable. In front of us the long leg of the L extended at least a hundred-and-twenty feet beyond the porch.

Mary Barbara showed me in herself, apologizing for not having staff on site this time of year. A deep, pine resin smell dominated the main room. A comfortable-looking sofa and arm chairs done in blond-wood frames with green leather cushions shared the polished-pine flooring with two Persian rugs. In the far corner of the room sat a very serious looking gun cabinet. Three heads – two antlered and one tusked – looked sightlessly at us from above a massive stone fire place.

"What a beautiful, beautiful home," I said.

"Thank you so much." Mary Barbara closed the front door behind us.

"I recognize the deer and the moose." I nodded towards the fireplace. "What's the third one?"

"Boar," she said. "Chad found a hunting preserve in Arkansas that guarantees you three clear shots at a wild boar; and he brought home his trophy. Speaking of whom, he should be here in about forty-five minutes, and he'll be hungry. Assuming that Bax got the refrigerator stocked, we should have just enough time to whip up something to nibble on."

"Can I help?" I asked.

"Consider yourself *sous chef*."

My maitre d'hotel butter was already done and the steaks had one minute left under the broiler when we heard Chad Bilbo coming in the front door.

Chapter 67

An hour later we were sitting in sated comfort in the living room. Courvoisier and a Davidoff for Bilbo; Courvoisier and a Silk Cut for Mary Barbara; Courvoisier and second-hand smoke for me. After the meal, Bilbo had exiled Bax to the basement to "keep an eye on things."

"I really wish Bax could be with us," Bilbo said, half-apologetically, as we settled in. "I love that boy. Guts. Loyalty. The whole package."

"Yes, I like him too," I said, partly to be polite but mostly because I really did like Bax. I saw him as an icon of the real America, the America that fights wars and raises children and pays the taxes that keep the Rayburn Building air conditioned in July.

"The thing is," Bilbo said, "that CNN smear may be having consequences beyond just pissing me off. I've gotten some unofficial hints from fellas with badges about serious let's-ice-Bilbo talk among certain activists prone to violence. Ten to one it's all just talk, but it can't hurt to take some prudent precautions."

Serious gut-flutter for Josie. Not just because of Eugene Simpson Stadium Park, although that was part of it. Card could have found out by now that his silent partner, Kappa, had used Bilbo to murder Slow Willie. In itself, that probably wouldn't infuriate him all too much: snitches die young. But Card figured to be super-pissed about Kappa imperiling the Bedford Industries money-laundering front by playing power games with White House cowboys. Because Bilbo was a politician who had provided cover for Kappa during the DEA's internal investigation, Card could easily have concluded that Bilbo was somehow involved in Kappa's political machinations. Had he decided to send a message to Kappa by taking Bilbo out? That possibility chilled me. Unlike the clowns who shout down speakers and vandalize political displays they don't like on college campuses, Card actually knew which end of a gun bullets come out of.

I kept concern from showing on my face. Bilbo moved smoothly on to other things while Mary Barbara and I listened. As the clock ticked and the shadows lengthened outside, I hoped I was about to find out why I was here. I was.

"Did my gal go over the analytics with you?" Bilbo asked at last.

"Yes, she did. Even with the CNN story and the independent counsel investigation, they make you look strong."

He chuckled appreciatively, settling back against green leather and exuding effortless confidence.

"You wanna know something funny?" he asked. "In some parts of the district, the CNN smear is actually helping. 'Shot that thug down like a dog! Yesss! Didn't hand him over to the cops so some candy-ass judge could give him probation.' That analytics gal says it might net out five thousand votes to the good."

You and President Hillary Clinton should talk about analytics in the Oval Office sometime. My Lord, how I wanted to say that. I said something else instead.

"If she's right, you have nothing to worry about."

"I'll tell you who's got something to worry about," Bilbo said. "Professor Letitia Dejean. She doesn't have anything close to the money she had last time. 'Crowd funding'. What a joke. She's sleeping on supporters' couches."

"I've heard rumors like that myself."

He sat up and jabbed his cigar in my direction.

"Letitia Dejean is two hundred thousand dollars upside down. That's the rumor *I* hear. At that little cow college she runs, that's two years' salary for her. She can't pay it! Can't! And it's only going to get worse."

"In that case," I said, "you may not have to worry about the numbers at all. She might have to shut down her campaign. Maybe even drop out of the race."

"I've had a thought or two about that," he said, settling back again with a complacent puff. "I kind of like Professor Letitia. I know I shouldn't, but I can't help it. I just do. She's got *balls*. I *love* balls."

"Healthy respect for the opposition," I said. "Always a good thing."

"I would surely hate for her to come out of this with a debt that would spoil the rest of her life. I've seen candidates stay in hopeless races just so they could keep raising money to retire the campaign debt. Never works. Contributors read the same polls everyone else does. The debt just gets bigger."

"So, your advice to Doctor Dejean would be to bail right now," I said.

He grinned at me behind a cloud of smoke.

"Suppose someone else gave the good professor some advice," he said. "Suppose this person said she had seen the numbers and knows how to read numbers and, frankly, the cat's in the bag and the bag's in the river."

"I suspect that Doctor Dejean wouldn't find such advice constructive."

"I know lots of kind, big-hearted people. Suppose this person were to add that, if the professor were to quit pouring money down a rathole, there might be a way to raise enough funds to get rid of that campaign debt."

"That would be a felony," I said. *I'm not doing that*

"Not a felony anyone could prove."

"In fact, Just sitting here talking it over might be criminal."

"It's not," he said. "I've had that checked. This isn't the Catholic Church. It's not a sin just to think about it."

"Well, I have *not* had it checked. So I think the most sensible thing for me to do is not make any further comment on this subject."

"I don't blame you for that. Prudent. But while you're not talking, I will. If a person chose to offer the very sound advice we have discussed, I would be delighted to introduce that person to some of those kind, big-hearted friends I mentioned."

"That's clear enough." I tried for a tone of finality. Apparently I didn't try hard enough.

"You can check this out with anyone you'd like – boss, lawyer, shrink, priest – but there has to be a legal way to do it. People do it every blessed election year."

Everybody does it isn't a defense. Didn't say *that*, either. In fact, I didn't say anything. But my silence caused no conversational slack. Bilbo kept right on going as twilight fell outside and the room lights automatically got brighter.

"I thought about running for governor this year. Probably could have won, but I decided not to take the plunge. The smear may be a net positive in the district, but it could look like major baggage in a statewide race."

"You're in a better position to make that judgment than I am," I said.

"So my thought is, I'll do one more term in the House. A nice solid win in the district, with no runoff, will put that smear to rest for good."

"I can see your logic," I said.

"When I do make that run for governor, of course, I'll need some professional assistance. MVC has an outstanding reputation in that area."

Then he winked. I didn't wink back.

Chapter 68

"Well," Mary Barbara said, deftly changing the subject, "since this is your first time here, how about a tour?"

It would have been rude to say no, and I welcomed the break from Bilbo's ego. Ten minutes later I knew that the upstairs had a master bedroom with two bathrooms, and five guest/staff bedrooms sharing two bathrooms among them. Also, a study with a wet bar and a Chesterfield sofa the size of a casting couch. And a "sewing room" where, judging from almost subliminal background odors filtered through undergraduate memories, Mary Barbara went when she felt like smoking a little weed.

Downstairs Mary Barbara showed me a butler's pantry and a den with the usual slew of up-to-the-second electronics. Screened-in porch along the back of the house. No tennis court or pool, though. I guess Bilbo didn't want to look like he was flaunting his wealth.

I'd clicked into belle mode thirty seconds into the tour. I stayed on message.

"I am simply blown away by this magnificent home," I gushed.

"Would you like to see the basement?"

"Of course."

Not sure what I'd expected, but what I saw wasn't it. No billiard or Ping-Pong table. No walls covered with family and vacation photos. Instead it had bedrooms for staff, a full bathroom and a half-bath, and L-shaped desks separated by low partitions where up to three aides could beaver away.

Bax Haskel sat in the center cubicle, in the glowing blue light of security monitors. We waved at him, he returned the wave, and we headed for the stairs. We'd just about reached them when we heard Haskel talking – and not to us.

"Intruders on the southeast perimeter, Congressman. At least two."

"Any visuals?" Bilbo's surprisingly calm response came over a speaker.

"Negative, sir. Just blips from the motion detector."

"How far is that from the gate?"

"At least three hundred yards east. Would you like me to run down there and check it out? Might just be kids messing around."

"Negative. Kids aren't going to go over an eight-foot fence with six inches of razor wire on top of it. And I can't risk you getting shot. What I want is everybody up here pronto – and call the sheriff on your way."

"Copy that," Haskel said as he jumped up and unholstered his mobile phone in almost the same motion. "We have to see the congressman ASAP," he told Mary Barbara and me, making urgent shooing motions with his prosthesis.

I felt myself pale, and with a glance at Mary Barbara I saw blood draining from her face as well. Her lips tightened into a thin determined line, and her muscles tensed. So did mine.

By the time we made it up to the living room, Bilbo had the gun cabinet wide open. While Haskel spoke in clipped tones into his phone, Bilbo took a black, clip-on holster holding a revolver with a four-inch barrel and fit it over his belt near his left hip. Then he reached for a much smaller, short-strapped holster with a gun that looked a lot like Mama's palm-sized twenty-five-caliber automatic. He strapped that to his left wrist, with the pistol on the inside.

"No one would know we're here unless they went to a lot of trouble to find out," Bilbo muttered. "That's not good news."

"Sheriff says he'll have someone here to look things over within twenty minutes, Congressman," Haskel called.

"Just in time to notify our next of kin," Bilbo said disgustedly.

He pulled an assault rifle with a banana clip from the vertical rack in the cabinet, looking over at Haskel while he did.

"Tell the sheriff to go ahead, but we're evacuating," he said.

"Copy that, Congressman," Haskel said.

"Do you have your weapon, Mary Barbara?" Bilbo asked.

"It's in the car," she answered.

No undue haste nor any suggestion of panic in Bilbo's voice or movements. He just *acted.* No hesitation, no wasted motion. *Maybe he has some combat chops after all.*

Haskel put his phone away and joined us.

"How much time do you figure until they're near the lodge?" Bilbo asked.

"Almost a mile over uneven ground and it's getting dark," Haskel mused. "That's fifteen minutes minimum, even if they're in good shape. So we've got more than ten minutes."

"That's more than we'll need," Bilbo said, handing Haskel the assault rifle. "Eighty-shot clip on a semi-automatic rifle. Just to be safe, though, grab an extra clip from the drawer on your way out."

"Got it," Haskel said.

Bilbo handed me a light, short-barreled rifle with a dinky little clip. The stock wasn't real wood, so it felt almost like a toy in my hand. Taking the thing and fussing with it gave me something to do besides think about how scared I was. I automatically checked for the safety. Bilbo nodded his approval.

"Have you ever fired a weapon?" he asked.

Fired a weapon? When Seamus decided to go after the NRA as a client, I showed up on Youtube blowing targets away with a snub-nosed Colt .32 revolver.

"Sure have."

"Here's how we'll roll," Bilbo said, his voice still steady and authoritative. "I'll go first, down the drive like greased lightning, with my brights on. Bax, you and the others follow in Mrs. Bilbo's car. About two hundred yards behind, lights off, and not fast. Mary Barbara, you drive, but put your seat as far back as you can, and incline the seatback, so that you're less of a target and Bax will have a clear shot through your window."

"Hold on," Mary Barbara said. "You need someone riding shotgun. Why don't I go with you and Ms. Kendall can drive Bax in my car?"

"At least one of us has to come out of this alive, darlin'," Bilbo said, "and Bax riding shotgun can protect you better than I can driving."

I took a good, deep breath. Only one answer here. I hated it, but I forced the words out around a golf-ball sized lump in my throat.

"Mary Barbara can drive her car better than I can," I told Bilbo, "especially in the dark without lights. I'll come with you."

Bilbo nodded decisively.

"You keep that Smith and Wesson of yours in your lap," he told Mary Barbara. "If you absolutely have to, you can shoot through the window on Bax's side. Leave the window on your side to Bax."

"Fine." Mary Barbara didn't sound happy.

"Now listen tight to this part," Bilbo said. "If our intruders are in a shooting mood, then I figure to draw fire. If I don't, that should mean the coast is clear all the way to the gate. If you hear gunshot one, though, then you turn that crate around the best way you know how, circle back around the lodge, drive overland about four hundred yards, and then crash through the fence to whatever that backroad is. That last part won't be easy, but the Escalade has enough muscle to handle it. Clear enough?"

"Sure," Mary Barbara said.

"Copy," Haskel said.

"If we all make it to the gate without incident, then we head for Baton Rouge," Bilbo said. "If there's gunfire and we have to separate, rally to HQ. Clear?"

"B-R if nothing happens, HQ if there's a scrap," Haskel said. "Got it."

"All right, then," Bilbo said, "boots and saddles."

Chapter 69

I followed Bilbo out the front door and through hot, damp twilight toward the garage. He jogged pretty spryly for a guy in his sixties. I kept up without huffing and puffing, the carbine muzzle down under my right arm, half expecting a muzzle-flash and a gunshot. Nothing. The prayer I breathed wasn't, *please get me out of this alive.* It was, *please don't let me wet my pants.*

Bilbo hustled into the garage through the service door, with me right behind him. I heard the sound of the garage door going up after he hit a switch, but no light came on. Feeling my way along the passenger side of his Yukon Denali with my left hand while I gripped the carbine with my right, I stumbled, fell to one knee, cussed, and pulled myself back up. I scraped the inside of one finger on something jagged in the rear door and cussed again. Trying to shake off the pain, I found my way to the front door and clambered into the front passenger seat.

Bilbo already had the engine going and both of our windows down.

"Adjust your seat to the rear as far as you can," he yelled as he accelerated backwards. "And slant the seatback."

No need to say it twice.

We came out of the garage fast, in a tire-squealing reverse that kicked crushed stone every which way. Spinning the steering wheel like an Indy veteran, Bilbo rocketed away from the lodge and onto the long, curving road to the gate in a jolting, bone-rattling rush. It was a narrow, tree-lined drive without much margin for error, but Bilbo had to be doing forty miles an hour. Haskel and Mary Barbara were waiting for us in the Escalade on the other side of the drive. They fell in behind us, driving at least fifteen miles an hour slower than we were.

Bilbo's head swiveled, scanning an arc from his left shoulder to his right. I didn't see anything but trees and rocks. By now we were thirty seconds or so into a drive that shouldn't last more than two minutes. *Maybe I'm overdoing the drama.*

No sooner had that thought teased me than Bilbo suddenly pulled the Colt from his hip with his right hand, holding the wheel with his left, yelling "Back! Sit back!" as he brought the weapon out. I pressed my spine as hard as I could against my seatback, dropping the rifle between my legs, as if my very soul hung in the balance. Bilbo straightened his arm and pointed the revolver directly at the window opening on my side, his knuckles less than six inches from my face.

He fired. I yelled, as much in surprise as in fear. A deafening roar split my eardrums. I reflexively squeezed my eyes shut at the yellow flash.

He fired again. He wasn't panic-shooting; he was firing deliberately and seemed to be aiming at something. This time I gasped instead of yelling. He squeezed off a third shot. Feeling the car swerve to the right, I forced my eyes open in time to see us bearing off the crushed rock, toward the mud and the trees.

"Road!" I screamed.

Bilbo jerked the steering wheel to the left, overcorrecting, but when all four tires found gravel again, he turned it more smoothly back to the right. The rich, sweet smell of burnt gunpowder filled the Deanli's front cabin. Bilbo lowered the Colt and laid it carefully in his lap. When he spoke, his voice was calm.

"Pop a couple of rounds out your window, just to give them something to think about."

Give WHO something to think about?

Propelled by adrenaline, I leaned forward, lifted the carbine's stock and pressed it against my left shoulder, pointing out the window. No way was I going to pump bullets blindly into the woods. The one thing I could see to my right was the muddy margin haloed by the Denali's strobe-like headlights beyond the west edge of the road. I aimed the carbine at that. Clicked the safety off and fired two shots. Didn't even notice the carbine's modest kick.

"Worm killers," I called to Bilbo.

"That's fine. Keeping their heads down is all we need to do."

Another thirty seconds, tops, and we'd be off Bilbo's property and onto the access road. *I'm pretty sure no one has shot at us yet.*

And just like that, from at least twenty feet into the woods on my side, three leaf-screened muzzle flashes suddenly lit up the gloaming just behind us. The bark of the guns cracked in my ears. I cringed back in my seat as far as I could go. I heard a couple of ugly *thonks* and felt the car shake.

Holy shit! For an instant my fury at getting shot at overwhelmed my fear of getting hit. I pulled myself forward with the childish idea of firing the carbine into the part of the woods now rapidly falling behind us.

"No!" Bilbo yelled. "Sit back! Hunker down! They're behind us now, and they shoot like Yankees anyhow!"

The last time Yankees did much shooting around here was during the Siege of Vicksburg in the Civil War, and they pretty much owned the place when the shooting was done. I knew what Bilbo meant, though, and I did exactly what he said. Closed my eyes and methodically counted off seconds in my head. By the time I reached twelve, we had screeched roughly onto the parish access road running past the lodge property, side-swiping both ends of a gate that hadn't opened fast enough to suit Bilbo when he'd pushed the remote clipped to his sun-visor. He made a tire-squealing left turn onto a public road, where I felt safe for the first time since I'd heard Haskel say "intruders."

Chapter 70

LEFT turn. Of course. If there's gunfire go to HQ, not Baton Rouge – whatever HQ was.

I brought my seatback closer to vertical and started fussing with the carbine. Clicked the safety back on. Popped the clip out. Muscled the bolt back to eject the cartridge already in the chamber. Found a place on the floor for the now unloaded weapon. Buckled my seat belt. With that there was nothing left for me to do but start thinking and feeling. Didn't care much for either.

I felt . . . *let down*. Sort of like post-coital, no-cuddle blahs after the kind of casual hook-up I'd outgrown around twenty. Action, excitement, danger and now – safety, security, *meh*.

But also . . . why was I getting an off-beat vibe from this thing? Why—

A buzz from Bilbo's phone put my thinking on hold. He jerked the phone from a clip near his right hip and handed it to me.

"Congressman Bilbo's phone," I said.

"Bax," Haskel's voice barked. "Status?"

"We're all clear. Shots fired. Couple of dings but no casualties that we know of. How about you."

"Clear and undamaged. Headed for HQ."

"They're safe," I told Bilbo, then swiveled the phone back up toward my mouth. "Would Mary Barbara like to talk to the Congressman?"

"Uh . . . she's driving . . . uh, yeah, here she is."

I handed the phone to Bilbo, whispering "Your wife."

"Y'all okay, then, dumplin' ?" he asked. After a ten second pause for her answer he continued. "Naw, we're all fine . . . . Not even a scratch. Little excitement is all. Looks to me like those boys were firin' with their heads down . . . . That's the problem with liberals. They don't know how to shoot . . . . No, Ms. Kendall is also just as fit as she can be. Gave as good as she got and not a squeal in the bargain . . . . Love you too. Can you put Bax back on?"

After a five second interval, Bilbo started talking again.

"Listen, Bax, call the sheriff, will ya? Give him an update, and make him promise to tell you what his deputies find on the grounds. Tell him the intruders were definitely armed and not shy about shooting, so have his boys be careful. . . . Yeah, we returned fire, but I don't think we got any of 'em . . . . Give him my number so he can call me later tonight if he has some questions. . . . Oh, almost forgot. Give Solly Eccles a head's up, willya? . . . . Real good. See you at HQ."

Back to thinking now, as we rolled through the inky night that had finally banished the twilight.

"Returned fire . . . ." No, actually we hadn't *returned* fire. We had *opened* fire. Semantics? Whomever Bilbo fired at was hostile enough to shoot back. And those muzzle flashes and gunshots sure weren't figments of my imagination. Good thing we were a moving target.

But why were we moving? Why the rush to evacuate? Why not just hunker down at the lodge with its military-grade arsenal and wait for the intruders, keeping track of them with Bilbo's world-class security system? Why not hold the fort while we waited half an hour for the deputies?

Had Bilbo panicked? Overreacted? But he hadn't shown any panic at all. Just the opposite. Cool as they come.

Why had Bilbo told Bax to notify someone named Solly Eccles? As discreetly as I could I pulled my phone out and Googled the name. "Did you mean *Solomon J. Eccles*?" Google asked. Well, let's say I did, just for fun. Three hits. Baseball player who'd spent a few seasons in the majors back in the '80's. Broker in Tampa who'd love for me to join his Linked-In group. And the owner of SJE News Service in Jackson, Mississippi – in other words, a stringer for the Associated Press and local newspapers.

As I clicked the off button on my phone, I noticed a smear of blood on my screen just before it went dark. Checked my left index finger, where I saw a pretty noticeable gash that was bleeding. I remembered the stumble I'd taken in the garage and cutting my finger on something jagged, like a hole, in the Denali's side. It wasn't a wound you'd go to the emergency room for, but it wasn't just a paper cut either. Now that I'd focused on the thing, it began to hurt. A lot. I wrapped my other hand around the fingers and pressed to try to stop the bleeding.

"By the way, little lady," Bilbo said as I put my phone away, "you did real good. *Real good.*"

"Thank you. What's 'HQ'?"

"Oh, that's headquarters for the bridges and highways subsidiary of the Bilbo family business," he said. "It's in Ville Fleuve."

"Mmmm," I said.

Ville Fleuve. Wow. That's awfully convenient to Vicksburg, Mississippi, where the President of the United States would be making a speech tomorrow.

Chapter 71

I found pretty much what I expected when we rendezvoused almost an hour later in the main parking lot at Bilbo Infrastructure Industries, Inc. – BI3, according to the black-on-red sign over its front door. The fence Mary Barbara and Haskel had crashed through had done a real number on the Escalade's front, but Bilbo told her not to worry, he'd buy her another one twice as good. Hugs, congratulations, giddy laughter, and basking in the glow of coming unscathed through gunfire. Bilbo lauded me like he was bucking for the Pulitzer Prize for Fiction: "Didn't flinch." "Didn't bat an eye." "Steady as Stonewall Jackson at Manassas."

I quietly examined the passenger side of Bilbo's Denali. Three holes, unevenly spaced, all well behind the front passenger door. They looked identical, but I had clearly cut my finger on one of them because I couldn't see anything else that looked like it would do the job. And I'd cut it *before* we'd left the lodge, which meant that the shots fired during our hell-for-leather drive just now didn't explain it. How did the bullet hole I'd cut my finger on get there? More important, why? Had Bilbo fired a shot into the Denali before he'd even gotten to the lodge, ensuring at least one battle scar if gunfire from the woods completely missed? Was that why the garage light was turned off – so anyone who came into the garage with him wouldn't notice the hole that was already there?

No other answers worked for me but 'yes' two times. A realization burst in my head like a high-powered camera flash: *the whole thing had been a fake attack.* Bilbo had made a desperation move so he could pose once again as a Hollywood hero, keeping his head in a crisis and saving a damsel in distress while he was at it. He'd summoned me down here, rather than just talking to me in his D.C. office, because he wanted an independent witness to verify the shooting.

The pieces fell into place for me even as Bilbo, Haskel, and Mary Barbara continued talking nearby.

Bilbo hadn't been aiming at anyone with his Colt. He'd fired those three shots as a signal to people already in place to get ready to fire their own carefully misplaced shots. No wonder he'd so easily managed his calm and commanding pose. He'd scripted the whole thing ahead of time, and just like with Slow Willie Woodbine, he'd never been in the slightest danger. Our wild ride was the live-fire equivalent of a professional wrestling match.

With a few location hints from Bilbo, deputies would eventually find ejected shell casings in the area the shots came from. Solly Eccles would hustle up here to get the story and pass on Bilbo's spin practically verbatim. He'd take pictures of the bullet holes. Every media outlet in the country would pick up the story. The big boys would rush in. They wouldn't roll over as easily as Eccles, but everyone who'd actually been there would back up Bilbo's version.

Wouldn't we?

Mary Barbara sidled over to me.

"I'm sorry, but we don't have a home here," she said. "Chad just sleeps in his office when he has to be on site for several days."

She was serious. She was apologizing because the Bilbos didn't have a fourth home to go along with the lodge and the ones in Baton Rouge and D.C.

"No problem. It's not your fault that some bad guys messed things up."

"Bax has been his usual efficient self," she said. "Most places anywhere near here are sold out, but he found a room at a Motel Six. I'm sure you're used to plusher accommodations, but –"

"Not at all," I said. "A bed and indoor plumbing are all I need."

"Once Chad gets through with him, Bax can drive you there in the Escalade. Your suitcase is still in the car, so at least that part works out."

Warm smile, mini-hug, and then she politely pattered away when I said I'd better call my husband. My phone showed that I'd missed three calls from Rafe. I put about twenty feet between myself and the Bilbo cluster. I figured Rafe would understand the delay in hearing from me: clinical shock is a pretty good excuse.

"What in the living *hell* is going down out there, woman?" That was Rafe's idea of 'Hello.' "CNN crawls say 'reports of intruders spotted at Congressman Bilbo's hunting lodge, and the congressman is believed to be safe.'"

"He's safe and so am I. I know you have media friends who require care and feeding, but for now, don't get out in front of this story, okay?"

"You got it," he said. No argument, no push-back, no questions. My guy is a jewel.

"And please have Phoebe give me a call ASAP."

"I'm to have her call you, so if someone looks at your phone it will show that Phoebe initiated the contact."

"Bingo," I said.

"What should I tell her you want to talk to her about?"

"The same fake news we've just talked about.'"

We signed off with declarations of fervent love. Phoebe called me three minutes later.

"What's up?" she asked.

"If you haven't heard it yet, there's breaking news about intruders on the grounds of Congressman Bilbo's hunting lodge. All hell is going to break loose on that by tomorrow morning. I'd advise CNN not to commit to anything too soon. Report all the accounts you want to, but throw in 'unconfirmed' and 'not yet corroborated' every chance you get."

"And why is that?" Phoebe asked.

"Because the reports you'll get will be unconfirmed and not yet corroborated. And because, off the record – repeat, off the record – it's a hundred to one those reports are unmitigated bullshit."

"Gotcha. I hate unmitigated bullshit. It's even worse than the mitigated variety. Anything else?"

"Sure," I said. "Let's just talk for a few more minutes. Anything you like, as long as it eats up some time. Recite the Gettysburg Address if you want to."

"That's a cliché," she said. "Let's go with Lincoln's Second Inaugural: 'Both read the same Bible and pray to the same God; and each invokes His aid against the other. It may seem strange that any men should dare to ask a just God's assistance in wringing their bread from the sweat of other men's faces; but let us judge not that we be not judged. . . . '"

I gaped at my phone as she continued.

"That's very impressive, Phoebe, but Frauen Congressperson Mary Barbara just handed her fob to Haskel, so I won't be on much longer."

"' . . . gives to both North and South this terrible war, as the woe due to those by whom the offence came . . . .'"

"He's about four healthy strides from me, so, you know, gotta go."

"' . . . every drop of blood drawn with the lash, shall be paid by another, drawn with the sword . . . .'"

"Profuse gratitude, Phoebe, but I'm signing off."

Chapter 72

About 20 minutes into my ride with Haskel I glanced over at him. I was ninety percent sure that he didn't know the attack was fake, and I'd call it a hard ninety. If it's loyalty versus honor with a guy like Haskel, honor wins.

"I'm assuming you know that Congressman Bilbo's Warrior Princess stuff was nonsense," I said.

"I figured it for gallant exaggeration." Haskel didn't take his eyes off the road. He didn't crack a smile, either.

"I screamed," I said. "I squealed. I was good and scared. I fired the carbine, but not at anyone who could shoot back. Not like some Hollywood heroine who's brave because a script says so."

"The important thing is that you got through it in one piece."

Wariness emanated from Haskel like heat from asphalt in August. Wariness of me. He'd read the Bible long before *The Federalist Papers*. To him, I wasn't just Josie Kendall. I might be Jezebel. Delilah. Bathsheba. Bearer of the insidious feminine power that saps a warrior's strength. His mother had probably warned him about women like me when he'd headed off to college with that ROTC scholarship, and a girl he was sweet on back home probably prayed every night that the likes of me wouldn't lure him away from her.

I let things sit there for a few minutes. Didn't want to rush this. Subtle, that's Josie. When I saw the Motel 6 sign, maybe half a mile away, I spoke again.

"There's something Congressman Bilbo needs to know."

"What's that?"

"Do you know who Phoebe Riverdale is?"

"I sure do," he said sharply. "She's the bi— uh, the *reporter* who smeared the congressman over the Willy Woodbine shooting."

"She called me tonight, sniffing around for something, and digging hard for an inside scoop."

"Like what?"

"From what she asked, I'd say she's wondering if tonight's whole attack was staged. A charade to pump up the macho vote."

"That's bull— uh, baloney." Second time in the conversation he'd charmingly self-censored to avoid vulgarities in my vicinity.

"I was there and I heard the shots," I said with deliberate ambiguity. "But she didn't dream that angle up all by herself. If she's asking about it this early in the game, someone started shopping the idea around as soon as the first scanner picked up a police band call with 'Bilbo lodge' in it. Anyway, I thought I'd better tell you in case you feel the congressman should know."

Knitted brow, twisted frown, options being tracked down a decision tree in his glass head. Abruptly, he pulled onto the verge of the frontage road we'd reached. In another ninety seconds, tops, he could have gotten us parked in front of the Motel 6 entrance. But he had 'THIS IS NO DRILL!' blaring in his brain.

"I hate to ask you this," he said, "but would you please just step outside and wait while I phone Congressman Bilbo?"

"You got it."

I felt my way gingerly out the passenger side door, hanging onto the handle to keep from slipping on the muddy gravel covering the slight incline on the Escalade's right. As soon as I had my footing, I walked carefully to the front of the SUV, so that he could see me through the windshield. Then I put a good twenty feet between its grill and my shameless self. I kept my back toward him. *All secure, congressman. She can't even read my lips.*

I only had to stand there a minute or so. When I heard the driver side window schussing smoothly down, I didn't even have to wait for the polite little beep on his horn to know he was about to make me part of the conversation.

"The congressman wants to talk to you," Haskel said, proffering his phone out the window.

I walked over to the opened window and took Haskel's phone.

"What can I do for you, congressman?" I asked.

"Exactly what did that pervert whore want to know?"

"Whether I actually heard the shots. I said for sure I had. That was after she'd asked me for a quick version of how it all went down. Then she asked whether I'd heard the shots hit the car, and I said I absolutely had. Then she started going off on why did I think everyone had hightailed it from the lodge instead of just lockin', loadin', and waitin' for the police. I said I didn't think much about it one way or another. First off, I was pretty scared myself. And second, I don't get paid for tactical opinions."

"Anything else?" Only a hint of agitation infected his voice.

"Not that she asked me," I said. "But I asked her where all this stuff was coming from. She said, 'A source.'"

Pause. *Three . . . four . . . five.*

"You sure about that?" Bilbo demanded then. "Not '*sources*' but '*a source*'?"

"Yessir, I sure am."

"Now isn't that interesting?" he muttered.

"Congressman," I said, "if you need to meet with your brain trust, don't worry about me. We're within sight of the motel. Just have Bax drop me off and then he can go wherever you need him."

"You are a pearl of great price," Bilbo said. "Your value is greater than rubies. And Ruby don't come cheap." I smiled gamely through the dirty-old-man cackle that followed. "But if you don't mind, I think I'd like you to drive back with Bax. My first string needs to hear your critical information first hand."

Gulp. I did *not* want to spend the rest of the night saying, 'Don't shoot the messenger.'

My left foot twitched. I was leaning, itching to take off, like a runner on first base about to break for second. I didn't have to do what Bilbo asked. *Thank you for your kind invitation, but I regret that I will be otherwise engaged for the remainder of the evening.* I didn't think he'd force the issue. I was a key witness for him, and if I insisted, it wouldn't make sense for him to alienate me by having Haskel drive me back to BI3 against my will instead of dropping me at the hotel. But I made a different choice.

"Well sure, Congressman, if you need me there I'll be happy to come."

Chapter 73

I hadn't suffered a sudden attack of idealism. The country wouldn't be much better or much worse off if Louisiana's seventh congressional district were represented by Chad Bilbo or Letitia Dejean or someone else. True, Chad Bilbo dead would be a marked improvement over Chad Bilbo alive, but that wouldn't spill many cornflakes on my breakfast table either way.

Near the end of my chat with Bilbo, though, I knew that I had to say yes, even though at that instant I couldn't have said why. It took a good five minutes after I climbed back into the Escalade beside Haskel for the kaleidoscopic profusion of chaotic thought in my head to click into a coherent insight about the mystery acronym 'VIMNAPA' from Hank's triple-encrypted notes. Ville Neuve being convenient to Vicksburg. Bilbo's crack about our supposed attackers shooting like Yankees. Siege of Vicksburg during the Civil War. Bits and pieces of 'If You Shoot at the King.' Trump campaign appearance at 'the Vicksburg Battlefield Site.'

There wasn't any such place as 'the Vicksburg Battlefield Site.' The opposing armies had fought battles all over the place, but Vicksburg was a seven-week siege, not a discrete, set-piece battle. The historic site was 'Vicksburg Military National Park – 'VMNP' for normal people, but that could very easily have become 'VIMNAPA' in the hands of Washington image-makers, who like to shoehorn vowels into acronyms so that they can be pronounced like words.

Vicksburg Military National Park is a memorial stretching twenty miles along the Mississippi, tracing the siege line and encampments, with monuments to the regiments involved on both sides. The Union Army identified regiments by state. Wisconsin, Illinois, Michigan, and West Virginia, for example.

Holy fucking shit! I damn near said that out loud. My gut twisted. Bile rose in my throat. I felt a fierce combination of horror and disgust distort my face. I remembered that split-second back in October, 2018 when I'd thought I'd seen Kappa's face in my own reflection. I felt like I was two fingers from vomiting.

President Trump would appear tomorrow at Vicksburg Military National Park, near the memorial for one of those four Union states, and when he did something awful was going to happen. A near miss by a sniper wouldn't be dramatic enough. The *modus operandi* for the fake assassination attempt would have to be more telegenic, generating impressive visuals. More important, even though it wouldn't kill the president, the whole point would be maximum media impact that would provoke national outrage and fury. That meant it would have to kill innocent Americans. Maybe dozens, maybe hundreds.

It would be classic confected news: an event staged for the sole purpose of being reported on. But if I were right, it would be confected news with a body count and flags at half-staff when it was over. It wouldn't be my doing, but I couldn't let myself completely off the hook, either. One of the reasons someone thought he could make a trick like that work was that D.C. hustlers like me had been ginning up confected news for quite a while now. I could just possibly do something about the plan that nobody else could. Maybe pick up some careless comment, some detail, that would get my theory down from a thirty-thousand-foot view to treetop level.

It was a long shot for sure. The alternative, though, was to curl up in a Motel 6 bed and pray that somehow there'd be no victims tomorrow or, if there were, that they'd die quickly and without too much pain. I'm not sure when it happened, exactly, but somewhere along the way I'd reached a point where that would take more swallowing than I could manage.

Okay, Josie, enough with the navel-gazing. Show time, starting with a stab at divide and conquer.

I held out my hand to show Haskel the nasty gash on my finger. It wasn't bleeding anymore, but the dried and smeared blood that I hadn't cleaned up yet made it look pretty ugly.

"Could you stop at the Rite-Aid in that strip mall at the next light so that I can get a bandage for this?" I asked.

Instead of shifting to the right lane for a turn, he reached under his seat and pulled out a hard-plastic white case with a muscular red cross embossed on its front.

"Should be tweezers in there to pluck out any foreign matter, plus disinfectant and bandages," he said. "Yell if you need help."

"Thanks."

Guess that's one more for the 'nice try' file. I found what he'd said I'd find. There was only one bandage, but that's all I needed. Although a single bandage in such a serious first-aid kit seemed odd, I was too busy wiping dried blood off my finger to think much about it. Rubbing the cut made it bleed again, so I swabbed it with a cotton ball, sprayed the cut with a stinging mist from a small plastic container, and finally bandaged the wound.

Something teased my brain, as one loose idea cascaded over another in seemingly random fashion. Maybe with a little patience I'd find some kind of pattern to them. Right now, though, it was just free association.

We drove in silence the rest of the way, making it back to BI3 in about fifteen more minutes. The first thing I saw in the parking lot was a black Lexus SUV that hadn't been there when we'd left. Whoever belonged to it was out of sight.

I thought of Kappa. Inferences from the files I'd teased out of Hank Sinclair made Kappa the subject of naughty-narc snitches by Slow Willie Woodbine. *That* made Kappa the principal beneficiary of Slow Willie's murder by Bilbo. If I assumed that confidential pro-Kappa noises by Bilbo were what got CI stamped on Kappa's DEA file (after all, who else would be carrying water for a dirty narc?), that meant that Kappa had probably worked with Bilbo to set Slow Willie up. If Kappa was in bed with Bilbo on the Slow Willie murder, he was a much more plausible source than Card for the trigger men Bilbo had used for the fake *bang-bang* stuff at the lodge tonight.

I didn't like the idea of Kappa joining our party at all. *Well, other people in the world drive black Lexus SUVs.* I prayed that someone not named Kappa was driving this one.

Bilbo stepped forward as Haskel and I climbed out of the Escalade.

"Nice work, boy," Bilbo said, clapping Haskel on his left bicep. "Welcome to you, too, little lady. I appreciate your accommodating us."

"Happy to be of service, Congressman."

"Now let's get inside and get to work," Bilbo said.

Kappa was waiting for us in the lobby. I recognized Tug and his playmate from my alley encounter in Baton Rouge as the two guys flanking him. In Tug's eyes I saw again the eerie true-believer glint I'd picked up before. I shivered. Give me a pure mercenary like Kappa any day, someone who's just in it for the money.

"Tug and Pug, you two stay here and watch the door," Kappa said.

Bilbo led us through a door to the right, down a hallway, and into a brightly lit, windowless conference room. We sat down around an oval table, with Bilbo between Kappa and Haskel on one side of the table and me on the other side, facing them.

"If you don't mind, Ms. Kendall," Bilbo said, "would you just run over for all three of us the conversation you had with Phoebe Whatsername?"

"Sure. Phoebe Riverdale at CNN. I've worked with her before. She called me at –"

"So she called you?" Kappa demanded.

"She did." I pulled out my phone and pulled up Recent Calls. "It was 10:48."

"Mind if I take a look at that?" Kappa asked.

"Go ahead. Her call is the most recent one listed." Standing up, I leaned over to hand the phone to him.

"So the two of you talked, it looks like, for something like four minutes?"

"I wasn't timing it, but that sounds about right," I said.

"Okay, then," Bilbo said after a glance at Kappa that seemed to ask, *anything else?* "Why don't you just recap what you told me about that phone conversation one more time?"

I repeated what I'd already told Bilbo, not quite word for word but without any substantive difference. Bilbo nodded thoughtfully. Kappa nodded skeptically. Haskel sat poker faced.

"And that's all you said to her?" Kappa asked.

"That's it. I mean, the congressman saved my life and there wasn't much else to say. Apparently, I wasn't telling her what she wanted to hear, but that was her problem."

Bilbo beamed. Kappa smiled knowingly.

"And you're sure she said '*a* source'?" Kappa asked.

"Absolutely. I get paid to talk to reporters."

Bilbo and Kappa looked at each other. I'd seen both looks in half a dozen campaigns and I read them like a book. Bilbo's said, *one anonymous source isn't enough for a story; you need two.* Kappa's said, *I wonder if we have a mole.*

"All right, then," Bilbo said, "Air Force One won't land in New Orleans until eleven o'clock tomorrow morning, and Trump will spend some time pressing flesh there before he choppers to Vicksburg. That gives us a decent window. I figure if we do a presser here around ten we can chase Miss Phoebe back into her hole and be sharing bloody marys before CNN gets its head out of its ass."

"I get that," I said. "Most of the media won't show up for us because they'll be focused on the president's arrival, but whoever comes will be first out of the gate with the story. You'll control the initial narrative. When other media want to play catch-up you can just refer them to your remarks at the press conference."

"*Our* remarks," he said with a wicked grin. "We'll have you, Mary Barbara, and Bax all make statements, along with mine, then I'll handle any questions."

What could possibly go wrong?

No matter. Our next agenda item had just become prepping for a press conference. That's at the heart of my skill set, moving me suddenly from dubious status at this meeting to key player.

I jumped in with both feet. There's only so much you can do with an uncoachable egomaniac, but things went well enough for me to think, *Phillipe Reines can kiss my Creole ass* as I drifted off to sleep an hour later on a couch in the executive lounge. Before lying down, though, and once I was sure I had the room to myself, I texted Rafe: "'Shoot/King' = Vburg 2mrrow. Phone off til further notice." As soon as I'd sent the text, I deleted it.

Chapter 74

"Finally," Bilbo said in a tinny, amplified voice around 10:20 the following morning, "I was advised by Sheriff Antoine a few minutes before we started that his deputies found, I believe, three, or perhaps four shell casings in a wooded area just west of the lodge road. They were 7.62 millimeters. I am sure I don't need to remind most of you that 7.62 is a standard caliber for the most common version of the Kalashnikov assault rifle."

Right. Because how could terrorists possibly get their hands on firearms in Louisiana without importing Russian weapons?

Scrub your mental image of "press conference." We were standing outdoors, in front of the main entrance to BI3. Bilbo was speaking over a cheesy little portable PA system that might have been used to announce the three-legged races at a Rotarian picnic. Haskel, Mary Barbara, and I had gathered in an awkward semicircle behind The Man. Eight reporters, mostly print but one guy holding a shoulder-mounted camera with TV station call letters on it, stood in a restless, slightly curved line ten feet or so in front of the microphone.

I will *not* take the rap for this lameburger. Or the credit, depending on how you're scoring. I had told Bilbo to meet the press in a BI3 conference room.

"That would be *way* too crowded, little lady."

"Crowded is *good*, Congressman. You *want* them cheek by jowl."

He had just smiled condescendingly and shaken his head. So here we were, with media attention slightly greater than you'd get for a mall opening and Bilbo trying to hide his disappointment. I kept my statement short and sweet: I'd heard shots, I'd felt something hit the Denali, I'd been scared out of my wits, I'd seen the congressman shoot, and I'd thanked the Lord for getting me through it alive. Then I faded gratefully into the background.

When the questions started, I shifted my focus to a black limo turning onto BI3 Drive with a small American flag on the driver-side fender-mast. The blue pennant on the passenger side mast might have sported a presidential seal, but I couldn't tell from sixty feet away. Wouldn't have meant much anyway. A single limo out in the middle of nowhere does *not* have the president in it.

I blinked. One of the reporters was apparently asking *me* a question.

"One more time on that one, darlin'," I called as I stepped toward the mic.

"Did you actually see any shooters during your escape?"

The question came from a male reporter whom I didn't recognize, which probably meant he didn't work in D.C. Interesting that someone outside the Beltway was already tip-toeing into *did-this-really-happen?* territory.

"No," I replied. "I was real busy keeping my head down. All I saw was trees and darkness. I did see muzzle flashes."

"Are you sure they were muzzle flashes? Could they have been, maybe, fire crackers or flashlights or something?"

"Honey, I grew up in Louisiana. I own a gun and I know how to shoot it. I know what muzzle flashes look like. What I saw were muzzle flashes."

Muzzle flashes from rifles fired by a couple of Kappa's rent-a-goons, deliberately aiming to hit the car but not the people in it? I was just about certain of that by now. Bilbo and Kappa had a violent-crime track record, and you don't find rent-a-goons by looking in the Yellow Pages under R. I didn't say that to the reporter, of course. I kept it to what I'd actually seen and heard, and left out what I'd figured out after the fact.

There were no more questions for me. Good thing, because the limo had now parked and the respite gave me a chance to watch Hank Sinclair climb out of it.

He took about five steps toward our group and stopped. I raised my eyebrows at him. He nodded minimally. I slipped away from the Bilbo group and strolled toward Hank. I caught Bax Haskel's eye and tilted my head toward the limo, hinting that he should follow me. A bit tentatively at first, Haskel started walking toward Hank as well, though he didn't seem to have any idea who he was. When we reached Hank, I introduced them.

"Courtesy of the White House," Hank said, gesturing toward the limo. "A ride to this afternoon's event in Vicksburg for Congressman Bilbo. Security will be super-tight and private car traffic will be chock-a-block."

I tried to send Haskel an urgent telepathic message: *Beware of geeks bearing gifts.*

Predictably, it didn't work. Haskel nodded vigorously as a mile-wide beam split his lips.

"No hurry," Hank told Haskel. "But as soon as the newsies get through with the congressman, you might want to bring him on over here."

"Sure," Haskel said. "And Ms. Bilbo too?"

"Uh, actually, no on that one," Hank said. "No family or aides. Not even I get to join the trip to Vicksburg in this limo. If you'll get me the fob for the Congressman's Denali, in fact, I'll drive over in it. That way, I'll have his suitcase and computer right there for him so we can get him on Marine One with them."

For some reason I couldn't put my finger on, Hank tooling around in the Denali gave me a bad feeling.

"I imagine the cops investigating the lodge shooting will want to have a look at the Bilbomobile," I said. "What with the bullet holes and all."

"They can have it as soon as Marine One lifts off," Hank said, with his patented smirk.

Haskel nodded again before scurrying away. He'd apparently bought Hank's patter.

"So what's really going on, Hank?" I asked him quietly.

"Bilbo has to get out of the race. On top of everything else, this 'terrorist attack' at the lodge stinks out loud. Phoebe Riverdale is already tearing into it. My guess is that it totally falls apart by Monday."

"Seems like an incredible risk for Bilbo to take when he had all the analytics in his favor," I mused out loud. I was teasing, but with a straight face.

"Analytics are bullshit." Hank shook his head disgustedly. "Word is Bilbo paid north of eighty thousand dollars for a poll. A real one. Old school, shoe-leather, knocking on doors to crosscheck what the phone polling turned up. Those numbers show him in serious trouble. Also, the special prosecutor on the Slow Willy Woodbine thing can't close the deal, but he has his teeth in the bird and he won't let go. The fake attack last night was a Hail Mary pass from eight yards deep in his end zone."

"I see." I glanced over at the presser, still going strong. "So how does the limo ride fit into it?"

"Buys you a good long time to talk him out of the race."

"Me? How in the world do you expect me to bring that off?"

"I'll leave that up to you," he said. "All you need to know is this: if he has bought into the graceful-exit scenario when I see him in Vicksburg, then you can ride Marine One from Vicksburg to New Orleans, and Air Force One from New Orleans to D.C. That's a long flight, and there are a couple of people it would be in your long-term interest to talk to on the way."

I'm not Bax Haskel. I did *not* buy it. I was the second person Hank had offered the same presidential perk to in five minutes, and that was one too many.

But that didn't matter. Not quite two years ago, a big-time false flag operation had fallen apart while I was in the neighborhood. Kappa figured to hold a grudge. Bilbo still needed me, and Kappa didn't. For the next several hours, the safest place in the world for me would be within three feet of Chad Bilbo.

Plus, a bunch of synapses were making another slow-motion connection in my brain.

Chapter 75

I found the limo's first-aid kit in the trunk when I swung my suitcase into it. The limo driver apparently saw me in the sideview mirror as I wheeled the thing up, and popped the trunk for me. If he'd hopped out himself to throw it in I might have avoided a lot of aggravation. But he didn't.

Magnets clamped the white kit to a sidewall of the trunk's passenger side. I opened it long enough to take out a handful of bandages. A handful – the quantity you'd expect in a first-aid kit. Then I climbed into the ample rear seat to update Rafe while I waited for Bilbo. Before I could dial Rafe, though, my phone chirped with a call from Seamus.

"What's up, chief?"

"Josie," he said in a voice without a drop of his characteristic warmth and humor, "I have a question you can answer yes or no. Are you planning on meeting up with Calvin Kirby while you're down there?"

"No." Pause. "Where did that come from?"

"It's just that he's down there in his souped-up Kirby Enterprises helicopter with its checkered-flag paint job, and *you're* down there, and he thinks you're the greatest thing since sliced bread, and . . . ."

"Seamus," I said, in a hybrid patient/exasperated voice that I might use with a four-year-old, "*I'm* down here because *you* sent me."

"I know, I know. But you're so good you might have manipulated me into sending you without my realizing what was happening. Anyway, Kirby is a huge client, and if you took him away to start your own shop . . . . I guess I'm paranoid."

"No – repeat – no, Seamus. I'm not down here to meet with Calvin Kirby, or any other Kirby."

"Thank you. I'm sorry, Josie, it's just . . . . ."

"Wait a minute," I said as my brain unfroze. "There has to be something else that triggered you on this. You're a world-class worry wart, but you're too smart to go nuts just because I'm in the same time zone as Calvin Kirby's helicopter."

Probably five seconds passed, but it seemed like five minutes. It was irritating at my end and, as far as I could tell, agonizing at Seamus's. Finally words cane out of his mouth, accompanied by a huge sigh.

"Okay. Okay. I got a call from junior, what's-his-name, Alan Kirby. He said he'd tried to call you late last night, but you weren't answering your phone."

"Yeah, I had my phone turned off from just before I went to sleep last night. I've been in unfriendly company for over twelve hours."

"Fine," Seamus said. "Anyway, he said he had to reach this Card character. Urgent."

"Did he say why?"

"Very cryptic. Something about he'd heard that Card's car had been stolen. I mean, you can see why I thought it had to be some kind of code, right?"

"The son of one of the richest and most politically savvy men in the country is jumping through hoops over a pusher's pimpmobile?" I demanded. "I have no idea what that could be code for, but taking it literally doesn't make much sense either."

Actually, it might make sense. If the Kirbys financed Bedford, as I'd begun to suspect, that would put Card in their orbit, because he was a Bedford silent partner. That would put them within three degrees of a mobster, which they themselves had said should be expected of any major politician, and it would fit in with their conviction that narcotics laws are idiotic public policy.

"I'm just telling you what the man said."

"I'll see what I can do."

Ending the call, I quickly found what had to be Alan Kirby's call on my phone's memory and called him back. He answered himself, on the first ring. I could hear chopper noise in the background.

"Josie Kendall," I said. "I understand you're trying to get in touch with a Baton Rouge badass who goes by Card."

"Thanks for calling back," he said in a bright, sunny voice. "I reached him by another route a good four hours ago. Everything is under control. Appreciate your willingness to help."

"Give my best to your dad," I said, a little deflated because I'd kind of hoped that Alan

269

might shed a little light on why any Kirby gave two raps about Card's wheels, and Alan's quick dismissal nixed that hope.

"Always. Later."

I dialed Rafe.

"How are things in D.C.?" I asked when he picked up.

"No worse than usual when I left," he said.

"When you left? Where are you going?"

"I landed in Baton Rouge two hours ago. Your Uncle Darius picked me up and we have been on the road to Vicksburg ever since."

"To rescue me?" I demanded. "You mean I get to be a damsel in distress two days in a row?"

"Theo called me at four o'clock this morning. Word got out that the Secret Service is flying reinforcements in for the president's Vicksburg jaunt. Top gun crew. Not planned in advance and not the usual protocol."

"So maybe 'If You Shoot at the King' has gotten through to someone," I said. "But I'd feel better if you were moving away from Vicksburg instead of toward it."

"'Ride to the sound of the guns,'" he said. "Where are *you* right now?"

I gave him a rundown on the latest itinerary. I had to cut it short when I noticed Haskel and Bilbo approaching the limo.

"You take good care of Mary Barbara, now," Bilbo said to Haskel as he hung his suit coat on a hook and slipped into the rear seat. "And make sure that turd-blossom Sinclair gets my bag and computer onto Marine One like he said he would."

"Yessir, Congressman," Haskel said. He stepped away as the limo started to roll.

I waited until we were about three minutes into the ride with the A/C humming along before I started on Bilbo.

"First thing this morning I contacted the Dejean campaign about the topic we discussed at the lodge," I said. "I asked for a meeting."

"You get one?"

"Nope. GG Mason said, 'Don't bother. Waste of our time and your breath.' Direct quote. Then he said they'd spent every penny they had left on a top-drawer poll. Claimed that poll shows they have it in the bag – even with a big ad buy for one of the fringe candidates."

I could tell that hit him in the gut. I'd just fed him imaginary poll results from the Dejean camp that tracked the results his own campaign's real poll had turned up. The shrug he gave me was apparently his idea of a quick recovery.

"We know from 2016 how good polls are."

"There are polls and then there are *polls*," I replied. "Sixteen guys in Orem, Utah calling random telephone numbers spit out by a computer for a given area code then, yeah, half the time you get crap. But this poll was apparently several steps above that. At least that's what Dejean's donors think. Heavy hitters are buying in again."

I braced myself for a rage fest, but didn't get one. Bilbo just settled into the far corner of his seat with a thoughtful scowl decorating his face. I tore the paper wrapping off one of the bandages I had cadged from the first aid kit. Then I peeled away the slick tabs protecting its ends and wrapped it around the tip of my right index finger. Picked up a second bandage and started on that one.

"Any chance of that special prosecutor finally letting go before the primary?" I asked innocently, as I began to apply the second bandage to the tip of my middle finger. "Might help if the Slow Willie mess came off the table."

Bilbo shook his head disgustedly.

"You pay a lawyer humpty hundred dollars an hour with taxpayer money and tell him he can take as long as he wants to, no hurry, just send us your bill every month and we'll pay it. No way *anything* is gonna happen fast."

"Bummer," I said as I finished bandaging my third finger-tip.

Now he looked at me.

"What in the Sam Hill are you doin'?" he demanded.

"An experiment. Someone told me you could bandage the tips of your thumb and all four fingers on one hand without losing any manual dexterity. You could still cook, or iron, or play the guitar. Even put a latex glove on and fire a handgun. Thought I'd give it a try and see if they're right. You know, just to pass the time."

Full scowl. Not thoughtful this time. Angry.

"Listen," he said in a voice that would have chilled a coffin plate, "if you're tryin' to get at somethin', why don't you just say it plain?"

"Okay." I looked directly at him. Full eye contact. "I make a nice living selling my political judgment. Here's a free sample. You should haul your ass out of the race for re-election to Congress. There are some folks willing to arrange a graceful exit for you – a nice little glide path instead of the crash and burn you're heading into right now."

I held my right hand up, palm out, with the tips of all five digits taped.

Bilbo's face turned red. Real red, and real fast.

"Are you threatening me?" he demanded.

"If I ever threaten you, Congressman, you won't have to ask. You'll know."

Silence for three beats. Then words started spewing from his mouth in a torrent you could have gone white-water rafting on.

"I have never run away from a fight in my life! I know some things about *Doctor* Letitia Dejean that will definitely interest CD-seven voters – and you can bet your sassy ass they're going to hear those things."

"I'll take that as a 'no' on the graceful exit thing," I said.

"Not only no but hell no! And so help me God, little lady, if you start sniffing around that special prosecutor with any half-assed speculation, then you're gonna get your tits caught in a one-way ratchet."

"See, Congressman, that's just what I was talking about. You're threatening me. I don't have to ask *if* you're threatening me. You are. Plain as day. Also, 'one-way ratchet' is redundant."

Theory confirmed. No way my bandage stunt would have triggered this kind of rage and threats from Bilbo unless he knew what I was implying: that he'd bandaged his fingertips to eliminate any risk of his own prints showing up on the inside of a latex glove when he fired the Walther at his garage joist to get gunpowder residue on that glove. And I'll give you a hundred to one odds that the only way he would have picked up that implication was if it were true.

Folding his arms across his chest, he pushed his body as far away from mine on the limo's leather seat as it could get. A Potemkin tough guy: swaggering, macho front with nothing but a pitiful *poseur* behind it. We lapsed into icy silence. Fine with me.

About ten minutes later, the driver's voice, distorted by amplification, came over the speaker from the front seat.

"Just a head's up. Traffic gets real heavy in about three miles, so they're sending a motorcycle escort for us. We'll pull into the first weigh station on the Mississippi side to wait for it."

My eyes shot wide open. *That* didn't pass the smell test. Couldn't imagine any way Bilbo could have signaled the limo driver after my demonstration – but that wouldn't be much consolation if I suddenly had to remember how to make a perfect Act of Contrition.

Bilbo turned a triumphant leer toward me. It took every ounce of nerve I could muster to keep raw fear from flooding my face.

"Guess there's *someone* pretty high up who doesn't think I'm toast yet," he said smugly.

Sweet Mother of Mercy! He really thinks we're going to cool our heels until a couple of Mississippi highway patrolmen tool up to validate his importance by escorting us the rest of the way to Vicksburg! Terrifying thought: this guy who helps set my tax rates is an idiot. Comforting thought: this stop can't be something he set up to silence me. *So what the hell is it?*

I felt the limo moving smoothly to the right, toward an exit. Looking out my window, I could make out a sign ahead:

WEIGH STATION CLOSED
PROCEED TO NEXT STATION

But the barrier arm at the highway end of the exit was raised, as it would be if the station were open. How had *that* happened?

The limo rolled past the raised barrier arm and along the exit ramp. It pulled to a gentle stop directly in front of a squat, rectangular building where attendants would have been working if the weigh station had been open. The driver's voice came over the speaker again.

"We have about a fifteen-minute wait. Boss won't let me keep the A/C on that long with the engine idling. They told me that they've electronically opened the building, though, and it has an air conditioner, so we can wait in there."

Engine off. A/C off. The driver stepped out of the limo. Sweat was already popping out on Bilbo's forehead. Mine too, presumably, but I didn't have a vote. As soon as the driver opened Bilbo's door for him, he bolted out.

I don't think Bilbo even looked at the driver as he quick-stepped around the back of the limo toward the long, low brick building. I looked at him, though. Opened my door, climbed out of the back seat, and stared at the driver through the heat-waves shimmering from the limo's roof. Vernon Czlewski winked at me.

Chapter 76

A nanosecond after Vernon's wink, my fast-but-not-deep brain flashed on an ugly truth. Kappa had laid a trap and I'd walked right into it. Hadn't figured out the details yet, but I knew the bottom line: no one who'd driven off in that limo was supposed to come out of this alive.

Option one was to run like a rabbit and take my chances on foot. That was out. First, no one will ever confuse me with Jack Reacher. Second, I'd decided the night before to do whatever I could to stop a fake attempted presidential assassination – and running away wouldn't stop anything. That left making it up as I went along – not a first for me.

I fell into step with Vernon, about ten feet behind Bilbo. .

"You don't want to be doing that shit up there any favors," I said, nodding in Bilbo's direction.

"What I have in mind for him won't pass for a favor," he muttered.

"You're handing him the gift of martyrdom," I said, keeping my voice low. "If you shoot him, he'll be dead in five seconds. He deserves to die by inches, over years. Asking for immunity and not getting it. Taking the Fifth Amendment over and over again in front of congressional committees. Hoping his lawyer can work out a plea deal with special prosecutors – the one in Baton Rouge *and* one that will be appointed in Washington. Losing his business. Having his wife divorce him and his friends lose his telephone number. Sweating out the pre-sentence report. Sitting there near tears while a judge reams him a new one. Then hearing the big steel door slam and knowing he'll never breathe free air again."

Bilbo had reached the building and found a side door unlocked, as promised. He went in.

"That was all supposed to happen when Phoebe Riverdale blew the whistle on him," Vernon said bitterly as we approached the door ourselves. "All it got was a special prosecutor who isn't prosecuting anyone. Bilbo is riding higher than ever."

I pushed the door open and stood aside so that I could go in behind him. Bilbo had already found the air conditioner and gotten it going. I walked into a single, large room, about sixteen feet long and ten feet deep, with a waist-high desk and monitors taking up most of the length in front, beneath a huge picture window that would let attendants see trucks that pulled up. I pushed a button on the inside doorknob. I hoped that would lock the door behind me when I pushed it shut.

"Whatinhell?"

As Bilbo yelped, I swiveled my head toward him. At first all I saw were bulging eyes and a gaping, startled mouth, looking like three black holes that dominated his otherwise chalk white face. Apparently, he had just recognized Vernon Czlewski. Or maybe he'd recognized the muscular automatic pistol Vernon held.

"Walther CC," Vernon said. "Just like the one you planted on Slow Willie."

Backed against the wall at the far end of the building, Bilbo raised his hands to chest level, palms out, looking for all the world as if he were trying to placate a furious wife. A dark stain spread across the crotch of his trousers as he lost control of his bladder. Then he fainted, crumpling to the floor like a southern belle in a romance novel.

A trace of pity splashed across Vernon's face, diluting the determined rage that dominated his expression. It was the first chink in his armor I'd seen since I'd recognized him outside the limo. Pistol still pointed at Bilbo, Vernon turned and looked at me.

"Don't worry," he said. "I'm not going to shoot you."

"You won't have to," I snapped, whispering fiercely. "The same guy who's going to shoot you will take care of me too."

"What are you talking about?" Vernon seemed genuinely baffled.

"Did Nick Kappa give you that gun?"

"What if he did?"

"And I'm guessing that he arranged for you to drive the limo, and gave you the whole run-down for this closed but mysteriously accessible weigh station and the fairy tale about the motorcycle escort. How am I doing?"

"Yes, that was Kappa too. So what?"

"We've been set up, Vernon!" I still kept my voice low, expecting Kappa to burst in any second. "Kappa is using you to eliminate Bilbo because Bilbo knows about Slow Willie, even if he doesn't know about anything else, and that's enough to start toppling dominoes right there. Kappa has been trying to stage a false flag terrorist attack for over two years. His first effort failed. The second one is going down today. When it's over, there's going to be one *hell* of an investigation – and Bilbo is the weak link. Kappa knows he'll fold at the first hint of an indictment and spill his guts all over the floor. The whole house of cards falls down then, because they'll use the threat of a death sentence to squeeze the false flag plots out of Kappa. So Kappa wants Bilbo dead."

"Quite a coincidence, then," Vernon said. "I want him dead too."

"Can't blame you for that, but you and I are gonna be collateral damage," I whispered with even greater intensity. "If I'm right, then Kappa is on his way here, and right after you kill Bilbo, he's gonna bust in here, take the gun you used on Bilbo, and use it to kill you and me. Then I see him planting the gun on someone with a foreign accent, and no one the wiser – especially us, because we'll be in a morgue freezer with tags on our toes."

"*If* you're right," Vernon said.

End of debate. I figured I had one chance in a thousand if I acted, and zero if I didn't. Always go with the odds.

Deliberately, and looking Vernon in the eye, I reached out carefully and wrapped my hands around Vernon's right fist and the gun it held. I pushed it up and to the left, and he let me do it.

"Fire a shot into the wall," I whispered urgently.

Vernon fired. A deafening roar filled the small room, followed by a scary whine as the bullet ricocheted off metal paneling about three feet over Bilbo's head. An instant later I heard the door rattling. No script, no plan, no talking points. I was on my own now, with nothing to go on but pure instinct and raw adrenaline.

"Oh my God!" I shrieked. "You've shot him!"

I darted over to Bilbo and fell to my knees beside his body. With my left hand, I seized his left wrist as if I were feeling for a pulse. Meanwhile, I snaked my right hand through the wrist vent on his dress shirt, remembering the palm-sized automatic that he'd stashed there when he was playing Chad Commando, just before our dash from the lodge.

I heard the door being kicked open behind me, followed by screeching metal and howling hinges as it swung abruptly open into the room.

"Hands up!" Kappa's voice yelled. "Give me that gun and get back across the room!"

Vernon's weapon clattered to the floor. His shoes squeaked on the linoleum as he retreated.

Got it! I found the pistol in Bilbo's wrist holster. I pulled it from the holster but kept my hand under the shirtsleeve. I snapped the safety off by feel.

"Pulse!" I yelled over my shoulder. "He's still alive! Call an ambulance!"

"If you want something done right . . . . ," Kappa muttered disgustedly.

Two strides brought him to where Vernon had dropped his pistol. Keeping his head up and his own gun ready, his eyes shifting rapidly from Vernon to me and back, Kappa squatted to pick up the Walther CC.

As soon as he had his left hand on it, I whipped out Bilbo's Colt .25 and pointed it at Kappa's bent torso, six feet away from me. Just as Kappa began to straighten up, I squeezed off three shots. With a vastly surprised look on his face, Kappa gaped toward me and started to turn his gun in my direction as he reeled awkwardly backward against the weigh station's control desk. I saw two dark red circles growing on his white shirt. I fired two more shots, still at his torso. Then I kept pulling the trigger, dry-snapping without realizing it, just mechanically jerking the trigger over and over. Kappa's eyes went vacant. His right elbow slipped from the control desk and he fell to the floor, stretched out on his right side.

"Close the door!" I told Vernon. "There have to be more of them out there, and they'll be charging in here before we know it."

Vernon jumped to comply. He managed to nudge the door with his left hand so that it rattled shut on its own momentum just before a volley of bullets hemstitched it.

"Get down!" I yelled.

He flattened himself on the floor, barely in time. A fusillade of shots shattered the station's front window and rattled off the back wall. Flying glass sprayed around the small room, sprinkling my hair and stinging my arms and face. Sliding over linoleum and glass shards toward Kappa's body, I found Vernon's gun and slid it across the floor to him. Then I pried Kappa's weapon from his lifeless fingers.

Whoever was shooting at us figured to rush the door any second. They were pros with automatic weapons, and we were amateurs with pea-shooters, but that didn't mean we had to just lie there and take it. Guns ready and pointed at the door, we braced ourselves.

Another shot rang out, from farther away. Maybe five seconds passed. A second blast, this one a bit closer. Then, three seconds later, a third roar from closer yet, followed by a feral yowl just outside.

Hurried footsteps slapped pavement. Another ten seconds. Then a familiar voice shouted, "Who's in there?"

"Bax, is that you?" I yelled back. "It's Josie, Bilbo, and . . . our driver."

"Affirmative, this is Bax. I'm coming in. Don't shoot me. Say again: DO NOT FIRE."

"Copy that," I yelled.

Scurrying around, I picked up the empty twenty-five caliber, thanked God that I still had those bandages on my fingertips, and laid it next to Bilbo's limp right hand. Just as I'd finished doing that, I heard Haskel's wary voice coming through the crack in the door.

"All clear in there?"

"Yes. I mean, affirmative. Or whatever."

He stepped cautiously through the door, a revolver in his right hand, pointed at the ground. Chrome barrel and cylinder.

"Is the congressman dead?" he asked, alarmed.

"No," I said as Haskel strode over to check for himself. "Just in shock. Is that Mary Barbara's gun?"

"Mm-hmm," he said absently, resting the first two fingers of his right hand against Bilbo's throat. "We saw that limo sitting here. Looked funny, so we pulled off at the next exit and doubled back to check it out. By the time we got here two hostiles were spraying lead every which way. Lucky for us, they apparently weren't expecting a flank attack. After I winged one of them they hightailed it."

Enter Mary Barbara, face stricken and eyes frantic.

"Alive and well," Haskel said to her. "Maybe a little shaken up, but it looks like the bad guy missed and he didn't."

She took in the tableau at a glance. Two survivors, Bax in the role of first responder, a dead body, a bullet gouge a few feet above her man, and a pistol near his right hand.

"Chad!" she screamed, rushing to him and kneeling to cradle his head and neck. "You did it again, Chad!"

I could have wallowed in the irony, or shaken my head at the schmaltz, or teared up a little at the unconditional spousal devotion, or something. But I didn't. Because at that moment my memory turned up a Bilbo sound bite: 'And make sure that turd blossom Sinclair gets my bag and computer on Marine One like he said he would.'

Chapter 77

I smacked Vernon on the shoulder.

"We've gotta roll. Leave the hardware here."

Without an eyeblink Vernon put his gun on the floor and hustled toward the door. Killing Kappa had apparently given me some street cred with him.

I looked over my shoulder at Haskel on my way out the door. "You take care of the cops. Let me know if they need anything from us."

"Where are you going?" Haskel demanded.

"Vicksburg Military National Park," I yelled. "And God help us get there before the president."

A fierce urgency burnt my gut like Johnny Walker Red neat. *The bad guys always have a Plan B.* I didn't even have a Plan A.

Thirty seconds later we were in the limo. A minute after that we were tooling down I-20, south of Vicksburg Military National Park, at a safe, sane, infuriating fifty miles an hour. No sense cussing about it. A stretch limo going fifty is doing the best it can.

I called Rafe.

"What's up?" he asked.

"How long before the president is supposed to reach the park?"

"Give me a sec. . . . Fifty-eight minutes," he said. "Still right on schedule."

I looked at my watch. 1:02. *Keep cool, Josie. Nice and calm.*

"Hank Sinclair probably doesn't know it, but he's hauling a computer bomb toward the president's appearance," I said. "He's in Congressman Bilbo's Denali. The one with at least three bullet holes on the passenger side. The FBI should be able to find it in five minutes flat."

"And you know this how?" He sounded calm, unruffled, and supremely aggravating in the way that only calm, unruffled males can be.

"Hank told Bilbo that he'd get Bilbo's computer aboard Marine One. Based on Bilbo's instruction to Bax Haskel to make sure Hank accomplished that, Bilbo bought it. It looks like Kappa is running Hank, so Hank's access to the computer means Kappa had access to it as well."

"I get it," Rafe said. "That stuff plus the references to explosives on the 'Shoot at the King' notes equals computer bomb."

I looked at the clock: 1:09.

"X-rays, metal detectors, bomb-sniffing dogs, and guys with guns will protect the president and Marine One," I said. "But nothing is protecting the people coming to hear him speak."

"Right. With enough photogenic damage, terrorism will preempt every other issue for seventy percent of the country. Your brilliant theory is one thing, though, and actionable intelligence is something else."

"'Actionable intelligence'," I said crossly. "Like what, for example?"

"PETN, for example," Rafe said. "That and Semtex were entries on the 'Shoot at the King' scenario. PETN is moldable. Years ago, terrorists used it to blow up a passenger plane over Lockerbie, Scotland with a computer bomb."

"Shit."

"So," Rafe said, "did Kappa say anything suggestive before he passed away? You couldn't be expected to have a perfect memory of it, given the stress, but did a helpful tidbit maybe slip out?"

I almost flubbed that one, coming within a hair's breadth of telling the truth. I caught myself just in time.

"'PETN' definitely refreshes my recollection," I said. "Yes. Kappa made some crack about getting the congressman's 'fancy new PETN computer' to Marine One. Then he gave kind of a sick laugh." I paused and glanced toward Vernon. "Do you remember that? Kappa saying something about the congressman's 'fancy new PETN computer'?"

"Yessir. 'Fancy new PETN computer.' Yessir."

Clock-check: 1:13.

"Close enough," Rafe said. "I'll contact Theo and ask him to call any FBI higher-ups who might listen to him. Then I'll jump start some protégés with channels to the Secret

Service. You call the FBI field office in New Orleans. Theo and I will give everyone we call your phone number. While all this is going on, you and I and Uncle Darius will all keep our eyes peeled for that Denali."

"Given when you landed in BR, and the way Uncle D drives, you have to be ahead of us. Are you still driving east, or have you turned north yet?"

"No one's doing much driving from any direction anywhere near the park right now. We're about a mile away, and we're making our way on foot."

ON FOOT!

"Raphael Taylor Kendall," I said in the most menacing voice I could muster, "*please* tell me that Uncle Darius does *not* have his forty-five with him."

"Uncle Darius does not have his forty-five with him."

"Thank God."

I signed off. Clock check: 1:16. We drove on. I noticed a road sign:

EXIT 4B to

VICKSBURG MILITARY NATIONAL PARK

VIA CLAY STREET

3 MILES

I jabbed Vernon's arm to be sure he saw it too. He had already started to change lanes.

Next I called the FBI New Orleans Field Office. Secretary, then duty agent. I'd just started my spiel when he cut me off:

"Name, please."

"Josephine Kendall. I'm –"

"Address?"

"I've made reports before. You already have all that. I need to –"

"Ma'am, this is my interview. I am controlling the conversation. The way this works is, I ask questions and you answer the questions I ask. So: address."

I threw a frustrated punch at the dashboard. Gritting my teeth, I rattled off address, social security number, date of birth, home telephone, office telephone, and mobile telephone.

"Thank you. Now, what do you wish to report?"

I launched into it, trying not to talk too fast, but not to waste any time, either. I'd just gotten the PETN part out when he broke in again.

"Wait a minute. Did you say there's been some kind of shoot-out at an interstate truck weigh station?"

"Yes. It has been reported by now –"

"Reported to whom?"

"Local law enforcement," I said, as I felt exasperation rising in my throat.

"And where are you?"

"On Interstate Twenty looking for the car THAT I TOLD YOU IS CARRYING A COMPUTER BOMB TO A PRESIDENTIAL APPEARANCE!"

"You should go back to the weigh station," he said.

"Bullshit. I mean negative. Please focus. Computer bomb. President. Vicksburg."

"Yeah, I got all that. PETN, congressman's computer, Denali. I'm sending an alert. Thank you for your report. If you see something, say something."

Click. *Well THAT accomplished a hell of a lot. He didn't believe a word I said. Whoever gets his alert will probably see 'Crank Call from Crazy Chick' in the subject line.* I cut loose with some ripe blasphemy.

1:21.

There's still time. They can't set the thing off until the president has landed.

As we got closer to Exit 4B, heavier traffic started slowing us down. We'd clearly have plenty of company the rest of the way.

I looked through the windshield, scanning the traffic for a Yukon Denali XL. Nothing. I glared at my phone, willing it to ring with a follow-up call from one of the people in the network Rafe and Theo were stimulating. Again, nothing.

I punched in Hank's mobile phone number. Voice-mail. Took a deep breath and left my message:

"Hank, this is Josie Kendall. I'm sure you don't know it, but the baggage in Congressman Bilbo's Denali includes a bomb. You need to drive the Denali as far into open countryside as you can get. Make sure it's at least five-hundred yards from any house or building, and run like your life depends on it – because it does. You've been played, buddy. Kappa, the guy who's pulling your strings, and who you presumably thought was some kind of undercover operative, is dead. Everyone with a badge in northeast Louisiana and western Mississippi is looking for that Denali. So do it NOW, Tiger. Say again, NOW."

1:26. *Still time. Chill, Josie. You've got this.*

My phone started playing "Jambalaya." No Caller ID. I punched ANSWER.

"Josie Kendall."

"Is this Josephine Kendall?" a clipped, no-nonsense female voice asked. I thought I was staying cool, but this lady registered twenty degrees below me. I've heard more excitement from insurance adjusters.

"Yes, this is Josephine Kendall!"

"Officer Tereska, Secret Service. I'm told that you have actionable intelligence about a threat to the president."

"Yes." I went through the scenario again.

"We have confirmation of gunfire and one death at the weigh station, with a congressman on the scene," she said. "Are you sure the decedent referred to 'PETN'?"

"Yes." *No hedging, no ass-covering.*

"Where are you at this point in time?"

"On Interstate Twenty, bearing north, now, but one to two miles from Exit 4B, and not moving very fast."

"We would like to speak with you face-to-face. The Secret Service has set up a command post inside the park. Exit 4B will take you to Clay Street, a quarter-mile from the park. Continue on that route until and unless you hear from me. I will call you back at this number if we can arrange for expedited transport to the command post for an interview."

"Okay." Going through that much hassle probably meant that Tereska was even now filling cyberspace with something about a Credible and Immediate Threat to POTUS. I'll take it.

"What is your level of confidence about the Denali?" Tereska asked.

Swallowed hard on that one. She didn't have to spell it out for me. The higher the number I gave her, the more likely it was that they'd blow the Denali to smithereens if they spotted it and couldn't stop it any other way.

Hundred percent? No. A pro would never say a hundred percent. But I can't equivocate, either.

"Ninety percent," I said. "And that's a hard ninety." I felt worse than I had all day, including when I'd come within an eyelash of eternity.

"Stand by." She broke the connection.

1:34.

We had finally exited onto Clay Street, but traffic had now slowed to a crawl.

1:42. *Okay, this is getting tight.*

I hauled out my iPad, praying the president was running late. No luck. CNN and Fox agreed: the visit was proceeding right on schedule. I did learn that the podium would be set up in front of the Wisconsin memorial, which was well up toward the north end of the park. Anyone coming to the park through the main entrance would have to cross what looked like a massive stretch of land labeled 'Battery DeGolyer' to get to the monument. Well, that's *something*.

I looked through the windshield again, searching for anything vaguely resembling a Denali. Nothing and more nothing.

I called Hank's number again. I got voice-mail again. I left another message, this one tumbling out fast and loud, with urgency dripping from every syllable:

"Hank, Josie again. You have to move *now*, as in five minutes ago. The Secret Service is looking for you, and if you get anywhere close to the president, even by accident, they're gonna blow you all the way back to Boston. I know you were duped, Hank. I know you have no idea that you're carrying a bomb. But trust me on this, you are. You have one chance to do one supremely good and selfless thing for your country and save your ass at the same time. Don't choke."

I guess I could have phrased that more diplomatically, but Miss Manners is never around when I need her.

1:51: *Shit! This is no longer plenty of time!* Inspiration struck.

"Open the sun roof," I told Vernon. "And unlock all the doors."

He complied. With the limo barely moving, I had no trouble stepping out, opening the rear door, and slipping back in, as if I were back at Carondalet doing a Chinese Fire Drill. I brought my iPad with me. By standing on the mini-fridge right behind the front seat, I could wedge my head and elbows through the sun roof and get a better view of the cars packed chock-a-block on Clay Street and the park entrance beyond, which was now between two hundred and three hundred yards away.

Putting the iPad in camera mode, I zoomed in on the entrance. Hazily but unmistakably I could make out phalanxes of National Park Service Police, uniformed Secret Service officers with dogs, Mississippi Highway Patrolmen, and Vicksburg police officers inspecting cars and trucks at a checkpoint just inside the park. *Serious* inspections: looking inside, checking trunks, sliding giant mirrors on wheels under the chassis, giving those dogs a chance to go on point if they smelled something. Then they'd direct the cars to temporary parking.

I spotted at least two drones, one chopper, and a single-engine reconnaissance plane circling over the park. At maximum zoom, I could make out moving black specks among the Civil War era canon on mounds twenty feet apart. Officers patrolling the park's outer perimeter? I sure hoped so. .

Now I turned the iPad toward the crawling traffic ahead of us. Still no Denali in sight. A sedan up ahead, maybe fifty feet in front of us, though, rang a bell: Kelly green Cadillac El Dorado, white trim with gold glitter and bumpers and hubcaps polished to a high gleam.

Zoomed in. Gasped. It was the same car I'd spotted that night in Baton Rouge when Card had saved my ass from Kappa's thugs in the alley. It had to be Card's, so it also had to be the car Alan Kirby had cryptically told Seamus had been stolen from Card, making Alan anxious to get in touch with him.

This could not *possibly* be a coincidence. *They pulled a switch! That's it! They put Hank in Card's car instead of the Denali!* But who was 'they'? Kappa, of course, because he'd been handling the operational stuff before he passed away. But did 'they' include Alan Kirby with some hare-brained scheme to use the trumpkins' own false flag attack scheme to *actually* take Trump out? Did they want to create a vacuum for Calvin to fill at the GOP Convention, galloping in as a last-minute savior on a white horse? With a shivering gut-chill I thought of the chopper noise in the background during my chat with Alan Kirby. Or was it someone well above Hank in the West Wing, with a talent for flying under the radar?

The sound of distant cheers jerked my head up. Helicopters at about two-o'clock, not all that far off and getting closer. Three of them – not whirlybirds like the one surveilling the park. They were "whitetops," as we call them in Washington. Marine One and two decoys.

The park entrance was now less than two hundred yards ahead. And sitting off the road to the right a hundred feet or so from that entrance, I could now see a satin black Chevy Suburban SUV with red and blue flashing lights and a blue presidential pennant on the right fender mast. It looked like a Secret Service battle wagon – except that I'd never seen a Secret Service battle wagon fly a presidential pennant unless it was part of a motorcade.

The scenario got real clear, real fast. Whoever was engineering this scenario would have Hank transfer from Card's car to that SUV. The SUV would then drive him into the park, off-road, unimpeded by traffic. Security would stop the SUV at the first checkpoint, like everyone else, and there the dogs figured to sniff the explosive in the computer he was carrying. That's when someone in Card's car, or in another car in the vicinity, would remotely detonate the bomb. They'd try to hold off on the explosion until Marine One had landed, but they'd default into detonating the bomb at the last possible moment before dogs reacted, even if the president's helicopter were still in the air.

I lowered myself down from the sunroof opening and slipped out the barely moving car's rear door, ditching the iPad in the car and raising my phone. I punched in Tereska's number as I ran awkwardly in between lines of cars creeping on either side of me.

"Tereska," the icy voice barked.

"Josie Kendall. They switched cars! No Deanali! Kelly green and white El Dorado that's now about –"

"Slow down, Kendall. Now your story is that it's not –"

"That's right, it's not the Denali, it's a green El Dorado – Kelly green – roughly a football field from the entrance. The one with a crazy chick pounding on it."

I didn't have any digital clock to check any more, but I didn't need one. My brain was keeping time with pitiless efficiency. By now it had to be 1:56.

I reached the El Dorado's front door on the driver's side. Rapped the tinted glass.

"Card! Open your window! I've got to tell you something!"

That earned me a contemptuous stare and a middle finger – but not from Card. A beefy white guy in a dark hoodie – in Mississippi in June. I banged on the window with the heel of my right hand. Hard. The window came down. Tug's hard eyes contemptuously took my measure.

"Don't be fuckin' with me, bitch," Tug said – and right at that moment I saw Hank Sinclair in the passenger seat, mouth agape, lowering his mobile phone from his right ear, and cradling a computer on his lap.

Next thing I knew, four knuckles on a meaty left hand were smashing into my lips. It wasn't a conventional punch. Tug just sort of pulled his balled left hand back about four inches, then snapped it into my face. My ears rang, while black and red and yellow op-art flashed behind my eyes. I tasted a rush of blood on my lips, and my hips smacked the car behind me. I didn't sprawl on the pavement, only because a desperate grab won me a four-finger grip on Tug's door handle.

1:58 flashed in my mind. Rotors roared as the whitetops descended inside the park. The Secret Service would take the president by battle wagon from the landing site to the Wisconsin memorial where he'd speak.

The window started to roll up. Last hope.

"Listen to my goddamn messages, Hank, or you're totally screwed!"

I prayed that he already had – that he had been listening to my messages just before Tug punched me. Prayer was all I had left.

The passenger door on the El Dorado suddenly sprang open. Tug barked something angrily as his head twisted to his right. Hank clambered out with the laptop hugged to his chest. He ran toward the front of the car. Apparently expecting Hank to run west, across the southbound lanes and toward the park, Tug sent the El Dorado lurching forward into the Confederate flag decal on the bumper of a Ford Bronco in order to block his path. Gripping the computer in his left arm, though, Hank ran *east*. He used his right hand to hoist himself to the hood of the car next to them in the outside lane. He scooted to the other side on his hips.

Dismounting neatly on the other side, Hank sprinted away from the park and the highway where all those people were just sitting, trapped in their cars, oblivious to their imminent peril. Going full tilt, running fast and smooth like a natural athlete, even in a suit and dress shoes he seemed to glide across a vast expanse of grass. A park ranger in green and khaki and a uniformed Secret Service officer noticed Hank and started in hasty pursuit, drawing their weapons as they ran.

The distant cheering got louder. Marine One had to be close to touchdown.

1:59.

My head and face still throbbing in pain from Tug's punch, I turned away from Hank's sprint to glance at Tug, afraid that he might be reaching for a gun. He wasn't. He was fingering a mobile phone, his window up, his doors locked.

"Don't do it, you bastard!" I screamed, pulling on the door handle and then banging on his window as hard as I could with my balled fists.

"Heya, lemme he'p you wi' dat, ma'am."

Startled, I looked up to see a refrigerator in human form. He was coiling a massive, fleshy fist near his shoulder. Crew-cut under his red Make America Great Again cap, his neck thick with rage, cords of muscle straining the threads of his MAGA t-shirt. It had to be the Bronco's driver.

One massive punch instantly starred the window with cracks and created a jagged gap where shredded glass had rocketed into the car.

A uniformed Secret Service officer began running from the park entrance toward us.

"Don't!" I yelled at Tug. "You're dead if you do!"

Too late. With a finger now coated crimson by flowing blood, the true-believer thug pushed one more button.

I looked toward Hank's sprinting figure as it began to disappear down an incline. A split-second of nauseating suspense passed before a muffled explosion rocked the landscape. Flaring from the other side of the slope at least thirty yards away, an orange and black fireball gave way to silver-streaked gray smoke.

Oh my God. Hank!

The ranger and the agent who had been running across the field pitched to the ground. After two seconds, they warily climbed to their feet and began jogging toward the site of the explosion. No particular hurry any more.

Tug slammed his door open, knocking me to the pavement like a rag doll and even pushing the human refrigerator back a couple of steps. Tug's right hand reached inside his half-buttoned shirt. As it came out, I saw the butt of an automatic pistol maybe one size down from Uncle D's .45.

"Gun!" I yelled. The Bronco driver looked like he already knew.

"Drop your weapon and put your hands in the air!"

The command came from two car-lengths ahead of us, from the uniformed Secret Service officer who had run from the park entrance.

"Fuck you, pig." Tug kept his gun on us instead of turning it toward the agent. He seemed to hesitate, unsure about whether to kill me or the human refrigerator first.

Fire! I mentally screamed at officer. But I knew he couldn't fire yet. No clear shot and civilians at risk. I heard leather-on-metal *clumping* as the officer pulled himself onto the Bronco's hood.

Tug fixed his beady eyes on me.

Too late, I thought. The officer would need one more second to aim, and that was a second I didn't have.

Just as Tug's finger tensed on the trigger, the front of his head suddenly burst open. Blood exploded all over everything – me, the Bronco driver, the pavement, and the car behind us – as Tug lurched forward. *Someone had shot him from behind.*

A succession of sharp *bangs!* from the Secret Service officer's gun immediately followed, but those were just target practice. Now riddled with bullets, Tug finally crumpled and fell on top of me.

Pinned underneath Tug's two hundred-plus pounds, I couldn't see who had fired the fatal shot. I could hear okay, though, and what I heard was Uncle D's delighted roar.

"HOO RAW! Helluva shot, buddy! Looks like that punk done fucked with the wrong man!"

The response came more as a rumble than a roar, but I heard it just fine.

"Mothafucka boosted my ride." Card's voice. "Plumb fo'got to read him his rights."

I worked my way to a standing position in time to see Card four cars back, standing beside Bilbo's Yukon Denali with his hands up and a handgun – I learned later it was a Glok – lying on the Denali's roof. I put the story together provisionally, subject to revision if I ever got any actual facts.

Kappa's goons had stolen Card's El Dorado so they could implicate him in the bombing. While the Secret Service, the FBI, and I were shuffling paper and filling out bureaucratic forms, Kirby *pere* and *fils* had found out, tracked down Card, and choppered him here with some hardware. The rest was history – or would be if anyone ever wrote it right. But no one ever will.

Two cars behind Card and one lane over stood Rafe and Uncle D, both looking like they'd just finished a marathon. Rafe was setting a pistol on the roof of the car next to him and raising his hands. He had told me the Gospel truth. Uncle D wasn't carrying his .45. Rafe was. He hadn't used it, thank God, because Card's shot had mooted the issue.

When I hadn't heard another shot after two panting gulps of air and one prayer, I figured the Secret Service officer wasn't going to blow any of them away. I would have put the odds on that at no better than even.

I couldn't see much of what looked at first like barely controlled chaos inside the park and just outside its entrance. I'd pick it up later, watching news clips running on endless loops: Four different kinds of cops moving forward simultaneously, heads on swivels, each group yelling its own version of the same basic order: "Lockdown!" "Shelter in place!" "Stay *in* your vehicles, repeat, stay *in* your vehicles!" "Engines off!" "No movement, say again, no movement!"

Same with the choreography deeper inside the park, which had nothing chaotic about it. The Secret Service agents there wore suits rather than uniforms, and in the news clips they moved with the elegance of a well trained dance troupe. Two of them had the President of the United States lifted almost off the ground but with his head forced down as they hustled him toward the middle of three jet-black armored battle wagons. Four more surrounded him front, back, and each side, putting their bodies in between him and any bad guy who might be out there, each of them ready to take a bullet for the president. Not for Donald Trump – for the President of the United States.

One of the whitetop decoy helicopters started to rise, to draw any fire that might come.

Few things on Earth are as vulnerable as a helicopter in low altitude flight, so the Secret Service would evacuate the president by land. They loaded him like a mail bag into the middle battle wagon. Blue and red lights flashing, all three started rumbling north in a line, with agents running alongside and one agent on a fender-step, clinging to a handle on the chassis. I watched it over and over, and it never stopped blowing my mind: no scrambling; no improvisation. They knew exactly what they were doing, exactly where they were going, and exactly how to get there.

Only one of the clips would show another battle wagon, the one moving in the opposite direction, toward us and the southern park perimeter. It was driving deliberately, toward the area where I'd seen the fireball, and then stopped just short of the incline Hank had disappeared over. Two people in Secret Service uniforms got out and headed down the hill. One of them carried a body bag.

Chapter 78

"Bilbo has officially dropped out of the race," Phoebe said to me not quite three weeks later, as we sat over Saturday morning coffee around my kitchen table. "So I guess you made a deal."

"How about those Nationals!" I said. In Washington's dripping-wet July heat, baseball struck me as a saner conversational topic than electoral politics – at least until we were off the record. "Second season without Bryce Harper, and it looks like they might have a shot at the playoffs!"

"This would be on deepest background, of course."

"Good pitching, solid hitting, strong defense, and sound fundamentals."

"Okay," Phoebe sighed. "Off the record. And I think real fans call them 'the Nats', not 'the Nationals.'"

I took a long sip of coffee. My lips had healed by now, so I did it without agony – not that the agony had slowed me down much even before they healed. I'll take pain over drinking coffee through a straw any day of the week.

"Off the record," I said, "Bilbo and I didn't shake on it or anything. Never even talked to each other. Reached a tacit understanding, through intermediaries."

"That's a deal," Phoebe said.

"He withdraws from the race. I will not challenge the official conclusion that he saved Vernon and me by shooting Kappa while he was under fire. He'll end his political career the way he began it: with a phony heroic homicide."

"After all," Phoebe said, "how could you challenge that account?"

"It would be hard, wouldn't it?"

"How could either you or Vernon have fired that twenty-five caliber automatic without leaving finger-prints on it?"

"That's a real good point," I said. Just to stay in practice, we were pretending that Phoebe didn't know about the bandages on my fingertips.

"How about the special prosecutor?" Phoebe asked then.

"Seasoned professionals don't need any help from an amateur like me on a criminal investigation." I paused, looking steadily at her. "Naturally, of course, I will truthfully answer any questions I am asked by law enforcement."

Phoebe's minute nod told me she got it. Her next chat would be with Special Prosecutor Lamarr. If he followed up with me, he'd get the truth – well, most of it.

"Then," she said, "there's the joint select congressional committee that will be investigating a bomb exploding less than a quarter of a mile from the president, who was saved by the selfless heroism of my ex-husband, a patriotic American named Hank Sinclair."

"Bilbo is on his own there. May his lawyers prosper and grow rich."

"You're okay with the Hank part?" she pressed. "The posthumous Presidential Medal of Freedom?"

"God bless his patriotic soul. 'Pin that medal upon his chest/Tell his mama he done his best.'"

Another pause. I think Phoebe was hoping that the heavy silence would make me blurt something out. Good luck with that. *Not my first rodeo, honey.*

"Any idea who the ultimate string-puller on this operation was?" she asked then. "The one who was running Kappa and coming up with all the scenarios?"

"Nope. All I know for sure is that it wasn't Steve Bannon, because he's way too smart to get involved in something like this. That leaves about two dozen people who are deeply committed MAGA economic populists and were either once on the White House staff – or still are."

"So, we just deferred the Apocalypse," Phoebe said at last.

"Yep. A handful of political hustlers, an *apparatchik* from the D.C. swamp, a Grade A asshole in a moment of grace, a one-handed Marine veteran, an ambitious reporter hungry for a big score, a fence, and just some regular decent folks – as motley a crew of allies as anyone ever saw."

"You choose your enemies," Phoebe said. "You don't choose your allies."

About an hour after Phoebe left, Rafe caught me crying. Not bawling my eyes out. Just little sobs that I tried to hide from him. I thought I'd gotten that stuff wrung out of my system in the two or three days after returning from Vicksburg, but the chat with Phoebe brought back the soul-wracking memory of the part I'd played; the sheer enormity of the choices I'd made; the doubts about what I'd done and hadn't done and could have done and maybe should have done (or not). Phoebe was right: I'd helped to defer the Apocalypse, and I was as proud as hell of that. But my pride came wrapped in guilt that I wouldn't let myself just shrug off.

Rafe didn't say a word. He just pulled me gently from my chair, wrapped his arms around me, and held me against his body for a few minutes, until I'd gotten it out of my system.

"I get it," he whispered then. "You'd never even pointed a gun at anyone before and now you've killed a human being. You're not supposed to feel okay about it. It should bother you."

"Kappa doesn't bother me at all. Not a whisper of remorse. I did it, I'm glad I did it, and if I had it to do over, I'd do it again."

"Hank, then? No matter how you spin it, his blood isn't on *your* hands."

"I fingered him, Rafe. I gave Tereska a 'hard ninety percent,' knowing full well that might get Hank a Hellfire missile straight up his gut. I looked it square in the face and I went ahead and did it – just as Trump would have."

"Barack Obama would have done the same thing," Rafe said. "So would Hillary Clinton, or her husband, or either Bush, or Reagan. Even Carter would have given a kill order in that situation."

"Would Phoebe? Or Father Kempton? Or my Papa, if he were still alive? Or the pair of reverends at the Holiness Full Gospel Church?"

"Can't say." Rafe kept his eyes locked on mine. "But if the answer is no, that just means they aren't cut out to run the country."

"Rafe, that's just it. That's really why I was crying. Because I *am* – I *am* fit to run this country. That's a helluva thing to see when you look in the mirror."

Sometimes there isn't anything more to say. So we didn't say any more. We just cuddle-hugged for another few minutes until I said I'd better get back to planning the project I'd start on Monday.

"What will you be working on?" Rafe asked.

"After investing all that money in finessing Bilbo into a fracking flip-flop, Calvin Kirby and his clan are pissed about him leaving Congress. Kirby thinks he might be able to do something with the fringe candidate he'd already dumped some money on so he could take a bite out of Dejean's vote and ensure a run-off. He's hoping that another two hundred thousand dollars and a week of Josie boot camp can make the guy credible enough to flip Dejean on fracking. I told Seamus I'd get right on it."

CPSIA information can be obtained
at www.ICGtesting.com
Printed in the USA
JSHW021743240919
1590JS00002B/2